DENZIL QUARRIER

Other novels by George Gissing also published by Harvester

DENZIL QUARRIER

George Gissing

Edited and with an introduction and notes by
JOHN HALPERIN
Professor of English,
University of Southern California

THE HARVESTER PRESS

This edition first published in 1979 by
THE HARVESTER PRESS LIMITED
Publisher: John Spiers
2 Stanford Terrace, Hassocks, Sussex

© New editorial material, John Halperin, 1979

British Library Cataloguing in Publication Data
Gissing, George
Denzil Quarrier.
I.   Title II. Halperin, John
823'.8 PR4716.D/

ISBN 0-85527-712-2

Printed and bound in England by Redwood Burn Limited,
Trowbridge and Esher

Contents

Acknowledgements

Grateful acknowledgement is made to Pierre Coustillas for nurturing my interest in Gissing and for helping to answer a number of questions about *Denzil Quarrier;* to Donald Greene for putting at my disposal his encyclopedic knowledge of English history and literature; to Heddy Richter of the library staff, University of Southern California, for help in gathering and making available books needed in connection with this and other writing projects of mine on Gissing; and to James Thorp, Director of the Huntington Library, for making my access to the holograph manuscript of *Denzil Quarrier* so uncomplicated.

John Halperin
Los Angeles, September 1978

Bibliographical Note

Denzil Quarrier, originally entitled 'The Radical Candidate', was commissioned by Arthur Henry Bullen for Lawrence & Bullen in the autumn of 1891. Gissing wrote the novel from 6 October to 12 November, and changed the title reluctantly, a week after completing the book, because of Bullen's wish to placate the booksellers' fears that female readers would be put off by a political title. The first edition was published on 5 February 1892 in green cloth gilt and priced at six shillings. A portion of the sheets was left unbound until after the dissolution of the partnership between Lawrence & Bullen in 1899, as is testified by the existence of copies of the first edition bound in red cloth with A.H. Bullen's name alone on the spine.

In 1892 Heinemann & Balestier brought out a Continental edition, in stiff brown wrappers, and George Robertson & Co., the Melbourne firm, a colonial edition, which consisted of sheets of the first English edition. Strangely enough Edward Augustus Petherick, the Australian publisher, also published the novel in his 'Collection of Favourite and Approved Authors' in the same year. The first American edition appeared in Macmillan & Co.'s Dollar Series in February 1892. The two states of the first edition in light-brown cloth with red titling and in dark-brown cloth with brown titling clearly indicate that Macmillan bound the sheets in at least two batches.

Reprints of the book include a colonial edition issued by George Bell and Sons (1894), English and Continental reissues respectively by Sidgwick & Jackson and Heinemann & Balestier in 1911, and the AMS edition of 1969. No translation of the novel is on record.

The original handwritten manuscript contains 133 leaves which are very lightly corrected. It is held, together with the MSS. of seven other Gissing novels, by the Huntington Library, at San Marino, California.

Pierre Coustillas

Introduction

Gissing's anomalous position among the Victorian novelists may be glimpsed by placing *Denzil Quarrier* (1892) next to another novel on the same subject, *Dr Wortle's School* (1881). Trollope's brilliant little story is about a man and woman who live together as though married when in fact no legal ceremony has been performed. In each novel it is the woman who is, technically, the bigamist, yet in each she is given a reason for doing what she does (Mrs Peacocke in *Dr Wortle's School* had thought her first husband was dead when she 'married' Mr Peacocke). Trollope, whose opinions on many matters were identical with those of most of his contemporaries, introduces his story gingerly. 'It may be that when I shall have told the mystery [of the Peacockes' relationship] there will no longer be any room for interest in the tale to you,' he tells the reader, with characteristic directness. Nor, he is quick to point out, does he himself condone bigamy. 'There is no one who reads this but will say that they should have parted,' Trollope declares—with an eye, perhaps, on Mudie's reader. 'Every day passed together as man and wife must be a falsehood and a sin.' Though there would be misery in their parting—still, 'there is no law from God or man entitling a man to escape from misery at the expense of falsehood and sin.' But Trollope goes on to juggle the odds by having his hero, Dr Wortle, defend the Peacockes (his employees at a school) against the hysterical ravings of vengeful morality, which declares loudly that a man should be married to his wife. Trollope sympathises, and means us to sympathise, with Wortle and the victimized pair, all of whom act in good faith, while their critics, often enough, do not. The power of social convention upon the mind of the novelist may be measured, however, in Trollope's ambivalent attitude toward the Peacockes, who in fact are exemplary people. Trollope's unclouded admiration is reserved for Dr Wortle, who ably defends the pair in the teeth of society's voracious propriety. For a major theme of *Dr Wortle's School* is that the conventions society finds proper should be observed—even when, as here, the attempted enforcement of conventional behaviour is carried on with so little restraint and generosity. The novel condemns mysteries and secrets, which are said to be accompanied always by fear and guilt, and tells us that few things are worse than a lie (in his novels Trollope declared again and again that he scorned to keep any secrets from his reader—though certainly he kept his share). What counts, Peacocke ultimately decides, is 'not what the drunken priest might think of himself, but what others might think of him'. 'It is not enough to be innocent,' says the local bishop, 'men must know that we are so'. Trollope in his own voice puts it this way: 'So much in this world depends upon character that attention has to be paid to bad character even when it is not deserved. In dealing with men and women, we have to consider what they believe, as well as what we believe ourselves'. In the novel's most dramatic scene, Dr Wortle tells Peacocke that 'no man [has] a right to regard his own moral life as isolated from the lives of others around him . . .a man cannot isolate the morals, the manners, the ways of his life from the morals of others. Men, if they live together, must live together by certain laws.' Those who deceive their neighbours, with or without cause, are dangerous in a world in which bad faith or deception or dishonesty is likely to weaken the links by which all men and women are so closely joined together. George Eliot uses the metaphor of the web of humanity to argue this same point in several of her novels.

Mrs Wade's attack on George Eliot in *Denzil Quarrier* for being so outspokenly conventional—despite a very unconventional private life—should tell us, if we need to be told, that Gissing (1857-1903) does not share Trollope's belief in the essential wisdom of the Voice of Society. Indeed, it is the couple with the 'guilty secret' (a well-worn device of Victorian novelists, especially Dickens) who are meant to command most of our sympathy in *Denzil Quarrier*—and this despite the fact that Lilian cannot claim, as Mrs Peacocke can, that she thought her first husband was dead. Northway's arrest on the heels of their wedding impels her neither to defend nor to follow him—or even to remain loyal for more than a minute or two—but rather to abandon him on the spot (Gissing, who was once arrested, knew what it was to be alone in such circumstances). Ultimately Lilian goes to live as Quarrier's wife without benefit of any ceremony, legal or otherwise. She is a mistress masquerading as a wife. As such her crime, if crime it is, is surely a more spectacular one than Mrs Peacocke's. But Gissing's defence of Lilian is more spirited than Trollope's of Mrs Peacocke and, more importantly, it is rooted in wholly different ground. Gissing's argument is that society and its rules are usually unreasonable. 'What we have to do is clear away the obvious lies and superstitions that hold a great part of the people in degrading bondage,' Quarrier announces in Chapter III. Gissing's point of view is the obverse of Trollope's ('I cannot read him; the man is such a terrible Philistine,' Gissing remarked of Trollope in an 1887 letter to his friend Eduard Bertz). When it injures no one, Quarrier says (XIV), 'conventional wrong-doing . . . [is] not wrong-doing at all, unless discovered." It is not wrong *unless discovered*— tht is to say, it cannot be wrong at all if convention declares it to be wrong: but God help you if you are found out. Gissing presses his attack on 'imbecile prejudice' by declaring, again through Quarrier, that 'Social law is stupid and unjust, imposing its obligations without regard to person or circumstance. It presumes no one can be *trusted*' (IX; if it does presume that, then it is certainly right to do so in the case of Lilian and Denzil). Quarrier insists that society by its laws forces people to tell lies by making them hide their real feelings while they observe the proprieties. He himself lies about his relationship with Lilian because he craves respectability, society's approval, and, ultimately, a political career. To achieve these things lies must be told. Gissing's subterranean feeling that such things may indeed by worth having—a feeling that seeps through in all of his novels, no matter how anti-Establishment they may at first seem to be—can be glimpsed here too in the character of Quarrier himself, who, despite the lies he tells and the various sorts of hypocrisy he practises on others, is presented to us for the most part sympathetically. This, however, cannot muffle the attack on Society and those who represent its values—such as the Rev. Scatchard Vialls, who is 'ignorant and foolish,' has 'eyes like a ferret's,' an 'insinuating' manner, and an eye for heiresses; and the Mumbrays, who are 'regarded as a centre of moral and religious influence' in Polterham despite their well-known 'reciprocal disgust...physical, mental, moral' for one another. 'These people,' observes William Glazzard, 'think themselves pillars of society, and the best of the joke is, that they really *are* what they imagine' (X). As in Ibsen's play of 1877, the pillars of the community are seen by Gissing to be very hollow indeed, supporting a society, moreover, that would prefer not to look too deeply into any questions of leverage. The pronouncements of such an Establishment are therefore seen as morally unimportant, though they may have a paralysing effect upon one's life. Lilian, says Quarrier (IX), '*is* my wife, in every sense of the word that merits the consideration of a rational creature '

It is typical of the relationship between Gissing's fiction and his private life that a few years later he would find himself saying more or less the same thing to his friends about Gabrielle Fleury, the woman with whom he lived during the last years of his life in a common-law union (there was a marriage ceremony for the benefit of Gabrielle's mother, but there was also another Mrs Gissing — like Northway, conveniently institutionalized). Of course Gissing, as he was writing *Denzil Quarrier* in 1891, could not know what was going to happen several years later (he did not meet Gabrielle until 1898). But generally he is like so many of his characters — there is so much of himself in his work — that such bizarre 'coincidences' are not unusual. In *In the Year of Jubilee*, published in 1894, Arthur Peachey, having had enough of Mrs

Peachey, waits until she is out of the house and then packs up and
leaves, taking their child to his sister to care for and moving himself into
bachelor quarters, the location of which he keeps secret from his wife.
Three years *later* Gissing played exactly this same role opposite his
second wife Edith.

The marriage question is at the centre of *Denzil Quarrier*, as it is at the
centre of so much of Gissing's fiction. He wrote about it obsessively
because it was so important in his own life — especially, if one may judge
from his letters and other private writings, his mental life. Like a good
Victorian novel-hero, Gissing too had a 'guilty secret': as a young man
he had gone briefly to jail for robbing the locker room of his college. He
had done this to help the young prostitute with whom he was living (and
from whom he had contracted gonorrhea); the crime cost him a university education — and, so he came to think, the love of any respectable
woman. He went off to America, began to write stories, and became a
novelist instead of what he was most temperamentally suited to be —
a teacher of classics at one of the universities. The classics have
survived without him; the chief beneficiary of such misery and mis-
calculation has been English fiction.

Two years after he returned to England, Gissing, still in his early
twenties, made the mistake of marrying Nell Harrison, the prostitute he
had tried to help some years earlier. She was alcoholic, violent,
promiscuous, and a pathological liar. Of course the marriage was a
disaster, and Gissing finally left her. After her death in 1888 (the death
certificate euphemistically listed the cause as chronic laryngitis) he was
free to marry again, but hesitated. Should he try once more? If so, what
sort of girl would marry him? Gissing in the late 1880s had little money
and few prospects; he was still struggling, and he was in his thirties. He
had been in jail for, of all horrors, a working-class crime. Could he
possibly marry a social equal? Gissing complained to Bertz that he was
too poor to marry a respectable woman and that he could not live alone.
He threatened to run out into the street and propose to the first decent
working girl he saw.

It is unclear whether Edith Underwood was the first, but propose to
her he certainly did, shortly after picking her up in a restaurant. Again,
the results were catastrophic. She was stupid, she wouldn't learn, he
grew ashamed of her, he refused to take her out, she grew violent, and
ultimately Gissing walked out on her too — in the manner described
(before the event) in *In the Year of Jubilee*. Gabrielle, whom he met the
following year, was both intelligent and attractive, eminently respectable and solidly middle-class — he couldn't believe his luck. But there was
Mrs Gissing. So Gissing and Gabrielle lived together in France, after

walking through a farcical marriage ceremony — and Gissing, though he could not exist without complaining, had at any rate finally found a woman to live with who was his intellectual equal. The final tragedy was that his health failed before he had had time to enjoy his new life for more than a few years.

These bare facts — the striving for respectability, the guilty secret, the liaisons with inferior women, the final flouting of convention — may help us to understand why, in *Denzil Quarrier* as in many of Gissing's other novels, there is an obsessive hatred of society's formal rules, a hatred generated largely by the novelist's suspicion that he could never live up to them, that they would be too much for him in the end. Like Dickens, Gissing saw himself as an outsider trying to get in; and when it became clear that poverty, bad luck, his own sense of inferiority and his self-destructive urges were going to make his whole life a desperate battle, a struggle to the death with superior forces, the logical result for Gissing the novelist was to fight back through his fiction, and in it to attack the thing that had always barred his way — society itself and all of its conventions. These are the roots of Gissing's anti-Establishment bias in *Denzil Quarrier*. He is at once the most radical and the most conventional of the Victorian novelists — yearning for conventional respectability yet hating society for not letting him have it. It is in this sense that his position among the novelists is anomalous. Nor is it any accident that he wrote a monograph and a number of essays on Dickens, whom he saw as being very much in the same mould.

Gissing plays with the marriage theme in every novel, looking at it from various angles and trying out different fictional situations. If the relationships between men and women have anything in common throughout his books it is that, as in the novels of Henry James, none of these relationships comes out right. Sometimes it is because the woman lacks the domestic virtues (as both Nell and Edith did) and the result is domestic disorder. Sometimes a discrepancy in social position or origins causes problems. Often one of the partners (usually the man) has more education than the other, which is at the root of a temperamental incompatability. Sometimes the man does not earn enought to satisfy the woman, who is used to (or simply wants) better things. No matter what the causes of inequality, the theme of the unequal marriage runs through all of the novels without exception. Exogamy is Gissing's great subject, and he was an expert on it. In Trollope's novels the marriage question is an important subject, but the lovers are usually of the same class; their problems are to choose correctly among several suitable possibilities and/or to brave and conquer parents' or guardians' opposition to their choice. Jane Austen's treatment of the marriage theme is generally like Trollope's; so is Thackerary's, and Meredith's, and indeed that of most of the English novelists who have much to do with the subject. Rarely is there any question of class, and this is because Jane Austen and Thackeray and Trollope and Meredith do not have many poor or uneducated people in their novels. A gentleman does not marry beneath him, nor does a lady: to do so would be to betray society's trust. Such betrayals were not the stock-in-trade of the nineteenth-century novelists, most of whom found themselves having to massage the expectations of their mostly female and decidedly middle-class readers, who had their own ideas about heroes and heroines and made these feelings felt, often at close range. So in *Dr Wortle's School* the central problem is not class or suitability but rather the reconciliation of private conduct with public standards. In *Denzil Quarrier* the point is made that often one must lie in order to live as one likes, society's rules being frequently unreasonable or irrational. That deception, unconventional behaviour, and liaisons outside of one's class usually end in disaster is what Lilian's story tells us. Her fate scuttles the hypothesis, sometimes advanced by commentators on this novel, that *Denzil Quarrier* is in fact a defence of the conventions. The novel may be an acknowledgement of the power of convention–but not, surely, a defence of that power. For how can we admire what destroys Lilian? Gissing in his novels almost always leads the things he likes to defeat; it is his way of expressing his view of things, as it was Hardy's. Indeed, Lilian's end rivals that of a Hardy heroine: the climactic scene of *Denzil Quarrier* (pp. 308-9) suggests that Gissing had read *The Return of the Native* (1878) with care (his Diary, as a matter of fact, shows that he reread it in September 1890, just a year before he began to write *Denzil Quarrier*); surely he was no less contemptuous of society's moral judgments than his great contemporary, though certainly Gissing was more frightened of them. In the novels of both writers people are ground in the mill of the conventional, whose precepts they transgress only at great peril. *Denzil Quarrier*, Gissing wrote to Bertz in February 1892, might well 'give some offence to the extreme philistine wing'–which shows, at least, where he thought the novel stood (and where he thought Trollope stood too).

The political story, and especially the question of female emancipation, lies behind these other issues, and Gissing moves between them with some skill in *Denzil Quarrier*. The 1870s, following the founding of women's colleges at London and Oxford and the publication of Mill's *The Subjection of Women* (1869), saw the agitation for women's rights reach a sort of crescendo, and Gissing, whose novel is set in the years 1879-80, was very much interested in the subject. Dickens had advised women to stay at home, and Trollope treated the feminists with great irreverence — especially in *He Knew He Was Right* (1868-9) and *Is He Popenjoy?* (1877–8), which depicts them as masculine, rude, unattractive, hypocritical, petty, and even criminal. George Eliot, as Mrs Wade complains, gave the feminists no encouragement. As Quarrier's lecture shows plainly, Gissing was ambivalent on the subject of women's rights. His own life-experiences told him that well-educated women were hard to find. He wanted women to receive the sort of education that would make them fit wives for educated men and enable them to take a more intelligent part in the political and intellectual debates of the day. Young women, Quarrier declares, should not be sent ignorant into the world – a ubiquitous complaint of Gissing's. Quarrier goes on:

> The ordinary girl [is] sent forth into life with a mind scarcely more developed than that of a child. Hence those monstrous errors she constantly [commits] when called upon to accept a husband. Not one marriage in fifty thousand [is] an alliance on terms fair to the woman. In the vast majority of cases she [weds] a sort of man in the moon. Of him and all his world she [knows] nothing. (VII)

And yet the prospect of women abandoning the kitchens and linen closets of England scared Gissing to death. He knew how slatternly housekeeping could affect a man's life and work. He wound up feeling, all in all, something like this: when the dishes were washed and the beds made, then – and then only – women should be free to go to meetings and gather material enough to converse intelligently with their husbands over supper. This was Gissing's version of female emancipation – notably more sympathetic, actually, than the position taken on the issue by many of his contemporaries, yet surprisingly moderate given his passion for educating women. When women get involved in public affairs the result is 'scandalous neglect of the house', Toby Liversedge declares in Chapter V; he goes on to tell the story of a man who locks up his wife to keep her at home, at the conclusion of which everyone laughs uproariously. In his lecture, Quarrier says that if a woman doesn't become a 'wife and mother' her life is 'imperfect'. Still, he finds woman's aspirations 'beyond the physical' utterly natural.

Gissing's complicated attitude toward the female sex has many manifestations in *Denzil Quarrier*. Certainly it is no accident that it is Mrs Wade, the novel's leading feminist, who cold-bloodedly watches Lilian go to her death when she could have intervened. She refuses to act because she wants Quarrier for herself; throughout the novel she is obsessed by him. A woman who thinks that most other women are silly and worthless and generally a 'great reactionary force' (XV), who spends much of her time chasing after another woman's husband, and who ultimately 'assists' at the death of his wife, is by any odds an unusual representative of the women's-rights movement – unless, of course, the novelist is making a point.

Mrs Wade's questionable political credentials are part of the leisurely commentary in *Denzil Quarrier* upon politics itself. As in *Our Friend the Charlatan* (1902), Gissing equates political aspirations with various kinds of moral charlatanism. The Liberal–Radical candidate, Quarrier, is living a lie. Eustace Glazzard, having extorted money from a dying friend, goes on to sublimate his frustrated political ambition in treachery and sadism (Glazzard equates politics with 'excitement', and Gissing seems to suggest that political and treacherous impulses are generated from similar sources). Northway, another would-be politician, is also an extortionist, with the emphasis on blackmail. Still another frustrated politico, Mumbray, is a living embodiment of cant and humbug. The Tory candidate, Welwyn-Baker, is lazy (too lazy, as a matter of fact, to appear in the novel) and incompetent. Gissing regarded the political process as another manifestation of society's hollowness–a charade in the course of which honest people are hoodwinked by hypocrites and only pretensions are taken seriously. Politics, for him, is a game played at by people who would like to be thought respectable; but the louder they talk the less they mean. Gissing had touched on this theme in the person of Dalmaine in an earlier novel, *Thyrza* (1887), and he was to take it up even more earnestly in *Our Friend the Charlatan*.

No one would argue that *Denzil Quarrier* is one of Gissing's best novels, or even one of his better ones. In October 1891, as he was working on *Denzil Quarrier*, Gissing told Bertz only that 'the book won't be bad.' Four months later, having sent a copy of the first edition off to Bertz, Gissing wrote to his friend: 'If you don't much care for it, just make a cross at the head of your next letter, and never mind further comment' (usually Gissing was anxious for Bertz's opinion of his work). The novelist was encouraged by favourable notices in *The Times* and the *Saturday Review* and by the quick publication of the book in America, but he soon lost interest in it and never considered it one of his better novels. In this he was certainly right. Some writers, unable at first to escape the distorting lens of self-interest, can write effectively only after exorcising personal demons. But Gissing's passion, power, and sometime brilliance as a novelist derive largely from personal experience and out of subjects (poverty, unhappy marriage, the importance of class, for example) with which he feels a close involvement. His best books contain a character or two very much like himself, written about with an eloquence and a depth of feeling never achieved when the *personae* or the subject are less familiar. Novels like *The Unclassed* (1884) and *Thyrza*, written relatively early in his career and containing monumental Gissingesque alter-egos, continued to haunt him for years after he had penned their final words. But *Denzil Quarrier*, like *Our Friend the Charlatan*, has fewer connections to the novelist's life, and in both novels the political story has no connection whatsoever. It is really fiction. Gissing cared nothing about politics and was contemptuous of politicians; unlike some of his fellow Victorian novelists, he had no political ambitions. His two political novels suffer accordingly. *Demos* (1886), which is first-rate, has sometimes been called a political novel, but it is really about class and not at all about politics. While there are situations in *Denzil Quarrier* and *Our Friend the Charlatan* that are clearly autobiographical, there are no Gissing alter-egos in them – and thus there is little passion in them. In both novels Gissing's posture is that of the satirist, and there is a corresponding reduction in sympathetic observation and even in authorial interest. In his best novels Gissing writes brilliantly of his own experiences and feelings – both past and, sometimes, those to come; it is when his fiction most nearly approaches autobiography that he reaches his highest achievements. In *New Grub Street* (1891) and *Born in Exile* (1892), the novels preceding *Denzil Quarrier* in the parade of generally first-rate books Gissing produced in the early 1890s, he does indeed write affectingly of himself. *Denzil Quarrier*, by moving over to public questions, gave him a breathing space, and for this reason it is a falling off – or perhaps, more precisely, a falling away from.

Yet at the heart of the story lies the theme of the unequal marriage and the guilty secret it hides, vintage Gissing and the best thing in the book. It is the domestic scenes rather than the public ones that give this so-called political novel both its chief interest and its intermittent power, and this is undoubtedly because Lilian has something of Edith Gissing in her. On 7 November 1891 Gissing, who still considered Edith gentle and pliable, wrote to his sister Ellen: 'Edith does very well – improves much in every way. I am more than satisfied with her. The house is orderly, everything punctual.' This letter (still unpublished), dated exactly five days before he finished writing *Denzil Quarrier*, may help to explain why Gissing will never be considered a great radical; more importantly, it may also help to explain why his relations with women were often stormy – stormy enough, indeed, to find their way inevitably into his fictional autobiographies, one after another.

John Halperin

DENZIL QUARRIER

DENZIL QUARRIER

𝔄 𝔑𝔬𝔳𝔢𝔩

BY

GEORGE GISSING

AUTHOR OF

" New Grub Street," " The Nether World," " Thyrza," &c.

LONDON

LAWRENCE & BULLEN

169 NEW BOND STREET, W.

1892

DENZIL QUARRIER.

I.

For half an hour there had been perfect silence in the
room. The cat upon the hearthrug slept profoundly;
the fire was sunk to a still red glow; the cold light of
the autumn afternoon thickened into dusk.

Lilian seemed to be reading. She sat on a footstool,
her arm resting on the seat of a basket-chair, which
supported a large open volume. But her hand was
never raised to turn a page, and it was long since her
eyes had gathered the sense of the lines on which they
were fixed. This attitude had been a favourite one
with her in childhood, and nowadays, in her long
hours of solitude, she often fell into the old habit. It
was a way of inviting reverie, which was a way of
passing the time.

She stirred at length; glanced at the windows, at
the fire, and rose.

A pleasant little sitting-room, furnished in the taste
of our time; with harmonies and contrasts of subdued colour, with pictures intelligently chosen, with

store of graceful knick-knacks. Lilian's person was in keeping with such a background; her dark gold hair, her pale, pensive, youthful features, her slight figure in its loose raiment, could not have been more suitably displayed.   In a room of statelier proportions she would have looked too frail, too young for significance; out of doors she was seldom seen to advantage; here one recognized her as the presiding spirit in a home fragrant of womanhood.   The face, at this moment, was a sad one, but its lines expressed no weak surrender to dolefulness; her lips were courageous, and her eyes such as brighten readily with joy.

A small table bore a tea-tray with a kettle and spirit-lamp; the service for two persons only. Lilian, after looking at her watch, ignited the lamp and then went to the window as if in expectation of some one's arrival.

The house stood in a row of small new dwellings on the outskirts of Clapham Common; there was little traffic along the road at any time, and in this hour of twilight even a passing footstep became a thing to notice. Some one approached on her side of the way; she listened, but with disappointment; it was not the step for which she waited. None the less it paused at this house, and she was startled to perceive a telegraph messenger on the point of knocking. At once she hastened to the front door.

"Mrs. Quarrier?" inquired the boy, holding out his missive.

Lilian drew back with it into the passage. But there was not light enough to read by; she had to enter the sitting-room and hold the sheet of paper close to the kettle-lamp.

"Very sorry that I cannot get home before ten. Unexpected business."

She read it carefully, then turned with a sigh and dismissed the messenger.

In a quarter of an hour she had made tea, and sat down to take a cup. The cat, refreshed after slumber, jumped on to her lap and lay there pawing playfully at the trimming of her sleeves. Lilian at first rewarded this friendliness only with absent stroking, but when she had drunk her tea and eaten a slice of bread and butter the melancholy mood dispersed; pussy's sportiveness was then abundantly indulged, and for awhile Lilian seemed no less merry than her companion.

The game was interrupted by another knock at the house-door; this time it was but the delivery of the evening paper. Lilian settled herself in a chair by the fireside, and addressed herself with a serious countenance to the study of the freshly-printed columns. Beginning with the leading-article, she read page after page in the most conscientious way, often pausing to reflect, and once even to pencil a note on the margin. The paper finished, she found it necessary for the clear understanding of a certain subject to consult a book of reference, and for this purpose she went to a room in the rear—a small study, comfortably but plainly furnished, smelling of tobacco. It was very chilly, and she did not spend much time over her researches.

A sound from the lower part of the house checked her
returning steps; some one was rapping at the door down
in the area. It happened that she was to-day without
a servant; she must needs descend into the kitchen herself and answer the summons. When the nether
regions were illumined and the door thrown open,
Lilian beheld a familiar figure, that of a scraggy and
wretchedly clad woman with a moaning infant in her
arms.

"Oh, it's you, Mrs. Wilson!" she exclaimed.
"Please to come in. How have you been getting on?
And how is baby?"

The woman took a seat by the kitchen fire, and began
to talk in a whining, mendicant tone. From the conversation it appeared that this was by no means the
first time she had visited Lilian and sought to arouse
her compassion; the stories she poured forth consisted
in a great measure of excuses for not having profited
more substantially by the help already given her. The
eye and the ear of experience would readily enough
have perceived in Mrs. Wilson a very coarse type of
impostor, and even Lilian, though showing a face of
distress at what she heard, seemed to hesitate in her
replies and to entertain troublesome doubts. But the
objection she ventured to make to a flagrant inconsistency in the tale called forth such loud indignation,
such a noisy mixture of insolence and grovelling entreaty,
that her moral courage gave way and Mrs. Wilson
whined for another quarter of an hour in complete
security from cross-examination. In the end Lilian

brought out her purse and took from it half-a-sovereign.

"Now, if I give you this, Mrs. Wilson, I do hope to have a better account "——

Her admonitions were cut short, and with difficulty she managed to obtain hearing for a word or two of what was meant for grave counsel whilst taking leave of her visitor. Mrs. Wilson, a gleam in her red eyes, vanished up the area steps, and left Lilian to meditate on the interview.

The evening passed on, and her solitude was undisturbed. When dinner-time came, she sat down to the wing of a cold chicken and a thimbleful of claret much diluted; the repast was laid out with perfection of neatness, and at its conclusion she cleared the table like the handiest of parlour-maids. Whatever she did was done gracefully; she loved order, and when alone was no less scrupulous in satisfying her idea of the becoming than when her actions were all observed.

After dinner, she played a little on the piano. Here, as over her book in the afternoon, the absent fit came upon her. Her fingers had rested idly on the keyboard for some minutes, when they began to touch solemn chords, and at length there sounded the first notes of a homely strain, one of the most familiar of the Church's hymns. It ceased abruptly; Lilian rose and went to another part of the room.

A few minutes later her ear caught the sound for which she was now waiting—that of a latch-key at the front door. She stepped quickly out into the passage, where the lamp-light fell upon a tall and robust man with dark, comely, bearded visage.

"Poor little girl!" he addressed her, affectionately, as he pulled off his overcoat. "I couldn't help it, Lily; bound to stay."

"Never mind!" was her laughing reply, as she stood on tip-toe and drew down his face to hers. "I was disappointed, but it's as well you didn't come to dinner. Sarah had to go away this morning."

"Oh! How's that? How have *you* managed then?"

They passed into the front room, and Quarrier repeated his inquiries.

"She had a letter from Birmingham," Lilian explained. "Her brother has been all but killed in some dreadful accident, and he's in a hospital. I saw she wished to go—so I gave her some money and sent her off as soon as possible. Perhaps it was her only chance of seeing him alive, Denzil."

"Yes, yes—of course you did right," he answered, after a moment's hesitation.

"I knew you wouldn't mind a dinner of my cooking—under the circumstances."

"But what are we to do? You can't take her place in the kitchen till she comes back."

"I'll get some one for a few days."

"But, confound it! how about to-morrow morning? It's very awkward"——

"Oh, I shall easily manage."

"What?—go down at eight o'clock and light fires!

Hang it, no! All right; I'll turn out and see to breakfast. But you must get another girl; a second servant, I mean. Yes, you ought really to have two. Get a decent cook."

" Do you think it necessary ? "

Quarrier was musing, a look of annoyance on his face.

"It couldn't have happened more inconveniently," he said, without regard to Lilian's objection. "I had better tell you at once, Lily: I've asked a friend of mine to come and dine with us to-morrow."

She started and looked at him with anxious eyes.

" A friend ? "

" Yes; Glazzard—the man who spoke to me at Kew Station the other day—you remember ? "

" Oh yes ! "

Lilian seated herself by the piano and stroked the keys with the tips of her fingers. Standing on the hearth-rug, her companion watched her closely for a moment; his forehead was wrinkled, and he did not seem quite at ease.

" Glazzard is a very good fellow," he pursued, looking about the room and thrusting his hands into his trouser-pockets. "I've known him since I was a boy—a well-read man, thoughtful, clever. A good musician; something more than an amateur with the violin, I believe. An artist, too; he had a bust in the Academy a few years ago, and I've seen some capital etchings of his."

" A universal genius !" said Lilian, with a forced laugh.

"Well, there's no doubt he has come very near success in a good many directions. Never *quite* succeeded; there's the misfortune. I suppose he lacks perseverance. But he doesn't care; takes everything with a laugh and a joke."

He reached for the evening newspaper, and glanced absently over the columns. For a minute or two there was silence.

"What have you told him?" Lilian asked at length, in an undertone.

"Why, simply that I have had reasons for keeping my marriage secret."

He spoke in a blunt, authoritative way, but with his usual kindly smile.

"I thought it better," he added, "after that chance meeting the other day. He's a fellow one can trust, I assure you. Thoroughly good-hearted. As you know, I don't readily make friends, and I'm the last man to give my confidence to any one who doesn't deserve it. But Glazzard and I have always understood each other pretty well, and—at all events, he knows me well enough to be satisfied with as much as I choose to tell him."

Quarrier had the air of a man who, without any vulgar patronage, and in a spirit of abundant good-nature, classifies his acquaintance in various degrees of subordination to himself. He was too healthy, too vigorous of frame and frank in manner to appear conceited, but it was evident that his experience of life had encouraged a favourable estimate of his own standing and resources. The ring of his voice was sound; no affectation or insincerity marred its notes. For all that, he seemed just now not entirely comfortable; his pretence of looking over the paper in the intervals of talk was meant to cover a certain awkwardness in discussing the subject he had broached.

"You don't object to his coming, Lily?"

"No; whatever you think best, dear."

"I'm quite sure you'll find him pleasant company. But we must get him a dinner, somehow. I'll go to some hotel to-morrow morning and put the thing in their hands; they'll send a cook, or do something or other. If the girl had been here we should have managed well enough; Glazzard is no snob.—I want to smoke; come into my study, will you? No fire? Get up some wood, there's a good girl, we'll soon set it going. I'd fetch it myself, but I shouldn't know where to look for it."

A flame was soon roaring up the chimney in the little back room, and Quarrier's pipe filled the air with fragrant mist.

"How is it," he exclaimed, settling in the arm-chair, "that there are so many beggars in this region? Two or three times this last week I've been assailed along the street. I'll put a stop to that; I told a great hulking fellow to-night that if he spoke to me again (it was the second time) I would take the trouble of marching him to the nearest police station."

"Poor creatures!" sighed Lilian.

"Pooh! Loafing blackguards, with scarcely an

exception! Well, I was going to tell you: Glazzard comes from my own town, Polterham. We were at the Grammar School there together; but he read Æschylus and Tacitus whilst I was grubbing over Eutropius and the Greek declensions."

"Is he so much older then? He seemed to me "——

"Six years older—about five-and-thirty. He's going down to Polterham on Saturday, and I think I shall go with him."

" Go with him? For long?"

" A week, I think. I want to see my brother-in-law. You won't mind being left alone? "

" No; I shall do my best to keep in good spirits."

" I'll get you a batch of new books. I may as well tell you, Liversedge has been persuaded to stand as Liberal candidate for Polterham at the next election. It surprised me rather; I shouldn't have thought he was the kind of fellow to go in for politics. It always seemed to be as little in his line as it is in mine."

" And do you wish to advise him against it? "

" Oh no; there's no harm in it. I suppose Beacons-field and crew have roused him. I confess I should enjoy helping to kick them into space. No, I just want to talk it over with him. And I owe them a visit; they took it rather ill that I couldn't go with them to Ireland."

Lilian sat with bent head. Casting a quick glance at her, Quarrier talked on in a cheerful strain.

" I'm afraid he isn't likely to get in. The present member is an old fogey called Welwyn-Baker; a fatheaded Tory; this is his third Parliament. They think he's going to set up his son next time—a fool, no doubt, but I have no knowledge of him. I'm afraid Liversedge isn't the man to stir enthusiasm."

"But is there any one to be made enthusiastic on that side?" asked Lilian.

"Well, it's a town that has changed a good deal of late years. It used to be only an agricultural market, but about twenty years ago a man started a blanket factory, and since then several other industries have shot up. There's a huge sugar-refinery, and a place where they make jams. That kind of thing, you know, affects the spirit of a place. Manufacturers are generally go-ahead people, and mill-hands don't support high Tory doctrine. It'll be interesting to see how they muster. If Liversedge knows how to go to work"— he broke into laughter. "Suppose, when the time comes, I go down and harangue the mob in his favour?"

Lilian smiled and shook her head.

"I'm afraid you would be calling them 'the mob' to their faces."

"Well, why not? I dare say I should do more that way than by talking fudge about the glorious and enlightened people. 'Look here, you blockheads!' I should shout, 'can't you see on which side your interests lie? Are you going to let England be thrown into war and taxes just to please a theatrical Jew and the howling riff-raff of London?' I tell you what, Lily, it seems to me I could make a rattling good speech if I gave my mind to it. Don't you think so?"

"There's nothing you couldn't do," she answered, with soft fervour, fixing her eyes upon him.

"And yet I do nothing—isn't that what you would like to add?"

"Oh, but your book is getting on!"

"Yes, yes; so it is. A capital book it'll be, too; a breezy book—smelling of the sea-foam! But, after all, that's only pen-work. I have a notion that I was meant for active life, after all. If I had remained in the Navy, I should have been high up by now. I should have been hoping for war, I dare say. What possibilities there are in every man!"

He grew silent, and Lilian, her face shadowed once more, conversed with her own thoughts.

II.

In a room in the west of London—a room full of pictures and bric-à-brac, of quaint and luxurious furniture, with volumes abundant, with a piano in a shadowed corner, a violin and a mandoline laid carelessly aside—two men sat facing each other, their looks expressive of anything but mutual confidence. The one (he wore an overcoat, and had muddy boots) was past middle age, bald, round-shouldered, dressed like a country gentleman; upon his knees lay a small hand-bag, which he seemed about to open. He leaned forward with a face of stern reproach, and put a short, sharp question:

"Then why haven't I heard from you since my nephew's death?"

The other was not ready with a reply. Younger, and more fashionably attired, he had assumed a lounging attitude which seemed natural to him, though it served also to indicate a mood of resentful superiority. His figure was slight, and not ungraceful; his features—pale, thin, with heavy nose, high forehead—were intellectual and noteworthy, but lacked charm.

"I have been abroad till quite recently," he said at length, his fine accent contrasting with that of the questioner, which had a provincial note. "Why did you expect me to communicate with you?"

"Don't disgrace yourself by speaking in that way, Mr. Glazzard!" exclaimed the other, his voice uncertain with strong, angry feeling. "You know quite well why I have come here, and why you ought to have seen me long ago!"

Thereupon he opened the bag and took out a manuscript-book.

"I found this only the other day among Harry's odds and ends. It's a diary that he kept. Will you explain to me the meaning of this entry, dated in June of last year: 'Lent E. G. a hundred pounds'?"

Glazzard made no answer, but his self-command was not sufficient to check a quivering of the lips.

"There can be no doubt who these initials refer to. Throughout, ever since my nephew's intimacy with you began, you are mentioned here as 'E. G.' Please to explain another entry, dated August: 'Lent E. G. two hundred pounds.' And then again, February of this year: 'Lent E. G. a hundred and fifty pounds'—and yet again, three months later: 'Lent E. G. a hundred pounds'—what is the meaning of all this?"

"The meaning, Mr. Charnock," replied Glazzard, "is indisputable."

"You astound me!" cried the elder man, shutting up the diary and straightening himself to an attitude of indignation. "Am I to understand, then, that *this* is the reason why Harry left no money? You mean to say you have allowed his relatives to believe that he had wasted a large sum, whilst they supposed that he was studying soberly in London"——

"If you are astounded," returned the other, raising his eyebrows, "I certainly am no less so. As your nephew made note of these lendings, wasn't he equally careful to jot down a memorandum when the debt was discharged?"

Mr. Charnock regarded him fixedly, and for a moment seemed in doubt.

"You paid back these sums?"

"With what kind of action did you credit me?" said Glazzard, quietly.

The other hesitated, but wore no less stern a look.

"I am obliged to declare, Mr. Glazzard, that I can't trust your word. That's a very strong thing to have to say to a man such as I have thought you—a man of whom Harry always spoke as if there wasn't his like on earth. My acquaintance with you is very slight; I know very little indeed about you, except what Harry told me. But the man who could deliberately borrow hundreds of pounds from a lad only just of age —a simple, trustful, good-natured country lad, who had little but his own exertions to depend upon—*such* a man will tell a lie to screen himself! This money was *not* paid back; there isn't a word about it in the diary, and there's the fact that Harry had got rid of his money in a way no one could explain. You had it, and you have kept it, sir!"

Glazzard let his eyes stray about the room. He uncrossed his legs, tapped on the arm of his easy-chair, and said at length:

"I have no liking for violence, and I shall try to

keep my temper. Please to tell me the date of the last entry in that journal."

Mr. Charnock opened the book again, and replied at once :

" June 5th of this year—1879."

" I see. Allow me a moment." He unlocked a drawer in a writing-table, and referred to some paper. " On the 1st of June—we were together the whole day—I paid your nephew five hundred and fifty pounds in bank-notes. Please refer to the diary."

" You *were* together on that day, but there is no note of such a transaction. ' With E. G. Much talk about pictures, books, and music—delightful ! ' That's all."

" Have you added up the sums mentioned previously ? "

" Yes. They come to what you say. How did it happen, Mr. Glazzard, that you had so large a sum in bank-notes ? It isn't usual."

" It is not unheard of, Mr. Charnock, with men who sometimes play for money."

" What ! Then you mean to tell me that Harry learnt from you to be a gambler ? "

" Certainly not. He never had the least suspicion that I played."

" And pray, what became of those notes after he received them ? "

" I have no idea. For anything I know, you may still find the money."

Mr. Charnock rose from his seat.

" I see," he said, " that we needn't talk any longer.

I don't believe your story, and there's an end of it. The fact of your borrowing was utterly disgraceful; it shows me that the poor boy had fallen in a trap, instead of meeting with a friend who was likely to guide and improve him. You confess yourself a gambler, and I go away with the conviction that you are something yet worse."

Glazzard set his lips hard, but fell back into the lounging attitude.

"The matter doesn't end here," went on his accuser, "be sure of that! I shall light upon evidence sooner or later. Do you know, sir, that Harry had a sister, and that she earns her own living by giving lessons? You have robbed her—think it over at your leisure. Why, less than a fortnight after that day you and he spent together—the 1st of June—the lad lay dying; yet you could deliberately plan to rob him. Your denial is utterly vain; I would pledge my life on the charge! I read guilt in your face when I entered—you were afraid of me, Mr. Glazzard! I understand now why you never came to see the lad on his death-bed, though he sent for you—and of course I know why he was anxious to speak to you. Oh, you have plenty of plausible excuses, but they are lies! You felt pretty sure, I dare say, that the lad would not betray you; you knew his fine sense of honour; you calculated upon it. All your conduct is of a piece!"

Glazzard rose.

"Mr. Charnock, please to leave me.—I oughtn't to have borrowed that money; but having paid it back, I can't submit to any more of your abuse. My patience has its limits."

" I am no brawler," replied the other, " and I can do no good by talking to you. But if ever I come across any of your acquaintances, they shall know, very plainly, what opinion I have of you. Prosecute me for slander, Mr. Glazzard, if you dare—I desire nothing better ! "

And Mr. Charnock went hurriedly from the room.

For several minutes Glazzard kept the same attitude, his eyes fixed on the floor, one hand behind his back, the other thrust into his waistcoat. Then he uttered an inarticulate exclamation, and walked with hurried, jerky step across the room ; his facial muscles quivered ceaselessly, distorting the features into all manner of grotesque and ugly expressions. Again the harsh sound escaped him, and again he changed his place as though impelled by a sudden pain. It was a long time before he took a seat ; on doing so, he threw up his feet, and rested them against the side of the fireplace. His hands were thrust into his trouser-pockets, and his head fell back, so that he stared at the ceiling. At one moment he gave out a short mocking laugh, but no look of mirth followed the explosion. Little by little he grew motionless, and sat with closed eyes.

From the walls about him looked down many a sweet and noble countenance, such as should have made the room a temple of serenity. Nowhere was there a token of vulgar sensualism ; the actress, the ballet-nymph had no place among these chosen gems of art. On the

dwarf book-cases were none but works of pure
inspiration, the best of old and new, the kings of
intellect and their gentlest courtiers. Fifteen years
had gone to the adorning of this sanctuary ; of money,
no great sum, for Glazzard had never commanded
more than his younger-brother's portion of a yearly five
hundred pounds, and all his tastes were far from being
represented in the retreat where he spent his hours of
highest enjoyment and endeavour. Of late he had
been beset by embarrassments which a man of his stamp
could ill endure : depreciation of investments, need of
sordid calculation, humiliating encounters. To-day he
tasted the very dregs of ignoble anguish, and it seemed
to him that he should never again look with delight
upon a picture, or feast his soul with music, or care to
open a book.

A knock at the door aroused him. It was a civil-
tongued serving-woman who came to ask if he purposed
having luncheon at home to-day. No ; he was on the
point of going forth.

Big Ben was striking twelve. At a quarter-past,
Glazzard took a cab which conveyed him to one of the
Inns of Court. He ascended stairs, and reached a door
on which was inscribed the name of Mr. Stark, Solicitor.
An office-boy at once admitted him to the innermost
room, where he was greeted with much friendliness by
a short, stout man, with gleaming visage, full lips,
chubby hands.

"Well, what is it now?" inquired the visitor, who
had been summoned hither by a note that morning.

Mr. Stark, with an air of solemnity not wholly jocose, took his friend's arm and led him to a corner of the room, where, resting against a chair-back, was a small ill-framed oil painting.

" What have you to say to that ? "

" The ugliest thing I've seen for a long time."

" But—but— " the solicitor stammered, with indignant eagerness—" but do know whose it is ? "

The picture represented a bit of country road, with a dung-heap, a duck-pond, a pig asleep, and some barn-door fowls.

" I know whose you *think* it is," replied Glazzard, coldly. His face still had an unhealthy pallor, and his eyes looked as if they had but just opened after the oppression of nightmare. " But it isn't."

" Come, come, Glazzard ! you are too dictatorial, my boy."

Mr. Stark kept turning a heavy ring upon his finger, showing in face and tone that the connoisseur's dogmatism troubled him more than he wished to have it thought.

" Winterbottom warrants it," he added, with a triumphant jerk of his plump body.

" Then Winterbottom is either cheating or cheated. That is no Morland ; take my word for it. Was that all you wanted me for ? "

Mr Stark's good-nature was severely tried. Mental suffering had made Glazzard worse than impolite ; his familiar tone of authority on questions of art had become too frankly contemptuous.

"You're out of sorts this morning," conjectured his legal friend. "Let Morland be for the present. I had another reason for asking you to call, but don't stay unless you like."

Glazzard looked round the office.

"Well?" he asked, more gently.

"Quarrier tells me you are going down to Polterham. Any special reason?"

"Yes. But I can't talk about it."

"I was down there myself last Sunday. I talked politics with the local wiseacres, and—do you know, it has made me think of you ever since?"

"How so?"

Mr. Stark consulted his watch.

"I'm at leisure for just nineteen minutes. If you care to sit down, I have an idea I should like to put before you."

The visitor seated himself and crossed his legs. His countenance gave small promise of attention.

"You know," resumed Mr. Stark, leaning forward and twiddling his thumbs, "that they're hoping to get rid of Welwyn-Baker at the next election?"

"What of that?"

"Toby Liversedge talks of coming forward—but *that* won't do."

"Probably not."

The solicitor bent still more and tapped his friend's knee.

"Glazzard, here is your moment. Here is your chance of getting what you want. Liversedge is reluctant to stand; I know that for certain. To a more promising man he'll yield with pleasure.—St! st! listen to me!—you are that man. Go down; see Toby; see the wiseacres and wire-pullers; get your name in vogue! It's cut out for you. Act now, or never again pretend that you want a chance."

A smile of disdain settled upon Glazzard's lips, but his eyes had lost their vacancy.

"On the Radical side?" he asked, mockingly. "For Manchester and Brummagem?"

"For Parliament, my dear boy! For Westminster, St. Stephen's, distinction, a career! I should perhaps have thought of your taking Welwyn-Baker's place, but there are many reasons against it. You would lose the support of your brother and all his friends. Above all, Polterham will go Liberal—mark my prediction!"

"I doubt it."

"I haven't time to give you all my reasons. Dine with me this evening, will you?"

"Can't. Engaged to Quarrier."

"All right!" said the latter. "To-morrow, then?"

"Yes, I will dine to-morrow."

Mr. Stark jumped up.

"Think of it. I can't talk longer now; there's the voice of a client I'm expecting. Eight sharp to-morrow!"

Glazzard took his leave.

III.

LIKE so many other gentlemen whose function in the world remains indefinite, chiefly because of the patrimony they have inherited, Denzil Quarrier had eaten his dinners, and been called to the Bar; he went so far in specification as to style himself Equity barrister. But the Courts had never heard his voice. Having begun the studies, he carried them through just for consistency, but long before bowing to the Benchers of his Inn he foresaw that nothing practical would come of it. This was his second futile attempt to class himself with a recognized order of society. Nay, strictly speaking, the third. The close of his thirteenth year had seen him a pupil at Polterham Grammar School; not an unpromising pupil by any means, but with a turn for insubordination, much disposed to pursue with zeal anything save the tasks that were set him. Inspired by Cooper and Captain Marryat, he came to the conclusion that his destiny was the Navy, and stuck so firmly to it that his father, who happened to have a friend on the Board of Admiralty, procured him a nomination, and speedily saw the boy a cadet on the " Britannia." Denzil wore Her Majesty's uniform for some five years; then he tired of the service and went back to Polterham to reconsider his bent and aptitudes.

His father no longer dwelt in the old home, but had recently gone over to Norway, where he pursued his calling of timber-merchant. Denzil's uncle—Samuel Quarrier—busied in establishing a sugar-refinery in his native town, received the young man with amiable welcome, and entertained him for half a year. The ex-seaman then resolved to join his parents abroad, as a good way of looking about him. He found his mother on her death-bed. In consequence of her decease, Denzil became possessed of means amply sufficient for a bachelor. As far as ever from really knowing what he desired to be at, he began to make a show of interesting himself in timber. Perhaps, after all, commerce was his *forte*. This, then, might be called a second endeavour to establish himself.

Mr. Quarrier laughed at the idea, and would not take it seriously. And of course was in the right, for Denzil, on pretence of studying forestry, began to ramble about Scandinavia like a gentleman at large. Here, however, he did ultimately hit on a pursuit into which he could throw himself with decided energy. The old Norsemen laid their spell upon him; he was bitten with a zeal for saga-hunting, studied vigorously the Northern tongues, went off to Iceland, returned to rummage in the libraries of Copenhagen, began to translate the Heimskringla, planned a History of the Vikings. Emphatically, this kind of thing suited him. No one was less likely to turn out a bookworm, yet in the study of Norse literature he found that combination of mental and muscular interests which was perchance what he had been seeking.

But his father was dissatisfied; a very practical man, he saw in this odd enthusiasm a mere waste of time. Denzil's secession from the Navy had sorely disappointed him; constantly he uttered his wish that the young man should attach himself to some vocation that became a gentleman. Denzil, a little weary for the time of his Sea-Kings, at length consented to go to London and enter himself as a student of law. Perhaps his father was right. "Yes, I need discipline—intellectual and moral. I am beginning to perceive my defects. There's something in me not quite civilized. I'll go in for the law."

Yet Scandinavia had not seen the last of him. He was backwards and forwards pretty frequently across the North Sea. He kept up a correspondence with learned Swedes, Norwegians, Danes, and men of Iceland; when they came to England he entertained them with hearty hospitality, and searched with them at the British Museum. These gentlemen liked him, though they felt occasionally that he was wont to lay down the law when the attitude of a disciple would rather have become him.

He had rooms in Clement's Inn, retaining them even when his abode, strictly speaking, was at the little house by Clapham Common. To that house no one was invited. Old Mr. Quarrier knew not of its existence; neither did Mr. Sam Quarrier of Polterham, nor any other of Denzil's kinsfolk. The first person to

whom Denzil revealed that feature of his life was
Eustace Glazzard—a discreet, upright friend, the very
man to entrust with such a secret.

It was now early in the autumn of 1879. Six
months ago Denzil had lost his father, who died
suddenly on a journey from Christiania up the country,
leaving the barrister in London a substantial fortune.

This change of circumstances had in no way out-
wardly affected Denzil's life. As before, he spent a
good deal of his time in the rooms at Clement's Inn,
and cultivated domesticity at Clapham. He was
again working in earnest at his History of the Vikings.
Something would at last come of it; a heap of manuscript attested his solid progress.

To-day he had come to town only for an hour or
two. Glazzard was to call at half-past six, and they
would go together to dine with Lilian. In his report
to her, Quarrier had spoken nothing less than truth.
" The lady with whom you chanced to see me the other
day was my wife. I have been married for a year and
a half—a strictly private matter. Be so good as to
respect my confidence." That was all Glazzard had
learnt; sufficient to excite no little curiosity in the
connoisseur.

Denzil's chambers had a marked characteristic; they
were full of objects and pictures which declared his love
of Northern lands and seas. At work he sat in the
midst of a little museum. To the bear, the elk, the
seal, he was indebted for comforts and ornaments; on
his shelves were quaint collections of crockery; coins of

historical value displayed themselves in cases on the walls; shoes and garments of outlandish fashion lay here and there. Probably few private libraries in England could boast such an array of Scandinavian literature as was here exhibited. As a matter of course the rooms had accumulated even more dirt than one expects in a bachelor's retreat; they were redolent of the fume of many pipes.

When Glazzard tapped at the inner door and entered, his friend, who sat at the writing-table in evening costume, threw up his arms, stretched himself, and yawned noisily.

" Working at your book ? " asked the other.

" No ; letters. I don't care for the Sea-Kings just now. They're rather remote old dogs, after all, you know."

" Distinctly, I should say."

" A queer thing, on the whole, that I can stick so to them. But I like their spirit. You're not a pugnacious fellow, I think, Glazzard ? "

" No, I think not."

" But I am, you know. I mean it literally. Every now and then I feel I should like to thrash some one. I read in the paper this morning of some son of a "—— (Denzil's language occasionally reminded one that he had been a sailor) " who had cheated a lot of poor servant-girls out of their savings. My fists itched to be at that lubber ! There's a good deal to be said for the fighting instinct in man, you know."

" So thinks 'Arry of the music-halls."

" Well, we have heard before of an ass opening its mouth to prophesy. I tell you what: on my way here this afternoon I passed the office of some journal or other in the Strand, where they're exhibiting a copy of their paper returned to them by a subscriber in Russia. Two columns are completely obliterated with the censor's lamp-black,—that's how it reaches the subscriber's hands. As I stood looking at that, my blood rose to boiling-point ! I could have hurrah'd for war with Russia on that one account alone. That contemptible idiot of a Czar, sitting there on his ant-hill throne, and bidding Time stand still ! "

He laughed long and loud in scornful wrath.

" The Czar can't help it," remarked Glazzard, smiling calmly, " and perhaps knows nothing about it. The man is a slave of slaves."

" The more contemptible and criminal, then ! " roared Denzil. " If a man in his position can't rule, he should be kicked out of the back-door of his palace. I have no objection to an autocrat ; I think most countries need one. I should make a good autocrat myself—a benevolent despot."

" We live in stirring times," said the other, with a fine curl of the lips. " Who knows what destiny has in store for you ? "

Quarrier burst into good-natured merriment, and thereupon made ready to set forth.

When they reached the house by Clapham Common, Denzil opened the door with his latch-key, talked loud whilst he was removing his overcoat, and then led the way into the sitting-room. Lilian was there; she rose and laid down a book; her smile of welcome did not conceal the extreme nervousness from which she was suffering. Quarrier's genial contempt of ceremony, as he performed the introduction, allowed it to be seen that he too experienced some constraint. But the guest bore himself with perfect grace and decorum. Though not a fluent talker, he fell at once into a strain of agreeable chat on subjects which seemed likely to be of interest; his success was soon manifest in the change of Lilian's countenance. Denzil, attentive to both, grew more genuinely at ease. When Lilian caught his eye, he smiled at her with warmth of approving kindness. It must have been a fastidious man who felt dissatisfied with the way in which the young hostess discharged her duties; timidity led her into no *gaucherie,* but was rather an added charm among the many with which nature had endowed her. Speech and manner, though they had nothing of the conventional adornment that is gathered in London drawing-rooms, were those of gentle breeding and bright intelligence; her education seemed better than is looked for among ladies in general. Glazzard perceived that she had read diligently, and with scope beyond that of the circulating library; the book with which she had been engaged when they entered was a Danish novel.

"Do you also look for salvation to the Scandinavians?" he asked.

"I read the languages—the modern. They have a very interesting literature of to-day; the old battle-stories don't appeal to me quite so much as they do to Denzil."

"You ought to know this fellow Jacobsen," said Quarrier, taking up the novel. "'Marie Grubbe' doesn't sound a very æsthetic title, but the book is quite in your line—a wonderfully delicate bit of work."

"Don't imagine, Mrs. Quarrier," pleaded Glazzard, "that I am what is called an æsthete. The thing is an abomination to me."

"Oh, you go tolerably far in that direction!" cried Denzil, laughing. "True, you don't let your hair grow, and in general make an ass of yourself; but there's a good deal of preciosity about you, you know."

Seeing that Mr. Glazzard's crown showed an incipient baldness, the allusion to his hair was perhaps unfortunate. Lilian fancied that her guest betrayed a slight annoyance; she at once interposed with a remark that led away from such dangerous ground. It seemed to her (she had already received the impression from Quarrier's talk of the evening before) that Denzil behaved to his friend with an air of bantering superiority which it was not easy to account for. Mr. Glazzard, so far as she could yet judge, was by no means the kind of man to be dealt with in this tone; she thought him rather disposed to pride than to an excess of humility, and saw in his face an occasional melancholy which inspired her with interest and respect.

A female servant (the vacancy made by Lilian's self-denying kindness had been hastily supplied) appeared with summons to dinner. Mr. Glazzard offered an arm to his hostess, and Quarrier followed with a look of smiling pleasure.

Hospitality had been duly cared for. Not at all inclined to the simple fare which Denzil chose to believe would suffice for him, Glazzard found more satisfaction in the meal than he had anticipated. If Mrs. Quarrier were responsible for the *menu* (he doubted it), she revealed yet another virtue. The mysterious circumstances of this household puzzled him more and more; occasionally he forgot to speak, or to listen, in the intensity of his preoccupation; and at such moments his countenance darkened.

On the whole, however, he seemed in better spirits than of wont. Quarrier was in the habit of seeing him perhaps once a month, and it was long since he had heard the connoisseur discourse so freely, so unconcernedly. As soon as they were seated at table, Denzil began to talk of politics.

" If my brother-in-law really stands for Polterham," he exclaimed, " we must set you canvassing among the mill-hands, Glazzard ! "

" H'm !—not impossible."

" As much as to say," remarked the other to Lilian, " that he would see them all consumed in furnaces before he stretched forth a hand to save them."

" I know very well how to understand Denzil's exaggerations," said Lilian, with a smile to her guest.

" He thinks," was Glazzard's reply, " that I am something worse than a high Tory. It's quite a mistake, and I don't know how his belief originated."

"My dear fellow, you are so naturally a Tory that you never troubled to think to what party you belong. And I can understand you well enough; I have leanings that way myself. Still, when I get down to Polterham I shall call myself a Radical. What sensible man swears by a party? There's more foolery and dishonesty than enough on both sides, when you come to party quarrelling; but as for the broad principles concerned, why, Radicalism of course means justice. I put it in this way: If *I* were a poor devil, half starved and overworked, I should be a savage Radical; so I'll go in for helping the poor devils."

"You don't always act on that principle, Denzil," said Lilian, with a rallying smile. "Not, for instance, when beggars are concerned."

"Beggars! Would you have me support trading impostors? As for the genuine cases—why, if I found myself penniless in the streets, I would make such a row that all the country should hear of it! Do you think I would go whining to individuals? If I hadn't food, it would be the duty of society to provide me with it—and I would take good care that I *was* provided; whether in workhouse or gaol wouldn't matter much. At all events, the business should be managed with the maximum of noise."

He emptied his wine-glass, and went on in the same vigorous tone.

"We know very well that there are no such things as natural rights. Nature gives no rights; she will produce an infinite number of creatures only to torture and eventually destroy them. But civilization is at war with nature, and as civilized beings we *have* rights. Every man is justified in claiming food and shelter and repose. As things are, many thousands of people in every English county either lack these necessaries altogether, or get them only in return for the accursed badge of pauperdom. I, for one, am against this state of things, and I sympathize with the men who think that nothing can go right until the fundamental injustice is done away with."

Glazzard listened with an inscrutable smile, content to throw in a word of acquiescence from time to time. But when the necessity of appeasing his robust appetite held Quarrier silent for a few minutes, the guest turned to Lilian and asked her if she made a study of political questions.

"I have been trying to follow them lately," she replied, with simple directness.

"Do you feel it a grievance that you have no vote and no chance of representing a borough?"

"No, I really don't."

"I defy any one to find a dozen women who sincerely do," broke in Denzil. "That's all humbug! Such twaddle only serves to obscure the great questions at issue. What we have to do is to clear away the obvious lies and superstitions that hold a great part of the people in a degrading bondage. Our need is of statesmen who are bold enough and strong enough to cast off the restraints of party, of imbecile fears, of words that answer to no reality, and legislate with

honest zeal for the general good. How many men are
there in Parliament who represent anything more
respectable than the interest of a trade, or a faction, or
their own bloated person ?"

"This would rouse the echoes in an East-end club,"
interposed Glazzard, with an air of good-humoured
jesting.

"The difference is, my dear fellow, that it is given
as an honest opinion in a private dining-room. There's
Welwyn-Baker now—thick-headed old jackass!—what
right has *he* to be sitting in a national assembly ? Call
himself what he may, it's clearly our business to get rid
of *him*. There's something infuriating in the thought
that such a man can give his hee-haw for or against a
proposal that concerns the nation. His mere existence
is a lie ! "

" He has hardly progressed with the times," assented
Glazzard.

Lilian was listening so attentively that she forgot
her dinner.

" I didn't think you cared so much about politics,"
she remarked, gravely.

"Oh, it comes out now and then. I suppose Glazzard's æsthetic neutrality stirs me up."

"I am neither æsthetic nor neutral," remarked the
guest, as if casually.

Denzil laughed.

Lilian, after waiting for a further declaration from
Glazzard, which did not come, said, in her soft tones:

" You express yourself so vehemently, Denzil."

"Why not? These are obvious truths. Of course I could speak just as strongly on the Conservative side with regard to many things. I can't say that I have much faith in the capacity or honesty of the mass of Radical voters. If I found myself at one of the clubs of which Glazzard speaks, I should very likely get hooted down as an insolent aristocrat. I don't go in for crazy extremes. There'll never be a Utopia, and it's only a form of lying to set such ideals before the multitude. I believe in the distinction of classes; the only class I would altogether abolish is that of the hungry and the ragged. So long as nature doles out the gift of brains in different proportions, there must exist social subordination. The true Radical is the man who wishes so to order things that no one will be urged by misery to try and get out of the class he is born in."

Glazzard agreed that this was a good way of putting it, and thereupon broached a subject so totally different that politics were finally laid aside.

When Lilian rose and withdrew, the friends remained for several minutes in silence. They lighted cigarettes, and contemplatively watched the smoke. Of a sudden, Quarrier bent forward upon the table.

"You shall have the explanation of this some day," he said, in a low friendly voice, his eyes lighting with a gleam of heartfelt confidence.

"Thanks!" murmured the other.

"Tell me—does she impress you favourably?"

"Very. I am disposed to think highly of her."

Denzil held out his hand, and pressed the one which Glazzard offered in return.

"You cannot think too highly—cannot possibly! She has a remarkable character. For one thing, I never knew a girl with such strong sympathies—so large-hearted and compassionate. You heard her remark about the beggars; if she had her own way, she would support a colony of pensioners. Let the sentimentalists say what they like, that isn't a common weakness in women, you know. Her imagination is painfully active; I'm afraid it causes her a great deal of misery. The other day I found her in tears, and what do you think was the reason?—she had been reading in some history about a poor fellow who was persecuted for his religion in Charles the First's time—some dissenter who got into the grip of Laud, was imprisoned, and then brought to destitution by being forbidden to exercise each calling that he took to in hope of earning bread. The end was, he went mad and died. Lilian was crying over the story; it made her wretched for a whole day."

"Rather morbid, that, I'm afraid."

"I don't know; most of us would be better for a little of such morbidness. You mustn't suppose that fiction would have the same effect on her—not at all. That poor devil (his name, I remember, was Workman) was really and truly hounded to insanity and the grave, and she saw the thing in all its dreadful details. I would rather she had got into a rage about it, as I should—but that isn't her nature."

" Let us hope she could rejoice when Laud was laid by the heels."

" I fear not. I'm afraid she would forget, and make excuses for the blackguard."

Glazzard smiled at the ceiling, and smoked silently. Turning his eyes at length, and seeing Quarrier in a brown study, he contemplated the honest face, then asked :

" How old is she ? "

" Just one-and-twenty."

" I should have thought younger."

Nothing more was said of Lilian, and very soon they went to the room where she awaited them.

"I know you are a musician, Mr. Glazzard," said Lilian before long. " Will you let me have the pleasure of hearing you play something ? "

"Some enemy hath done this," the guest made reply, looking towards Denzil.

But without further protest he went to the piano and played two or three short pieces. Any one with more technical knowledge than the hearers would have perceived that he was doing his best. As it was, Lilian frequently turned to Denzil with a look of intense delight.

" Glazzard," exclaimed his friend at length, " it puzzles me how such a lazy fellow as you are has managed to do so much in so many directions."

The musician laughed carelessly, and, not deigning any other reply, went to talk with his hostess.

IV.

THE Polterham Literary Institute was a "hot-bed of Radicalism." For the last year or two this had been generally understood. Originating in the editorial columns of the *Polterham Mercury*, the remark was now a commonplace on the lips of good Conservatives, and the Liberals themselves were not unwilling to smile an admission of its truth. At the founding of the Institute no such thing was foreseen; but in 1859 Polterham was hardly conscious of the stirrings of that new life which, in the course of twenty years, was to transform the town. In those days a traveller descending the slope of the Banwell Hills sought out the slim spire of Polterham parish church amid a tract of woodland, mead and tillage; now the site of the thriving little borough was but too distinctly marked by trails of smoke from several gaunt chimneys —that of Messrs. Dimes & Nevison's blanket-factory, that of Quarrier & Son's sugar-refinery, and, higher still (said, indeed, to be one of the tallest chimneys in England), that of Thomas & Liversedge's soap-works. With the character of Polterham itself, the Literary Institute had suffered a noteworthy change. Ostensibly it remained non-political : a library, reading-room and lecture-hall, for the benefit of all the townsfolk ; but by a subtle process the executive authority had passed into the hands of new men with new ideas. A mere enumeration of the committee sufficed to frighten away all who held by Church, State, and Mr. Welwyn-Baker: the Institute was no longer an Institute, but a "hot-bed."

How could respectable people make use of a library which admitted works of irreligious and immoral tendency? It was an undoubted fact (the *Mercury* made it known) that of late there had been added to the catalogue not only the "Essays of David Hume" and that notorious book Buckle's "History of Civilization," but even a large collection of the writings of George Sand and Balzac—these latter in the original tongue; for who, indeed, would ever venture to publish an English translation? As for the reading-room, was it not characterization enough to state that two Sunday newspapers, reeking fresh from Fleet Street, regularly appeared on the tables? What possibility of perusing the *Standard* or the *Spectator* in such an atmosphere? It was clear that the supporters of law and decency must bestir themselves to establish a new Society. Mr. Mumbray, long prominent in the municipal and political life of the town, had already made the generous offer of a large house at a low rental—one of the ancient buildings which had been spoilt for family residence by the erection of a mill close by. The revered Member for the borough was willing to start the new library with a gift of one hundred volumes of "sterling literature." With dissolution of Parliament in view, not a day should be lost in establishing this centre of intellectual life for right-thinking inhabitants.

It was a strange thing, a very strange thing indeed, that interlopers should have been permitted to oust the wealth and reputability of Polterham from an Institute which ought to have been one of the bulwarks of Conservatism. Laxity in the original constitution, and a spirit of supine confidence, had led to this sad result. It seemed impossible that Polterham could ever fall from its honourable position among the Conservative strongholds of the country; but the times were corrupt, a revolutionary miasma was spreading to every corner of the land. Polterham must no longer repose in the security of conscious virtue, for if it *did* happen that, at the coming election, the unprincipled multitude even came near to achieving a triumph, oh what a fall were there!

Thus spoke the *Mercury.* And in the same week Mr. Mumbray's vacant house was secured by a provisional committee on behalf of the Polterham Constitutional Literary Society.

The fine old crusted party had some reason for their alarm. Since Polterham was a borough it had returned a Tory Member as a matter of course. Political organization was quite unknown to the supporters of Mr. Welwyn-Baker; such trouble had never seemed necessary. Through the anxious year of 1868 Mr. Welwyn-Baker sat firm as a rock; an endeavour to unseat him ended amid contemptuous laughter. In 1874 the high-tide of Toryism caused only a slight increase of congratulatory gurgling in the Polterham backwater; the triumphant party hardly cared to notice that a Liberal candidate had scored an unprecedented proportion of votes. Welwyn-Baker sat on, stolidly oblivious of the change that was affecting his constituency, denying indeed the possibility of mutation in human things. Yet even now the Literary Institute was passing into the hands of people who aimed at making it something more than a place where retired tradesmen could play draughts and doze over *Good Words;* already had offensive volumes found harbourage on the shelves, and revolutionary periodicals been introduced into the reading-room. From time to time the *Mercury* uttered a note of warning, of protest, but with no echo from the respectable middle-class abodes where Polterham Conservatism dozed in self-satisfaction. It needed another five years of Liberal activity throughout the borough to awaken the good people whose influence had seemed unassailable, and to set them uttering sleepy snorts of indignation. But the *Mercury* had a new editor, a man who was determined to gain journalistic credit by making a good fight in a desperate cause. Mr. Mumbray, who held the post of Mayor, had at length learnt that even in municipal matters the old order was threatened ; on the Town Council were several men who gave a great deal of trouble, and who openly boasted that in a very short time all the affairs of the town would be managed by members of the Progressive party. If so, farewell public morality ! farewell religion !

The reading-room of the Literary Institute heard many an animated conversation among the zealous

partisans who hoped great things from the approaching
contest. The talkers were not men of recognized
standing, the manufacturers and landowners whose
influence was of most importance—for these personages
were seldom seen at the Institute; but certain "small"
people, fidgety, or effervescent, or enthusiastic, eager to
hear their own voices raised in declamation, and to get
spoken of in the town as representatives of public
opinion. Such a group had gathered early one afternoon in this month of October. The hour was unusual,
for between one o'clock and four the reading-room was
generally abandoned to a few very quiet, somnolent
persons; but to-day an exciting piece of news had got
about in Polterham, and two or three ardent politicians
hastened from their dinner-tables to discuss the situation
with Mr. Wykes, secretary of the Institute, or any one
else who might present himself. It was reported that
Mr. Welwyn-Baker had had a seizure of some kind,
and that he lay in a dangerous state at his house just
outside the town.

"It's perfectly true," affirmed Mr. Wykes. "I saw
Dr. Staple on his way there. He'll never survive it.
We shall have a bye-election—the very last thing
desirable."

The Secretary was a man of intelligent features but
painfully distorted body; his right leg, permanently
bent double, was supported at the knee by metal
mechanism, and his arm on the opposite side ended at
the elbow. None the less he moved with much activity,
gesticulated frequently with the normal arm, and

seemed always to be in excellent spirits. He was a Cambridge graduate, but had never been able to make much use of his education and abilities; having reached middle age, and finding himself without resources, he was glad to accept this post at the Institute.

About him stood three Polterham worthies: Mr. Chown, draper, a member of the Corporation; Mr. Vawdrey, coal-merchant; and Mr. Murgatroyd, dentist. The draper—tall, bearded, with goggle eyes and prominent cheek-bones—had just rushed in; as soon as Mr. Wykes had spoken, he exclaimed in a hard, positive voice:

"It's nothing! it's nothing! I have it on the best assurance that it was only a fall over a footstool. Muscles strained—a bruise or two—nothing worse."

"I'm very glad to hear it, on every ground," said Wykes. "But even if that is quite correct, it'll be a warning. A fall at that age generally dates the beginning of decrepitude. He won't come forward again—I'm convinced he won't."

"Let us hope they'll be foolish enough to set up his son," remarked Mr. Vawdrey, in deep tones, which harmonized with his broad, stunted body and lowering visage. "It'll be their ruin."

Mr. Wykes agreed.

"The waverers can hardly doubt—between Tobias Liversedge and Hugh Welwyn-Baker."

"Bear in mind," rang Mr. Chown's brassy voice, "that it's by no means certain Liversedge is to be our candidate. I am in a position to assure you that many of our most reliable men are not at all satisfied with that choice—not at all satisfied. I don't mind going so far as to declare that I share this dissatisfaction."

" Really," put in Mr. Murgatroyd, the dentist, " it's rather late in the day, Mr. Chown" ——

His accents of studious moderation were interrupted by a shout from the dogmatic draper.

" Late ? late ? I consider that nothing whatever has been decided. I protest—I protest, most emphatically, against any attempt to force a candidate on the advanced section of the Liberal party ! I will even go so far as to say—purely on my own responsibility—that the advanced section of the Liberal party is the *essence* of the Liberal party, and must be recognized as such, if we are to fight this campaign in union. I personally—I speak for myself—do *not* feel prepared to vote for Tobias Liversedge. I say it boldly, caring not who may report my words. I compromise no man, and no body of men ; but my view is that, if we are to win the next election against the Tory candidate, it must be with the help, and in the name, of a *Radical* candidate ! "

At the close of each period Mr. Chown raised his hand and made it vibrate in the air, his head vibrating in company therewith. His eyes glared, and his beard wagged up and down.

" Speaking as an individual," replied Mr. Murgatroyd, who, among other signs of nervousness, had the habit of constantly pulling down his waistcoat, " I can't say that I should regret to be called upon to vote for a really advanced man. But I may say—I really must say—and I think Mr. Wykes will support me— I think Mr. Vawdrey will bear me out—that it wouldn't be easy to find a candidate who would unite all suffrages in the way that Mr. Liversedge does. We have to remember "——

" Well," broke in the coal-merchant, with his muffled bass, " if any one cares to know what I think, I should say that we want a local man, a popular man, and a Christian man. I don't know whom you would set up in preference to Liversedge; but Liversedge suits me well enough. If the Tories are going to put forward such a specimen as Hugh Welwyn-Baker, a gambler, a drinker, and a profligate, I don't know, I say, who would look better opposed to him than Toby Liversedge."

Mr. Chown could not restrain himself.

" I fail altogether to see what Christianity has to do with politics ! Christianity is all very well, but where will you find it ? Old Welwyn-Baker calls himself a Christian, and so does his son. And I suppose the Rev. Scatchard Vialls calls himself a Christian ! Let us have done with this disgusting hypocrisy ! I say with all deliberation—I affirm it—that Radicalism must break with religion that has become a sham ! Radicalism is a religion in itself. We have no right—no right, I say—to impose any such test as Mr. Vawdrey insists upon ! "

"I won't quarrel about names," returned Vawdrey,

stolidly, "What I meant to say was that we must have a man of clean life, a moral man."

"And do you imply," cried Chown, "that such men are hard to find among Radicals?"

"I rather think they're hard to find anywhere nowadays."

Mr. Wykes had made a gesture requesting attention, and was about to speak, when a boy came up to him and held out a telegram.

"What's this?" murmured the Secretary, as he opened the envelope. "Well, well, how very annoying! Our lecturer of to-morrow evening can't possibly keep his engagement. No reason given; says he will write."

"Another blank evening!" exclaimed Chown. "This is most unsatisfactory, I must say."

"We must fill it up," replied the Secretary. "I have an idea; it connects with something I was on the point of saying." He looked round the room cautiously, but saw only a young lad bent over an illustrated paper. "There *is* some one," he continued, subduing his voice, "who might possibly be willing to stand if Mr. Liversedge isn't finally adopted as our candidate—some one who, in my opinion, would suit us very well indeed. I am thinking of young Mr. Quarrier, Liversedge's brother-in-law, Mr. Sam Quarrier's nephew."

"I can't say I know much for or against him," said the draper.

"A barrister, I believe?" questioned Murgatroyd.

"Yes, but not practising his profession. I happened

to meet him in the train yesterday; he was coming to spend a few days with his relatives. It occurs to me that he's the man to give us a lecture to-morrow evening."

The others lent ear, and Mr. Wykes talked at some length of Mr. Denzil Quarrier, with whom he had a slight personal acquaintance dating from a year or two ago. He represented that the young man was of late become wealthy, that he was closely connected with people in high local esteem, that his views were those of a highly cultured Radical. Mr. Chown, distrustful regarding any proposition that did not originate with himself, meditated with some intensity. Mr. Vawdrey's face indicated nothing whatever. It was the dentist who put the first question.

"I should like to know," he said, in his usual voice of studied inoffensiveness, " whether Mr. Quarrier is disposed to support the Female Suffrage movement ? "

"If he is," growled Mr. Vawdrey, with sudden emphasis, " he mustn't expect *my* vote and interest. We've seen enough in Polterham lately of the Female question."

"Let it wait ! Let it wait ! " came from the draper. "The man," he glared at little Murgatroyd, " who divides his party on matters of detail, beyond the range of practical politics, is an enemy of popular progress. What *I* should desire to know is, whether Mr. Quarrier will go in heartily for Church Disestablishment ? If not—well, I for my humble self must Decline to consider him a Radical at all."

"That, it seems to me," began the dentist, "is distinctly beyond "——

But politic Mr. Wykes interrupted the discussion.

" I shall go at once," he said, " and try to see Mr. Quarrier. A lecture to-morrow we must have, and I think he can be persuaded to help us. If so, we shall have an opportunity of seeing what figure he makes on the platform."

Mr. Vawdrey looked at his watch and hurried away without a word. The draper and the dentist were each reminded of the calls of business. In a minute or two the youth dozing over an illustrated paper had the room to himself.

V.

For a characteristic scene of English life one could not do better than take Mr. Liversedge's dining-room when the family had assembled for the midday meal. Picture a long and lofty room, lighted by windows which opened upon a lawn and flower-garden, adorned with large oil paintings (cattle-pieces and portraits) in massive and, for the most part, tarnished frames, and furnished in the solidest of British styles—mahogany chairs and table, an immense sideboard, a white marble fireplace, and a chandelier hanging with ponderous menace above the gleaming expanse of table-cloth. Here were seated eleven persons: Mr. Liversedge and his wife, their seven children (four girls and three boys), Miss Pope the governess, and Mr. Denzil Quarrier; waited upon by two maid-servants, with ruddy cheeks, and in spotless attire. Odours of roast meat filled the air. There was a jolly sound of knife-and-fork play, of young voices laughing and chattering, of older ones in genial colloquy. A great fire blazed and crackled up the chimney. Without, a roaring wind stripped the autumnal leafage of the garden, and from time to time drenched the windows with volleys of rain.

Tobias Liversedge was a man of substance, but in domestic habits he followed the rule of the unpretentious middle-class. Breakfast at eight, dinner at one, tea at five, supper at nine—such was the order of the day that he had known in boyhood, and it suited him well enough now that he was at the head of a household. The fare was simple, but various and abundant; no dishes with foreign names, no drinks more luxurious than sherry and claret. If he entertained guests, they were people of his own kind, who thought more of the hearty welcome than of what was set before them. His children were neither cockered nor held in too strait a discipline; they learnt from their parents that laughter was better than sighing, that it was good to be generous, that they had superiors in the world as well as inferiors, that hard work was the saving grace, and a lie the accursed thing. This training seemed to agree with them, for one and all were pictures of health. Tom, the first-born, numbered fifteen years; Daisy, the latest arrival, had seen but three summers, yet she already occupied a high chair at the dinner-table, and conducted herself with much propriety. The two elder boys went to the Grammar School morning and afternoon; for the other children there was Miss Pope, with her smile of decorum, eyes of intelligence, and clear, decided voice.

Mrs. Liversedge was obviously Denzil Quarrier's sister; she had his eyes and his nose—not uncomely features. It did not appear that her seven children were robust at their mother's expense; she ate with undisguised appetite, laughed readily (just showing excellent teeth), and kept a shapely figure, clad with simple becomingness. Her age was about eight-and-thirty, that of her husband forty-five. This couple—if any in England—probably knew the meaning of happiness. Neither had experienced narrow circumstances, and the future could but confirm their security from sordid cares. Even if seven more children were added to their family, all would be brought up amid abundance, and sent forth into the world as well equipped for its struggles as the tenderest heart could desire. Father and mother were admirably matched; they knew each other perfectly, thought the same thoughts on all essential matters, exchanged the glances of an absolute and unshakeable confidence.

Seeing him thus at the end of his table, one would not have thought Mr. Liversedge a likely man to stand forth on political platforms and appeal to the populace of the borough for their electoral favour. He looked modest and reticent; his person was the reverse of commanding. A kind and thoughtful man, undoubtedly; but in his eye was no gleam of ambition, and it seemed doubtful whether he would care to trouble himself much about questions of public policy. Granted his position and origin, it was natural enough that he should take a stand on the Liberal side, but it could hardly be expected that he should come up to Mr. Chown's ideal of a Progressive leader.

He was talking lightly on the subject with his brother-in-law.

"I should have thought," he said, "that William Glazzard might have had views that way. He's a man with no ties and, I should say, too much leisure."

"Oh," exclaimed Mrs. Liversedge, "the idea of his getting up to make speeches! It always seems to me as if he found it a trouble even to talk. His brother would be far more likely, wouldn't he, Denzil?"

"What, Eustace Glazzard?" replied Quarrier. "He regards Parliament and everything connected with it with supreme contempt. Suggest the thing when he comes this evening, and watch his face."

"What is he doing?" Mr. Liversedge asked.

"Collecting pictures, playing the fiddle, gazing at sunflowers, and so on. He'll never do anything else."

"How contradictory you are in speaking about him!" said his sister. "One time you seem to admire and like him extremely, and another "——

"Why, so I do. A capital fellow! He's weak, that's all. I don't mean weak in the worst way, you know; a more honourable and trustworthy man doesn't live. But—well, he's rather womanish, I suppose."

Mrs. Liversedge laughed.

"Many thanks! It's always so pleasing to a woman to hear that comparison. Do you mean he reminds you of Mrs. Wade?"

The boy Tom, who had been attentive, broke into merriment.

"Uncle Denzil wouldn't dare to have said it in *her* presence!" he cried.

"Perhaps not," conceded Denzil, with a smile. "By-the-bye, is that wonderful person still in Polterham?"

"Oh yes!" Mrs. Liversedge replied. "She has been very prominent lately."

" How ? "

The lady glanced at her husband, who said quietly,
" We'll talk over it some other time."

But Tom was not to be repressed.

" Mother means that Revivalist business," he
exclaimed.   " Mrs. Wade went against it."

" My boy, no meddling with things of that kind,"
said his father, smiling, but firm.   He turned to
Denzil.   " Has Glazzard exhibited anything lately ? "

" No ; he gave up his modelling, and he doesn't
seem to paint much nowadays.   The poor fellow has no
object in life, that's the worst of it."

The meal was nearly at an end, and presently the
two men found themselves alone at the table.   Mr.
Liversedge generally smoked a cigar before returning
for an hour or two to the soap-works.

" Any more wine ? " he asked.   " Then come into
my snuggery and let us chat."

They repaired to a room of very homely appearance.
The furniture was old and ugly ; the carpet seemed to
have been beaten so often that it was growing thread-
bare by force of purification.   There was a fair
collection of books, none of very recent date, and on the
walls several maps and prints.   The most striking
object was a great stuffed bird that stood in a glass-case
before the window—a capercailzie shot by Quarrier
long ago in Norway, and presented to his brother-in-
law.   Tobias settled himself in a chair, and kicked a
coal from the bars of the grate.

" Tom is very strong against religious fanaticism,"

he said, laughing. "I have to pull him up now and then. I suppose you heard about the crazy goings-on down here in the summer?"

"Not I. Revivalist meetings?"

"The whole town was turned upside down. Such frenzy among the women I never witnessed. Three times a day they flocked in swarms to the Public Hall, and there screeched and wept and fainted, till it really looked as if some authority ought to interfere. If I had had my way, I would have drummed the preachers out of the town. Mary and Mrs. Wade and one or two others were about the only women who escaped the epidemic. Seriously, it led to a good deal of domestic misery. Poor Tomkins's wife drove him to such a pass by her scandalous neglect of the house, that one morning he locked her into her bedroom, and there he kept her on very plain diet for three days. We thought of getting up a meeting to render public thanks to Tomkins, and to give him some little testimonial."

Denzil uttered roars of laughter; the story was exactly of the kind that made appeal to his humorous instincts.

"Has the ferment subsided?" he asked.

"Tolerably well; leaving a good deal of froth and scum, however. The worst of it was that, in the very week when those makebates had departed, there came down on us a second plague, in the shape of Mrs. Hitchin, the apostle of—I don't quite know what, but she calls it Purity. Of course, you know her by repute. She, too, had the Public Hall, and gave addresses to which only women were admitted. I have a very strong opinion as to the tendency of those addresses, and if Rabelais had come to life among us just then—but never mind. The fact is, old Polterham got into a thoroughly unwholesome condition, and we're anything but right yet. Perhaps a little honest fighting between Liberal and Tory may help to clear the air.—Well, now, that brings me to what I really wish to talk about. To tell you the truth, I don't feel half satisfied with what I have done. My promise to stand, you know, was only conditional, and I think I must get out of it."

" Why ? "

" Mary was rather tickled with the idea at first ; naturally she had no objection to be Mrs. M.P., and she persuaded herself that I was just the man to represent Polterham. I felt rather less sure of it, and now I am getting pretty well convinced that I had better draw back before I make a fool of myself."

" What about your chances ? Is there any hope of a majority ? "

" That's more than I can tell you. The long-headed men, like your Uncle Sam (an unwilling witness) and Edward Coke, say that the day has come for the Liberals. I don't know, but I suspect that a really brisk and popular man might carry it against either of the Welwyn-Bakers. That fellow Hugh will never do—by the way, that might be the beginning of an election rhyme ! He's too much of a blackguard, and nowadays, you know, even a Tory candidate must preserve the decencies of life."

Denzil mused, and muttered something indistinct.

"Now listen," pursued the speaker, shifting about in his chair. "What I want to say is this : why shouldn't *you* come forward ? "

Quarrier pursed his lips, knit his brows, and grunted.

"I am very serious in thinking that you might be the best man we could find."

And Mr. Liversedge went on to exhibit his reasons at some length. As he listened, Denzil became restless, crossing and recrossing his legs, spreading his shoulders, smiling, frowning, coughing ; and at length he jumped up.

"Look here, Toby ! " he exclaimed, "is this a self-denying ordinance ? Have you and Molly put your heads together to do me what you think a good turn ? "

"I haven't spoken to her, I assure you. I am sincere in saying that I don't wish to go through with it. And I should be right heartily glad to see you come out instead."

The face of the younger man worked with subdued excitement. There was a flush in his cheeks, and he breathed rapidly. The emotion that possessed him could not be altogether pleasurable, for at moments he cast his eyes about him with a pained, almost a desperate look. He walked up and down with clenched fist, occasionally digging himself in the side.

"Toby," he burst out at length, "let me think this over! I can't possibly decide at once. The notion is absolutely new to me; I must roll it about, and examine it on all sides."

Mr. Liversedge cheerfully agreed, and, after a little more talk, he went his way to business, leaving Denzil alone in the snuggery. There sat the young man in deep but troubled meditation. He sat for nearly an hour. Then his sister came in.

"Denzil, you are wanted. Mr. Wykes wishes to see you. Shall I send him here?"

"Mr. Wykes! What about, I wonder? Yes, let him come."

A clumping was heard without, and the bright face of the Institute's Secretary, so strongly in contrast with his wretched body, presented itself in the doorway. Quarrier received him with a friendly consideration due rather to pity than to any particular interest in the man himself. He placed him in a comfortable chair, and waited in attentive attitude for an explanation of the call. Mr. Wykes lost no time in making known his business; he told what had happened at the Institute, and respectfully begged for Mr. Quarrier's aid in averting disappointment on the next evening.

"I am sure, sir, that your appearance on our platform would give very general pleasure. I should have time to post announcements here and there. We should have a splendid hall."

"The deuce! But, Mr. Wykes, it is no such simple

matter to prepare a lecture in four-and-twenty hours.
What am I to talk about?"

"Any subject, sir, that would be of interest to a
wide-awake audience. If I might suggest, there are
your travels, for instance. And I understand that you
are deeply conversant with the Northern literatures; I
am sure something" ——

"Pardon me. I hardly think I should care to go so
far away for a theme."

The Secretary heard this with pleasure.

"All the better, sir! Any subject of the day;
nothing could be more acceptable. You probably know
our position at the Institute. In practice, we are something like a Liberal Club. You have heard that the
other party are going to start a Society of their own?"

"I have—a Society with an imbecile name." He
pondered. "Suppose I were to talk about 'The
Position of Woman in our Time'?"

"Capital, Mr. Quarrier! Couldn't be better, sir!
Do permit me to announce it at once!"

"It's rather a ticklish responsibility I'm undertaking
—but—very well, I will do my best, Mr. Wykes.
Who is chairman?"

"Mr. William Glazzard, sir."

"Ho ho! All right; I'll turn up to time. Eight
o'clock, I suppose? Evening dress, or not? Oh, of
course, if it's usual; I didn't know your custom."

Mr. Wykes did not linger. Left alone again, Denzil
walked about in excited mood. At length, with a wave
of the arm which seemed to announce a resolution, he

went to the drawing-room. His sister was reading there in solitude.

"Molly, I'm going to lecture at the Institute to-morrow, *vice* somebody or other who can't turn up. What subject, think you?"

"The Sagas, probably?"

"The Sagas be blowed! 'Woman's Place in our Time,' that's the title."

Mrs. Liversedge laughed, and showed astonishment.

"And what have you to say about her?"

"Wait and see!"

VI.

AT the distance of a mile and a half from Polterham
lay an estate which had long borne the name of Highmead.   Here had dwelt three successive generations of
Glazzards.   The present possessor, by name William,
was, like his father and grandfather, simply a country
gentleman, but, unlike those respectable ancestors, had
seen a good deal of the world, and only settled down
amid his acres when he was tired of wandering.   His
age at present was nearing fifty.   When quite a
young man, he had married rather rashly—a girl
whose acquaintance he had made during a voyage.
In a few years' time, he and his wife agreed to differ on
a great many topics of moment, and consequently to
live apart.   Mrs. Glazzard died abroad.   William, when
the desire for retirement came upon him, was glad of
the society of a son and a daughter in their early teens.
But the lad died of consumption, and the girl, whose
name was Ivy, for a long time seemed to be clinging
to life with but doubtful tenure.   She still lived, however, and kept her father's house.

Ivy Glazzard cared little for the pleasures of the
world—knew, indeed, scarcely more about them than she
had gathered from books.   Her disposition was serious,
inclined to a morbid melancholy ;   she spent much time
over devotional literature, but very seldom was heard to

speak of religion. Probably her father's avowed in-
differentism imposed upon her a timid silence. When the
Revivalist services were being held in Polterham, she
visited the Hall and the churches with assiduity, and
from that period dated her friendship with the daughter
of Mr. Mumbray, Mayor of the town. Serena
Mumbray was so uncomfortable at home that she
engaged eagerly in any occupation which could excuse
her absence for as many hours a day as possible.
Prior to the outbreak of Revivalism no one had
supposed her particularly pious, and, indeed, she had
often suffered Mrs. Mumbray's rebukes for levity of
speech and indifference to the conventional norm of
feminine behaviour. Though her parents had always
been prominent in Polterham society, she was ill-
educated, and of late years had endeavoured, in a
fitful, fretful way, to make amends to herself for this
injustice. Disregarding paternal censure, she subscribed
to the Literary Institute, and read at hap-hazard
with little enough profit. Twenty-three years old, she
was now doubly independent, for the will of a maiden
aunt (a lady always on the worst of terms with Mr. and
Mrs. Mumbray, and therefore glad to encourage
Serena against them) had made her an heiress of no
slight consideration. Young men of Polterham regarded
her as the greatest prize within view, though none
could flatter himself that he stood in any sensible
degree of favour with her. There seemed no reason
why Miss Mumbray should not marry, but it was
certain that as yet she behaved disdainfully to all who

approached her with the show of intention. She was not handsome, but had agreeable features. As though to prove her contempt of female vanity and vulgar display, she dressed plainly, often carelessly—a fact which of course served to emphasize her importance in the eyes of people who tried to seem richer than they were.

Miss Glazzard rarely came into the town, but Serena visited Highmead at least once a week. According to the state of the weather, the friends either sat talking in Ivy's room or rambled about the grounds, where many a pretty and sheltered spot was discoverable. At such times the master of the house seldom showed himself, and, on the whole, Highmead reminded one of a mansion left in the care of servants whilst the family are abroad. Miss Mumbray was surprised when, on her arrival one afternoon, she was conducted into the presence of three persons, who sat conversing in the large drawing-room. With Ivy and her father was a gentleman whose identity she could only guess; he proved to be Mr. Eustace Glazzard, her friend's uncle.

To the greetings with which she was received Serena responded formally. It happened that her attire was to-day even more careless than usual, for, the weather being wet and cold, she had just thrown a cloak over the frock in which she lounged at home, and driven out in a cab with the thought of stepping directly into Ivy's sanctum. So far from this, she found herself under the scrutiny of two well-dressed men, whose faces, however courteous, manifested the signature of a critical spirit.

The elder Mr. Glazzard was bald, wrinkled, and of aristocratic bearing; he wore gold-rimmed glasses, which accentuated the keenness of his gaze. The younger man, though altogether less formidable, had a smile which Miss Mumbray instinctively resented; he seemed to be regarding her with some special interest, and it was clear that her costume did not escape mental comment.

Ivy did her best to overcome the restraint of the situation, and for a quarter of an hour something like conversation was maintained, but, of a sudden, Miss Mumbray rose.

"We will go to my room," said Ivy, regarding her nervously.

"Thank you," was the reply, "I mustn't stay longer to-day."

"Oh, why not? But indeed you must come for a moment; I have something to show you."

Serena took leave of the gentlemen, and with show of reluctance suffered herself to be led to the familiar retreat.

"I'm afraid I have displeased you," Ivy addressed her, when the door was closed. "I ought to have asked your permission."

"It doesn't matter, dear—not a bit. But I wasn't quite in the humour for—for that kind of thing. I came here for quietness, as I always do."

"Do forgive me! I thought—to tell the truth, it was my uncle—I had spoken of you to him, and he said he should so much like to meet you."

" It really doesn't matter ; but I look rather like the woman who comes to buy old dresses, don't I ? "

Ivy laughed.

" Of course not ! "

" And what if I do ? " exclaimed the other, seating herself by the fire. " I don't know that I've any claim to look better than Mrs. Moss. I suppose she and I are about on a level in understanding and education, if the truth were told. Your uncle would see that, of course."

" Now, don't—don't ! " pleaded Ivy, bending over the chair and stroking her friend's shoulder. " It's so wrong of you, dear. My father and Uncle Eustace are both quite capable of judging you rightly."

" What did you tell him about me—your uncle ? " asked Serena, pettishly.

" That you were my friend, and that we read together "——

" Oh, of course ! What else ? "

Ivy faltered.

" I explained who you were."

" That I had a ridiculous name, and was the daughter of silly people ! "

" Oh, it *is* unkind of you ! "

" Well, and what else ? I insist on knowing, Ivy."

" Indeed, I didn't say one word that you mightn't have heard yourself. I think you can believe me, dear ? "

" To be sure I can. But then no doubt your father told him the rest, or has done by this time. There's

no harm in that. I like people to know that I am
independent. Well, now tell me about *him*. He isn't
a great favourite of yours, is he?"

"No, not a great favourite." Ivy seemed always to
weigh her words. "I don't know him very well. He
has always lived in London, and I've never seen him
more than once a year. I'm afraid he doesn't care
much about the things that I prize most, but he is kind
and very clever, I believe. Father always says he
might have been a great artist if he had chosen."

"Then why didn't he choose?"

"I can't say. So many people seem to fall far short
of what they might have been."

"Women do—what else can you expect? But men
are free. I suppose he is rich?"

"No, not rich. He seems to have enough for his
needs."

Serena indulged her thoughts.

"I felt I disliked him at first," she said, presently.
"But he is improved. He can talk well, I should
think. I suppose he is always in clever society?"

"I suppose so."

"And why doesn't he invite you to London, and
take you to see people?"

"Oh, he knows me better than that!" replied Ivy,
with a laugh.

Whilst the girls talked thus, Eustace Glazzard and
his brother were also in confidential chat. They had
gone to the library and made themselves comfortable
with cigars—a cellaret and glasses standing within

reach.   The rooms at Highmead gave evidence of neglect.   Guests were seldom entertained; the servants were few, and not well looked after.

"She has, I dare say, thirty thousand," William Glazzard was saying, with an air of indifference.   " I suppose she'll marry some parson.   Let us hope it's one of the fifty-pound curates."

"Deep in the old slough ? "

"Hopelessly—or Ivy wouldn't be so thick with her."

When he had spoken, William turned with an expressive smile.

"Still, who knows ?   I rather like the girl.   She has no humbug about her—no pretence, that's to say. You see how she dresses."

" A bad sign, I'm afraid."

" Well, no, not in this case, I think.   Her home accounts for it.   That old ass, Mumbray, and his wife make things pretty sour for her, as the Germans say ; at least, I guess so."

" I don't dislike her appearance—intelligent at bottom, I should imagine."

There followed a long silence.   Eustace broke it by asking softly :

" And how do things go with you ? "

"The same as ever.   Steadily down-hill.   I had better let the place before it gets into a thoroughly bad state.   And you ? "

His brother made no answer, but sat with bent head.

"You remember Stark," he said at length, "the lawyer? He wants me to stand for Polterham at the next election."

"You? In place of Welwyn-Baker?"

"No; as Liberal candidate; or Radical, if you like."

"You're joking, I suppose!"

"Where's the impossibility?"

Their eyes met.

"There's no absurdity," said William, "in your standing for Parliament; *au contraire.* But I can't imagine you on the Radical side. And I don't see the necessity of that. Welwyn-Baker is breaking up; they won't let him come forward again, even if he wishes. His son is disliked, and would have a very poor chance. If you cared to put yourself in touch with Mumbray and the rest of them—by Jove! I believe they would welcome you. I don't know of any one but the Welwyn-Bakers at all likely to stand."

"But," objected his brother, "what's the use of my standing for a party that is pretty sure to be beaten?"

"You think that's the case?"

Eustace repeated Mr. Stark's opinions, and what he had heard from Quarrier. It seemed to cost William an effort to fix his mind on the question; but at length he admitted that the contest would probably be a very close one, even granting that the Conservatives secured a good candidate.

"That's as much as to say," observed his brother, "that the Liberals stand to win, as things are. Now, there seems to be no doubt that Liversedge would gladly withdraw in favour of a better man. What I want you to do is to set this thing in train for me. I am in earnest."

"You astonish me! I can't reconcile such an ambition with "——

"No, no; of course not." Glazzard spoke with unwonted animation. "You don't know what my life is and has been. Look! I must do something to make my blood circulate, or I shall furnish a case for the coroner one of these mornings. I want excitement. I have taken up one thing after another, and gone just far enough to understand that there's no hope of reaching what I aimed at—superlative excellence; then the thing began to nauseate me. I'm like poor Jackson, the novelist, who groaned to me once that for fifteen years the reviewers had been describing his books as 'above the average.' In whatever I have undertaken the results were 'above the average,' and that's all. This is damned poor consolation for a man with a temperament like mine!"

His voice broke down. He had talked himself into a tremor, and the exhibition of feeling astonished his brother, who—as is so often the case between brothers —had never suspected what lay beneath the surface of Eustace's *dilettante* life.

"I can enter into that," said the elder, slowly. "But do you imagine that in politics you have found your real line?"

"No such thing. But it offers me a chance of *living*

for a few years. I don't flatter myself that I could make a figure in the House of Commons; but I want to sit there, and be in the full current of existence. I had never dreamt of such a thing until Stark suggested it. But he's a shrewd fellow, and he has guessed my need."

" What about the financial matter?" asked William, after reflection.

"I see no insuperable difficulty. You, I understand, are in no position to help me?"

" Oh, I won't say that," interrupted the other. " A few hundreds will make no difference to me. I suppose you see your way for the ordinary expenses of life?"

" With care, yes. I've been throwing money away, but that shall stop; there'll be no need for it when my nerves are put in tone."

" Well, it strikes me in a comical light, but you must act as you think best. I'll go to work for you. It's a pity I stand so much apart, but I suppose my name is worth something. The Radicals have often tried to draw me into their camp, and of course it's taken for granted that I am rather for than against them. By-the-bye, what is the date? Ah! that's fortunate. To-morrow I am booked to take the chair at the Institute ; a lecture—I don't know by whom, or about what. A good opportunity for setting things astir."

" Then you do take some part in town life?"

"Most exceptional thing. I must have refused to lecture and to chairmanize twenty times. But those fellows are persistent ; they caught me in a weak moment a few days ago. I suppose you realize the kind of speechifying that would be expected of you? Are you prepared to blaze away against Beaconsfield, and all that sort of thing?"

"I'm not afraid. There are more sides to my character than you suppose."

Eustace spoke excitedly, and tossed off a glass of liqueur. His manner had become more youthful than of wont; his face showed more colour.

"The fact is," he went on, "if I talk politics at all, I can manage the Radical standpoint much more easily than the Tory. I have precious little sympathy with anything popular, that's true; but it's easier for me to adopt the heroic strain of popular leaders than to put my own sentiments into the language of squires and parsons. I should feel I was doing a baser thing if I talked vulgar Toryism than in roaring the democratic note. Do you understand?"

"I have an inkling of what you mean."

Eustace refilled the little glass.

"Of course," he went on, "my true life stands altogether outside popular contention. I am an artist, though only half-baked. But I admit most heartily that our form of government is a good one—the most favourable that exists to individual freedom. We are ruled by the balance of two parties; neither could do without the other. This being the case, a man of my mind may conscientiously support either side. Nowadays neither is a foe to liberty; we know that party tall-talk means nothing—mere playing to the gallery.

If I throw whatever weight I represent into the Liberal scales, I am only helping, like every other Member of Parliament, to maintain the constitutional equilibrium. You see, this view is not even cynical; any one might proclaim it seriously."

"Yes; but don't do so in Polterham."

The other laughed, and at the same moment remembered how long it was since such an expression of mirth had escaped his lips.

"Well," he exclaimed, "I feel better to-day than for long enough. I've been going through a devilish bad time, I can tell you. To make things worse, some one has fixed an infernal accusation on me—an abominable calumny. I won't talk about it now, but it may be necessary some day."

"Calumny?—nothing that could be made use against you in public?"

"No danger of that, I think. I didn't mean to speak of it."

"You know that a man on the hustings must look out for mud?"

"Of course, of course!—How do you spend your afternoons? What shall we do?"

William threw away the end of a cigar, and stretched himself.

"I do very little but read," he answered. "A man gets the reading habit, just like the morphia habit, or anything else of that kind. I think my average is six novels a week: French, Russian, German, Italian. No English, unless I'm in need of an emetic. What else should I do? It's a way of watching contemporary life.—Would you like to go and talk with Ivy? Oh, I forgot that girl."

"You wouldn't care to ask some people to dinner one of these days—the right kind of people?"

"Yes, yes; we'll do that. I must warn you not to talk much about art, and above all not to play the piano. It would make a bad impression."

"All right. How shall I deal with Liversedge? I go there this evening, you remember."

"Sound him, if opportunity offers. No hurry, you know. We have probably several months before us. You'll have to live here a good deal."

As the rain had ceased, they presently went out into the garden and strolled aimlessly about.

VII.

No sooner had Mr. Liversedge become aware of his brother-in-law's promise to appear on the platform, than he despatched a note to Mr. Wykes, recommending exceptional industry in spreading the announcement. These addresses were not commonly of a kind to excite much interest, nor had the name of Mr. Denzil Quarrier any prestige in Polterham; it occasioned surprise when messengers ran about the town distributing handbills, which gave a general invitation (independent of membership) to that evening's lecture at the Institute. At the doors of the building itself was a large placard, attracting the eye by its bold inscription : " Woman : Her Place in Modern Life "—so had the title been ultimately shaped. Politicians guessed at once that something was in the wind, and before the afternoon there was a distinct rumour that this young man from London would be brought forward as Liberal candidate (Radical, said the Tories) in the place of Mr. Liversedge, who had withdrawn his name. The reading-room was beset. This chanced to be the day on which the Polterham Liberal newspaper was published, and at the head of its " general " column appeared a long paragraph on the subject under discussion. " At the moment of going to press, we learn that unforeseen circumstances have necessitated a change in this evening's programme at the Literary Institute. The indefatigable Secretary, Mr. Wykes, has been fortunate enough to fill the threatened vacancy, and that in a way which gives promise of a rare intellectual treat." Then followed a description of the lecturer (consisting of laudatory generalities), and a few sounding phrases on the subject he had chosen. Mr. Chown, who came and went twenty times in the course of the day, talked to all and sundry with his familiar vehemence.

"If it is true," he thundered, "that Tobias Liversedge has already surrendered his place to this young man, I want to know why these things have been done in a corner? If you ask my opinion, it looks uncommonly like a conspiracy. The Radical electors of Polterham are not going to be made the slaves of a secret caucus! The choice may be a very suitable one. I don't say "——

"Then wait till we know something definite," growled Mr. Vawdrey. "All I can say is that if this Mr. Quarrier is going in for extreme views about women, I'll have nothing to do with him."

"What do you mean by 'extreme views'?" screeched a thin man in dirty clothing.

Thereupon began a furious controversy, lasting half an hour. (It may be noted that a card hung in several parts of the room, requesting members not to converse in audible tones.)

Mr. Liversedge had gone to work like a man of decision. Between six and eight on the previous evening he had seen the members of that "secret caucus" whose existence outraged Mr. Chown—in other words, the half-dozen capable citizens who practically managed the affairs of Liberal Polterham—and had arrived at an understanding with them which made it all but a settled thing that Denzil Quarrier should be their prospective candidate. Tobias was eager to back out of the engagement into which he had unadvisedly entered. Denzil's arrival at this juncture seemed to him providential— impossible to find a better man for their purpose. At eight o'clock an informal meeting was held at the office of the *Polterham Examiner*, with the result that Mr. Hammond, the editor, subsequently penned that significant paragraph which next morning attracted all eyes.

On returning to supper, Mr. Liversedge found his wife and Denzil in conversation with Eustace Glazzard. With the latter he had a bare acquaintance; from Denzil's report, he was disposed to think of him as a rather effeminate old-young man of metropolitan type.

"Well," he exclaimed, when greetings were over, " I don't think you will want for an audience to-morrow, Denzil. We are summoning Polterham indiscriminately."

Glazzard had of course heard of the coming lecture. He wore a smile, but was taciturn.

"Pray heaven I don't make an exhibition of myself ! " cried Denzil, with an air of sufficient confidence.

" Shall I send coffee to your bedroom, to-night ? " asked his sister, with merry eyes.

" Too late for writing it out. It must be inspiration. I know what I want to say, and I don't think the sea of Polterham faces will disturb me."

He turned sharply to his brother-in-law.

" Are you still in the same mind on that matter we spoke of this afternoon ? "

" Decidedly ! "

" Glazzard, what should you say if I came forward as Radical candidate for Polterham ? "

There was silence. Glazzard fixed his eyes on the opposite wall; his smile was unchanged.

" I see no objection," he at length replied. The tones were rather thick, and ended in a slight cough. Feeling that all eyes were fixed upon him, Glazzard made an uneasy movement, and rose from his chair.

" It doesn't astonish you ? " said Quarrier, with a broad grin.

" Not overpoweringly."

" Then let us regard the thing as settled. Mr. Liversedge has no stomach for the fight, and makes room for me. In a week's time I shall be a man of distinction."

In the midst of his self-banter he found Glazzard's gaze turned upon him with steady concentration. Their eyes met, and Denzil's expression became graver.

" You will take up your abode here ? " Glazzard asked.

" Shortly," was the reply, given with more emphasis

than seemed necessary, and accompanied with an earnest look.

Again there was silence, and before the conversation could be renewed there came a summons to supper.

A vivacious political dialogue between Mr. Liversedge and his relative allowed Glazzard to keep silence, save when he exchanged a few words with his hostess or Miss Pope. He had a look of extreme weariness; his eyes were heavy and without expression, the lines of his face slack, sullen; he seemed to maintain with difficulty his upright position at the table, and his eating was only pretence. At the close of the meal he bent towards Mrs. Liversedge, declared that he was suffering from an intolerable headache, and begged her to permit his immediate departure.

Denzil went with him out into the road.

"I could see you were not well," he said, kindly. "I want to have a long and very serious talk with you; it must wait till after to-morrow. You know, of course, what I have on my mind. Come and hear my balderdash if you are all right again."

All the next day Denzil was in extravagant spirits. In the morning he made a show of shutting himself up to meditate the theme of his discourse, but his sister presently saw him straying about the garden, and as soon as her household duties left her at leisure she was called upon to gossip and laugh with him. The *Polterham Examiner* furnished material for endless jesting. In the midst of a flow of grotesque fancies, he broke off to say:

"By-the-bye, I shall have to run over to Paris for a few weeks."

"What to do there?"

"A private affair. You shall hear about it afterwards."

And he went on with his mirthful fantasia. This mood had been frequent with him in earlier years, and his sister was delighted to see that he preserved so much of youth. After all, it might be that he had found his vocation ere it was too late. Certainly he had the gift of speech, and his personality was not a common one. He might strike out a special line for himself in Parliament. They must make his election a sure thing.

The lecture was at eight. About seven, Mr. Liversedge and his relative walked off to the Institute, and entered the committee-room. Two or three gentlemen had already arrived; they were no strangers to Denzil, and a lively conversation at once sprang up. In a few minutes the door again opened to admit Mr. William Glazzard. The chairman of the evening came forward with lounging steps. Regardless of the others present, he fixed his eye upon Quarrier, and examined him from head to foot. In this case, also, introduction was unnecessary.

"You have lost no time," he remarked, holding out his hand, and glancing from the young man to Mr. Liversedge.

"Your brother has given you a hint?" said the latter.

"Oh yes! How am I to phrase my introductory remarks?"

"Quite without reference to the political topic."

The others murmured an approval.

"Eustace well again?" asked Quarrier. "He went home with a bad headache last night."

"He'll be here," answered Mr. Glazzard, laconically. "Liversedge, a word with you."

The two stepped apart and conversed under cover of the chat that went on in front of the fire. Mr. Glazzard merely wished for a few hints to direct him when he introduced the lecturer; he was silent about his brother's frustrated project.

Fresh members of the committee kept appearing. The room resounded with talk and laughter. Denzil had a higher colour than usual, but he seemed perfectly self-possessed; his appearance and colloquial abilities made a very favourable impression. "Distinct improvement on friend Toby," whispered one committee-man to another; and this was the general opinion. Yet there was some anxiety regarding the address they were about to hear. Denzil did not look like a man who would mince his words and go half-way in his opinions. The Woman question was rather a dangerous one in Polterham just now; that period of Revivalism, and the subsequent campaign of Mrs. Hitchin, had left a sore feeling in not a few of the townsfolk. An old gentleman (he had known Denzil as a boy) ventured to speak of this to the lecturer.

"Don't be afraid, Mr. Toft," was the laughing reply.

" You will stand amazed at my moderation; I am dead against Female Suffrage."

"That is safe, I think. You'll find Mrs. Wade down upon you—but that doesn't matter."

" Will she attack me in the hall ? "

"No, no; we don't have public discussion; but prepare for an assault to-morrow."

"I shall enjoy it ! "

The hall was rapidly filling. Already twice as many people as attended an ordinary lecture had taken seats, and among them were numerous faces altogether strange at the Institute, though familiar enough in the streets of Polterham. Among early arrivals was Mr. Samuel Quarrier, Denzil's uncle, a white-headed but stalwart figure. He abominated Radicalism, and was one of the very few " new " men who supported the old political dynasty of the town. But his countenance manifested no sour displeasure ; he exchanged cheery greetings on all hands, and marched steadily to the front chairs, his two daughters following. The Mayor, accompanied by his wife, Miss Mumbray, and young Mr. Raglan Mumbray, was seen moving forward ; he acknowledged salutations with a heavy bow and a wave of the hand. Decidedly it was a field-day. From the street below sounded a constant roll of carriages and clatter of hoofs coming to a standstill before the Institute. Never, perhaps, had so many people in evening costume gathered under this roof. Even Mr. Chown, the draper, though scornful of such fopperies, had thought it due to his position as a town-councillor

to don the invidious garb; he was not disposed to herd
among the undistinguished at the back of the room.
Ladies were in great force, though many of them
sought places with an abashed movement, not quite
sure whether what they were about to hear would be
strictly "proper." One there was who betrayed no
such tremors; the position she assumed was about the
middle of the hall, and from time to time curious looks
were cast in that direction.

The clock pointed to eight. Punctually to the
moment a side door was thrown open, and a procession
of gentlemen ascended the platform. Members of the
committee seated themselves in a row of arm-chairs;
Mr. William Glazzard took his place not far from the
reading-desk, and behind it subsided the lecturer.

In these instants Denzil Quarrier was the prey of
sudden panic. He had imagined that his fortitude
was proof against stage-fright, but between the door and
his seat on the platform he suffered horribly. His
throat was parched and constricted; his eyes dazzled, so
that he could see nothing; his limbs were mere auto-
matic mechanism; he felt as though some one had set
his ears on fire. He strove wildly to recollect his
opening sentences; but they were gone. How was he
to fill up a mortal hour with coherent talk when he
had not command of one phrase? He had often
reproved himself for temerity, and now the weakness had
brought its punishment. What possessed him to run
into such a —— ?

The chairman had risen and was speaking. "Plea-

sure — — — introduce — — — Mr. Denzil Quarrier,
— — — not unknown to many of you — — — almost
at a moment's notice — — — much indebted — — —"

An outbreak of applause, and then dead silence.
The ticking of the clock became audible. Some external
force took hold upon him, lifted him from the chair, and
impelled him a few steps forward. Some voice, decidedly not his own, though it appeared to issue from his
throat, uttered the words: "Mr. Chairman, Ladies
and Gentlemen." And before the sound had ceased,
there flashed into his thoughts a story concerning an
enlightened young lady of Stockholm, who gave a
lecture to advance the theory that woman's intellect
suffered from the habit of allowing her hair to grow so
long. It was years since this trifle had recurred to his
mind; it came he knew not how, and he clutched at it
like the drowning man at a straw. Before he really
understood what he was about, he had begun to narrate
the anecdote, and suddenly, to his astonishment, he was
rewarded with universal peals of laughter. The noise
dispelled his anguish of nervousness; he drew a deep
breath, grasped the table before him, and was able to
speak as freely as if he had been on his own hearth-rug
in Clement's Inn.

Make a popular audience laugh, and you have a hold
upon its attention. Able now to distinguish the faces
that were gazing at him, Denzil perceived that he had
begun with a lucky stroke; the people were in expectation of more merriment, and sat beaming with good-
humour. He saw the Mayor spread himself and

stroke his beard, and the Mayoress simper as she caught a friend's eye. Now he might venture to change his tone and become serious.

Decidedly, his views were moderate. From the beginning he allowed it to be understood that, whatever might be the effect of long hair, he for one considered it becoming, and was by no means in favour of reducing it to the male type. The young lady of Stockholm might or might not have been indebted for her wider mental scope to the practice of curtailing her locks, yet he had known many Swedish ladies (and ladies of England, too) who, in spite of lovely hair, managed to preserve an exquisite sense of the distinctions of womanhood, and this (advanced opinion notwithstanding) he maintained was the principal thing. But, the fact that so many women were nowadays lifting up their voices in a demand for various degrees of emancipation seemed to show that the long tresses and the flowing garb had really, by process of civilization, come to symbolize certain traditions of inferiority which weighed upon the general female consciousness. "Let us, then, ask what these traditions are, and what is to be said for or against them from the standpoint of a liberal age."

Denzil no longer looked with horror at the face of the clock; his only fear was lest the hands should move too rapidly, and forbid him to utter in spacious periods all he had on his mind. By half-past eight he was in the midst of a vehement plea for an enlargement of female education, in the course of which he uttered several

things rather disturbing to the nerves of Mrs. Mumbray,
and other ladies present.—Woman, it was true, lived an
imperfect life if she did not become wife and mother;
but this truism had been insisted on to the exclusion of
another verity quite as important: that wifehood and
motherhood, among civilized people, implied qualifica-
tions beyond the physical. The ordinary girl was sent
forth into life with a mind scarcely more developed
than that of a child. Hence those monstrous errors she
constantly committed when called upon to accept a
husband. Not one marriage in fifty thousand was an
alliance on terms fair to the woman. In the vast
majority of cases, she wedded a sort of man in the
moon. Of him and of his world she knew nothing;
whereas the bridegroom had almost always a very
sufficient acquaintance with the circumstances, habits,
antecedents, characteristics, of the girl he espoused.
Her parents, her guardians, should assure themselves
—pooh! even if these people were conscientious
and capable, the task was in most cases beyond their
power.

" I have no scheme for rendering marriages universally happy. On the contrary, I believe that marriages
in general will always serve as a test of human
patience." (Outbreak of masculine laughter.) "But
assuredly it is possible, by judicious training of young
girls, to guard them against some of the worst perils
which now threaten their going forth into the world.
It is possible to put them on something like an equality
in knowledge of life with the young men of correspond-

ing social station." (" Oh, shameful ! " murmured Mrs.
Mumbray. " Shocking ! ") " They must be treated,
not like ornaments under glass-cases, but like human
beings who, physiologists assure us, are born with
mental apparatus, even as men are. I repeat that I
don't want to see them trained for politics " (many
faces turned towards the middle of the hall) " and that
I lament the necessity imposed on so many of them of
struggling with men in the labour-market. What I
demand is an education in the true sense of the word,
and that as much at the hands of their mothers as of
the school-teacher. When that custom has been established, be sure that it will affect enormously the habits
and views of the male population. The mass of men at
present regard women as creatures hoodwinked for
them by nature—or at all events by society. When
they can no longer act on that assumption, interest and,
let us hope, an expanding sense of honour will lead
them to see the marriage contract, and all connected
with it, in altogether a different light."

He drank off a glass of water, listening the while to
resonant applause. There was still twenty minutes,
and he decided to use the time in offering solace to the
army of women who, by force of mere statistics, are
fated to the frustration of their *raison d'être*. On this
subject he had nothing very remarkable to say, and,
indeed, the maiden ladies who heard him must have
felt that it all amounted to a pitying shrug of the
shoulders. But he could not speak otherwise than
vigorously, and at times his words were eloquent.

"We know not how things may improve in the future,"
(thus he perorated), " but let celibate ladies of the present
bear in mind that the chances are enormously against
their making a marriage worthy of the name." (" Oh ! "
from some man at the back.)   " Let them remember, too,
if they are disposed to altruism, that though most men
manage to find a wife, very few indeed, as things are,
do not ultimately wish that they had remained single."
(A roar of laughter, and many protests.)   "This being
so, let women who have no family of their own devote
themselves, whenever possible, to the generous and
high task of training the new female generation,
so that they may help to mitigate one of the greatest
ills of civilized existence, and prepare for women of
the future the possibility of a life truly emancipated."

Denzil sat down with a glow of exulting triumph.
His lecture was a success, not a doubt of it.   He saw
the chairman rise, and heard slow, languid phrases
which contrasted strangely with his own fire and rush.
A vote of thanks was being proposed.   When silence
came, he was aware of some fluster in the body of the
hall ; people were whispering, tittering, turning round
to look.   Two persons had stood up with the intention
of seconding the vote of gratitude ; one was Mr. Chown,
the other that lady who had a place in the middle of
the assemblage, and who seemed to be so well known.
The Radical draper did not immediately give way, but
his neighbours reminded him of propriety.   Quarrier
had just scrutinized the person of the lady about to

speak, when her voice fell upon his ears with a pleasant distinctness.

"As it is certainly right," she began, "that a woman should be one of those who return thanks to our lecturer, and as I fear that no other woman present will be inclined to undertake this duty, I will make no apology for trying to perform it. And that in very few words. Speaking for myself, I cannot pretend to agree with the whole of Mr. Quarrier's address ; I think his views were frequently timid "—laughter and hushing—" frequently timid, and occasionally quite too masculine. I heard once of a lady who proposed to give a series of lectures on 'Astronomy from a Female Point of View'" (a laugh from two or three people only), " and I should prefer to entitle Mr. Quarrier's lecture, 'Woman from a Male Point of View.' However, it was certainly well-meaning, undoubtedly eloquent, and on the whole, in this time of small mercies, something for which a member of the struggling sex may reasonably be grateful. I wish, therefore, to add my voice to the proposal that a vote of thanks be offered to our lecturer, with all sincerity and all heartiness."

"A devilish good little speech ! " Denzil murmured to himself, as the applause and merriment broke forth.

The show of hands seemed to be universal. Denzil was enjoying an enormous happiness. He had proved to himself that he could speak, and henceforth the platform was his own. Now let the dissolution of

Parliament come with all convenient speed; he longed to begin the political conflict.

Committee-men crowded about him, offering hands, and brimming with facetious eulogy.

"You were on very thin ice now and then," said Mr. Liversedge. "You made me shake in my shoes. But the skating was admirable."

"I never knew Mrs. Wade so complimentary," remarked old Mr. Toft. "I expected half an hour's diatribe, 'the rapt oration flowing free,' as Tennyson says. You have taught her good manners."

Down in the hall was proceeding an animated conversazione. In one group stood the Mayor and his wife, Miss Mumbray, and Ivy Glazzard. Serena was turning aside to throw a shawl over her shoulders, when Eustace Glizzard stepped up.

"Pray let me assist you, Miss Mumbray." He placed the wrap. "I hope you have been amused?"

"I have, really," answered the girl, with a glance towards Ivy, who had heard her uncle's voice.

"You, Ivy," he continued, "are rather on Mrs. Wade's side, I think?"

"Oh, uncle—how *can* you!"

Mr. Mumbray was looking on, trying to determine who the gentleman might be. Glazzard, desirous of presentation to the Mayor, gave Ivy a glance, and she, with much nervousness, uncertain whether she might do such a thing, said to her friend's father:

"I think, Mr. Mumbray, you don't know my uncle, Mr. Eustace Glazzard?"

"Ha! very glad to meet you, Mr. Glazzard. My love," he turned to the Mayoress, "let me present to you Mr. Eustace Glazzard—Mr. William's brother."

The Mayoress laid her fan on her bosom, and inclined graciously. She was a portly and high-coloured woman, with hanging nether lip. Glazzard conversed with her and her husband in a tone of amiable liveliness.

"Remarkable," he said, smiling to the Mayoress, "how patiently women in general support this ancient yoke of tyranny!"

Mrs. Mumbray looked at him with condescending eyes, in doubt as to his real meaning. Her husband, ponderously literal, answered in his head-voice:

"I fail to recognize the grievance.—How do you do, Mr. Lovett?—I am conscious of no tyranny."

"But that is just what Mr. Glazzard meant, papa," put in Serena, with scarcely disguised contempt.

"Ha! oh! To be sure—to be sure! Quite so, Mr. Glazzard.—A very amoosing lecture, all the same. Not of course to be taken seriously.—Good evening, Mr. Glazzard—good evening!"

The Mayoress again inclined. Serena gave her acquaintance an enigmatic look, murmured a leave-taking, and, with an affectionate nod to Ivy, passed on. Glazzard drew near to his niece.

"Your friend is not a disciple of Mrs. Wade?"

"Oh dear no, uncle!"

"Not just a little bit?" he smiled, encouragingly.

"Perhaps she would agree with what Mr. Quarrier said about girls having a right to better instruction."

"I see. Don't wait with me if there's any one you would like to speak to."

Ivy shook her head. She had a troubled expression, as if the experience of the evening had agitated her.

Close at hand, a circle of men had formed about Mr. Chown, who was haranguing on the Woman question. What he wanted was to emancipate the female mind from the yoke of superstition and of priestcraft. Time enough to talk about giving women votes when they were no longer the slaves of an obstructive religion. There were good things in the lecture, but, on the whole, it was flabby—flabby. A man who would discourse on this topic must be courageous; he must dare to shock and give offence. Now, if *he* had been lecturing——

Glazzard beckoned to his niece, and led her out of ear-shot of these utterances. In a minute or two they were joined by the chairman, who had already equipped himself for departure.

"Bah! I have a splitting headache," said William. "Let us get home."

Quarrier was still on the platform, but at this moment he caught Glazzard's eye, and came hastening down. His friend stepped forward to meet him.

"Well, how did it go?" Denzil asked, gaily.

"You have great aptitude for that kind of thing."

"So it strikes me.—Will you engage yourself to dine with me the day after to-morrow?"

"Willingly."

"I have an idea. You remember the Coach and Horses—over at Rickstead?"

It was a fine old country inn, associated in their memories of boyhood with hare-and-hounds and other sportive excursions. Glazzard nodded.

"Let us have a quiet dinner there; six-thirty· They can drive us back."

Glazzard rejoined his relatives. Denzil, turning away, came face to face with Mr. Samuel Quarrier.

"So you took the trouble to come and hear me?"

"To be sure," replied the old man, in a gruff but good-natured voice. "Is it true what they are saying? Is it to be you instead of Toby?"

"I believe so."

"I shall do my best to get you a licking. All in good part, you know."

"Perfectly natural. But I shall win!"

VIII.

"Do you know of any good house to let in or near the town?" inquired Denzil of his sister the next morning, as they chatted after Toby's departure to business.

"A house! What do you want with one?"

"Oh, I must have a local habitation—the more solid the better."

Mrs. Liversedge examined him.

"What is going on, Denzil?"

"My candidature—that's all. Any houses advertised in this rag?" He took up yesterday's *Examiner*, and began to search the pages.

"You can live very well with us."

Denzil did not reply, and his sister, summoned by a servant, left him. There was indeed an advertisement such as he sought. An old and pleasant family residence, situated on the outskirts of Polterham (he remembered it very well), would be vacant at Christmas. Application could be made on the premises. Still in a state of very high pressure, unable to keep still or engage in any quiet pursuit, he set off on the instant to view this house. It stood in a high-walled garden, which was entered through heavy iron-barred gates, one of them now open. The place had rather a forlorn look, due in part to the decay of the foliage which in summer shaded the lawn; blinds were drawn on all the front windows; the porch needed repair. He rang at the door, and was quickly answered by a dame of the housekeeper species. On learning his business, she began to conduct him through the rooms, which were in habitable state, though with furniture muffled.

"The next room, sir, is the library. A lady is there at present. Perhaps you know her?—Mrs. Wade."

"Mrs. Wade! Yes, I know her slightly."

The coincidence amused him.

"She comes here to study, sir—being a friend of the family. Will you go in?"

Foreseeing a lively dialogue, he released his attendant till she should hear his voice again, and, with preface of a discreet knock, entered the room. An agreeable warmth met him, and the aspect of the interior contrasted cheerfully with that of the chambers into which he had looked. There was no great collection of books, but some fine engravings filled the vacancies around. At the smaller of two writing-tables sat the person he was prepared to discover; she had several volumes open before her, and appeared to be making notes. At his entrance she turned and gazed at him fixedly.

"Forgive my intrusion, Mrs. Wade," Denzil began, in a genial voice. "I have come to look over the house, and was just told that you were here. As we are not absolute strangers "——

He had never met her in the social way, though she had been a resident at Polterham for some six years.

Through Mrs. Liversedge, her repute had long ago reached him; she was universally considered eccentric, and, by many people, hardly proper for an acquaintance. On her first arrival in the town she wore the garb of recent widowhood; relatives here she had none, but an old friendship existed between her and the occupants of this house, a childless couple named Hornibrook. Her age was now about thirty.

Quarrier was far from regarding her as an attractive woman. He thought better of her intelligence than before hearing her speak, and it was not difficult for him to imagine that the rumour of Polterham went much astray when it concerned itself with her characteristics; but the face now directed to him had no power whatever over his sensibilities. It might be that of a high-spirited and large-brained woman; beautiful it could not be called. There was something amiss with the eyes. All the other features might pass; they were neither plain nor comely: a forehead of good type, a very ordinary nose, largish lips, chin suggesting the masculine; but the eyes, to begin with, were prominent, and they glistened in a way which made it very difficult to determine their colour. They impressed Denzil as of a steely-grey, and seemed hard as the metal itself. His preference was distinctly for soft feminine eyes—such as Lilian gazed with.

Her figure was slight, but seemed strong and active. He had noticed the evening before that, in standing to address an audience, she looked anything but ridiculous —spite of bonnet. Here too, though allowing her surprise to be seen, she had the bearing of perfect self-possession, and perhaps of conscious superiority. Fawn-coloured hair, less than luxuriant, lay in soft folds and plaits on the top of her head; possibly (the thought was not incongruous) she hoped to gain half an inch of seeming stature.

They shook hands, and Denzil explained his object in calling.

"Then you are going to settle at Polterham?"

"Probably—that is, to keep an abode here."

"You are not married, I think, Mr. Quarrier?"

"No."

"There was a report at the Institute last night—may I speak of it?"

"Political? I don't think it need be kept a secret. My brother-in-law wishes me to make friends with the Liberals, in his place."

"I dare say you will find them very willing to meet your advances. On one question you have taken a pretty safe line."

"Much to your disgust," said Denzil, who found himself speaking very freely and inclined to face debatable points.

"Disgust is hardly the word. Will you sit down? In Mrs. Hornibrook's absence, I must represent her. They are good enough to let me use the library; my own is poorly supplied."

Denzil took a chair.

"Are you busy with any particular subject?" he asked.

"The history of woman in Greece."

"Profound! I have as good as forgotten my classics. You read the originals?"

"After a fashion. I don't know much about the enclitic *de*, and I couldn't pass an exam. in the hypothetical sentences; but I pick up the sense as I read on."

Her tone seemed to imply that, after all, she was not ill-versed in grammatical niceties. She curtailed the the word "examination" in an off-hand way which smacked of an undergraduate, and her attitude on the chair suggested that she had half a mind to cross her legs and throw her hands behind her head.

"Then," said Quarrier, "you have a good deal more right to speak of woman's claims to independence than most female orators."

She looked at him with a good-humoured curl of the lip.

"Excuse me if I mention it—your tone reminds me of that with which you began last evening. It was rather patronizing."

"Heaven forbid! I am very sorry to have been guilty of such ill-manners."

"In a measure you atoned for it afterwards. When I got up to offer you my thanks, I was thinking of the best part of your lecture—that where you spoke of girls being entrapped into monstrous marriages. That was generous, and splendidly put. It seemed to me that you must have had cases in mind."

For the second time Denzil was unable to meet the steely gaze. He looked away and laughed.

" Oh, of course I had ; who hasn't—that knows anything of the world ? But," he changed the subject,
" don't you find it rather dull, living in a place like
Polterham ? "

" I have my work here."

" Work ?—the work of propagandism ? "

" Precisely. It would be pleasant enough to live in
London, and associate with people of my own way of
thinking ; but what's the good ?—there's too much of
that centralization. The obscurantists take very good
care to spread themselves. Why shouldn't those who
love the light try to keep little beacons going in out-of-
the-way places ? "

" Well, do you make any progress ? "

" Oh, I think so. The mere fact of my existence
here ensures that. I dare say you have heard tell of
me, as the countryfolk say ? "

The question helped Denzil to understand why Mrs.
Wade was content with Polterham. He smiled.

" Your influence won't be exerted against me, I
hope, when the time comes ? "

" By no means. Don't you see that I have already
begun to help you ? "

" By making it clear that my Radicalism is not of
the most dangerous type ? "

They laughed together, and Quarrier, though the
dialogue entertained him, rose as if to depart.

" I will leave you with your Greeks, Mrs. Wade ;
though I fear you haven't much pleasure in them from
that special point of view."

"I don't know; they have given us important types of womanhood. The astonishing thing is that we have got so little ahead of them in the facts of female life. Woman is still enslaved, though men nowadays think it necessary to disguise it."

"Do you really attach much importance to the right of voting, and so on?"

"'And so on!' That covers a great deal, Mr. Quarrier. I attach all importance to a state of things which takes for granted that women stand on a level with children."

"So they do—with an inappreciable number of exceptions. You must be perfectly well aware of that."

"And so you expect me to be satisfied with it?—I insist on the franchise, because it symbolizes full citizenship. I won't aim at anything less than that. Women must be taught to keep their eyes on that, as the irreducible minimum of their demands."

"We mustn't argue. You know that I think they must be taught to look at quite different things."

"Yes; but what those things are you have left me in doubt. We will talk it over when you have more time to spare. Do you know my address? Pear-tree Cottage, Rickstead Road. I shall be very glad to see you if ever you care to call."

Denzil made his acknowledgments, shook hands, and left the room.

When his step sounded in the hall, the housekeeper appeared and conducted him to the upper stories. He examined everything attentively, but in silence; his features expressed grave thought. Mr. and Mrs. Hornibrook, he was told, were living in Guernsey, and had resolved to make that island their permanent abode. A Polterham solicitor was their agent for the property.

Denzil was given to acting on the spur of the moment. There might be dwellings obtainable that would suit him better than this, but he did not care to linger in the business. As he passed out of the iron gates he made up his mind that the house, with necessary repairs, would do very well; and straightway he turned his steps to the office of the agent.

IX.

THE village of Rickstead lay at some five miles' distance from that suburb of Polterham where dwelt Mr. Toby Liversedge, Mr. Mumbray (the Mayor), Mr. Samuel Quarrier, and sundry other distinguished townsfolk. A walk along the Rickstead Road was a familiar form of exercise with the less-favoured people who had their homes in narrow streets; for on either side of the highway lay an expanse of meadows, crossed here and there by pleasant paths which led to the surrounding hamlets. In this direction no factories had as yet risen to deform the scene.

Darkness was falling when Quarrier set forth to keep his appointment with Eustace Glazzard at the Coach and Horses Inn. The road-lamps already glimmered; there would be no moon, but a soft dusky glow lingered over half the sky, and gave promise of a fair night. Denzil felt his boyhood revive as he got clear of the new houses, and began to recognize gates, trees, banks, and stiles; he could not say whether he enjoyed the sensation, but it served to combat certain troublesome thoughts which had beset him since the morning. He was experiencing reaction after the excitement of the last two days. A change from the orderly domesticities of his sister's house had become necessary to him, and he looked forward with satisfaction to the evening he had planned.

At a turn of the road, which, as he well remembered, had been a frequent limit of his nurse-guarded walk five-and-twenty years ago, his eye fell upon a garden gate marked with the white inscription, " Pear-tree Cottage." It brought him to a pause. This must be Mrs. Wade's dwelling ; the intellectual lady had quite slipped out of his thoughts, and with amusement he stopped to examine the cottage as well as dusk permitted. The front was overgrown with some creeper; the low roof made an irregular line against the sky ; one window on the ground-floor showed light through a red blind. Mrs. Wade, he had learnt, enjoyed but a small income; the interior was probably very modest. There she sat behind the red blind and meditated on the servitude of her sex. Repressing an inclination to laugh aloud, he stepped briskly forward.

Rickstead consisted of twenty or thirty scattered houses ; an ancient, slumberous place, remarkable chiefly for its time-honoured inn, which stood at the crossing of two high roads. The landlord had received notice that two gentlemen would dine under his roof, and the unwonted event was making quite a stir in the hostelry. Quarrier walked in at about a quarter-past six; savoury odours saluted him from the threshold. Glazzard had not yet arrived, but in less than five minutes a private carriage drew up to the door, and the friends hailed each other.

The room prepared for them lay well apart from the bar, with its small traffic. A great fire had been blazing for an hour or two ; and the table, not too large, was laid with the best service the house could afford—nothing very grand, to be sure, in these days of its decline, but the general effect was inviting to men with a good appetite and some historical imagination.

"A happy idea of yours!" said Glazzard, as he rubbed his hands before the great hearth. "Are we to begin with a cup of sack?"

Punctually the meal was served; the liquor provided therewith, though of small dignity, did no discredit to the host. They talked and laughed over old Grammar School days, old acquaintances long since dead or lost to sight, boyish ambitions and achievements. Dinner dismissed, a bottle of whisky on the table, a kettle steaming by the fire, Denzil's pipe and Glazzard's cigar comfortably glowing, there came a long pause.

"Well, I have a story to tell you," said Quarrier, at length.

"So I supposed," murmured the other, without eagerness.

"I don't know that I *should* have told it but for that chance encounter at Kew. But I'm not sorry. I think, Glazzard, you are the one man in the world in whom I have perfect confidence."

The listener just bent his head. His features were impassive.

"It concerns Lilian, of course," Quarrier pursued, when he had taken a few puffs less composedly than hitherto. "I am telling the story without her leave, but—well, in a way, as I said, the necessity is forced upon me. I can't help doing many things just now that I should avoid if I had my choice. I have under-taken to fight society by stratagem. For my own part, I would rather deal it a plain blow in the face, and bid it do its worst; but "—— He waved his hand.

Glazzard murmured and nodded comprehension.

"I'll go back to the beginning. That was about three years ago. I was crossing the North Sea (you remember the time; I said good-bye to you in the Academy, where your bust was), and on the boat I got into conversation with a decent kind of man who had his wife and family with him, going to settle for a time at Stockholm; a merchant of some sort. There were three children, and they had a governess—Lilian, in fact, who was then not much more than eighteen. I liked the look of her from the first. She was very still and grave,—the kind of thing that takes me in a woman, provided she has good features. I managed to get a word or two with her, and I liked her way of speaking. Well, I was sufficiently interested to say to myself that I might as well spend a week or two at Stockholm and keep up the acquaintance of these people; Becket, their name was. I'm not exactly the kind of fellow who goes about falling in love with nursery governesses, and at that time (perhaps you recollect?) I had somebody else in mind. I dare say it was partly the contrast between that shark of a woman and this modest girl; at all events, I wanted to see more of Lilian, and I did. I was in Stockholm, off and on, for a couple of months. I became good friends with the Beckets, and before coming back to England I made an

offer to Miss Allen—that was the governess's name.
She refused me, and I was conceited enough to wonder
what the deuce she meant."

Glazzard laughed.   He was listening with more
show of interest.

" Well," pursued Quarrier, after puffing vainly at his
extinguished pipe, "there was reason for wondering.
Before I took the plunge, I had a confidential talk with
Mrs. Becket, who as good as assured me that I had only
to speak; in fact, she was rather angry with me for disturbing her family arrangements.   Miss Allen, I learnt
from her, was an uncommonly good girl—everything I
imagined her.   Mrs. Becket didn't know her family,
but she had engaged her on the strength of excellent
testimonials, which didn't seem exaggerated.   Yet
after that I was floored—told that the thing couldn't
be.   No weeping and wailing; but a face and a voice
that puzzled me.   The girl liked me well enough; I
felt sure of it.   All the same I had to come back to
England alone, and in a devilish bad temper.   You
remember that I half quarrelled with you about something at our first meeting."

" You were rather bearish," remarked Glazzard,
knocking the ash off his cigar.

" As I often am.   Forgive me, old fellow ! "

Denzil relit his pipe.

" The next summer I went over to Sweden again.
Miss Allen was still with the Beckets, as I knew; but
she was only going to stay a few months more.   One of
the children had died, and the other two were to be sent

to a boarding-school in England. Again I went through the proposing ordeal, and again it was useless. 'Confound it!' I shouted, 'do deal honestly with me! What's the matter? Are you engaged already?' She kept silent for a long time, then said 'Yes!' 'Then why in the name of the Jötuns didn't you tell me so before?' I was brutal (as I often am), and the poor girl began to cry. Then there was a scene— positive stage business. I wouldn't take her refusal. 'This other man, you don't really care for him—you are going to sacrifice yourself! I won't have it!' She wept and moaned, and threatened hysterics; and at last, when I was losing patience (I can't stand women's idiotic way of flinging themselves about and making a disturbance, instead of discussing difficulties calmly), she said at last that, if ever we met in England, she would explain her position. 'Why not now?'—no, not in the Beckets' house. Very well then, at least she might make it certain that I *should* see her in England. After trouble enough, she at last consented to this. She was to come back with Mr. Becket and the boys, and then go to her people. I got her promise that she would write to me and make an appointment somewhere or other.—More whisky?"

Glazzard declined; so Denzil replenished his own glass, and went on. He was now tremulous with the excitement of his reminiscences; he fidgeted on the chair, and his narrative became more jerky than ever.

"Her letter came, posted in London. She had taken leave of the Becket party, and was supposed to be travelling homewards; but she would keep her word with me. I was to go and see her at an hotel in the West End. Go, I did, punctually enough; I believe I would have gone to Yokohama for half an hour of her society. I found her in a private sitting-room, looking wretched enough, confoundedly ill. And then and there she told me her story. It was a queer one; no one could have guessed it."

He seized the poker and stirred the fire savagely.

"I shall just give you the plain facts. Her father was a builder in a small way, living at Bristol. He had made a little money, and was able to give his children a decent education. There was a son, who died young, and then two girls, Lilian the elder of them. The old man must have been rather eccentric; he brought up the girls very strictly (their mother died when they were children)—would scarcely let them go out of his sight, preached to them a sort of mixture of Christianity and Pantheism, forbade all pleasures except those of home, didn't like them to make acquaintances. Their mother's sister kept the house; a feeble, very pious creature, probably knowing as much about life as the cat or the canary—so Lilian describes her. The man came to a sudden end; a brick fell on his head whilst he was going over a new building. Lilian was then about fifteen. She had passed the Oxford Local, and was preparing herself to teach—or rather, being prepared at a good school.

"Allen left enough money to provide his daughters with about a hundred a year each; this was to be theirs absolutely when they came of age, or when they married. The will had been carefully drawn up, and provided against all sorts of real and imaginary dangers. The one thing it couldn't provide against was the imbecility of the old aunt, who still had the girls in her care.

" A couple of years went by, and Lilian became a teacher in the school she had attended. Do you know anything about Bristol and the neighbourhood? It seems that the people there are in the habit of going to a place called Weston-super-Mare—excursion steamers, and so on. Well, the girls and their aunt went to spend a day at Weston, and on the boat they somehow made acquaintance with a young man named Northway. That means, of course, he made up to them, and the aunt was idiot enough to let him keep talking. He stuck by them all day, and accompanied them back to Bristol.—Pah! it sickens me to tell the story! "

He took the glass to drink, but it slipped from his nervous fingers and crashed on the ground.

" Never mind; let it be there. I have had whisky enough. This damned fellow Northway soon called upon them, and was allowed to come as often as he liked. He was a clerk in a commercial house—gave references which were found to be satisfactory enough, a great talker, and of course a consummate liar. His special interest was the condition of the lower classes; he made speeches here and there, went slumming, called himself a Christian Socialist. This kind of thing was no doubt attractive to Lilian—you know enough of her to understand that. She was a girl of seventeen, remember. In the end, Northway asked her to marry him, and she consented."

" Did he know of the money ? " inquired Glazzard.

" Undoubtedly. I shouldn't wonder if the block-head aunt told. Well, the wedding-day came; they were married; and—just as they came out of the church, up walks a detective, claps his hand on Northway's shoulder, and arrests him for forgery."

" H'm ! I see."

" The fellow was tried. Lilian wouldn't tell me the details; she gave me an old newspaper with full report. Northway had already, some years before, been in the hands of the police in London. It came out now that he was keeping a mistress; on the eve of marriage he had dispensed with her services, and the woman, in revenge, went to his employers to let them know certain suspicious facts. He was sent to penal servitude for three years."

" Three years ! " murmured Glazzard. " About so ago, I suppose ? "

" Yes; perhaps he is already restored to society. Pleasant reflection ! "

" Moral and discreet law," remarked the other, " which maintains the validity of such a marriage ! "

Denzil uttered a few violent oaths, reminiscences of the Navy.

" And she went at once to Sweden ? " Glazzard inquired.

" In a month or two the head-mistress of her

school, a sensible woman, helped her to get an engagement—with not a word said of the catastrophe. She went as Miss Allen. It was her firm resolve never again to see Northway. She would not acknowledge that that ceremony in the church made her a wife. Of course, you understand that it wasn't only the forgery that revolted her; that, I suppose, could have been pardoned. In a few days she had learnt more of herself and of the world than in all the previous years. She understood that Northway was really nothing to her. She accepted him because he was the first man who interested her and made love to her—like thousands of girls. Lilian is rather weak, unfortunately. She can't stand by herself. But for me, I am convinced she would now be at the mercy of that blackguard, when he comes out. Horror and despair enabled her to act firmly three years ago; but if she had no one to support her—well, she has!"

"What did you propose," asked Glazzard, "when you persuaded her to live with you?"

Denzil wrinkled his brow and looked gloomily at the fire.

"We agreed to live a life of our own, that was all. To tell you the truth, Glazzard, I had no clear plans. I was desperately in love, and—well, I thought of emigration some day. You know me too well to doubt my honesty. Lilian became my wife, for good and all—no doubt about that! But I didn't trouble much about the future—it's my way."

"She cut herself loose from the Bristol people?"

"No; she has corresponded with them at long

intervals. They think she is teaching in London. The tragedy excuses her from visiting them. Aunt and sister are sworn to secrecy concerning her whereabouts. A good thing she has no male relatives to hunt her up."

"Does she draw her income?—I beg your pardon, the question escaped me. Of course it's no business of mine."

"Never mind. Yes, the money is at her disposal; thanks to the settlement required by her father's will. I'm afraid she gives away a lot of it in indiscriminate charity. I needn't say," he added, with a characteristic movement of the head, "that *I* have nothing to do with it."

He paused.

"My real position she doesn't understand. I have never told her of how it was changed at my father's death.—Poor girl! About that time she was disappointed of a child, and had a month or two of black misery. I kept trying to make up my mind what course would be the wisest, and in the meanwhile said nothing. She is marvellously patient. In fact, what virtue hasn't she, except that of a strong will? Whatever happens, she and I stand together; nothing on earth would induce me to part from her! I want you to understand that. In what I am now going to do, I am led solely and absolutely by desire for our common good. You see, we are face to face with the world's immoral morality. To brave it would be possible, of course; but then we must either go to a foreign country or live here in isolation. I don't want to live permanently abroad, and I do want to go in for activity —political by preference. The result is we must set our faces, tell lies, and hope that fortune will favour us."

There was a strong contrast between Quarrier's glowing vehemence and the show of calm reflection which the other maintained as he listened. Denzil's face was fully lighted by the fire; his friend's received the shadow of an old-fashioned screen which Glazzard, finding the heat oppressive, had pulled forward a few minutes ago. The frank, fearless gaze with which Denzil's words were accompanied met no response ; but to this habit in the listener he was accustomed.

" Yes, we must tell lies!" Quarrier emphasized the words savagely. "Social law is stupid and unjust, imposing its obligation without regard to person or circumstance. It presumes that no one can be *trusted.* I decline to be levelled with the unthinking multitude. You and I can be a law to ourselves. What I shall do is this : On returning to town next week, I shall take Lilian over to Paris. We shall live there for several weeks, and about the end of the time I shall write to my people here, and tell them that I have just been married."

He paused. Glazzard made no motion, and uttered no sound.

" I have already dropped a mysterious word or two to my sister, which she will be able to interpret afterwards. Happily, I am thought a likely fellow to do odd, unconventional things. Again and again Mary has heard me rail against the idiocies of ordinary weddings; this private marriage will be quite in character. I shall state that Lilian has hitherto been a governess at Stockholm—that I made her acquaintance there—that I sent for her to meet me in Paris. Now, tell me, have you any objection to offer?"

Glazzard shifted his position, coughed, and drew from his case a new cigar, which he scrutinized closely from tip to end—even drawing it along under his nose. Then he spoke very quietly.

"It's feasible—but dangerous."

"But not *very* dangerous, I think?"

"I can't say. It depends greatly on your wife's character."

"Thank you for using that word, old fellow!" burst from Denzil. "She *is* my wife, in every sense of the word that merits the consideration of a rational creature!"

"I admit it; but I am afraid of lies."

"I am not only afraid of them; I hate them bitterly. I can say with a clear conscience that I abhor untruthfulness. I have never told a deliberate lie since I was old enough to understand the obligation of truth! But we have to do with monstrous social tyrannies. Lilian can no longer live in hiding. She must have a full and enjoyable life."

"Yes. But is it possible for her, under these conditions?"

"I think so. I have still to speak to her, but I know she will see things as I do."

A very faint smile flitted over Glazzard's lips.

" Good ! And you don't fear discovery by—what's his name—Northway ? "

" Not if Lilian can decide to break entirely with her relatives—at all events for some years. She must cease to draw her dividends, of course, and must announce to the Bristol people that she has determined on a step which makes it impossible for her to communicate with them henceforth. I don't think this will be a great sacrifice ; her aunt and her sister have no great hold upon her affections.—You must remember that her whole being is transformed since she last saw them. She thinks differently on all and every subject."

" You are assured of that ? "

" Absolutely sure ! I have educated her. I have freed her from superstitions and conventionalities. To her, as to me, the lies we shall have to tell will be burdensome in the extreme ; but we shall both forget in time."

" That is exactly what you can never do ! " said Glazzard, deliberately. " You enter upon a lifetime of dissimulation. Ten, twenty years hence you will have to act as careful a part as on the day when you and she first present yourselves in Polterham."

" Oh, in a sense ! " cried the other, impatiently.

" A very grave sense.—Quarrier, why have you taken up this political idea ? What's the good of it ? "

He leaned forward and spoke with a low earnest voice. Denzil could not instantly reply.

"Give it up!" pursued Glazzard. "Take Lilian abroad, and live a life of quiet happiness. Go on with your literary work "——

"Nonsense! I can't draw back now, and I don't wish to."

"Would you—if—if *I* were willing to become the Liberal candidate?"

Denzil stared in astonishment.

"You? Liberal candidate?"

"Yes, I!"

A peal of laughter rang through the room. Glazzard had spoken as if with a great effort, his voice indistinct, his eyes furtive. When the burst of merriment made answer to him, he fell back in his chair, crossed his legs, and set his features in a hard smile.

"You are joking, old fellow!" said Denzil.

"Yes, if you like."

Quarrier wished to discuss the point, but the other kept an obstinate silence.

"I understand," remarked Denzil, at length. "You hit upon that thought out of kindness to me. You don't like my project, and you wished to save me from its dangers. I understand. Hearty thanks, but I have made up my mind. I won't stunt my life out of regard for an imbecile superstition. The dangers are *not* great; and if they were, I should prefer to risk them. You electioneering! Ho, ho!"

Glazzard's lips were close drawn, his eyes veiled by the drooping lids. He had ceased to smoke, and when, a few minutes later, he threw away his cigar, it was all but squeezed flat by the two fingers which had seemed to hold it lightly.

"It is settled!" cried Denzil, jumping up, with a return of his extravagant spirits. "You, Glazzard, will stand by and watch—our truest friend. You on the hustings! Ha, ha, ha! Come, one more glass of whisky, and I will tell them to get our cab ready. I say, Glazzard, from this evening forth never a word between us about the secret. That is understood, of course. You may let people know that you were in my confidence about the private marriage. But I can trust your discretion as my own. Your glass—pledge me in the old style!"

Ten minutes more, and they were driving back to Polterham.

X.

But for domestic warfare, Mrs. Mumbray would often have been at a loss how to spend her time. The year of her husband's Mayoralty supplied, it is true, a good many unwonted distractions, but in the middle of the morning, and late in the evening (if there were no dinner-party), *ennui* too frequently weighed upon her. For relief in the former case, she could generally resort to a quarrel with Serena; in the latter, she preferred to wrangle with her spouse.

One morning early in December, having indulged her ill-humour with even more than usual freedom among the servants, she repaired to the smaller drawing-room, where, at this hour, her daughter often sat reading. Serena was at a table, a French book and dictionary open before her. After hovering for a few moments with eyes that gathered wrath, the Mayoress gave voice to her feelings.

"So you pay no attention to my wishes, Serena! I will not have you reading such books!"

Her daughter rustled the dictionary, impassive. Conscious of reduced authority, Mrs. Mumbray glared and breathed hard, her spacious bosom working like a troubled sea.

"Your behaviour astonishes me!—after what you heard Mr. Vialls say."

"Mr. Vialls is an ignorant and foolish man," remarked Serena, without looking up.

Then did the mother's rage burst forth without restraint, eloquent, horrisonous. As if to save her ears, Serena went to the piano and began to play. When the voice was silenced, she turned round.

"You had rather have me play than read that book? That shows how little you understand of either. This is an *immoral* piece of music! If you knew what it meant you would scream in horror. It is *immoral*, and I am going to practise it day after day."

The Mayoress stood awhile in mute astonishment, then, with purple face, swept from the room.

The family consisted of four persons. Serena's brother, a young gentleman of nineteen, articled to a solicitor in the town, was accustomed to appear at meals, but seldom deigned to devote any more of his leisure to the domestic circle. After luncheon to-day, as he stood at the window with a sporting newspaper, his mother addressed him.

"We have company this evening, Raglan. Take care that you're not late."

"Who's coming?" asked the young man, without looking up.

"Mr. Eustace Glazzard and Miss Glazzard."

"Any one else?"

"Mr. Vialls."

"Then you don't catch me here! I have an appointment at eight."

"I insist upon your dining with us! If you are not

at dinner, I will have your allowance stopped! I mean what I say. Not one penny more shall you receive until you have learnt to behave yourself! "

" We'll see about that," replied Raglan, with finished coolness; and, folding his newspaper, he walked off.

Nor did the hour of dinner see his return. The expected guests arrived; it was not strictly a dinner-party, but, as Mr. Mumbray described it, "a quiet evening *ong fammil*." The Rev. Scatchard Vialls came in at the last moment with perspiring brow, excusing himself on the ground of professional duties. He was thin, yet flabby, had a stoop in the shoulders, and walked without noticeably bending his knees. The crown of his head went to a peak; he had eyes like a ferret's; his speech was in a high, nasal note. For some years he had been a widower, a fact which perhaps accounted for his insinuating manner when he approached Miss Mumbray.

The dinner was portentously dull. Ivy Glazzard scarcely uttered a syllable. Her uncle exerted himself to shape phrases of perfect inoffensiveness, addressing now his hostess, now Serena. The burden of conversation fell upon Mr. Vialls, who was quite equal to its support; he spoke of the evil tendencies of the time as exhibited in a shameful attempt to establish Sunday evening concerts at a club of Polterham workmen. His discourse on this subject, systematically developed, lasted until the ladies withdrew. It allowed him scarcely any attention to his plate, but Mr. Vialls had the repute of an ascetic. In his buttonhole was a piece of blue ribbon, symbol of a ferocious total-abstinence; his face would have afforded sufficient proof that among the reverend man's failings were few distinctly of the flesh.

The Mayor did not pretend to asceticism. He ate largely and without much discrimination. His variously shaped and coloured glasses were not merely for display. When the door had closed behind the Mayoress and her two companions, he settled himself with an audible sigh, and for a few moments wore a look of meditation; then, leaning towards Glazzard, he inquired gravely:

" What is your opinion of the works of Bawlzac ? "

The guest was at a loss for an instant, but he quickly recovered himself.

" Ah, the French novelist? A man of great power, but—hardly according to English tastes."

"Should you consider him suitable reading for young ladies ? "

" Well, hardly. Some of his books are unobjectionable."

Mr. Vialls shot a fierce glance at him.

" In my opinion, his very name is pollution ! I would not permit a page of his writing, or of that of any French novelist, to enter my house. One and all are drenched with impurity ! "

" Certainly many of them are," conceded Glazzard.

"Lamentable," sighed the Mayor, raising his glass, "to think that quite a large number of his books have been put into the Institute library ! We must use our influence on all hands, Mr. Vialls. We live in sad times. Even the theatre—I am told that some of the plays produced in London are disgraceful, simply disgraceful ! "

The theatre was discussed, Mr. Vialls assailing it as a mere agent of popular corruption. On the mention of the name of Shakspere, Mr. Mumbray exclaimed :

" Shakspere needs a great deal of expurgating. But some of his plays teach a good lesson, I think. There is ' Romeo and Juliet,' for instance." Glazzard looked up in surprise. " I read ' Romeo and Juliet ' not long ago, and it struck me that its intention was decidedly moral. It points a lesson to disobedient young people. If Juliet had been properly submissive to her parents, such calamities would never have befallen her. Then, again, I was greatly struck with the fate that overtook Mercutio—a most suitable punishment for his persistent use of foul language. Did you ever see it in that light, Mr. Glazzard ? "

" I confess it is new to me. I shall think it over."

The Mayor beamed with gratification.

" No one denies," struck in Mr. Vialls, " that to a pure mind all things are pure. Shakspere is undoubtedly a great poet, and a soul bent on edification can extract much good from him. But for people in general, especially young people, assuredly he cannot be recommended, even in the study. I confess I have neither time nor much inclination for poetry— except that of the sacred volume, which is poetry indeed. I have occasionally found pleasure in Long- fellow "——

" Pardon me," interrupted the Mayor—"Longfellow? —the author of that poem called ' Excelsior ' ? "

" Yes."

" Now, really—I am surprised—I should have thought—the fact is, when Raglan was at school, he had to learn 'Excelsior,' and I happened to glance over it. I was slightly acquainted with the piece, but I had quite forgotten that it contained what seems to me very gross indelicacy—very gross indeed. Do you remember a verse beginning (I must ask your pardon for quoting it, Mr. Vialls)—

> ' Oh stay, the maiden cried, and rest
> Thy weary head upon this breast.'

Surely, that is all but indecency. In fact, I wrote at once to the master and drew his attention to the passage, requesting that my boy might never be asked to repeat such a poem. The force of my objection was not at once admitted, strange to say ; but in the end I gained my point."

Mr. Vialls screwed up his lips and frowned at the table-cloth, but said nothing.

" Our task nowadays," pursued the Mayor, with confidence, " is to preserve the purity of home. Our homes are being invaded by dangerous influences we must resist. The family should be a bulwark of virtue—of all the virtues—holiness, charity, peace."

He lingered on the last word, and his gaze became abstracted.

" Very true, very true indeed!" cried the clergyman. " For one thing, how careful a parent should be with regard to the periodical literature which is allowed to enter his house. This morning, in a home I will not mention, my eye fell upon a weekly paper which I should have thought perfectly sound in its teaching; yet, behold, there was an article of which the whole purport was to *excuse* the vices of the lower classes on the ground of their poverty and their temptations. Could anything be more immoral, more rotten in principle? *There* is the spirit we have to contend against—a spirit of accursed lenity in morals, often originating in so-called scientific considerations! Evil is evil—vice, vice—the devil is the devil—be circumstances what they may. I do not care to make mention of such monstrous aberrations as, for instance, the attacks we are occasionally forced to hear on the law of marriage. That is the mere reek of the bottomless pit, palpable to all. But I speak of subtler disguises of evil, such as may recommend themselves to persons well-intentioned but of weak understanding. Happily, I persuaded my friends to discontinue their countenance of that weekly paper, and I shall exert myself everywhere to the same end."

They rose at length, and went to the drawing-room. There Glazzard succeeding in seating himself by Miss Mumbray, and for a quarter of an hour he talked with her about art and literature. The girl's face brightened; she said little, but that little with very gracious smiles. Then Mr. Vialls approached, and the *tête-à-tête* was necessarily at an end.

When he was at length alone with his wife, the

Mayor saw what was in store for him; in fact, he had foreseen it throughout the evening.

"Yes," began the lady, with flashing eyes, "this is your Mr. Glazzard! He encourages Serena in her shameful behaviour! I overheard him talking to her."

"You are altogether wrong, as usual," replied Mr. Mumbray, with his wonted attempt at dignified self-assertion. "Glazzard distinctly disapproves of Bawlzac, and everything of that kind. His influence is as irreproachable as that of Mr. Vialls."

"Of course! You are determined to overthrow my plans at whatever cost to your daughter's happiness here and hereafter."

"I don't think Vialls a suitable husband for her, and I am not sorry she won't listen to him. He's all very well as a man and a clergyman, but—pshaw! what's the good of arguing with a pig-headed woman?"

This emphatic epithet had the result which was to be expected. The debate became a scolding-match, lasting well into the night. These two persons were not only on ill-terms, they disliked each other with the intensity which can only be engendered by thirty years of a marriage such as, but for public opinion, would not have lasted thirty weeks. Their reciprocal disgust was physical, mental, moral. It could not be concealed from their friends; all Polterham smiled over it; yet the Mumbrays were regarded as a centre of moral and religious influence, a power against the encroaches of rationalism and its attendant depravity. Neither of

them could point to dignified ancestry; by steady
persistence in cant and snobbishness—the genuine
expression of their natures—they had pushed to a
prominent place, and feared nothing so much as
depreciation in the eyes of the townsfolk. Raglan and
Serena were causing them no little anxiety; both,
though in different ways, might prove an occasion of
scandal. When Eustace Glazzard began to present
himself at the house, Mr. Mumbray welcomed the
significant calls. From his point of view, Serena could
not do better than marry a man of honourable name,
who would remove her to London. Out of mere
contrariety, Mrs. Mumbray thereupon began to encourage
the slow advances of her Rector, who thought of Serena's
fortune as a means to the wider activity, the greater
distinction, for which he was hungering.

Glazzard's self-contempt as he went home this evening
was not unmingled with pleasanter thoughts. For a
man in his position, Serena Mumbray and her thousands
did not represent a future of despair. He had always
aimed much higher, but defeat after defeat left him with
shaken nerves, and gloomy dialogues with his brother
had impressed upon him the necessity of guarding
against darkest possibilities. His state of mind was
singularly morbid; he could not trust the fixity of his
purposes for more than a day or two together; but just
at present he thought without distaste of Serena herself, and was soothed by the contemplation of her
(to him modest) fortune. During the past month he had
been several times to and from London; to-morrow he

would return to town again, and view his progress from a distance.

On reaching his brother's house, he found a letter waiting for him; it bore the Paris postmark. The contents were brief.

"DEAR GLAZZARD.

"I announce to you the fact of our marriage. The L.s will hear of it simultaneously. We are enjoying ourselves.

"Ever yours,

"D. Q."

He went at once to the room where William was sitting, and said, in a quiet voice:

"Quarrier has just got married—in Paris."

"Oh? To whom?"

"An English girl who has been a governess at Stockholm. I knew it was impending."

"Has he made a fool of himself?" asked William, dispassionately.

"I think not; she seems to be well educated, and good-looking—according to his report."

"Why didn't you mention it before?"

"Oh, his wish. We talked it all over when he was here. He has an idea that a man about to be married always cuts a ridiculous figure."

The elder man looked puzzled.

"No mysteries—eh?"

"None whatever, I believe. A decent girl without fortune, that's all. I suppose we shall see them before long."

The subject was shortly dismissed, and Eustace fell to reporting the remarkable conversation in which he had taken part at the Mayor's table. His brother was moved to no little mirth, but did not indulge in such savage contemptuousness as distinguished the narrator. William Glazzard viewed the world from a standpoint of philosophic calm; he expected so little of men in general, that disappointment or vexation could rarely befall him.

"These people," he observed, "think themselves pillars of society, and the best of the joke is, that they really *are* what they imagine. Without tolerably honest fools, we should fare badly at the hands of those who have neither wits nor honesty. Let us encourage them, by all means. I see no dawn as yet of the millennium of brains."

XI.

THE weather, for this time of year, was unusually bright in Paris. Each morning glistened with hoar-frost; by noon the sky shone blue over clean, dry streets, and gardens which made a season for themselves, leafless, yet defiant of winter's melancholy. Lilian saw it all with the eyes of a stranger, and often was able to forget her anxiety in the joy of wonderful, new impressions.

One afternoon she was resting in the room at the hotel, whilst Quarrier went about the town on some business or other. A long morning at the Louvre had tired her, and her spirits drooped. In imagination she went back to the days of silence and solitude in London; the memory affected her with something of home-sickness, a wish that the past could be restored. The little house by Clapham Common had grown dear to her; in its shelter she had shed many tears, but also had known much happiness: that sense of security which was now lost, the hope that there she might live always, hidden from the world's inquisitive gaze, justified to her own conscience by love and calm. What now was before her? Not only the elaborate deceit, the per-petual risk, weighed upon her heart; she was summoned to a position such as she had never foreseen, for which she had received no training. When Denzil revealed to her his real standing in the world, spoke laughingly of

the wealth he had inherited, and of his political
ambitions, her courage failed before the prospect. She
had not dared to let him see all her despondency, for his
impatient and sanguine temper would have resented it.
To please him and satisfy his utmost demands was the
one purpose of her life. But the task he had imposed
seemed to her, in these hours of faintness, no less than
terrible.

He entered, gay as usual, ready with tender words,
pet names and diminutives, the "little language" of
one who was still a lover. Seeing how things were
with her, he sat down to look over an English newspaper. Presently his attention strayed, he fell into
reverie.

"Well," he exclaimed at length, rousing himself,
"they have the news by now."

She gave no answer.

"I can imagine how Mary will talk. 'Oh, nothing
that Denzil does can surprise me! Whoever expected
him to marry in the ordinary way?' And then they'll
laugh, and shrug their shoulders, and hope I mayn't
have played the fool—good, charitable folks!"

Still she said nothing.

"Rather out of sorts to-day, Lily?"

"I wish we were going to stay here—never to go
back to England."

"Live the rest of our lives in a Paris hotel!"

"No, no—in some quiet place—a home of our own."

"That wouldn't suit me, by any means. Paris is
all very well for a holiday, but I couldn't make a home

here. There's no place like England. Don't you ever think what an unspeakable blessing it is to have been born in England? Every time I go abroad, I rejoice that I am not as these foreigners. Even my Scandinavian friends I can't help despising a little—and as for Frenchmen! There's a great deal of the old island prejudice in me."

Lilian smiled, raising herself slightly upon the sofa.

" These old Latin nations have had their day," he continued, with a wave of the arm. " France, Italy, Spain—they have played their part in civilization, and have nothing left now but old relics and modern bluster. The future's with us Teutons. If I were not an Englishman, I would be an American. The probability is that we shall have a hard fight one of these days with the Slavs—and all the better, perhaps; I don't think the world can do without fighting yet awhile."

" I should be sorry to hear you teaching people that," said Lilian.

" Oh," he laughed, " it wouldn't fit into our electoral campaign! No danger of my preaching bloodthirstiness. But how I shall enjoy the bloodless fight down at Polterham! I want you to look forward to it in the same way. Do cheer up, Lily!—you see I have been gradually moving in this direction. When I found myself a man of means, I knew that the time had come for stirring. Writing about the Sea-Kings is all very well in its way, but I am no born literary man. I must get that book finished and published, though. It might help me with the constituency. A book gives a man distinction."

"You seem to me to have changed very much."

"No; it's only that you didn't know me thoroughly. To tell you the truth, that life of hiding away in London wasn't a very good thing for me. I lived too much to myself. The half-dozen acquaintances I had were not the kind of men to profit me. Glazzard— well, Glazzard is an odd sort of fellow—helpful now and then, but on the whole musty. He has no ambition, thinks it enough to doze on among his pictures, and that kind of thing. The fact is, such companionship has made me conceited. I want to get among my equals and my superiors—as I shall do if I become a Member of Parliament."

"Your equals—perhaps."

"Confound it! *Your* influence has tended the same way. You spoil me—make me think myself a fine fellow. I suppose one's wife ought to talk like that—I don't dislike it, you know; but if I end by never doing anything at all, I should be confoundedly ashamed of myself. But the more I think of it, the better satisfied I am that a political career is the best thing for me. You see, this is the age of political progress—that before everything. We English are working out our revolution in a steady and sensible way, —no shrieking and slaughtering—we leave that to people who don't really know what they want, and will never get much to speak of. We go ahead soberly on the constitutional highway—with a little hearty swearing to clear the air now and then."

Lilian laughed.

"Well, I was saying it is a political age, and I think a man ought to go in for the first interest of his time. What have we to do just now with artistic aims? The English, at any time, care little or nothing for art; one has to recognize that. Our task in the world is practical—to secure all men a sufficiency of beef and beer, and honest freedom. I like to feel that I am on the advancing wave; I don't care for your picturesque ponds; they generally have a bad smell."

The effect of his vigorous talk was manifest in Lilian's face. She yielded her spirit to his, was borne whither he would.

"You talk of living in Paris—why, if you really knew Paris, you would hate the place. Underneath all this show of civilization, refinement, brilliancy—I'm glad to say you can't even guess what it covers. The town reeks with abominations. I'm getting sick of it."

The sincerity of his moral disgust was obvious. No one knew so well as Lilian the essential purity—even the puritanism—of Quarrier's temper.

"For all that," he added, merrily, "we'll go and dine at the restaurant, and then look in at the Français. They know how to cook here, and they know how to play the fool—no denying it."

When Lilian went forth with him she had once more succeeded in overcoming her despondent mood. The lights of the Boulevard exercised their wonted effect—cheering, inspiring. She pressed his arm, laughed at his mirthful talk; and Denzil looked down into her face with pride and delight in its loveliness. He had taken especial care to have her dressed in the manner that became his wife; Parisian science had gone to the making of her costume, and its efforts were not wasted. As they entered the restaurant, many eyes were turned with critical appreciation upon the modest face and figure, as undeniably English, in their way, as Quarrier's robust manhood.

Denzil's French was indifferently good, better perhaps than his capacity for picking out from the bill of fare a little dinner which should exalt him in the eyes of waiters. He went to work, however, with a noble disregard for consequences, whether to digestion or pocket. Where Lilian was concerned there could be no such thing as extravagance; he gloried in obtaining for her the best of everything that money could command. The final " *Bien, monsieur*," was, after all, sufficiently respectful, and our friend leaned back with the pleasant consciousness of duty performed.

He drank a good deal of wine, and talking with a spontaneity beyond the ordinary Briton. Towards the close of dinner his theme was the coming electoral contest.

" You know," he said, bending over the table, " you will be able to give me important help. The wife of a candidate—especially cf a Radical candidate—can find plenty of work, if she knows how to go about it. As little humbug as possible; and as little loss of self-respect; but we shall have to shake a good many dirty hands. Your turn for ' slumming' will serve us well, but I know the dangers of it. You'll be coming home *éplorée*, as they say here. I hope you'll grow stronger in that respect. One has to harden one's heart a little."

" I know it is wiser to do so."

" Of course! It's not only that you are constantly imposed upon; the indulgence of universal sympathy is incompatible with duty to one's self—unless you become at once a sister of mercy. One is bound, in common sense, to close eyes and ears against all but a trifling fraction of human misery. Why, look, we sit here, and laugh and talk and enjoy ourselves; yet at this instant what horrors are being enacted in every part of the world! Men are perishing by every conceivable form of cruelty and natural anguish. Sailors are gurgling out their life in sea-storms; soldiers are agonizing on battle-fields; men, women, and children are being burnt, boiled, hacked, squashed, rent, exploded to death in every town and almost every village of the globe. Here in Paris, and over there in London, there is no end to the forms of misery our knowledge suggests—all suffered while we eat and talk. But to sit down and think persistently of it would lead to madness in any one of imagination like yours. We have to say: It doesn't concern us! And no more it does. We haven't the ordering of the world; we can't alter the vile course of things. I like to swear over it now and then (especially when I pass a London hospital), but I soon force myself to think of something else. You must do the same—

even to the swearing, if you like. There's a tendency in our time to excess of humanitarianism—I mean a sort of lachrymose habit which really does no good. You represent it in some degree, I'm afraid—eh? Well, well, you've lived too much alone—you've got into the way of brooding; the habit of social life will strengthen you."

" I hope so, Denzil."

" Oh, undoubtedly! One more little drop of wine before the coffee. Nonsense! You need stimulus; your vitality is low. I shall prescribe for you hence-forth. Merciful heavens! how that French woman does talk! A hundred words to the minute for the last half hour."

A letter had arrived for him at the hotel in his absence. It was from Mr. Hornibrook's agent, announcing that the house at Polterham was now vacated, and that Mr. Quarrier might take possession just as soon as he chose.

" *That's* all right! " he exclaimed, after reading it to Lilian. " Now we'll think of getting back to London, to order our furniture, and all the rest of it. The place can be made habitable in a few weeks, I should say."

XII.

An emissary from Tottenham Court Road sped down
to Polterham, surveyed the vacant house, returned with
professional computations. Quarrier and Lilian abode
at the old home until everything should be ready for
them, and Mrs. Liversedge represented her brother on
the spot—solving the doubts of workmen, hiring
servants, making minor purchases. She invited Denzil
to bring his wife, and dwell for the present under the
Liversedge roof, but her brother preferred to wait. " I
don't like makeshifts; we must go straight into our
own house; the dignity of the Radical candidate
requires it." So the work glowed, and as little time as
possible was spent over its completion.

It was midway in January when the day and hour of
arrival were at last appointed. No one was to be in
the house but the servants. At four in the afternoon
Mr. and Mrs. Quarrier would receive Mr. and Mrs.
Liversedge, and thus make formal declaration of their
readiness to welcome friends. Since her return to
England, Lilian had seen no one. She begged Denzil
not to invite Glazzard to Clapham.

They reached Polterham at one o'clock, in the tumult
of a snowstorm; ten minutes more, and the whitened
cab deposited them at their doorway. Quarrier knew,
of course, what the general appearance of the interior

would be, and he was well satisfied with the way in which his directions had been carried out. His companion was at first overawed rather than pleased. He led her from room to room, saying frequently, " Do you like it?   Will it do?"

" It frightens me ! " murmured Lilian, at length. " How shall I manage such a house ? "

She was pale, and inclined to tearfulness, for the situation tired her fortitude in a degree Denzil could not estimate.   Fears which were all but terrors, self-reproach which had the poignancy of remorse, tormented her gentle, timid nature.   For a week and more she had not known unbroken sleep; dreams of fantastic misery awakened her to worse distress in the calculating of her perils and conflict with insidious doubts.   At the dead hour before dawn, faiths of child-hood revived before her conscience, upbraiding, menacing.   The common rules of every-day honour spoke to her with stern reproval.   Denzil's arguments, when she tried to muster them in her defence, answered with hollow, meaningless sound.   Love alone would stead her; she could but shut her eyes, and breathe, as if in prayer, the declaration that her love was a sacred thing, cancelling verbal untruth.

She changed her dress, and went down to luncheon. The large dining-room seemed to oppress her insignifi-cance; to eat was impossible, and with difficulty she conversed before the servants.   Fortunately, Denzil was in his best spirits; he enjoyed the wintery atmosphere, talked of skating on the ice which had known him as a boy, laughed over an old story about a snowball with a stone in it which had stunned him in one of the fights between town and Grammar School.

"Pity the election can't come on just now!—we should have lively times. A snowball is preferable to an addled egg any day. The Poltram folks "—this was the common pronunciation of the town's name—" have a liking for missiles at seasons of excitement."

From table, they went to the library—as yet unfurnished with volumes—and made themselves comfortable by the fireside. Through the windows nothing could be seen but a tempestuous whirl of flakes. Lilian's cat, which had accompanied her in a basket, could not as yet make itself at home on the hearthrug, and was glad of a welcome to its mistress's lap. Denzil lit a pipe and studied the political news of the day.

At four o'clock he waited impatiently the call of his relatives. Lilian, unable to command her agitation, had gone into another room, and was there counting the minutes as if each cost her a drop of heart's blood. If this first meeting were but over! All else seemed easy, could she but face Denzil's sister without betrayal of her shame and dread. At length she heard wheels roll up to the door; there were voices in the hall; Denzil came forth with loud and joyous greeting; he led his visitors into the library. Five minutes more of anguish, and the voices were again audible, approaching, at the door.

"Well, Lily, here is my sister and Mr. Liversedge," said Denzil. "No very formidable persons, either of them," he added merrily, as the best way of making apology for Lilian's too obvious tremor.

But she conquered her weakness. The man was of no account to her; upon the woman only her eyes were fixed, for *there* was the piercing scrutiny, the quick divination, the merciless censure—there, if anywhere, in one of her own sex. From men she might expect tolerance, justice; from women only a swift choice between the bowl and the dagger. Pride prompted her to hardihood, and when she had well looked upon Mrs. Liversedge's face a soothing confidence came to the support of desperation. She saw the frank fairness of Denzil's lineaments softened with the kindest of female smiles; a gaze keen indeed, but ingenuous as that of a child; an expression impossible to be interpreted save as that of heartfelt welcome, absolutely unsuspecting, touched even with admiring homage.

They kissed each other, and Lilian's face glowed. After that, she could turn almost joyously for Mr. Liversedge's hearty hand-shake.

"You have come like a sort of snow-queen," said Tobias, with unusual imaginativeness, pointing to the windows. "It must have begun just as you got here."

Perhaps the chill of her fingers prompted him to this poetical flight. His wife, who had noticed the same thing, added, with practical fervour:

"I only hope the house is thoroughly dry. We have had great fires everywhere for more than a fortnight. As for the snow and frost, you are pretty well used to that, no doubt."

Painfully on the alert, Lilian of course understood this allusion to the Northern land she was supposed to have quitted recently.

"Even at Stockholm," she replied, with a smile, "there is summer, you know."

"And in Russia, too, I have heard," laughed Mr. Liversedge. "But one doesn't put much faith in such reports. Denzil tries to persuade us now and then that the North Cape has quite a balmy atmosphere, especially from December to March. He is quite safe. We sha'n't go to test his statements."

Instead of a time of misery, this first half-hour proved so pleasant that Lilian all but forgot the shadow standing behind her. When tea was brought in, she felt none of the nervousness which had seemed to her inevitable amid such luxurious appliances. These relatives of Denzil's, henceforth her own, were people such as she had not dared to picture them—so unaffected, genial, easy to talk with; nor did she suffer from a necessity of uttering direct falsehoods; conversation dealt with the present and the future—partly, no doubt, owing to Quarrier's initiative. Mr. Liversedge made a report of local affairs as they concerned the political outlook; he saw every reason for hope.

"Welwyn-Baker," he said, "is quite set up again, and I am told he has no inclination to retire in favour of his son, or any one else. An obstinate old fellow— and may his obstinacy increase! The Tories are beginning to see that they ought to set up a new man; they are quarrelling among themselves. That bazaar at

the opening of the new Society's rooms—the Constitutional Literary, you know—seems to have been a failure.
No one was satisfied. The *Mercury* printed savage
letters from a lot of people—blaming this, that, and the
other person in authority. The *Examiner* chuckled,
and hasn't done referring to the matter yet."

Apart with Lilian, Mrs. Liversedge had begun to talk
of the society of Polterham. She did not try to be
witty at the expense of her neighbours, but confessed
with a sly smile that literature and the arts were not
quite so well appreciated as might be wished.

" You are a serious student, I know—very learned in
languages. I wish I had had more time for reading,
and a better head. But seven children, you know—oh
dear! Even my little bit of French has got so ragged
that I am really ashamed of it. But there *is* one woman
who studies. Has Denzil spoken to you of Mrs.
Wade ? "

" I don't remember."

" She is no great favourite of his, I believe. You
will soon hear of her, and no doubt see her. Denzil
admits that she is very clever—even a Greek scholar ! "

" Really ! And what fault does he find with
her ? "

" She is a great supporter of woman's rights, and
occasionally makes speeches. It's only of late that I
have seen much of her ; for some reason she seems to
have taken a liking to me, and I feel rather honoured.
I'm sure her intentions are very good indeed, and it
must be trying to live among people who have no

sympathy with you. They make sad fun of her, and altogether misunderstand her—at least I think so."

The snowstorm still raged. To spare their own horses, the Liversedges had come in a cab, and at half-past five the same vehicle returned to take them home. Lilian was sorry to see them go.

"Where are all your apprehensions now?" cried Denzil, coming back to her from the hall. "It's over, you see. Not another minute's uneasiness need you have!"

"They were kindness itself. I like them *very* much."

"As I knew and said you would. Now, no more chalky faces and frightened looks! Be jolly, and forget everything. Let us try your piano."

"Your sister was telling me about Mrs. Wade. Is she one of the people you would like me to be friends with?"

"Oh yes!" he answered, laughing, "Mrs. Wade will interest you, no doubt. Make a friend of her by all means. Did Mary whisper mysterious warnings?"

"Anything but that; she spoke very favourably."

"Indeed!"

"And she said Mrs. Wade seemed to have taken a liking to her lately."

"Oh! How's that, I wonder? She goes about seeking whom she may secure for the women's-vote movement; I suppose it's Molly's turn to be attacked. Oh, we shall have many a lively half-hour when Mrs. Wade calls!"

" What is her husband ? "

" Husband! She's a widow. I never thought of such a person as Mr. Wade, to this moment. To be sure, he must have existed. Perhaps she will confide in you, and then—— By-the-bye, is it right for women to tell their husbands what they learn from female friends ? "

He asked it jokingly, but Lilian seemed to reflect in earnest.

" I'm not sure "——

" Oh, you lily of the valley ! " he cried, interrupting her. " Do cultivate a sense of humour. Don't take things with such desperate seriousness ! Come and try your instrument. It ought to be a good one, if price-lists mean anything."

The next morning was clear and cold. Assuredly there would be good skating, and the prospect of this enjoyment seemed to engross Denzil's thoughts. After breakfast he barely glanced at the newspapers, then, leaving Lilian to enter upon her domestic rule, set forth for an examination of the localities which offered scope to Polterham skaters. Such youthful zeal proved his thorough harmony with the English spirit; it promised far more for his success as a politician than if he had spent the morning over blue-books and statistical treatises.

If only the snow were cleared away, the best skating near at hand was on a piece of water near the road to Rickstead. The origin of this pond or lakelet had caused discussion among local antiquaries ; for tradition said that it occupied the site of a meadow which many years ago mysteriously sank, owing perhaps to the un-suspected existence of an ancient mine. It connected with a little tributary of the River Bale, and was believed to be very deep, especially at one point, where the tree-shadowed bank overhung the water at a height of some ten feet. The way thither was by a field-path, starting from the high road within sight of Pear-tree Cottage. At a rapid walk Quarrier soon reached his goal, and saw with satisfaction that men and boys were sweeping the snowy surface, whilst a few people had already begun to disport themselves where the black ice came to view. In the afternoon he would come with Lilian; for the present, a second purpose occupied his thoughts. Standing on the bank of Bale Water (thus was it named), he could see the topmost branches of that pear-tree which grew in the garden behind Mrs. Wade's cottage; two meadows lay between—a stretch of about a quarter of a mile. It was scarcely the hour for calling upon ladies, but he knew that Mrs. Wade sat among her books through the morning, and he wished especially to see her as soon as possible.

Polterham clocks were counting eleven as he presented himself at the door of the cottage. Once already he had paid a call here, not many days after his meeting with the widow in Mr. Hornibrook's library; he came at three in the afternoon, and sat talking till nearly six. Not a few Polterham matrons would have considered that proceeding highly improper, but such a thought never occurred to Denzil; and Mrs. Wade would have spoken her mind very distinctly to any one who wished to circumscribe female freedom in such respects. They had conversed on a great variety of subjects with unflagging animation. Since then he had not seen his acquaintance.

A young girl opened to him, and left him standing in the porch for a minute or two. She returned, and asked him to walk into the sitting-room, where Mrs. Wade was studying with her feet on the fender.

" Do I come unseasonably ? " he asked, offering his hand.

" Not if you have anything interesting to say," was the curious reply.

The widow was not accoutred for reception of visitors. She wore an old though quite presentable dress, with a light shawl about her shoulders, and had evidently postponed the arrangement of her hair until the time of going abroad. Yet her appearance could hardly be called disconcerting, for it had nothing of slovenliness. She looked a student, that was all. For some reason, however, she gave Quarrier a less cordial welcome than he had anticipated. Her eyes avoided his, she shook hands in a perfunctory way.

" It depends what you call interesting," was his rejoinder to the unconventional reply. " I got here yesterday, and brought a wife with me—there, at all events, is a statement of fact."

" You have done me the honour to hasten here with the announcement ? "

" I came out to see if Bale Water was skateable, and

I thought I might venture to make a friendly call whilst I was so near. But I'm afraid I disturb you?"

"Not a bit! Pray sit down and talk. Of course I have heard of your marriage. Why didn't you let me know it was impending?"

"Because I told nobody. I chose to get married in my own way. You, Mrs. Wade, are not likely to find fault with me for that."

"Oh dear no!" she answered, with friendly indifference.

"I am told you see a good deal of the Liversedges?"
She nodded.

"Does my sister give any promise of reaching higher levels? Or is she a hopeless groveller?"

"Mrs. Liversedge is the kind of woman I can respect, independently of her views."

"I like to hear you say that, because I know you don't deal in complimentary phrases. The respect, I am sure, is reciprocated."

Mrs. Wade seemed to give slight attention; she was looking at a picture above the fireplace.

"You will count my wife among your friends, I hope?" he continued.

"I hope so. Do you think we shall understand each other?"

"If not, it won't be for lack of good will on her side. I mustn't begin to praise her, but I think you will find she has a very fair portion of brains."

"I'm glad to hear that."

"Do you imply that you had fears?"

"Men are occasionally odd in their choice of wives."

"Yes," Denzil replied, with a laugh; "I have seen remarkable illustrations of it."

"I didn't feel sure that you regarded brains as an essential."

"Indeed! Then you were a long way from understanding me. How can you say that, after my lecture, and our talks?"

"Oh, theory doesn't go for much. May I call shortly?"

"If you will be so good."

"She's very young, I think?"

"Not much more than one-and-twenty. I have known her for about three years."

There was a short silence, then Mrs. Wade said with some abruptness:

"I think of leaving Polterham before long. It was Mr. and Mrs. Hornibrook who decided me to come here, and now that they are gone I feel as if I too had better stir. I want books that are out of my reach."

"That will be a loss to us, Mrs. Wade. Society in Polterham has its limitations "——

"I'm aware of it. But you, of course, will have a home in London as well?"

"Well, yes—if I get sent to Parliament."

"I suppose we shall meet there some day."

Her voice grew careless and dreamy. She folded her hands upon her lap, and assumed a look which seemed to Denzil a hint that he might now depart. He stood up.

"So you are going to skate?" murmured Mrs. Wade. "I won't keep you. Thank you very much for looking in."

Denzil tried once more to read her countenance, and went away with a puzzled feeling. He could not conjecture the meaning of her changed tone.

XIII.

LAST November had turned the scale in the Polterham Town Council. It happened that the retiring members were all Conservatives, with the exception of Mr. Chown, who alone of them obtained re-election, the others giving place to men of the Progressive party. Mr. Mumbray bade farewell to his greatness. The new Mayor was a Liberal. As returning-officer, he would preside over the coming political contest. The Tories gloomed at each other, and whispered of evil omens.

For many years Mr. Mumbray had looked to the Mayoralty as the limit of his ambition. He now began to entertain larger projects, encouraged thereto by the dissensions of Conservative Polterham, and the promptings of men who were hoping to follow him up the civic ladder. He joined with those who murmured against the obstinacy of old Mr. Welwyn-Baker. To support such a candidate would be party suicide. Even Welwyn-Baker junior was preferable; but why not recognize that the old name had lost its prestige, and select a representative of enlightened Conservatism, who could really make a stand against Quarrier and his rampant Radicals? Mr. Mumbray saw no reason why he himself should not invite the confidence of the burgesses.

In a moment of domestic truce the ex-Mayor com-

municated this thought to his wife, and Mrs. Mumbray
gave ready ear. Like the ladies of Polterham in
general, she had not the faintest understanding of
political principles; to her, the distinction between
parties was the difference between bits of blue and
yellow ribbon, nothing more. But the social advantages
accruing to the wife of an M.P. impressed her very
strongly indeed. For such an end she was willing to
make sacrifices, and the first of these declared itself in
an abandonment of her opposition to Mr. Eustace
Glazzard. Her husband pointed out to her that a
connection with the family so long established at Highmead would be of distinct value. William Glazzard
nominally stood on the Liberal side, but he was very luke-
warm, and allowed to be seen that his political action
was much swayed by personal considerations. Eustace
made no pretence of Liberal leaning; though a friend
of the Radical candidate (so Quarrier was already
designated by his opponents), he joked at popular
enthusiasm, and could only be described as an independent aristocrat. Money, it appeared, he had none; and
his brother, it was suspected, kept up only a show of
the ancestral position. Nevertheless, their names had
weight in the borough.

Eustace spent Christmas at Highmead, and made
frequent calls at the house of the ex-Mayor. On one
of the occasions it happened that the ladies were from
home, but Mr. Mumbray, on the point of going out,
begged Glazzard to come and have a word with him in
his sanctum. After much roundabout talk, character-

istically pompous, he put the question whether Mr. Glazzard, as a friend of Mr. Denzil Quarrier, would "take it ill" if he, Mr. Mumbray, accepted an invitation to come forward as the candidate of the Conservative party.

"I hope you know me better," Glazzard replied. "I have nothing whatever to do with politics."

The ex-Mayor smiled thoughtfully, and went on to explain, "in strictest confidence," that there *was* a prospect of that contingency befalling.

"Of course I couldn't hope for Mr. William's support."

He paused on a note of magnanimous renunciation.

"Oh, I don't know," said Glazzard, abstractedly. "My brother is hardly to be called a Radical. I couldn't answer for the line he will take."

"Indeed? That is very interesting. Ha!"

Silence fell between them.

"I'm sure," remarked Mr. Mumbray, at length, "that my wife and daughter will be very sorry to have missed your call. Undoubtedly you can count on their being at home to-morrow."

The prediction was fulfilled, and before leaving the house Glazzard made Serena a proposal of marriage. That morning there had occurred a quarrel of more than usual bitterness between mother and daughter. Serena was sick of her life at home, and felt a longing, at any cost, for escape to a sphere of independence. The expected offer from Glazzard came just at the right moment; she accepted it, and consented that the marriage should be very soon.

But a few hours of reflection filled her with grave misgivings. She was not in love with Glazzard; personally, he had never charmed her, and in the progress of their acquaintance she had discovered many points of his character which excited her alarm. Serena, after all, was but a half-educated country girl; even in the whirlwind of rebellious moments she felt afraid of the words that came to her lips. The impulses towards emancipation which so grievously perturbed her were unjustified by her conscience; at heart, she believed with Ivy Glazzard that woman was a praying and subordinate creature; in her bedroom she recounted the day's sins of thought and speech, and wept out her desire for " conversion," for the life of humble faith. Accepting such a husband as Eustace, she had committed not only an error, but a sin. The man was without religion, and sometimes made himself guilty of hypocrisy; of this she felt a miserable assurance. How could she hope to be happy with him? What had interested her in him was that air of culture and refinement so conspicuously lacked by the men who had hitherto approached her. He had seemed to her the first *gentleman* who sought her favour. To countenance him, moreover, was to defy her mother's petty rule. But, no, she did not love him—did not like him.

Yet to retract her promise she was ashamed. Only girls of low social position played fast and loose in that way. She went through a night of misery.

On the morrow her betrothed, of course, came to see her. Woman-like, she had taken refuge in a resolve of postponement; the marriage must be sooner or later, but it was in her power to put it off. And, with show of regretful prudence, she made known this change in her mind.

"I hardly knew what I was saying. I ought to have remembered that our acquaintance has been very short."

"Yet long enough to enable me to win your promise," urged Glazzard.

"Yes, I have promised. It's only that we cannot be married so very soon."

"I must, of course, yield," he replied, gracefully, kissing her hand. "Decision as to the time shall rest entirely with you."

"Thank you—that is very kind."

He went away in a mood of extreme discontent. Was this little simpleton going to play with him? There were solid reasons of more than one kind why the marriage should not be long delayed. It would be best if he returned to London and communicated with her by letter. He could write eloquently, and to let her think of him as in the midst of gay society might not be amiss.

Shortly after Quarrier's arrival at Polterham, he was back again. Daily he had repented his engagement, yet as often had congratulated himself on the windfall thus assured to him. Before going to the Mumbrays, he called upon Mrs. Quarrier, whom, as it chanced, he found alone. To Lilian his appearance was a shock, for in the contentment of the past week she had practically forgotten the existence of this man who shared her secret. She could not look him in the face.

Glazzard could be trusted in points of tact. He entered with a bright face, and the greetings of an old friend, then at once began to speak of his own affairs.

" Have you heard that I am going to be married ? "

" Denzil told me when he received your letter."

" I am afraid Miss Mumbray will hardly belong to your circle, but as Mrs. Glazzard—that will be a different thing. You won't forbid me to come here because of this alliance ? "

Lilian showed surprise and perplexity.

" I mean, because I am engaged to the daughter of a Tory."

" Oh, what difference could that possibly make ? "

" None, I hope. You know that I am not very zealous as a party-man."

In this his second conversation with Lilian, Glazzard analysed more completely the charm which she had before exercised upon him. He was thoroughly aware of the trials her nature was enduring, and his power of sympathetic insight enabled him to read upon her countenance, in her tones, precisely what Lilian imagined she could conceal. Amid surroundings such as those of the newly furnished house, she seemed to him a priceless gem in a gaudy setting ; he felt (and with justice) that the little drawing-room at Clapham, which spoke in so many details of her own taste, was a much more suitable home for her. What could be said of the man who had thus transferred her, all (or chiefly) for the sake of getting elected to Parliament? Quarrier had no true appreciation of the woman with whose life and happiness he was entrusted. He was devoted to her, no doubt, but with a devotion not much more clairvoyant than would have distinguished one of his favourite Vikings.

Glazzard, whilst liking Denzil, had never held him in much esteem. Of late, his feelings had become strongly tinged with contempt. And now, with the contempt there blended a strain of jealousy.

True that he himself had caught eagerly at the hope of entering Parliament; but it was the impulse of a man who knew his life to be falling into ruin, who welcomed any suggestion that would save him from final and fatal apathy—of a man whose existence had always been loveless—who, with passionate ideals, had never known anything but a venal embrace. In Quarrier's position, with abounding resources, with the love of such a woman as this, what would he not have made of life? Would it ever have occurred to *him* to wear a mask of vulgar deceit, to condemn his exquisite companion to a hateful martyrdom, that he might attain the dizzy height of M. P.-ship for Polterham?

He compassionated Lilian, and at the same time he was angry with her. He looked upon her beauty, her gentle spirit, with tenderness, and therewithal he half hoped that she might some day repent of yielding to Quarrier's vulgar ambition.

" Have you made many acquaintances ? " he asked.

" A good many. Some, very pleasant people ; others —not so interesting."

" Polterham society will not absorb you, I think."

"I hope to have a good deal of quiet time. But Denzil wishes me to study more from life than from books, just now. I must understand all the subjects that interest him."

" Yes—the exact position, as a force in politics, of the licensed victuallers ; the demands of the newly enfranchised classes—that kind of thing."

He seemed to be jesting, and she laughed goodhumouredly.

"Those things are very important, Mr. Glazzard."

" Infinitely ! "

He did not stay long, and upon his departure Lilian gave a sigh of relief.

The next day he was to lunch with the Mumbrays. He went about twelve o'clock, to spend an hour with Serena. His welcome was not ardent, and he felt the oppression of a languor he hardly tried to disguise. Yet in truth his cause had benefited whilst he was away. The eloquent letters did not fail of their effect ; Serena had again sighed under domestic tyranny, had thought with longing of a life in London, and was once more swayed by her emotions towards an early marriage.

In dearth of matter for conversation (Glazzard sitting taciturn), she spoke of an event which had occupied Polterham for the last day or two. Some local genius had conceived the idea of wrecking an express train, and to that end had broken a portion of the line.

"What frightful wickedness!" she exclaimed. "What motive can there have been, do you think?"

"Probably none, in the sense you mean."

"Yes—such a man must be mad."

"I don't think that," said Glazzard, meditatively. "I can understand his doing it with no reason at all but the wish to see what would happen. No doubt he would have been standing somewhere in sight."

"You can *understand* that?"

"Very well indeed," he answered, in the same half-absent way. "Power of all kinds is a temptation to men. A certain kind of man—not necessarily cruel—would be fascinated with the thought of bringing about such a terrific end by such slight means."

"Not necessarily cruel? Oh, I can't follow you at all. You are not serious."

"I have shocked you." He saw that he had really done so, and felt that it was imprudent. His tact suggested a use for the situation. "Serena, why should you speak so conventionally? You are not really conventional in mind. You have thoughts and emotions infinitely above those of average girls. Do recognize your own superiority. I spoke in a speculative way. One may speculate about anything and everything—if one has the brains. You certainly are not made to go through life with veiled eyes and a tongue tuned to the common phrases. Do yourself justice, dear girl.

However other people regard you, *I* from the first have seen what it was in you to become."

It was adroit flattery; Serena reddened, averted her face, smiled a little, and kept silence.

That day he did not follow up his advantage. But on taking leave of Serena early in the afternoon, he looked into her eyes with expressive steadiness, and again she blushed.

A little later, several ladies were gathered in the drawing-room. On Thursdays Mrs. Mumbray received her friends; sat as an embodiment of the domestic virtues and graces. To-day the talk was principally on that recent addition to Polterham society, Mrs. Denzil Quarrier.

"I haven't seen her yet," said Mrs. Mumbray, with her air of superiority. "They say she is pretty but rather childish."

"But what is this mystery about the marriage?" inquired a lady who had just entered, and who threw herself upon the subject with eagerness. (It was Mrs. Roach, the wife of an alderman.) "Why was it abroad? She is English, I think?"

"Oh no!" put in Mrs. Tenterden, a large and very positive person. "She is a Dane—like the Princess of Wales. I have seen her. I recognized the cast of features at once."

An outcry from three ladies followed. They knew Mrs. Quarrier was English. They had seen her skating at Bale Water. One of them had heard her speak—it was pure English.

"I thought every one knew," returned Mrs. Tenterden, with stately deliberation, "that the Danes have a special gift for languages. The Princess of Wales"——

"But, indeed," urged the hostess, "she is of English birth. We know it from Mr. Eustace Glazzard, who is one of their friends."

"Then *why* were they married abroad?" came in Mrs. Roach's shrill voice. "*Can* English people be legitimately married abroad? I always understood that the ceremony had to be repeated in England."

"It was at Paris," said Mrs. Walker, the depressed widow of a bankrupt corn-merchant. "There is an English church there, I have heard."

The others, inclined to be contemptuous of this authority, regarded each other with doubt.

"Still," broke out Mrs. Roach again, "*why* was it at Paris? No one seems to have the slightest idea. It is really very strange!"

Mrs. Mumbray vouchsafed further information.

"I understood that she came from Stockholm."

"Didn't I *say* she came from Denmark?" interrupted Mrs. Tenterden, triumphantly.

There was a pause of uncertainty broken by Serena Mumbray's quiet voice.

"Dear Mrs. Tenterden, Stockholm is not in Denmark, but in Sweden. And we are told that Mrs. Quarrier was an English governess there."

"Ah! a governess!" cried two or three voices.

"To tell the truth," said Mrs. Mumbray, more

dignified than ever after her vindication, "it is probable that she belongs to some very poor family. I should be sorry to think any worse of her for *that*, but it would explain the private marriage."

"So you think people *can* be married legally in Paris?" persisted the alderman's wife, whose banns had been proclaimed in hearing of orthodox Polterham about a year ago.

" Of course they can," fell from Serena.

Lilian's age, personal appearance, dress, behaviour, underwent discussion at great length.

" What church do they go to ? " inquired some one, and the question excited general interest.

"They were at St. Luke's last Sunday," Mrs. Walker was able to declare, though her wonted timidity again threw some suspicion on the statement.

"St. Luke's ! Why St. Luke's ? " cried other voices. " It isn't their parish, is it ? "

" I think," suggested the widow, " it may be because the Liversedges go to St. Luke's. Mrs. Liversedge is "——

Her needless information was cut short by a remark from Mrs. Tenterden.

" I could never listen Sunday after Sunday to Mr. Garraway. I think him excessively tedious. And his voice is so very trying."

The incumbent of St. Luke's offered a brief diversion from the main theme. A mention of the Rev. Scatchard Vialls threatened to lead them too far, and Mrs. Roach interposed with firmness.

"I still think it a very singular thing that they went abroad to be married."

"But they *didn't* go abroad, my dear," objected the hostess. "That is to say, one of them was already abroad."

"Indeed! The whole thing seems very complicated. I think it needs explanation. I shouldn't feel justified in calling upon Mrs. Quarrier until"——

Her voice was overpowered by that of Mrs. Tenterden, who demanded loudly:

"Is it true that she has already become very intimate with *that person* Mrs. Wade?"

"Oh, I *do* hope not!" exclaimed several ladies.

Here was an inexhaustible topic. It occupied more than an hour, until the last tea-cup had been laid aside and the more discreet callers were already on their way home.

XIV.

THERE needed only two or three days of life at Polterham to allay the uneasiness with which, for all his
show of equanimity, Denzil entered upon so perilous a
career.   By the end of January he had practically
forgotten that his position was in any respect insecure.
The risk of betraying himself in an unguarded moment
was diminished by the mental habit established during
eighteen months of secrecy in London.   Lilian's name
was seldom upon his lips, and any inquiry concerning her at once awakened his caution.   Between
themselves they never spoke of the past.

Long ago he had silenced every conscientious scruple
regarding the relation between Lilian and himself; and
as for the man Northway, if ever he thought of him at
all, it was with impatient contempt.   That he was deceiving his Polterham acquaintances, and in a way which
they would deem an unpardonable outrage, no longer
caused him the least compunction.   Conventional wrong-
doing, he had satisfied himself, was not wrong-doing at
all, unless discovered.   He injured no one.   The society
of such a person as Lilian could be nothing but an
advantage to man, woman, and child.   Only the sub-
limation of imbecile prejudice would maintain that she
was an unfit companion for the purest creature living.
He had even ceased to smile at the success of his strata-

gem.   It was over and done with ; their social standing
was unassailable.

Anxious to complete his book on the Vikings, he
worked at it for several hours each morning; it would
be off his hands some time in February, and the spring
publishing season should send it forth to the world.
The rest of his leisure was given to politics.   Chests of
volumes were arriving from London, and his library
shelves began to make a respectable appearance ; as a
matter of principle, he bought largely from the local
bookseller, who rejoiced at the sudden fillip to his stag-
nant trade, and went about declaring that Mr. Denzil
Quarrier was evidently *the* man for the borough.

He fell upon history, economics, social speculation,
with characteristic vigour.   If he got into the House of
Commons, those worthies should speedily be aware of
his existence among them.   It was one of his favourite
boasts that whatever subject he choose to tackle, he
could master.   No smattering for him ; a solid foundation of knowledge, such as would ensure authority to
his lightest utterances.

In the meantime, he began to perceive that Lilian
was not likely to form many acquaintances in the town.
With the Liversedges she stood on excellent terms, and
one or two families closely connected with them gave
her a welcome from which she did not shrink.   But she
had no gift of social versatility ; it cost her painful efforts
to converse about bazaars and curates and fashions and
babies with the average Polterham matron ; she felt
that most of the women who came to see her went

away with distasteful impressions, and that they were anything but cordial when she returned their call. A life of solitude and study was the worst possible preparation for duties such as were now laid upon her.

" You are dissatisfied with me," she said to Denzil, as they returned from spending the evening with some empty but influential people who had made her exceedingly uncomfortable.

" Dissatisfied ? On the contrary, I am very proud of you. It does one good to contrast one's wife with women such as those."

" I tried to talk ; but I'm so ignorant of everything they care about. I shall do better when I know more of the people they refer to."

" Chattering apes ! Malicious idiots ! Heaven forbid that you should ever take a sincere part in their gabble ! That lot are about the worst we shall have to deal with. Decent simpletons you can get along with very well."

" How ought I to speak of Mrs. Wade ? When people tell downright falsehoods about her, may I contradict ? "

" It's a confoundedly difficult matter, that. I half wish Mrs. Wade would hasten her departure. Did she say anything about it when you saw her the other day ? "

" Nothing whatever."

It appeared that the widow wished to make a friend of Lilian. She had called several times, and on each occasion behaved so charmingly that Lilian was very ready to meet her advances. Though on intellectual and personal grounds he could feel no objection to such an intimacy, Denzil began to fear that it might affect his popularity with some voters who would take the Liberal side if it did not commit them to social heresies. This class is a very large one throughout England. Mrs. Wade had never given occasion of grave scandal; she was even seen, with moderate regularity, at one or other of the churches; but many of the anti-Tory bourgeois suspected her of sympathy with views so very "advanced" as to be socially dangerous. Already it had become known that she was on good terms with Quarrier and his wife. It was rumoured that Quarrier would reconsider the position he had publicly assumed, and stand forth as an advocate of Female Suffrage. For such extremes Polterham was not prepared.

"Mrs. Wade asks me to go and have tea with her to-morrow," Lilian announced one morning, showing a note. "Shall I, or not?"

"You would like to?"

"Not if you think it unwise."

"Hang it!—we can't be slaves. Go by all means, and refresh your mind."

At three o'clock on the day of invitation Lilian alighted from her brougham at Pear-tree Cottage. It was close upon the end of February; the declining sun shot a pleasant glow across the landscape, and in the air reigned a perfect stillness. Mrs. Wade threw open the door herself with laughing welcome.

"Let us have half-an-hour's walk, shall we? It's so dry and warm."

"I should enjoy it," Lilian answered, readily.

"Then allow me two minutes for bonnet and cloak."

She was scarcely longer. They went by the hedge-side path which led towards Bale Water. To-day the papers were full of exciting news. Sir Stafford North-cote had brought forward his resolution for making short work of obstructive Members, and Radicalism stood undecided. Mrs. Wade talked of these things in the liveliest strain, Lilian responding with a light-hearted freedom seldom possible to her.

"You skated here, didn't you?" said her companion, as they drew near to the large pond.

"Yes; a day or two after we came. How different it looks now."

They stood on the bank where it rose to a consider-able height above the water.

"The rails have spoilt this spot," said Mrs. Wade. "They were only put up last autumn, after an accident. I wonder it was never found necessary before. Some children were gathering blackberries from the bramble there, and one of them reached too far forward, and over she went! I witnessed it from the other side, where I happened to be walking. A great splash, and then a chorus of shrieks from the companions. I began to run forward, though of course I could have done nothing whatever; when all at once I saw a splendid sight. A man who was standing not far off ran to the edge and plunged in—a magnificent 'header!' He had only thrown away his hat and coat. They say it's very deep just here. He disappeared completely, and then in a few seconds I saw that he had hold of the child. He brought her out where the bank slopes yonder—no harm done. I can't tell you how I enjoyed that scene! It made me cry with delight."

As usual, when deeply moved, Lilian stood in a reverie, her eyes wide, her lips tremulous. Then she stepped forward, and, with her hand resting upon the wooden rail, looked down. There was no perceptible movement in the water; it showed a dark greenish surface, smooth to the edge, without a trace of weed.

"How I envy that man his courage!"

"His power, rather," suggested Mrs. Wade. "If we could swim well, and had no foolish petticoats, we should jump in just as readily. It was the power over circumstances that I admired and envied."

Lilian smiled thoughtfully.

"I suppose that is what most attracts us in men?"

"And makes us feel our own dependence. I can't say I like *that* feeling—do you?"

She seemed to wait for an answer.

"I'm afraid it's in the order of nature," replied Lilian at length with a laugh.

"Very likely. But I am not content with it on that account. I know of a thousand things quite in the order of nature which revolt me. I very often think of nature as an evil force, at war with the good principle of which we are conscious in our souls."

"But," Lilian faltered, "is your ideal an absolute independence?"

Mrs. Wade looked far across the water, and answered, "Yes, absolute!"

"Then you—I don't quite know what would result from that."

"Nor I," returned the other, laughing. "That doesn't affect my ideal. You have heard, of course, of that lecture your husband gave at the Institute before—before your marriage?"

"Yes; I wish I could have heard it."

"You would have sympathized with every word, I am sure. Mr. Quarrier is one of the strong men who find satisfaction in women's weakness."

It was said with perfect good-humour, with a certain indulgent kindness—a tone Mrs. Wade had used from the first in talking with Lilian. A manner of affectionate playfulness, occasionally of caressing protection, distinguished her in this intercourse; quite unlike that by which she was known to people in general. Lilian did not dislike it, rather was drawn by it into a mood of grateful confidence.

"I don't think 'weakness' expresses it," she objected. "He likes women to be subordinate, no doubt of that. His idea is that"——

"I know, I know!" Mrs. Wade turned away with a smile her companion did not observe. "Let us walk back again; it grows chilly. A beautiful sunset, if clouds don't gather. Perhaps it surprises you that I care for such sentimental things?"

"I think I understand you better."

"Frankly—do you think me what the French call *hommasse?* Just a little?"

"Nothing of the kind, Mrs. Wade," Lilian replied, with courage. "You are a very womanly woman."

The bright, hard eyes darted a quick glance at her.

"Really? That is how I strike you?"

"It is, indeed."

"How I like your way of speaking," said the other, after a moment's pause. "I mean, your voice—accent. Has it anything to do with the long time you have spent abroad, I wonder?"

Lilian smiled and was embarrassed.

"You are certainly not a Londoner?"

"Oh no! I was born in the west of England."

"And I at Newcastle. As a child I had a strong northern accent; you don't notice anything of it now? Oh, I have been about so much. My husband was in the Army. That is the first time I have mentioned him to you, and it will be the last, however long we know each other."

Lilian kept her eyes on the ground. The widow glanced off to a totally different subject, which occupied them the rest of the way back to the cottage.

Daylight lasted until they had finished tea, then a lamp was brought in and the red blind drawn down. Quarrier had gone to spend the day at a neighbouring town, and would not be back before late in the evening, so that Lilian had arranged to go from Mrs. Wade's to the Liversedges'. They still had a couple of hours'

talk to enjoy; on Lilian's side, at all events, it was un-
feigned enjoyment. The cosy little room put her at
ease. Its furniture was quite in keeping with the
simple appearance of the house, but books and pictures
told that no ordinary cottager dwelt here.

"I have had many an hour of happiness in this
room," said Mrs. Wade, as they seated themselves by
the fire. "The best of all between eleven at night and
two in the morning. You know the lines in 'Pen-
seroso.' Most men would declare that a woman can't
possibly appreciate them; I know better. I am by
nature a student; the life of society is nothing to me;
and, in reality, I care very little about politics."

Smiling, she watched the effect of her words.

"You are content with solitude?" said Lilian,
gazing at her with a look of deep interest.

"Quite. I have no relatives who care anything
about me, and only two or three people I call friends.
But I must have more books, and I shall be obliged to
go to London."

"Don't go just yet—won't our books be of use to
you?"

"I shall see. Have you read this?"

It was a novel from Smith's Library. Lilian knew
it, and they discussed its merits. Mrs. Wade mentioned
a book by the same author which had appeared more
than a year ago.

"Yes, I read that when it came out," said Lilian,
and began to talk of it.

Mrs. Wade kept silence, then remarked carelessly:

"You had them in the Tauchnitz series, I suppose?"

Had her eyes been turned that way, she must have observed the strange look which flashed across her companion's countenance. Lilian seemed to draw in her breath, though silently.

"Yes—Tauchnitz," she answered.

Mrs. Wade appeared quite unconscious of anything unusual in the tone. She was gazing at the fire.

"It isn't often I find time for novels," she said; "for new ones, that is. A few of the old are generally all I need. Can you read George Eliot? What a miserably conventional soul that woman has!"

"Conventional? But"——

"Oh, I know! But she is British conventionality to the core. I have heard people say that she hasn't the courage of her opinions; but that is precisely what she *has*, and every page of her work declares it flagrantly. She might have been a great power—she might have speeded the revolution of morals—if the true faith had been in her."

Lilian was still tremulous, and she listened with an intensity which gave her a look of pain. She was about to speak, but Mrs. Wade anticipated her.

"You mustn't trouble much about anything I say when it crosses your own judgment or feeling. There are so few people with whom I can indulge myself in free speech. I talk just for the pleasure of it; don't think I expect or hope that you will always go along with me. But you are not afraid of thinking—that's the great thing. Most women are such paltry creatures

that they daren't look into their own minds—for fear
nature should have put something ' improper ' there."

She broke off with laughter, and, as Lilian kept
silence, fell into thought.

In saying that she thought her companion a
" womanly woman," Lilian told the truth. Ever
quick with sympathy, she felt a sadness in Mrs.
Wade's situation, which led her to interpret all
her harsher peculiarities as the result of disappointment and loneliness. Now that the widow had
confessed her ill-fortune in marriage, Lilian was
assured of having judged rightly, and nursed her
sentiment of compassion. Mrs. Wade was still young ;
impossible that she should have accepted a fate which
forbade her the knowledge of woman's happiness. But
how difficult for such a one to escape from this narrow
and misleading way ! Her strong, highly-trained
intellect could find no satisfaction in the society of
every-day people, yet she was withheld by poverty
from seeking her natural sphere. With Lilian, to
understand a sorrow was to ask herself what she could
do for its assuagement. A thought of characteristic
generosity came to her. Why should she not (some
day or other, when their friendship was mature) offer
Mrs. Wade the money, her own property, which would
henceforth be lying idle? There would be practical
difficulties in the way, but surely they might be overcome. The idea brought a smile to her face. Yes;
she would think of this. She would presently talk of it
with Denzil.

" Come now," said Mrs. Wade, rousing herself from meditation, " let us talk about the Irish question."

Lilian addressed herself conscientiously to the subject, but it did not really interest her; she had no personal knowledge of Irish hardships, and was wearied by the endless Parliamentary debate. Her thoughts still busied themselves with the hopeful project for smoothing Mrs. Wade's path in life.

When the carriage came for her, she took her leave with regret, but full of happy imaginings. She had quite forgotten the all but self-betrayal into which she was led during that chat about novels.

Two days later Quarrier was again absent from home on business, and Lilian spent the evening with the Liversedges. Supper was over, and she had begun to think of departure, when the drawing-room door was burst open, and in rushed Denzil, wet from head to foot with rain, and his face a-stream with perspiration.

" They dissolve at Easter ! " he cried, waving his hat wildly. " Northcote announced it at five this afternoon. Hammond has a telegram; I met him at the station."

" Ho! ho! this is news!" answered Mr. Liversedge, starting up from his easy-chair.

" News, indeed! " said his wife; " but that's no reason, Denzil, why you should make my carpet all rain and mud. Do go and take your coat off, and clean your boots, there's a good boy! "

" How can I think of coat and boots ? Here, Lily, fling this garment somewhere. Give me a duster, or something, to stand on, Molly. Toby, we must have a meeting in a day or two. Can we get the Public Hall for Thursday or Friday? Shall we go round and see our committee-men to-night?"

"Time enough to-morrow; most of them are just going to bed. But how is it no one had an inkling of this? They have kept the secret uncommonly well."

"The blackguards! Ha, ha! Now for a good fight! It'll be old Welwyn-Baker, after all, you'll see. They won't have the courage to set up a new man at a moment's notice. The old buffer will come maudling once more, and we'll bowl him off his pins!"

Lilian sat with her eyes fixed upon him. His excitement infected her, and when they went home together she talked of the coming struggle with joyous animation.

XV.

The next morning—Tuesday, March 9th—there was a rush for the London papers. Every copy that reached the Polterham vendors was snapped up within a few minutes of it arrival. People who had no right of membership ran ravening to the Literary Institute and the Constitutional Literary Society, and peered over the shoulders of legitimate readers, on such a day as this unrebuked. Mr. Chown's drapery establishment presented a strange spectacle. For several hours it was thronged with sturdy Radicals eager to hear their eminent friend hold forth on the situation. At eleven o'clock Mr. Chown fairly mounted a chair behind his counter, and delivered a formal harangue—thus, as he boasted, opening the political campaign. He read aloud (for the seventh time) Lord Beaconsfield's public letter to the Duke of Marlborough, in which the country was warned, to begin with, against the perils of Home Rule. "It is to be hoped that all men of light and leading will resist this destructive doctrine. . . . . Rarely in this century has there been an occasion more critical. The power of England and the peace of Europe will largely depend on the verdict of the country. . . . . Peace rests on the presence, not to say the ascendancy, of England in the Councils of Europe."

"Here you have it," cried the orator, as he dashed

the newspaper to his feet, "pure, unadulterated Jingoism! 'Ascendancy in the Councils of Europe!' How are the European powers likely to hear *that*, do you think? I venture to tell my Lord Beaconfield—I venture to tell him on behalf of this constituency—aye, and on behalf of this country—that it is *he* who holds 'destructive doctrine'! I venture to tell my Lord Beaconsfield that England is not prepared to endorse any such insolent folly! We shall very soon have an opportunity of hearing how far such doctrine recommends itself to *our* man 'of light and leading'—to our Radical candidate—to our future member, Mr. Denzil Quarrier!"

A burst of cheering echoed from the drapery-laden shelves. Two servant-girls who had come to the door intent on purchase of hair-pins ran frightened away, and spread a report that Mr. Chown's shop was on fire.

At dinner-time the politician was faced by his angry wife.

"I know what the end of *this*'ll be!" cried Mrs. Chown. "You're ruining your business, that's what you're doing! Who do you think'll come to the shop if they find it full of shouting ragamuffins? They'll all go to Huxtable's, that's what they'll do! I've no patience"——

"There's no need to declare *that!*" replied Mr. Chown, rolling his great eyes at her with an expression of the loftiest scorn. "I have known it for thirteen years. You will be so good as to attend to your own affairs, and leave *me* to see to *mine!* What does a woman care for the interests of the country? Grovelling sex! Perhaps when I am called upon to shoulder a rifle and go forth to die on the field of battle, your dense understanding will begin to perceive what was at stake.—Not another syllable! I forbid it! Sit down and serve the potatoes!"

At the same hour Denzil Quarrier, at luncheon with Lilian, was giving utterance to his feelings on the great topic of the day.

"Now is the time for women to show whether their judgment is worthy of the least confidence. This letter of Beaconsfield's makes frank appeal to the spirit of Jingoism; he hopes to get at the fighting side of Englishmen, and go back to power on a wave of 'Rule, Britannia' bluster. If it is true that women are to be trusted in politics, their influence will be overwhelming against such irresponsible ambition. I have my serious doubts"——

He shook his head and laughed.

"I will do my utmost!" exclaimed Lilian, her face glowing with sympathetic enthusiasm. "I will go and talk to all the people we know"——

"Really! You feel equal to that?"

"I will begin this very afternoon! I think I understand the questions sufficiently. Suppose I begin with Mrs. Powell? She said her husband had always voted Conservative, but that she couldn't be quite sure what he would do this time. Perhaps I can persuade her to take our side."

" Have a try ! But you astonish me, Lily—you are transformed ! "

" Oh, I have felt that I might find courage when the time came." She put her head aside, and laughed with charming *naïveté*. " I can't sit idle at home whilst you are working with such zeal. And I really *feel* what you say : women have a clear duty. How excited Mrs. Wade must be ! "

" Have you written all the dinner-cards ? "

" They were all sent before twelve."

" Good ! Hammond will be here in half an hour to talk over the address with me. Dinner at seven prompt ; I am due at Toby's at eight. Well, it's worth going in for, after all, isn't it ? I am only just beginning to live."

" And I, too ! "

The meal was over. Denzil walked round the table and bent to lay his cheek against Lilian's.

" I admire you more than ever," he whispered, half laughing. " What a reserve of energy in this timid little girl ! Wait and see ; who knows what sort of table you will preside at some day ? I have found my vocation, and there's no saying how far it will lead me. Heavens ! what a speech I'll give them at the Public Hall ! It's bubbling over in me. I could stand up and thunder for three or four hours ! "

They gossiped a little longer, then Lilian went to prepare for her call upon Mrs. Powell, and Quarrier retired to the library. Here he was presently waited upon by Mr. Hammond, editor of the *Polterham*

Examiner. Denzil felt no need of assistance in drawing up the manifesto which would shortly be addressed to Liberal Polterham; but Hammond was a pleasant fellow of the go-ahead species, and his editorial pen would be none the less zealous for confidences such as this. The colloquy lasted an hour or so. Immediately upon the editor's departure, a servant appeared at the study door.

" Mrs. Wade wishes to see you, sir, if you are at leisure."

" Certainly ! "

The widow entered. Her costume—perhaps in anticipation of the sunny season—was more elaborate and striking than formerly. She looked a younger woman, and walked with lighter step.

" I came to see Mrs. Quarrier, but she is out. You, I'm afraid, are frightfully busy ? "

" No, no. This is the breathing time of the day with me. I've just got rid of our journalist. Sit down, pray."

" Oh, I won't stop. But tell Lilian I am eager to see her."

" She is off canvassing—really and truly ! Gone to assail Mrs. Powell. Astonishing enthusiasm ! "

" I'm delighted to hear it ! "

The exclamation lingered a little, and there was involuntary surprise on Mrs. Wade's features. She cast a glance round the room.

" Do sit down," urged Denzil, placing a chair. " What do you think of Dizzy's letter ? Did you ever

read such bunkum? And his 'men of light and leading'—ha, ha, ha!"

"He has stolen the phrase," remarked Mrs. Wade.
"Where from, I can't say; but I'm perfectly sure I
have come across it."

"Ha! I wish we could authenticate that! Search
your memory—do—and get a letter in the *Examiner* on
Saturday."

"Some one will be out with it before then. Besides,
I'm sure you don't wish for me to draw attention to
myself just now."

"Why not? I shall be disappointed if you don't
give me a great deal of help."

"I am hardly proper, you know."

She looked steadily at him, with an inscrutable
smile, then let her eyes again stray round the room.

"Bosh! As I was saying to Lily at lunch, women
ought to have a particular interest in this election. If
they are worth anything at all, they will declare that
England sha'n't go in for the chance of war just to
please that Jew phrase-monger. I'm ready enough
for a fight, on sound occasion, but I won't fight in
obedience to Dizzy and the music-halls! By jingo,
no!"

He laughed uproariously.

"You won't get many Polterham women to see it in
that light," observed the widow. "This talk about the
ascendency of England is just the thing to please them.
They adore Dizzy, because he is a fop who has succeeded brilliantly; they despise Gladstone, because he is

conscientious and an idealist. Surely I don't need to tell you this?"

She leaned forward, smiling into his face.

"Well," he exclaimed, with a laugh, "of course I can admit, if you like, that most women are *not* worth anything politically. But why should I be uncivil?"

Mrs. Wade answered in a low voice, strangely gentle.

"Don't I know their silliness and worthlessness? What woman has more reason to be ashamed of her sex?"

"Let us—hope!"

"For the millennium—yes." Her eyes gleamed, and she went on in a more accustomed tone.   "Women are the great reactionary force. In political and social matters their native baseness shows itself on a large scale. They worship the vulgar, the pretentious, the false. Here they will most of them pester their husbands to vote for Welwyn-Baker just because they hate change with the hatred of weak fear. Those of them who know anything at all about the Irish question are dead set against Ireland—simply because they are unimaginative and ungenerous; they can't sympathize with what seems a hopeless cause, and Ireland to them only suggests the dirty Irish of Polterham back streets. As for European war, the idiots are fond of drums and fifes and military swagger; they haven't brains enough to picture a battle-field."

"You are severe, Mrs. Wade. I should never have ventured"——

" You are still afraid of telling *me* the truth ! "

" Well, let us rejoice in the exceptions. Yourself, Lilian, my sister Mary, for instance."

The widow let her eyes fall and kept silence.

" We hope you will dine with us on Friday of next week," said Denzil. " Lilian posted you an invitation this morning. There will be a good many people."

" Seriously then, I am to work for you, openly and vigorously ? "

" What a contemptible fellow I should be if I wished you to hold aloof ! " He spoke sincerely, having overcome his misgivings of a short time ago. " The fight will be fought on large questions, you know. I want to win, but I have made up my mind to win honestly ; it's a fortunate thing that I probably sha'n't be called upon to declare my views on a thousand side-issues."

" Don't be so sure of that. Polterham is paltry, even amid national excitement."

" Confound it ! then I will say what I think, and risk it. If they want a man who will fight sincerely for the interests of the people, here he is ! I'm on the side of the poor devils ; I wish to see them better off ; I wish to promote honest government, and chuck the selfish lubbers overboard. Forgive the briny phrase ; you know why it comes natural to me."

Mrs. Wade gave him her kindest smile.

" You will win, no doubt of it ; and not this battle only."

She rose, and half turned away.

" By-the-bye, shall you be able to finish your book ? "

"It is finished. I wrote the last page yesterday morning. Wonderful, wasn't it?"

"A good omen. My love to Lilian."

As they shook hands, Mrs. Wade just raised her eyes for an instant, timorously. The look was quite unlike anything Denzil had yet seen on her face. It caused him to stand for a few moments musing.

From half-past four to half-past six he took a long walk; such exercise was a necessity with him, and the dwellers round about Polterham had become familiar with the sight of his robust figure striding at a great pace about roads and fields. Generally he made for some wayside inn, where he could refresh himself with a tankard of beer, after which he lit his pipe, and walked with it between his teeth. Toby Liversedge, becoming aware of this habit, was inclined to doubt its prudence. "Beware of the teetotalers, Denzil; they are a power among us." Whereto Quarrier replied that teetotalers might be eternally condemned; he would stick by his ale as tenaciously as the old farmer of Thornaby Waste.

"It's the first duty of a Radical to set his face against humbug. If I see no harm in a thing, I shall do it openly, and let people "——

At this point he checked himself, almost as if he had a sudden stitch in the side. Tobias asked for an explanation, but did not receive one.

On getting home again, he found Lilian in the drawing-room. (As an ordinary thing he did not "dress" for dinner, since his evenings were often spent in the company of people who would have disliked the conspicuousness of his appearance.) She rose to meet him with shining countenance, looking happier, indeed, and more rarely beautiful than he had ever seen her.

"What cheer? A triumph already?"

"I think so, Denzil; I really think so. Mrs. Powell has promised me to do her very best with her husband. Oh, if you could have heard our conversation! I hadn't thought it possible for any one to be so ignorant of the simplest political facts. One thing that she said—I was talking about war, and suddenly she asked me: 'Do you think it likely, Mrs. Quarrier, that there would be an *inscription*?' For a moment I couldn't see what she meant. 'An inscription?' 'Yes; if there's any danger of that, and—my four boys growing up!' Then, of course, I understood. Fortunately, she was so very much in earnest that I had no temptation to smile."

"And did you encourage her alarm?"

"I felt I had no right to do that. To avoid repeating the word, I said that I didn't think *that system* would ever find favour in England. At the same time, it was quite certain that our army would have to be greatly strengthened if this war-fever went on. Oh, we had an endless talk—and she was certainly impressed with my arguments."

"Bravo! Why, this is something like!"

"You can't think what courage it has given me! To-morrow I shall go to Mrs. Clifford—yes, I shall. She is far more formidable; but I want to try my strength."

"Ho, ho! What a pugnacious Lily—a sword-Lily! You ought to have had an heroic name—Deborah, or Joan, or Portia! Your eyes gleam like beacons."

"I feel more contented with myself.—Oh, I am told that Mrs. Wade called this afternoon?"

"Yes; anxious to see you. Burning with wrath against female Toryism. She was astonished when I told her of your expedition."

Lilian laughed merrily. Thereupon dinner was announced, and they left the room hand in hand.

That evening it was rumoured throughout the town that Mr. Welwyn-Baker had telegraphed a resolve *not* to offer himself for re-election. In a committee-room at the Constitutional Literary Society was held an informal meeting of Conservatives, but no one of them had definite intelligence to communicate. Somebody had told somebody else that Hugh Welwyn-Baker held that important telegram from his father; that was all. Mr. Mumbray's hopes rose high. On the morrow, at another meeting rather differently constituted (miserable lack of organization still evident among the Tories), it was made known on incontestable authority that the sitting Member *would* offer himself for re-election. Mr. Mumbray and his supporters held high language. "It would be party suicide," they went about repeating. With such a man as Denzil Quarrier on the Radical side, they *must* have a new and a strong candidate! But all was confusion; no one could take the responsibility of acting.

Already the affairs of the Liberals were in perfect

order, and it took but a day or two to decide even the minutiæ of the campaign. To Quarrier's candidature no one within the party offered the least opposition. Mr. Chown, who had for some time reserved his judgment, declared to all and sundry that "all things considered, a better man could scarcely have been chosen." Before thus committing himself he had twice called upon Quarrier, and been closeted with him for a long time. Now, in these days of arming, he received a card inviting him (and his wife) to dine at the candidate's house on a certain evening a fortnight ahead; it was the second dinner that Denzil had planned, but Mr. Chown was not aware of this, nor that the candidate had remarked of him to Lilian: "We must have that demagogue among his kind, of course." Denzil's agent (Hummerstone by name) instantly secured rooms in admirable situations, and the Public Hall was at the disposal of the party for their first great meeting a few days hence.

In facing that assembly (Toby Liversedge was chairman) Denzil had a very slight and very brief recurrence of his platform nervousness. Determined to risk nothing, he wrote out his speech with great care and committed it to memory. The oration occupied about two hours, with not a moment of faltering. It was true that he had discovered his vocation; he spoke like a man of long Parliamentary experience, to the astonished delight of his friends, and with enthusiastic applause from the mass of his hearers. Such eloquence had never been heard in

Polterham. If anything, he allowed himself too much
scope in vituperation, but it was a fault on the right
side. The only circumstance that troubled him was
when his eye fell upon Lilian, and he saw her crying
with excitement; a fear passed through his mind that
she might be overwrought and fall into hysterics, or
faint. The occasion proved indeed too much for her;
that night she did not close her eyes, and the next day
saw her prostrate in nervous exhaustion. But she
seemed to pick up her strength again very quickly,
and was soon hard at work canvassing among the
electors' wives.

"Don't overdo it," Denzil cautioned her. "Remember, if you are ill, I shall mope by your bedside."

" I can't stop now that I have begun," was her reply.
"If I try to sit idle, I *shall* be ill."

She could read nothing but newspapers; her piano
was silent; she talked politics, and politics only. Never
was seen such a change in woman, declared her
intimates; yet, in spite of probabilities, they thought
her more charming than ever. No word of animosity
ever fell from her lips; what inspired her was simple
ardour for Denzil's cause, and, as she considered it, that
of the oppressed multitude. In her way, said Toby
Liversedge, she was as eloquent as Quarrier himself,
and sundry other people were of the same opinion.

XVI.

WITH sullen acquiescence the supporters of Mr. Mumbray and "Progressive Conservatism"—what phrase is not good enough for the lips of party?— recognized that they must needs vote for the old name. Dissension at such a moment was more dangerous than an imbecile candidate. Mr. Sam Quarrier had declared that rather than give his voice for Mumbray he would remain neutral. "Old W.-B. is good enough for a figure-head; he signifies something. If we are to be beaten, let it be on the old ground." That defeat was likely enough, the more intelligent Conservatives could not help seeing. Many of them (Samuel among the number) had no enthusiasm for Beaconsfield, and *la haute politique* as the leader understood it, but they liked still less the principles represented by Councillor Chown and his vociferous regiment. So the familiar bills were once more posted about the streets, and once more the Tory canvassers urged men to vote for Welwyn-Baker in the name of Church and State.

At Salutary Mount (this was the name of the ex-Mayor's residence) personal disappointment left no leisure for lamenting the prospects of Conservatism. Mr. Mumbray shut himself up in the room known as his "study." Mrs. Mumbray stormed at her servants, wrangled with her children, and from her husband held apart

in sour contempt—feeble, pompous creature that he
was! With such an opportunity, and unable to make
use of it! But for *her*, he would never even have
become Mayor. She was enraged at having yielded
in the matter of Serena's betrothal. Glazzard had
fooled them; he was an unprincipled adventurer,
with an eye only to the fortune Serena would bring
him!

"If you marry that man," she asseverated, *à propos*
of a discussion with her daughter on a carpet which had
worn badly, " I shall have nothing whatever to do with
the affair—nothing ! "

Serena drew apart and kept silence.

" You hear what I say? You understand me?"

" You mean that you won't be present at the
wedding ? "

" I do ! " cried her mother, careless what she said so
long as it sounded emphatic. "You shall take all the
responsibility. If you like to throw yourself away on a
bald-headed, dissipated man—as I *know* he is—it shall
be entirely your own doing. I wash my hands of it
—and that's the last word you will hear from me on the
subject."

In consequence of which assertion she vilified
Glazzard and Serena for three-quarters of an hour,
until her daughter, who had sat in abstraction, slowly
rose and withdrew.

Alone in her bedroom, Serena shed many tears, as
she had often done of late. The poor girl was miserably
uncertain how to act. She foresaw that home would be

less than ever a home to her after this accumulation of
troubles, and indeed she had made up her mind to leave
it, but whether as a wife or as an independent woman
she could not decide. "On her own responsibility"—
yes, that was the one thing certain. And what experience had she whereon to form a judgment? It might
be that her mother's arraignment of Glazzard was
grounded in truth, but how could she determine one
way or the other? On the whole, she liked him better
than when she promised to marry him—yes, she liked
him better; she did not shrink from the thought of
wedlock with him. He was a highly educated and
clever man; he offered her a prospect of fuller life than
she had yet imagined; perhaps it was a choice between
him and the ordinary husband such as fell to Polterham
girls. Yet again, if he did not really care for her—
only for her money?

She remembered Denzil Quarrier's lecture on
"Woman," and all he had said about the monstrously
unfair position of girls who are asked in marriage by
men of the world. And thereupon an idea came into
her mind. Presently she had dried her tears, and in
half-an-hour's time she left the house.

Her purpose was to call upon Mrs. Quarrier, whom
she had met not long ago at Highmead. But the lady
was not at home. After a moment of indecision, she
wrote on the back of her visiting card: "Will you be
so kind as to let me know when I could see you? I
will come at any hour."

It was then midday. In the afternoon she received

a note, hand-delivered. Mrs. Quarrier would be at home from ten to twelve the next morning.

Again she called, and Lilian received her in the small drawing-room. They looked at each other with earnest faces, Lilian wondering whether this visit had anything to do with the election. Serena was nervous, and could not reply composedly to the ordinary phrases of politeness with which she was received. And yet the phrases were not quite ordinary; whomsoever she addressed, Lilian spoke with a softness, a kindness peculiar to herself, and chose words which seemed to have more than the common meaning.

The visitor grew sensible of this pleasant characteristic, and at length found voice for her intention.

" I wished to see you for a very strange reason, Mrs. Quarrier. I feel half afraid that I may even offend you. You will think me very strange indeed."

Lilian trembled. The old dread awoke in her. Had Miss Mumbray discovered something ?

"Do let me know what it is," she replied, in a low voice.

"It—it is about Mr. Eustace Glazzard. I think he is an intimate friend of Mr. Quarrier's ? "

" Yes, he is."

"You are surprised, of course. I came to you because I feel so alone and so helpless. You know that I am engaged to Mr. Glazzard ? "

Her voice faltered. Relieved from anxiety, Lilian looked and spoke in her kindest way.

" Do speak freely to me, Miss Mumbray. I shall be

so glad to—to help you in any way I can—so very glad."

"I am sure you mean that. My mother is very much against our marriage—against Mr. Glazzard. She wants me to break off. I can't do that without some better reason than I know of. Will you tell me what you think of Mr. Glazzard? Will you tell me in confidence? You know him probably much better than I do—though that sounds strange. You have known him much longer, haven't you?"

"Not much longer. I met him first in London."

"But you know him through your husband. I only wish to ask you whether you have a high opinion of him. How has he impressed you from the first?"

Lilian reflected for an instant, and spoke with grave conscientiousness.

"My husband considers him his best friend. He thinks very highly of him. They are unlike each other in many things. Mr. Quarrier sometimes wishes that he —that Mr. Glazzard were more active, less absorbed in art; but I have never heard him say anything worse than that. He likes him very much indeed. They have been friends since boyhood."

The listener sat with bowed head, and there was a brief silence.

"Then you think," she said at length, "that I shall be quite safe in—Oh, that is a bad way of putting it! Do forgive me for talking to you like this. You, Mrs. Quarrier, are very happily married; but I am sure you can sympathize with a girl's uncertainty. We have so few opportunities of—— Oh, it was so true what Mr. Quarrier said in his lecture at the Institute—before you came. He said that a girl had to take her husband so very much on trust—of course his words were better than those, but that's what he meant."

"Yes—I know—I have heard him say the same thing."

"I don't ask," pursued the other, quickly, "about his religious opinions, or anything of that kind. Nowadays, I suppose, there are very few men who believe as women do—as most women do." She glanced at Lilian timidly. "I only mean—do you think him a good man —an honourable man?"

"To that I can reply with confidence," said Lilian, sweetly. "I am quite sure he is an honourable man— quite sure! I believe he has very high thoughts. Have you heard him play? No man who hadn't a noble nature could play like that."

Serena drew a sigh of relief.

"Thank you, dear Mrs. Quarrier—thank you so very much! You have put my mind at rest."

These words gave delight to the hearer. To do good and to receive gratitude were all but the prime necessities of Lilian's heart. Obeying her impulse, she began to say all manner of kind, tender, hopeful things. Was there not a similarity between this girl's position and that in which she had herself stood when consenting to the wretched marriage which happily came to an end at the church door? Another woman might have been disposed to say, in the female parrot-language : " But do you love him or not ? That is the whole question." It was *not* the whole question, even granting that love had spoken plainly; and Lilian understood very well that it is possible for a girl to contemplate wedlock without passionate feeling such as could obscure her judgment.

They talked with much intimacy, much reciprocal good-will, and Serena took her leave with a comparatively cheerful mind. She had resolved what to do.

And the opportunity for action came that afternoon. Glazzard called upon her. He looked rather gloomy, but smiled in reply to the smile she gave him.

" Have you read Mr. Gladstone's address to the electors of Midlothian ? " Serena began by asking, with a roguish look.

" Pooh ! What is such stuff to me ? "

" I knew I should tease you. What do you think of Mr. Quarrier's chances ? "

" Oh, he will be elected, no doubt."

Glazzard spoke absently, his eyes on Serena's face, but seemingly not conscious of her expression.

" I hope he will," she rejoined.

" What !—you hope so ? "

" Yes, I do. I am convinced he is the right man. I agree with his principles. Henceforth I am a Radical."

Glazzard laughed mockingly, and Serena joined, but not in the same tone.

" I like him," she pursued, with a certain odd persistence. "If I could do it decently, I would canvass for him. He is a manly man and means what he says. I like his wife, too—she is very sweet."

He glanced at her and pursed his lips.

"I am sure," added Serena, "you like me to praise such good friends of yours?"

"Certainly."

They were in the room where the grand piano stood, for Mrs. Mumbray had gone to pass the day with friends at a distance. Serena said of a sudden:

"Will you please play me something—some serious piece—one of the best you know?"

"You mean it?"

"I do. I want to hear you play a really noble piece. You won't refuse."

He eyed her in a puzzled way, but smiled, and sat down to the instrument. His choice was from Beethoven. As he played, Serena stood in an attitude of profound attention. When the music ceased, she went up to him and held out her hand.

"Thank you, Eustace. I don't think many people can play like that."

"No; not very many," he replied quietly, and thereupon kissed her fingers.

He went to the window and looked out into the chill, damp garden.

"Serena, have you any idea what Sicily is like at this time of year?"

"A faint imagination. Very lovely, no doubt."

"I want to go there."

" Do you ? " she answered, carelessly, and added in lower tones, " So do I."

" There's no reason why you shouldn't. Marry me next week, and we will go straight to Messina."

" I will marry you in a fortnight from to-day," said Serena, in quivering voice.

" You will ? "

Glazzard walked back to Highmead with a countenance which alternated curiously between smiling and lowering. The smile was not agreeable, and the dark look showed his face at its worst. He was completely absorbed in thought, and when some one stopped full in front of him with jocose accost, he gave a start of alarm.

" I should be afraid of lamp-posts," said Quarrier, " if I had that somnambulistic habit. Why haven't you looked in lately ? Men of infinite leisure must wait upon the busy."

" My leisure, thank the destinies ! " replied Glazzard, " will very soon be spent out of hearing of election tumult."

" When ? Going abroad again ? "

" To Sicily."

" Ha !—that means, I conjecture," said Denzil, searching his friend's face, " that a certain affair will come to nothing after all ? "

" And what if you are right ? " returned the other, slowly, averting his eyes.

" I sha'n't grieve. No, to tell you the truth, I shall not ! So at last I may speak my real opinion. It wouldn't have done, Glazzard; it was a mistake, old fellow. I have never been able to understand it. You —a man of your standing—no, no, it was completely a mistake, believe me!"

Glazzard looked into the speaker's face, smiled again, and remarked calmly:

"That's unfortunate. I didn't say my engagement was at an end; and, in fact, I shall be married in a fortnight. We go to Sicily for the honeymoon."

A flush of embarrassment rose to Denzil's face. For a moment he could not command himself; then indignation possessed him.

"That's too bad!" he exclaimed. "You took advantage of me. You laid a trap. I'm damned if I feel able to apologize!"

Glazzard turned away, and it seemed as if he would walk on. But he faced about again abruptly, laughed, held out his hand.

"No, it is I who should apologize. I did lay a trap, and it was too bad. But I wished to know your real opinion."

No one more pliable than Denzil. At once he took the hand that was offered and pressed it heartily.

"I'm a blundering fellow. Do come and spend an hour with me to-night. From eleven to twelve. I dine out with fools, and shall rejoice to see you afterwards."

"Thanks, I can't. I go up to town by the 7.15."

They were in a suburban road, and at the moment some ladies approached. Quarrier, who was acquainted with them, raised his hat and spoke a few hasty words, after which he walked on by Glazzard's side.

"My opinion," he said, "is worth very little. I had no right whatever to express it, having such slight evidence to go upon. It was double impertinence. If *you* can't be trusted to choose a wife, who could? I see that—now that I have made a fool of myself."

"Don't say any more about it," replied the other, in a good-natured voice. "We have lived in the palace of truth for a few minutes, that's all."

"So you go to Sicily. There you will be in your element. Live in the South, Glazzard; I'm convinced you will be a happier man than in this mill-smoke atmosphere. You have the artist's temperament; indulge it to the utmost. After all, a man ought to live out what is in him. Your wedding will be here, of course?"

"Yes, but absolutely private."

"You won't reject me when I offer good wishes? There is no man living who likes you better than I do, or is more anxious for your happiness. Shake hands again, old fellow. I must hurry off."

So they parted, and in a couple of hours Glazzard was steaming towards London.

He lay back in the corner of a carriage, his arms hanging loose, his eyes on vacancy. Of course he had guessed Quarrier's opinion of the marriage he was making; he could imagine his speaking to Lilian about it with half-contemptuous amusement. The daughter of a man like Mumbray—an unformed, scarcely pretty girl, who had inherited a sort of fortune from some soap-boiling family—what a culmination to a career of fastidious dilettantism! "He has probably run through all his money," Quarrier would add. "Poor old fellow! he deserves better things."

He had come to hate Quarrier. Yet with no vulgar hatred; not with the vengeful rancour which would find delight in annihilating its object. His feeling was consistent with a measure of justice to Denzil's qualities, and even with a good deal of admiration; as it originated in mortified vanity, so it might have been replaced by the original kindness, if only some stroke of fortune or of power had set Glazzard in his original position of superiority. Quarrier as an ingenuous young fellow looking up to the older comrade, reverencing his dicta, holding him an authority on most subjects, was acceptable, lovable; as a self-assertive man, given to patronage (though perhaps unconsciously), and succeeding in life as his friend stood still or retrograded, he aroused dangerous emotions. Glazzard could no longer endure his presence, hated the sound of his voice, cursed his genial impudence; yet he did not wish for his final unhappiness—only for a temporary pulling-down, a wholesome castigation of over-blown pride.

The sound of the rushing wheels affected his thought, kept it on the one subject, shaped it to a monotony of verbal suggestion. Not a novel suggestion, by any means; something that his fancy had often played with; very much, perhaps, as that ingenious criminal spoken of by Serena amused himself with the picture of a wrecked train long before he resolved to enjoy the sight in reality.

"Live in the South," Quarrier had urged. "Precisely; in other words: Keep out of my way. You're a good, simple-hearted fellow, to be sure, but it was a pity I had to trust you with that secret. Leave England for a long time."

And why not? Certainly it was good counsel—if it had come from any one but Denzil Quarrier. Probably he should act upon it after all.

XVII.

His rooms were in readiness for him, and whilst the attendant prepared a light supper, he examined some letters which had arrived that evening. Two of the envelopes contained pressing invitations—with reference to accounts rendered and re-rendered ; he glanced over the writing and threw them into the fire. The third missive was more interesting; it came from a lady of high social position at whose house he had formerly been a frequent guest. " Why do we never see you ? " she wrote. " They tell me you have passed the winter in England ; why should you avoid your friends who have been condemned to the same endurance ? I am always at home on Thursday."

He held the dainty little note, and mused over it. At one time the sight of this handwriting had quickened his pulses with a delicious hope ; now it stimulated his gloomy reflections. Such a revival of the past was very unseasonable.

Before going to bed he wrote several letters. They were announcements of his coming marriage—brief, carelessly worded, giving as little information as possible.

The next morning was taken up with business. He saw, among other people, his friend Stark, the picture-collecting lawyer. Stark had letters from Polterham which assured him that the Liberals were confident of victory.

" Confounded pity that Quarrier just got the start of you ! " he exclaimed. " You could have kept that seat for the rest of your life."

"Better as it is," was the cheerful reply. " I should have been heartily sick of the business by now."

" There's no knowing. So you marry Miss Mumbray ? An excellent choice, I have no doubt. Hearty congratulations !—Oh, by-the-bye, Jacobs & Burrows have a capital Greuze—do look in if you are passing."

Glazzard perceived clearly enough that the lawyer regarded this marriage just as Quarrier did, the *pis-aller* of a disappointed and embarrassed man. There was no more interest in his career ; he had sunk finally into the commonplace.

At three o'clock he was at home again, and without occupation. The calendar on his writing-table reminded him that it was Thursday. After all, he might as well respond to the friendly invitation of last evening, and say good-bye to his stately acquaintances in Grosvenor Square. He paid a little attention to costume, and presently went forth.

In this drawing-room he had been wont to shine with the double radiance of artist and critic. Here he had talked pictures with the fashionable painters of the day ; music with men and women of resonant name. The accomplished hostess was ever ready with that smile she bestowed only upon a few favourites, and her daughter —well, he had misunderstood, and so came to grief one

evening of mid-season. A rebuff, the gentlest possible,
but leaving no scintilla of hope. At the end of the
same season she gave her hand to Sir Something
Somebody, the diplomatist.

And to-day the hostess was as kind as ever, smiled
quite in the old way, held his hand a moment longer
than was necessary. A dozen callers were in the room,
he had no opportunity for private speech, and went away
without having mentioned the step he was about to take.
Better so; he might have spoken indiscreetly, unbecom-
ingly, in a tone which would only have surprised and
shocked that gracious lady.

He reached his rooms again with brain and heart in
fiery tumult. Serena Mumbray!—he was tempted to
put an end to his life in some brutal fashion, such as
suited with his debasement.

Another letter had arrived during his absence. An
hour passed before he saw it, but when his eye at length
fell on the envelope he was roused to attention. He
took out a sheet of blue note-paper, covered with large,
clerkly writing.

"Dear Sir,

        "We have at length been able to trace the
person concerning whom you are in communication with
us. He is at present living in Bristol, and we think is
likely to remain there for a short time yet. Will you
favour us with a call, or make an appointment elsewhere?

"We have the honour to be, dear Sir,

                        "Yours faithfully,

                                "Tulks & Crowe."

He paced the room, holding the letter behind his back. It was more than three weeks since the investigation referred to had been committed to Messrs. Tulks & Crowe, private inquiry agents; and long before this he had grown careless whether they succeeded or not. An impulse of curiosity; nothing more. Well, yes; a fondness for playing with secrets, a disposition to get power into his hands—excited to activity just after a long pleasant talk with Lilian. He was sorry this letter had come; yet it made him smile, which perhaps nothing else would have done just now.

"To be weak is miserable, doing or suffering." The quotation was often in his mind, and he had never felt its force so profoundly as this afternoon. The worst of it was, he did not believe himself a victim of inherent weakness; rather of circumstances which persistently baffled him. But it came to the same thing. Was he never to know the joy of vigorous action ?—of asserting himself to some notable result ?

He could do so now, if he chose. In his hand were strings, which, if he liked to pull them, would topple down a goodly edifice, with uproar and dust and amazement indescribable : so slight an effort, so incommensurable an outcome ! He had it in his power to shock the conventional propriety of a whole town, and doubtless, to some extent, of all England. What a vast joke that would be—to look at no other aspect of the matter ! The screamings of imbecile morality—the confusion of party zeal—the roaring of indignant pulpits !

He laughed outright.

But no; of course it was only an amusing dream. He was not malignant enough. The old-fashioned sense of honour was too strong in him. Pooh! He would go and dine, and then laugh away his evening somewhere or other.

Carefully he burnt the letter. To-morrow he would look in at the office of those people, hear their story, and so have done with it.

Next morning he was still in the same mind. He went to Tulks & Crowe's, and spent about an hour closeted with the senior member of that useful firm. " A benevolent interest—anxious to help the poor devil if possible—miserable story, that of the marriage— was to be hoped that the girl would be persuaded to acknowledge him, and help him to lead an honest life —no idea where she was." The information he received was very full and satisfactory ; on the spot he paid for it, and issued into the street again with tolerably easy mind.

To-morrow he must run down to Polterham again. How to pass the rest of to-day? Pressing business was all off his hands, and he did not care to look up any of his acquaintances ; he was not in the mood for talk. Uncertain about the future, he had decided to warehouse the furniture, pictures, and so on, that belonged to him. Perhaps it would be well if he occupied himself in going through his papers—making a selection for the fire.

He did so, until midway in the afternoon. Perusal

of old letters will not generally conduce to cheerfulness, and Glazzard once more felt his spirits sink, his brain grow feverishly active. Within reach of where he sat was a railway time-table; he took it up, turned to the Great Western line, pondered, finally looked at his watch.

At two minutes to five he alighted from a cab at Paddington Station — rushed, bag in hand, to the booking-office—caught the Bristol train just as the guard had signalled for starting.

He was at Bristol soon after eight. The town being strange ground to him, he bade a cabman drive him to a good hotel, where he dined. Such glimpse as he had caught of the streets did not invite him forth, but neither could he sit unoccupied; as the weather was fair, he rambled for an hour or two. His mind was in a condition difficult to account for; instead of dwelling upon the purpose that had brought him hither, it busied itself with all manner of thoughts and fancies belonging to years long past. He recalled the first lines of a poem he had once attempted; it was suggested by a reading of Coleridge—and there, possibly, lay the point of association. Coleridge: then he fell upon literary reminiscences. Where, by the way, was St. Mary Redcliffe? He put the inquiry to a passer-by, and was directed. By dreary thoroughfares he came into view of the church, and stood gazing at the spire, dark against a blotchy sky. Then he mocked at himself for acting as if he had an interest in Chatterton, when in truth the name signified boredom to him. Oh, these

English provincial towns! What an atmosphere of deadly dulness hung over them all! And people were born, and lived, and died in Bristol—merciful powers!

He made his way back to the hotel, drank a glass of hot whisky, and went to bed.

After a sound sleep he awoke in the grey dawn, wondered awhile where he could be, then asked himself why on earth he had come here. It didn't matter much; he could strike off by the Midland to Polterham, and be there before noon. And again he slept.

When he had breakfasted, he called to the waiter and asked him how far it was to that part of the town called Hotwells. Learning that the road thither would bring him near to Clifton, he nodded with satisfaction. Clifton was a place to be seen; on a bright morning like this it would be pleasant to walk over the Downs and have a look at the gorge of the Avon.

A cab was called. With one foot raised he stood in uncertainty, whilst the driver asked him twice whither they were to go. At length he said "Hotwells," and named a street in that locality. He lay back and closed his eyes, remaining thus until the cab stopped.

Hastily he looked about him. He was among poor houses, and near to docks; the masts of great ships appeared above roofs. With a quick movement he drew a coin from his pocket, tossed it up, caught it between his hands. The driver had got down and was standing at the door.

"This the place? Thanks; I'll get out."

He looked at the half-crown, smiled, and handed it to the cabman.

In a few minutes he stood before an ugly but decent house, which had a card in the window intimating that lodgings were here to let. His knock brought a woman to the door.

" I think Mr. North lives here ? "

" Yes, sir, he do live yere," the woman answered, in a simple tone. " Would you wish for to see him ? "

" Please ask him if he could see a gentleman on business—Mr. Marks."

" But he ben't in, sir, not just now. He "—— she broke off and pointed up the street. " Why, there he come, I declare ! "

" The tall man ? "

" That be he, sir."

Glazzard moved towards the person indicated, a man of perhaps thirty, with a good figure, a thin, sallow face, clean-shaven, and in rather shabby clothes. He went close up to him and said gravely :

" Mr. North, I have just called to see you on business."

The young man suppressed a movement of uneasiness, drew in his lank cheeks, and looked steadily at the speaker.

" What name ? " he asked, curtly, with the accent which represents some degree of liberal education.

" Mr. Marks. I should like to speak to you in private."

" Has any one sent you ? "

"No, I have taken the trouble to find where you were living. It's purely my own affair. I think it will be to your interest to talk with me."

The other still eyed him suspiciously, but did not resist.

"I haven't a sitting-room," he said, "and we can't talk here. We can walk on a little, if you like."

"I'm a stranger. Is there a quiet spot anywhere about here?"

"If we jump on this omnibus that's coming, it'll take us to the Suspension Bridge—Clifton, you know. Plenty of quiet spots about there."

The suggestion was accepted. On the omnibus they conversed as any casual acquaintances might have done. Glazzard occasionally inspected his companion's features, which were not vulgar, yet not pleasing. The young man had a habit of sucking in his cheeks, and of half closing his eyes as if he suffered from weak sight; his limbs twitched now and then, and he constantly fingered his throat.

"A fine view," remarked Glazzard, as they came near to the great cliffs; "but the bridge spoils it, of course."

"Do you think so? Not to my mind. I always welcome the signs of civilization."

Glazzard looked at him with curiosity, and the speaker threw back his head in a self-conscious, conceited way.

"Picturesqueness is all very well," he added, "but it very often means hardships to human beings. I don't ask whether a country looks beautiful, but what it does for the inhabitants."

" Very right and proper," assented Glazzard, with a curl of the lip.

" I know very well," pursued the moralist, " that civilization doesn't necessarily mean benefit to the class which ought to be considered first. But that's another question. It *ought* to benefit them, and eventually it must."

" You lean towards Socialism ? "

" Christian Socialism if you know what that signifies."

" I have an idea. A very improving doctrine, no doubt."

They dismounted, and began the ascent of the hillside by a path which wound among trees. Not far from the summit they came to a bench which afforded a good view.

" Suppose we stop here," Glazzard suggested. " It doesn't look as if we should be disturbed."

" As you please."

" By-the-bye, you have abbreviated your name, I think ? "

The other again looked uneasy and clicked with his tongue.

" You had better say what you want with me, Mr. Marks," he replied, impatiently.

" My business is with Arthur James Northway. If you are he, I think I can do you a service."

" Why should you do me a service ? "

" From a motive I will explain if all else is satisfactory."

" How did you find out where I was ? "

" By private means which are at my command." Glazzard adopted the tone of a superior, but was still suave. " My information is pretty complete. Naturally, you are still looking about for employment. I can't promise you that, but I daresay you wouldn't object to earn a five-pound note ? "

" If it's anything—underhand, I'll have nothing to do with it."

" Nothing you can object to. In fact, it's an affair that concerns you more than any one else.—I believe you can't find any trace of your wife ? "

Northway turned his head, and peered at his neighbour with narrow eyes.

" It's about *her*, is it ? "

" Yes, about her."

Strangely enough, Glazzard could not feel as if this conversation greatly interested him. He kept gazing at the Suspension Bridge, at the woods beyond, at the sluggish river, and thought more of the view than of his interlocutor. The last words fell from his lips idly.

" You know where she is ? " Northway inquired.

" Quite well. I have seen her often of late—from a distance. To prove I am not mistaken, look at this portrait and tell me if you recognize the person ? "

He took from an inner pocket a mutilated photograph; originally of cabinet size, it was cut down to an oval, so that only the head remained. The portrait had been taken in London between Lilian's return from Paris and her arrival at Polterham. Glazzard was one of the few favoured people who received a copy.

Northway examined it and drew in his cheeks, breathing hard.

" There's no mistake, I think ? "

The reply was a gruff negative.

" I suppose you do care about discovering her ? "

The answer was delayed. Glazzard read it, however, in the man's countenance, which expressed various emotions.

" She has married again—eh ? "

" First, let me ask you another question. Have you seen her relatives ? "

" Yes, I have."

" With what result ? "

" They profess to know nothing about her. Of course, I don't believe them."

" But you may," said Glazzard, calmly. " They speak the truth, no doubt. From them you must hope for no information. In all likelihood, you might seek her for the rest of your life and never come upon her track."

" Then let me know what you propose."

" I offer to tell you where she is, and how situated, and to enable you to claim her. But you, for your part, must undertake to do this in a certain way, which I will describe when everything is ready, a week or so hence. As I have said, I am willing to reward you for agreeing to act as I direct. My reasons you shall understand when I go into the other details. You will see that I have no kind of selfish object in view—in fact, that I am quite justified in what looks like vulgar plotting."

Glazzard threw out the words with a careless condescension, keeping his eyes on the landscape.

" I'll take back the portrait, if you please."

He restored it to his pocket, and watched Northway's features, which were expressive of mental debate.

" At present," he went on, " I can do no more than give you an idea of what has been going on. Your wife has not been rash enough to marry a second time ; but she is supposed to be married to a man of wealth and position—is living publicly as his wife. They have deceived every one who knows them."

" Except you, it seems," remarked Northway, with a gleam from between his eyelids.

" Except me—but that doesn't concern you. Now, you see that your wife has done nothing illegal; you can doubtless divorce her, but have no other legal remedy. I mention this because it might occur to you that—you will excuse me—that the situation is a profitable one. It is nothing of the kind. On the threat of exposure they would simply leave England at once. Nothing could induce them to part—be quite sure of that. The man, as I said, has a high position, and you might be tempted to suppose that—to speak coarsely—he would pay blackmail. Don't think it for a moment. He is far too wise to persevere in what would be a lost game; they would at once go abroad. It is only on the stage that men consent to pay for the keeping of a secret which is quite certain not to be kept."

Northway had followed with eager attention, pinching his long throat and drawing in his cheeks.

"Well, what do you want me to do?" he asked.

"To remain here in Bristol for a week or so longer. I will then telegraph to you, and tell you where to meet me."

"Is it far from here?"

"A couple of hours' journey, or so. If you will allow me, I will pay your fare at once."

He took out a sovereign, which Northway, after a moment's hesitation, accepted.

"Do you take any interest in the elections?" Glazzard asked.

"Not much," replied the other, reassuming his intellectual air. "One party is as worthless as the other from my point of view."

"I'm glad to hear that—you'll understand why when we meet again. And, indeed, I quite agree with you."

"Politics are no use nowadays," pursued Northway. "The questions of the time are social. We want a party that is neither Liberal nor Tory."

"Exactly.—Well, now, may I depend upon you?"

"I'll come when you send for me."

"Very well. I have your address."

He stood up, hesitated a moment, and offered his hand, which Northway took without raising his eyes.

"I shall walk on into Clifton ; so here we say good-bye for the present.—A week or ten days."

"I suppose you won't alter your mind, Mr.—Mr. Marks ? "

"Not the least fear of that.   I have a public duty to discharge."

So speaking, and with a peculiar smile on his lips, Glazzard walked away.   Northway watched him and seemed tempted to follow, but at length went down the hill.

XVIII.

DISAPPOINTED in his matrimonial project, the Rev. Scatchard Vialls devoted himself with acrid zeal to the interests of the Conservative party. He was not the most influential of the Polterham clerics, for women in general rather feared than liked him ; a sincere ascetic, he moved but awkwardly in the regions of tea and tattle, and had an uncivil habit of speaking what he thought the truth without regard to time, place, or person. Some of his sermons had given offence, with the result that several ladies betook themselves to gentler preachers. But the awe inspired by his religious enthusiasm was practically useful now that he stood forward as an assailant of the political principles held in dislike by most Polterham church-goers. There was a little band of district-visitors who stood by him the more resolutely for the coldness with which worldly women regarded him ; and these persons, with their opportunities of making interest in poor households, constituted a party agency not to be despised. They worked among high and low with an unscrupulous energy to which it is not easy to do justice. Wheedling or menacing—doing everything indeed but argue—they blended the cause of Mr. Welwyn-Baker and that of the Christian religion so inextricably that the wives of humble electors came to regard the Tory candidate as

Christ's vicegerent upon earth, and were convinced
that their husbands' salvation depended upon a Tory
vote.

One Sunday, Mr. Vialls took for his text, " But
rather seek ye the kingdom of God, and all these things
shall be added unto you." He began by pointing out
how very improper it would be for a clergyman to
make the pulpit an ally of the hustings; far indeed be
it from him to discourse in that place of party questions
—to speak one word which should have for its motive
the advancements of any electioneering cause. But in
these times of social discontent and upheaval it must not
be forgotten that eternal verities were at stake. There
were men—there were multitudes, alas! who made it the
object of their life-long endeavour to oust Christianity
from the world; if not avowedly, at all events in fact.
Therefore would he describe to them in brief, clear
sentences what really was implied in a struggle between
the parties commonly known as Conservative and
Liberal. He judged no individual; he spoke only of
principles, of a spirit, an attitude. The designs of
Russia, the troubles in Ireland—of these things he
knew little and recked less; they were " party shib-
boleths," and did not concern a Christian minister in
his pulpit. But deeper lay the interests for which
parties nowadays were in truth contending. It had
come to this : are we to believe, or are we *not* to believe
that the " kingdom of God " must have precedence of
worldly goods? The working classes of this country
—ah, how sad to have to speak with condemnation of

the poor!—were being led to think that the only object worth striving after was an improvement of their material condition. Marvellous to say, they were encouraged in this view by people whom Providence had blessed with all the satisfactions that earth can give. When the wealthy, the educated thus repudiated the words of Christ, what could be expected of those whom supreme Goodness has destined to a subordinate lot? No! material improvement was *not* the first thing, even for those unhappy people (victims for the most part of their own improvident or vicious habits) who had scarcely bread to eat and raiment wherewith to clothe themselves. Let them seek the kingdom of God, and these paltry, temporal things shall surely be added unto them.

This sermon was printed at the office of the *Polterham Mercury*, and distributed freely throughout the town. He had desired no such thing, said Mr. Vialls, but the pressure of friends was irresistible. In private, meanwhile, he spoke fiercely against the Radical candidate, and never with such acrimony as in Mrs. Mumbray's drawing-room when Serena was present. One afternoon he stood up, tea-cup in hand, and, as his habit was, delivered a set harangue on the burning topic.

"In one respect," he urged, after many other accusations, "I consider that Mr. Quarrier is setting the very worst, the most debasing, the most demoralizing example to these working folk, whose best interests he professes to have at heart. I am assured (and the witness of my own eyes in one instance warrants me in

giving credit to the charge) that he constantly enters
public-houses, taverns, even low dram-shops, to satisfy
his thirst for strong liquor in the very face of day,
before the eyes of any one who may happen to be
passing. This is simply abominable! If an honourable man has one duty—one social duty—more incumbent upon him than another, it is to refrain from setting
an example of intemperance."

Serena had listened thus far with a look of growing
irritation. At length she could resist no longer the
impulse to speak out.

"But surely, Mr. Vialls, you don't charge Mr.
Quarrier with intemperance?"

"I do, Miss Mumbray," replied the clergyman,
sternly. "Intemperance does not necessarily imply
drunkenness. It is intemperate to enter public-houses
at all hours and in all places, even if the liquor partaken
of has no obvious effect upon the gait or speech of the
drinker. I maintain"——

"Mr. Quarrier does not go about as you would have
us believe."

"Serena!" interfered her mother. "Do you contradict Mr. Vialls?"

"Yes, mother, I do, and every one ought to who *knows*
that he is exaggerating. I have heard this calumny
before, and I have been told how it has arisen. Mr.
Quarrier takes a glass of beer when he is having a long
country walk; and why he shouldn't quench his thirst
I'm sure I can't understand."

"Miss Mumbray," said the clergyman, glaring at

her, yet affecting forbearance, "you seem to forget that our cottagers are not so inhospitable as to refuse a glass of water to the weary pedestrian who knocks at their door."

"I don't forget it, Mr. Vialls," replied Serena, who was trembling at her own boldness, but found a pleasure in persevering. "And I know very well what sort of water one generally gets at cottages about here. I remember the family at Rickstead that died one after another of their temperance beverage."

"Forgive me! That is not at all to the point. Granting that the quality of the water is suspicious, are there not pleasant little shops where lemonade can be obtained? But no; it is *not* merely to quench a natural thirst that Mr. Quarrier has recourse to those pestilent vendors of poison; the drinking of strong liquor has become a tyrant-habit with him."

"I deny it, Mr. Vialls!" exclaimed the girl, almost angrily. (Mrs. Mumbray in vain tried to interpose, and the other ladies present were partly shocked, partly amused, into silence.) "If so, then my father is a victim to the habit of drink — and so is Mr. Welwyn-Baker himself!"

This was laying a hand upon the Ark. Mrs. Mumbray gave a little scream, and several "Oh's!" were heard. Mr. Vialls shook his head and smiled with grim sadness.

"My dear young lady, I fear we shall not understand each other. I am far from being one of those who deny to ladies the logical faculty, but "——

"But you feel that I am right, and that party prejudice has carried you too far!" interrupted Serena, rising from her chair. "I had better go away, or I shall say disagreeable things about the Conservatives. I am not one of them, and I should like that to be understood."

She walked quietly from the room, and there ensued an awkward silence.

"Poor Serena!" breathed Mrs. Mumbray, with a deep sigh. "She has fallen under the influence of Mrs. Quarrier—a most dangerous person. How such things come to pass I cannot understand."

Mrs. Tenterden's deep voice chimed in:

"We must certainly guard our young people against Mrs. Quarrier. From the look of her, no one could have guessed what she would turn out. The idea of so young a woman going to people's houses and talking politics!"

"Oh, I think nothing of that!" remarked a lady who particularly wished to remind the company that she was still youthful. "I canvass myself; it's quite the proper thing for ladies to do. But I'm told she has rather an impertinent way of speaking to every one who doesn't fall down and worship her husband."

"Mrs. Lester," broke in the grave voice of the clergyman, "I trust you will pardon me, but you have inadvertently made use of a phrase which is, or should be, consecrated by a religious significance."

The lady apologized rather curtly, and Mr. Vialls made a stiff bow.

At this same moment the subject of their conversation was returning home from a bold expedition into the camp of the enemy. Encouraged by the personal friendliness that had been shown her in the family of Mr. Samuel Quarrier, Lilian conceived and nourished the hope that it was within her power to convert the sturdy old Tory himself. Samuel made a joke of this, and entertained himself with a pretence of lending ear to her arguments. This afternoon he had allowed her to talk to him for a long time. Lilian's sweetness was irresistible, and she came back in high spirits with report of progress. Denzil, who had just been badgered by a deputation of voters who wished to discover his mind on seven points of strictly non-practical politics, listened with idle amusement.

"Dear girl," he said presently, "the old fellow is fooling you! You can no more convert him than you could the Dalai-Lama to Christianity."

"But he speaks quite seriously, Denzil! He owns that he doesn't like Beaconsfield, and "——

"Don't waste your time and your patience. It's folly, I assure you. When you are gone he explodes with laughter."

Lilian gazed at him for a moment with wide eyes, then burst into tears.

"Good heavens! what is the matter with you, Lily?" cried Denzil, jumping up. "Come, come, this kind of thing won't do! You are overtaxing yourself. You are getting morbidly excited."

It was true enough, and Lilian was herself conscious

of it, but she obeyed an impulse from which there seemed no way of escape. Her conscience and her fears would not leave her at peace; every now and then she found herself starting at unusual sounds, trembling in mental agitation if any one approached her with an unwonted look, dreading the arrival of the post, the sight of a newspaper, faces in the street. Then she hastened to the excitement of canvassing, as another might have turned to more vulgar stimulants. Certainly her health had suffered. She could not engage in quiet study, still less could rest her mind in solitary musing, as in the old days.

Denzil seated himself by her on the sofa.

"If you are to suffer in this way, little girl, I shall repent sorely that ever I went in for politics."

"How absurd of me! I can't think why I behave so ridiculously!"

But still she sobbed, resting her head against him.

"I have an idea," he said at length, rendered clairvoyant by his affection, "that after next week you will feel much easier in your mind."

"After next week?"

"Yes; when Glazzard is married and gone away."

She would not confess that he was right, but her denials strengthened his surmise.

"I can perfectly understand it, Lily. It certainly was unfortunate; and if it had been any one but Glazzard, I might myself have been wishing the man away. But you know as well as I do that Glazzard would not breathe a syllable."

" Not even to his wife ? " she whispered.

"Not even to her! I assure you"—he smiled—
"men have no difficulty in keeping important secrets,
Samson notwithstanding. Glazzard would think himself for ever dishonoured. But in a week's time they
will be gone; and I shouldn't wonder if they remain
abroad for years. So brighten up, dearest dear, and leave
Sam alone; he's a cynical old fellow, past hope of
mending his ways. See more of Molly; she does you
good. And, by-the-bye, it's time you called on the
Catesbys. They will always be very glad to see you."

This family of Catesby was one of the few really
distinguished in the neighbourhood. Colonel Catesby,
a long-retired warrior, did not mingle much with local
society, but with his wife and daughter he had appeared
at Denzil's first political dinner; they all "took to"
their hostess, and had since manifested this liking in
sundry pleasant ways.

Indeed, Lilian was become a social success—that
is to say, with people who were at all capable of
appreciating her. Herein, as in other things, she had
agreeably surprised Denzil. He had resigned himself
to seeing her remain a loving, intelligent, but very un-
ambitious woman; of a sudden she proved equal to all
the social claims connected with his candidature—
unless the efforts, greater than appeared, were under-
mining her health. Having learned to trust herself in
conversation, she talked with a delightful blending of
seriousness and gentle merriment. Her culture
declared itself in every thought; there was much within

the ordinary knowledge of people trained to the world that she did not know, but the simplicity resulting from this could never be confused with want of education or of tact. When the Catesbys made it evident that they approved her, Quarrier rejoiced exceedingly ; he was flattered in his deepest sensibilities, and felt that henceforth nothing essential would be wanting to his happiness—whether Polterham returned him or not.

That he would be returned, he had no doubt. The campaign proceeded gloriously. Whilst Mr. Gladstone flowed on for ever in Midlothian rhetoric, Denzil lost no opportunity of following his leader, and was often astonished at the ease with which he harangued as long as Polterham patience would endure him. To get up and make a two hours' speech no longer cost him the least effort ; he played with the stock subjects of eloquence, sported among original jokes and catch-words, burned through perorations with the joy of an improvisatore in happiest mood. The *Examiner* could not report him for lack of space ; the *Mercury* complained of a headache caused by this "blatant youthfulness striving to emulate garrulous senility "—a phrase which moved Denzil to outrageous laughter. And on the whole he kept well within such limits of opinion as Polterham approved. Now and then Mr. Chown felt moved by the spirit to interrogate him as to the " scope and bearing and significance " of an over-bold expression, but the Radical section was too delighted with a prospect of victory to indulge in " heckling," and the milder Progressives considered their candidate as a man of whom

Polterham might be proud, a man pretty sure to "make his mark" at Westminster.

In the hostile ranks there was a good deal of loud talk and frequent cheering, but the speeches were in general made by lieutenants, and the shouts seemed intended to make up for the defective eloquence of their chief. Mr. Welwyn-Baker was too old and too stout and too shaky for the toil of personal electioneering. He gave a few dinners at his big house three miles away, and he addressed (laconically) one or two select meetings; for the rest, his name and fame had to suffice. There was no convincing him that his seat could possibly be in danger. He smiled urbanely over the reports of Quarrier's speeches, called his adversary "a sharp lad," and continued through all the excitement of the borough to conduct himself with this amiable fatuity.

" I vow and protest," said Mr. Mumbray, in a confidential ear, " that if it weren't for the look of the thing, I would withhold my vote altogether! W.-B. is in his dotage. And to think that we might have put new life into the party! Bah!"

Conservative canvassers did not fail to make use of the fact that Mr. Welwyn-Baker had always been regardful of the poor. His alms-houses were so pleasantly situated and so tastefully designed that many Polterham people wished they were for lease on ordinary terms. The Infirmary was indebted to his annual beneficence, and the Union had to thank him—especially through this past winter—for a lightening of its burden. Aware of these things, Lilian never felt able to speak harshly against the old Tory. In theory she acknowledged that the relief of a few families could not weigh against principles which enslaved a whole population (thus Quarrier put it), but her heart pleaded for the man who allayed suffering at his gates; and could Mr. Chown have heard the admissions she made to Welwyn-Baker's advocates, he would have charged her with criminal weakness, if not with secret treachery. She herself had as yet been able to do very little for the poor of the town; with the clergy she had no intimate relations (church-going was for her and Denzil only a politic conformity); and Polterham was not large enough to call for the organization of special efforts. But her face invited the necessitous; in the by-ways she had been appealed to for charity, with results which became known among people inclined to beg. So it happened that she was one day led on a benevolent mission into the poorest part of the town, and had an opportunity of indulging her helpful instincts.

This was in the afternoon. Between nine and ten that evening, as Denzil and she sat together in the library (for once they were alone and at peace), a servant informed her that Mrs. Wade wished to speak for a moment on urgent business. She went out and found her friend in the drawing-room.

" Can you give me a few minutes ? "

" As long as ever you like ! No one is here, for a wonder. Do you wish to talk privately, or will you come into the study ? We were sitting there."

" It's only politics."

" Oh, then come."

Quarrier would rather have been left in quiet over the proof-sheets of his book—it was already going through the press—but he welcomed the visitor with customary friendliness.

" Capital speech of Hartington's yesterday."

" Very good answer to Cross. What do you think of John Bright and the licensed victuallers ? "

" Oh," laughed Denzil, " he'll have to talk a good deal before he persuades them that temperance is money in their pockets! I don't see the good of that well-intentioned sophistry. But then, you know, I belong to the habitual drunkards! You have heard that Scatchard Vialls so represents me to all and sundry ? "

" I should proceed against him for slander."

" On the contrary, I think it does me good. All the honest topers will rally to me, and the sober Liberals will smile indulgently. Sir Wilfred Lawson would long ago have been stamped out as a bore of the first magnitude but for his saving humour."

Mrs. Wade presently made known her business ; but with a preface which disturbed the nerves of both her listeners.

" The enemy have a graver charge against you. I happened, an hour ago, to catch a most alarming rumour. Mr. Quarrier, your wife will be your ruin! "

Notwithstanding the tone of burlesque, Lilian turned pale, and Quarrier stood frowning. Mrs. Wade examined them both, her bright eyes glancing quickly from one face to the other and back again. She did not continue, until Quarrier exclaimed impatiently :

"What is it now?"

"Nothing less than an accusation of bribery and corruption."

Relief was audible in Denzil's laugh.

"It's reported," Mrs. Wade went on, "that Mrs. Quarrier has been distributing money—money in hand-fuls, through half-a-dozen streets down by the river."

"You don't really mean"—— began Lilian, who could not even yet quite command her voice.

"It's positively going about! I thought it my duty to come and tell you at once. What is the foundation?"

"I warned you, Lily," said Denzil, good-humouredly. "The fact is, Mrs. Wade, she gave half-a-crown to some old woman in Water Lane this afternoon. It was imprudent, of course. Who told you about it?"

"Mr. Rook, the stationer. It was talked of up and down High Street, he assures me. We may laugh, but this kind of misrepresentation goes a long way."

"Let the blackguards make the most of it!" cried Quarrier. "I have as good things in store for them. One of Jobson's workmen told me this morning that he and his fellows were being distinctly intimidated ; Jobson has told them several times that if the Radicals won, work would be scarce, and that the voters would have only themselves to thank for it. And Thomas Barker has been promising lowered rents at Lady-day."

"But who *could* have told such falsehoods about me?" asked Lilian.

" Some old woman who didn't get the half-crown, no doubt," replied Mrs. Wade.

" Those poor creatures I went to see have no vote."

" Oh, but handfuls of money, you know! It's the impression made on the neighbourhood. Seriously, they are driven to desperate resources ; and I believe there *is* a good deal of intimidation going on—especially on the part of district-visitors. Mrs. Alexander told me of several instances. And the wives (of course) are such wretched cowards! That great big carpenter, East, is under his wife's thumb, and she has been imploring him not to vote Liberal for fear of consequences—she sits weeping, and talking about the workhouse. Contemptible idiot! It would gratify me extremely to see her really going to the workhouse."

" And pray," asked Denzil, with a laugh, " what would be the result of giving the franchise to such women ? "

" The result *might* be that, in time to come, there wouldn't be so many of them."

" In time to come—possibly. In the meanwhile, send their girls to school to learn a wholesome contempt for their mothers."

" Oh, Denzil ! "

" Well, it sounds brutal, but it's very good sense. All progress involves disagreeable necessities."

Mrs. Wade was looking about the room, smiling, absent. She rose abruptly.

" I mustn't spoil your one quiet evening. How do the proofs go on ? "

" Would you care to take a batch of them ? " asked Quarrier. " These are revises—you might be able to make a useful suggestion."

She hesitated, but at length held out her hand.

You have rather a long walk," said Lilian. " I hope it's fine."

" No ; it drizzles."

" Oh, how kind of you to take so much trouble on our account ! "

Mrs. Wade went out into the darkness. It was as disagreeable a night as the time of year could produce ; black overhead, slimy under foot, with a cold wind to dash the colder rain in one's face. The walk home took more than half an hour, and she entered her cottage much fatigued. Without speaking to the girl who admitted her, she went upstairs to take off her out-of-door things ; on coming down to the sitting-room, she found her lamp lit, her fire burning, and supper on the table—a glass of milk and some slices of bread and butter. Her friends would have felt astonishment and compassion had they learned how plain and slight was the fare that supported her; only by reducing her household expenditure to the strict minimum could she afford to dress in the manner of a lady, supply herself with a few papers and books, and keep up the appearances without which it is difficult to enjoy any society at all.

To-night she ate and drank with a bitter sense of her poverty and loneliness. Before her mind's eye was the picture of Denzil Quarrier's study—its luxury, brightness, wealth of volumes; and Denzil's face made an inseparable part of the scene. That face had never ceased to occupy her imagination since the evening of his lecture at the Institute. Its haunting power was always greatest when she sat here alone in the stillness. This little room, in which she had known the pleasures of independence and retirement, seemed now but a prison. It was a mean dwelling, fit only for labouring folk; the red blind irritated her sight, and she had to turn away from it.

What a hope had come to her of a sudden last autumn! How recklessly she had indulged it, and how the disappointment rankled!

A disappointment which she could not accept with the resignation due to fate. At first she had done so; but then a singular surmise crept into her thoughts— a suspicion which came she knew not whence—and thereafter was no rest from fantastic suggestions. Her surmise did not remain baseless; evidence of undeniable strength came to its support, yet all was so vague— so unserviceable.

She opened the printed sheets that Quarrier had given her and for a few minutes read with interest. Then her eyes and thoughts wandered.

Her servant knocked and entered, asking if she should remove the supper-tray. In looking up at the girl, Mrs. Wade noticed red eyes and other traces of weeping.

" What is the matter? " she asked, sharply. " Have you any news? "

The girl answered with a faltering negative. She, too, had her unhappy story. A Polterham mechanic who made love to her lost his employment, went to London with hopes and promises, and now for more than half a year had given no sign of his existence. Mrs. Wade had been wont to speak sympathetically on the subject, but to-night it excited her anger.

"Don't be such a simpleton, Annie! If only you knew anything of life, you would be glad of what has happened. You are free again, and freedom is the one thing in the world worth having. To sit and cry because—I'm ashamed of you!"

Surprise and misery caused the tears to break forth again.

"Go to bed, and go to sleep!" said the mistress, harshly. "If ever you *are* married, you'll remember what I said, and look back to the time when you knew nothing worse than silly girlish troubles. Have you no pride? It's girls like you that make men think so lightly of all women—despise us—say we are unfit for anything but cooking and cradle-rocking! If you go on in this way you must leave me; I won't have a silly, moping creature before my eyes, to make me lose all patience!"

The girl took up the tray and hurried off. Her mistress sat till late in the night, now reading a page of the proofs, now brooding with dark countenance.

XIX.

THE polling would take place on the last day of March. On the day previous to that of nomination Glazzard and Serena Mumbray were to be married. Naturally, not at Mr. Vialls' church ; they made choice of St. Luke's, which was blessed with a mild, intellectual incumbent. Mrs. Mumbray, consistently obstinate on this one point, refused to be present at the ceremony.

" There will be no need of me," she said to Serena. " Since you choose to be married as if you were ashamed of it, your father's presence will be quite enough. I have always looked forward to very different things ; but when were *my* wishes and hopes consulted ? I am not angry with you ; we shall part on perfectly good terms, and I shall wish you every happiness. I hope to hear from you occasionally. But I cannot be a witness of what I so strongly disapprove."

William Glazzard—who saw nothing amiss in his brother's choice of a wife, and was greatly relieved by the thought of Serena's property—would readily have gone to the church, but it was decided, in deference to the bride's wish, that Ivy should come in his stead.

Ivy had felt herself neglected lately. Since the announcement that her uncle Eustace was to marry Serena, she had seen very little of the friend with whom alone she could enjoy intimate converse. But on the eve of the wedding-day they spent an hour or two together in Serena's room. Both were in a quiet mood, thoughtful rather than talkative.

"This day week," said Serena, breaking a long silence, "I shall be somewhere in Sicily—perhaps looking at Mount Etna. The change comes none to soon. I was getting into a thoroughly bad state of mind. Before long you would have refused to associate with me."

"I think not, dear."

"If not, then I should have done you harm—and that would be a burden on my conscience. I had begun to feel a pleasure in saying and doing things that I believed to be wrong. You never had that feeling?"

Ivy looked up with wonder in her gentle, dreamy eyes.

"It must be very strange."

"I have thought about it, and I believe it comes from ignorance. You know, perhaps what I said and did wasn't really wrong, after all—if one only understood."

The listener was puzzled.

"But we won't talk about it. Before long I shall understand so many things, and then you shall have the benefit of my experience. I believe I am going to be very happy."

It was said as if on a sudden impulse, with a tremulous movement of the body.

"I hope and believe so, dear," replied the other, warmly.

"And you—I don't like to think of you being so much alone. There's a piece of advice I should like to give you. Try and make friends with Mrs. Quarrier."

" Mrs. Quarrier ? "

" Yes—I have a good reason—I think she would suit you exactly. I had a long talk with her about a fortnight ago, and she seemed to me very nice—nicer than any one I have ever known, except you."

" Perhaps I shall have an opportunity "——

" Make one. Go and see her, and ask her to come and see you."

They fell again into musing, and the rest of their talk was mainly about the arrangements for the morrow.

About the time that Ivy Glazzard was going home, her uncle left Polterham by train. He travelled some thirty miles, and alighted at a large station, which, even thus late, was full of noise and bustle. After drinking a cup of coffee in the refreshment-room, he crossed to another platform, and then paced up and down for a quarter of an hour, until the ringing of a bell gave notice that a train which he awaited was just arriving. It steamed into the station, and Glazzard's eye, searching among the passengers who got out, quickly recognized a tall, thin figure.

" So, here you are," he said, holding his hand to Northway, who smiled doubtfully, and peered at him with sleepy eyes. " I have a room at the station hotel —come along."

They were presently at their ease in a sitting-room, with a hot supper on the table. Northway ate heartily; his entertainer with less gusto, though he looked in excellent spirits, and talked much of the impending elections. The meal dismissed, Glazzard lit a cigar (Northway did not smoke) and broached the topic of their meeting.

" Now, what I am going to propose to you may seem disagreeable. I take it for granted that we deal honourably—for my own purpose is nothing to be ashamed of; and if, after hearing what I ask, you don't care to undertake it, say so at once, and there's no harm done."

" Well, let me know what it is ? " replied the other, plucking at his throat.

" Plainly then, I am engaged in election work. My motives are political."

" Oh ! "

" The man of whom we spoke the other day is standing as candidate for a borough not very far from here—not *this* town. Not long ago I discovered that secret of his private life. I am going to use it against him—to floor him with this disgrace. You understand ? "

" Which side is he ? "

" Liberal. But to a man of your large views, that of course makes no difference."

" Not a bit ! " Northway replied, obviously flattered. " You are a Conservative, then ? "

" Yes; I am Conservative. I think (as I am sure

you do) that Liberalism is a mere name, used for the most part by men who want to make tools of the people."

"Yes, I agree with that," said Northway, putting his head aside and drawing in his cheeks.

Glazzard repressed a smile, and smoked for a moment.

"What I want you to do," he continued, "is this. To-morrow, by an early train, you will go down to this borough I speak of. You will find your way to the Court-house, and will get leave to make an appeal for the magistrate's advice. When you come forward, you will say that your wife has deserted you—that a friend of yours has seen her in that town, and has discovered that she has committed bigamy—that you wish for the magistrate's help—his advice how to take proceedings. And, finally, you will state in a particularly clear voice that your wife is Mrs. So-and-so, illegally married to Mr. So-and-so, Liberal candidate."

He spoke in hurrying accents, and as he ceased the cigar fell from his fingers.

"But I thought you said that they weren't married at all?"

"They are not. But you mustn't know it. Your friend—who informed you (say it was a man casually in the town, a commercial traveller, who knew your wife formerly by sight)—took it for granted they were married. If you knew she had not broken the law, you would have no excuse for going into Court, you see."

Northway pondered the matter, clicking with his tongue.

"You remember, I hope," pursued Glazzard, "all I told you at Clifton about the position of these people?"

"Yes, I remember. How long have they been together?"

"About two years."

"Has she a child?"

"No. Now, are you disposed to serve me? If you consent, you will gain the knowledge of your wife's whereabouts and the reward I promised—which I shall pay now. If you take the money and then spoil my scheme, you will find it has been useless dishonesty. To-morrow, in any case, the facts will be made public."

Northway glanced at him ill-humouredly.

"You needn't be so anxious about my honesty, Mr. Marks. But I should like to be made a little surer that you have been telling me the truth. How do I know that my wife is really living as you say? It seems to me I ought to have a sight of her before I go talking to magistrates."

Glazzard reflected.

"Nobody," pursued the other, "would make such a charge just on hearsay evidence. It would only be common sense for me to see her first."

"That objection is reasonable. If you knew how well-assured I am of this lady's identity, you would understand why your view of the matter never occurred to me. You must say that you *have* seen her, that's all—seen her coming out of her house."

But Northway was still unsatisfied. He desired to know how it was that a public man had succeeded in deceiving all his friends in such an affair as that of his marriage, and put various other questions, which reminded Glazzard how raw a hand he was at elaborate artifice. Whilst the discussion was going on, Northway took from his pocket an envelope, and from the envelope drew a small photograph.

"You showed me one the other day," he said. "Now, do you recognize that?"

"Undoubtedly. That is Miss Lilian Allen—four years ago, I dare say."

"H'm! not a bad guess. It's four years old, as near as can be. I see you know all about her, though how you found out I can't understand, unless she "——

He paused, peering at Glazzard suspiciously.

"It doesn't matter how I learnt what I know," said the latter, in a peremptory tone. "Let us stick to the point. It's lucky you have brought this carte-de-visite; it will enable you to assure yourself, before going to the Court-house, that you are not being fooled. As soon as you land in the town, ask your way to the shop of a bookseller called Ridge (make a note of the name)—tell Mr. Ridge that you have found a pocket-book with that photograph in it, and ask him if he can help you to identify the person. You'll hear his answer. And in this way, by-the-bye, you could dispense with telling the magistrate that you have seen your wife. Produce the portrait in Court, and declare that it has been recognized by people in the town."

Northway appeared content.

"Well, that sounds better. And what am I to do after speaking to the magistrate ? "

" I should advise you to have an interview with the man himself, the Liberal candidate, and ask him how it happens that your wife is living with him. In that way—when he learns what step you have already taken —you will no doubt get hold of the truth. And then," he smiled, "you can spend the rest of the day in contradicting your statement that Mrs. So-and-so has committed bigamy ; making it known that she is merely a counterfeit wife."

" Making known to whom ? "

Glazzard laughed.

"Why, to the hundreds of people who will crowd about you. My dear sir, you will be the most important person in the town ! You will turn an election—overthrow the hopes of a party ! Don't you want to know the taste of *power ?* Won't it amuse you to think, and to remember, that in the elections of 1880 you exercised an influence beyond that of Gladstone or Beaconsfield ? It's the wish for power that excites all this uproar throughout the country. I myself, now— do you think I am a political agent just for the money it brings me ? No, no; but because I have delight in ruling men ! If I am not mistaken, you have it in you to become a leader in your way, and some day you'll remember my words."

Northway opened his eyes very wide, and with a look of gratification.

" You think I'm cut out for that kind of thing?"

" Judging from what I have heard of your talk. But not in England, you understand. Try one of the new countries, where the popular cause goes ahead more boldly. You're young enough yet."

The listener mused, smiling in a self-conscious way that obliged Glazzard to avert his face for a moment lest he should betray contemptuous amusement.

" Shall you be there—in that town—to-morrow?" asked the young man.

" No, I have business in quite another part. That election," he added, with an air of importance, " is not the only one I am looking after."

There was silence, then Glazzard continued :

" It's indifferent to me whether it comes out that *I* planned this stratagem, or not. Still, in the interests of my party, I admit that I had rather it were kept quiet. So I'll tell you what. If, in a month's time, I find that you have kept the secret, you shall receive at any address you like a second five-pound note. It's just as you please. Of course, if you think you can get more by bargaining with the Liberals—but I doubt whether the secret will be worth anything after the explosion."

" All right. I'll give you an address, so that if you keep in the same mind "——

He mentioned it. And Glazzard made a note.

" Then we strike a bargain, Mr. Northway?"

" Yes, I'll go through with it," was the deliberate reply.

" Very well. Then you shall have the particulars."

Thereupon Glazzard made known the names he had kept in reserve. Northway jotted them down on the back of an envelope, his hand rather unsteady.

" There's a train to Polterham," said Glazzard, " at nine o'clock in the morning. You'll be there by ten— see Ridge the bookseller, and be at the Court-house in convenient time. I know there's a sitting to-morrow ; and on the second day after comes out the Polterham Tory paper. You will prepare them such an item of news in their police reports as they little look for. By that time the whole truth will be known, of course, and Mr. Quarrier's candidature will be impossible."

" What will the Liberals do ? "

" I can't imagine. We shall look on and enjoy the situation—unprecedented, I should think."

Northway again smiled ; he seemed to enter into the jest.

" You sleep here," said Glazzard. " Your expenses are paid. I'll take leave of you now, and I sha'n't see you again, as I have to leave by the 3.40 up-train."

The money he had promised was transferred to Northway's pocket, and they shook hands with much friendliness.

Glazzard quitted the hotel. His train back to Polterham left at 1.14, and it was past midnight.

He went into the station, now quiet and deserted. A footstep occasionally echoed under the vault, or a voice sounded from a distance. The gas was lowered ;

out at either end gleamed the coloured signal-lights, and above them a few faint stars.

It was bitterly cold. Glazzard began to walk up and down, his eyes straying vaguely. He felt a miserable sinking of the heart, a weariness as if after great exertion.

An engine came rolling slowly along one of the lines; it stopped just beyond the station, and then backed into a siding. There followed the thud of carriage against carriage : a train was being made up, he went to watch the operation. The clang of metal, the hiss of steam, the moving about of men with lanterns held his attention for some time, and so completely that he forgot all else.

Somewhere far away sounded a long-drawn whistle, now faint, now clearer, a modulated wail broken at moments by a tremolo on one high note. It was like a voice lamenting to the dead of night. Glazzard could not endure it; he turned back into the station and tramped noisily on the stone platform.

Then the air was disturbed by the dull roar of an approaching train, and presently a long string of loaded waggons passed without pause. The engine-fire glowed upon heavy puffs of smoke, making them a rich crimson. A freight of iron bars clanged and clashed intolerably. When remoteness at length stilled them, there rose again the long wailing whistle ; it was answered by another like it from still greater distance.

Glazzard could stand and walk no longer. He threw

himself on a seat, crossed his arms, and remained
motionless until the ringing of a bell and a sudden
turning on of lights warned him that his train drew
near.

On the way to Polterham he dozed, and only a
fortunate awaking at the last moment saved him from
passing his station. It was now close upon two o'clock,
and he had a two-mile walk to Highmead. His
brother believed that he was spending the evening with
an acquaintance in a neighbouring town; he had said
he should probably be very late, and a side door was to
be left unbarred that he might admit himself with a
latch-key.

But for a policeman here and there, the streets were
desolate. Wherever the lamplight fell upon a wall or
hoarding, it illumined election placards, with the names
of the candidates in staring letters, and all the familiar
vulgarities of party advertising. " Welwyn-Baker and
the Honour of Old England!"—" Vote for Quarrier, the
Friend of the Working Man!"—" No Jingoism!"—
" The Constitution in Danger! Polterham to the
Rescue!" These trumpetings to the battle restored
Glazzard's self-satisfaction; he smiled once more, and
walked on with lighter step.

Just outside the town, in a dark narrow road, he was
startled by the sudden rising of a man's figure. A voice
exclaimed, in thick, ebrious tones: " Who are you
for? What's you're colour?"

" Who are *you* for?" called out Glazzard, in return,
as he walked past.

The politician—who had seemingly been asleep in the ditch—raised himself to his full height and waved his arms about.

" I'm a Radical!—Quarrier for ever!—Come on, one and all of you—I'm ready : fist or argument, it's all one to me!—You and your Welwyn-Baker—gurr! What's *he* ever done for the people?—that's what *I* want to know!—Ya-oo-oo-oo! Quarrier for ever!— Down with the aristercrats as wants to make war at the expense of the working man! What's England coming to?—tell me that! You've no principles, you haven't, you Tory skunks; you've not half a principle among you.—I'm a man of principle, I am, and I vote for national morality, I do!—You're running away, are you?—Ya-oo-oo!—stop and fight it out, if you're a man!—Down with' em, boys! Down with 'em!— Quarrier for ever! "

The shouts of hiccoughy enthusiasm came suddenly to an end, and Glazzard, looking back, saw that, in an attempt to run, the orator had measured his length in the mud.

By three o'clock he was seated in his bedroom, very tired but not much disposed to turn into bed. He had put a match to the fire, for his feet were numbed with cold, in spite of a long walk. Travelling-bags and trunks in readiness for removal told of his journey on the morrow. All his arrangements were made; the marriage ceremony was to take place at ten o'clock, and shortly after eleven he and his wife would leave for London on their way to the Continent.

Too soon, of course, to hear the result of Northway's visit to the Court-house. There would be the pleasure of imagining all that he left behind him, and in a day or two the papers would bring news. He had always sympathized with Guy Fawkes and his fellow-conspirators : how delightful to have fired the train, and then, at a safe distance, have awaited the stupendous explosion.

Poor little Lilian! That was the only troublesome thought. Yet was he in truth harming her? Quarrier would take her abroad, and, in a life of retirement, she would have far more happiness than was possible to her under the present circumstances. Northway would sue for a divorce, and thus leave her free to enter upon legitimate marriage. Perhaps he was doing her the greatest kindness in his power.

When his feet were thoroughly warm he went to bed, and slept well until the servant call him at half-past seven. It was a very bright morning; he drew up the blind and let a flood of sunshine into the room. Contrary to his expectations, no despondency weighed upon him ; by breakfast time he was more than usually cheerful.

"Ivy," he said to his niece, "I have promised to call at the Quarriers' on our way. We had better start at a quarter to nine ; that will give us five minutes with them."

Of his brother he took leave with much cordiality. William would probably not be much longer at High-mead, and might perhaps join his relatives abroad before the end of the year. In that case, Ivy would accompany him; and she thought with timid pleasure of thus renewing her friendship with Serena under brighter skies.

Two vehicles came up to the door—in one the luggage was despatched to the station; the other carried the bridegroom and his niece into Polterham.

Quarrier awaited them on his threshold, watch in hand, for he had no time to lose on the eve of nomination-day.

"Come in!" he cried, joyously. "Such weather as this is a good omen. How do you do, Miss Glazzard? Here is Lilian all excitement to see you; she would give her little finger to go to the wedding."

They entered the house.

"Decidedly," said Denzil, turning to Lilian, "his appearance is a compliment to Miss Mumbray. When did you see him looking so well and animated?"

Lilian coloured, and tried to speak in the same tone, but it was with difficulty that she used her voice at all. Glazzard's departure from Polterham promised her such relief of mind that she could not face him without a sense of shame.

"Telegraph the result, if it is favourable," said Glazzard. "You shall have an address in time for that."

"If it is favourable? Why, my dear fellow, we shall poll two to one, at the lowest computation! I've half lost my pleasure in the fight; I feel ashamed to hit out with all my strength when I make a speech—it's like pounding an invalid!"

"Then I congratulate you in advance, Mrs. Quarrier. If we are long away from England, the chances are I shall have to make my next call upon you in Downing Street!"

"Some day, old boy—some day!" assented Denzil, with a superb smile.

There followed much handshaking, and the visitors returned to their carriage. As it moved away, Glazzard put his head out of the window, waved his hand, and cried merrily:

"Quarrier for ever!"

XX.

In the interviews with Mr. Marks, Arthur Northway did not show at his best. Whoever that scheming personage might be, his knowledge and his air of condescension oppressed the needy young man, made him conscious of a hang-dog look, and a helpless promptitude to sell himself for a few coins. It was not thus that Northway, even after his unpleasant experiences, viewed himself in relation to the world. He had decidedly more intellect than is often found in commercial clerks—the class to which he belonged by birth and breeding—and in spite of checks he believed himself destined to no common career. Long musing had taught him the rashness of his youthful endeavours to live largely ; he was now aware that his talents must ally themselves with patience, with a careful scrutiny of possibilities.

Lying awake in the night, he thought with anything but satisfaction of the bargain to which he had pledged himself. To discover the woman who was by law his wife would undoubtedly be a good beginning now that he had every disposition to fix himself in a steady course, but he saw no advantage whatever in coming before a bench of magistrates and re-opening the story of his past. It would be pleasant to deal a blow at this man Quarrier ; but, if Marks had told him the truth,

Quarrier was in any case doomed to exposure. Was it not possible to act at once with prudence and with self-respect, to gain some solid benefit without practice of rascality? It involved breaking his word, but was he bound to keep faith with a man who proceeded on the assumption that he was ready for any base dealing? The money in his pocket he might find an opportunity of paying back. In this matter before him, he was undeniably an injured man. Lilian was treating him very badly indeed, very unfairly. If she chose to repudiate her marriage with him, it was her duty to afford him the chance of freeing himself from the legal bond. What moralist could defend her behaviour?

He worked himself into a mood of righteous indignation, of self-pity. No; the very least Lilian should have done, in uniting herself to another man, moreover a wealthy man, was to make some provision for her forsaken husband. That little income of hers should have been transferred to him. Her action was unexpected; he had thought her too timid, too religious, too soft-hearted, for anything of this kind. Since the disastrous wedding-day, she had, it was true, declined to hold communication with him; but he always looked forward to a meeting when he regained his freedom, and had faith in his personal influence. It was not solely for the sake of her money that he wooed and won her; other connections notwithstanding, he felt something like genuine tenderness for Lilian, and even now this sentiment was not extinct.

The morning only confirmed his reluctance to follow

Mr. Marks's directions. Practically, he lost nothing by taking his own course but a five-pound note. Let the electioneering agent attack Quarrier by some other means. For a few hours, at all events, the secret would remain unpublished, and in that interval the way might be opened for an honest and promising career.

He breakfasted substantially, and left by the train appointed. Arrived at Polterham, after a walk up and down the nearest streets and an inspection of the party placards, he asked his way to the shop of Mr. Ridge, bookseller. At once he was directed thither.

"So far so good," he said to himself. "It seems pretty certain that Marks has not misled me. Shall I go into this shop, and play the trick that was recommended? I think it is hardly worth while. Better to inquire for Quarrier's house, and have a look at it."

He did so, and—it may be mentioned—on his way passed the doors of the church in which at that moment Glazzard was being married. At about half-past ten he was in sight of the high wall surrounding Quarrier's garden; he approached the gate, and cautiously took a view of what was within, then walked to a little distance.

His wife had not done badly for a little country girl. Whilst *he* prowled about the streets with his burden of disgrace, his blank future, Lilian sat at her ease in a mansion—doubtless had her carriages, perhaps her liveried servants—associated with important people. After all, there was something to be said for that appeal to the magistrate, with its consequence of scandal, ruin, to these people who thought themselves so secure from him. He recovered his mood of last night.

"Boy!"—an errand-lad was just passing—"whereabouts is the Court-house?"

He was bidden take a turning within sight and go straight on for about half a mile.

"And I will, too!" he said in his mind. "She shall suffer for it!"

He turned away and walked for some twenty yards. Then once more the doubt occurred to him. He had better go to the bookseller's and make sure of Mrs. Quarrier's identity. Turning to take the opposite direction, he saw some one coming forth from the gates by which he had just stood—a lady—and it might be——?

Agitation shook him from head to foot. Was not that Lilian's figure, her walk? She was moving away from him; he must have a glimpse of her face. Drawing carefully nearer, on the side opposite to hers—carefully—fearfully—he at length saw her features, then fell back. Yes, it was Lilian. Much disguised in that handsome walking-costume, but beyond doubt Lilian. Still, as of old, she walked with bowed head, modestly. Who could imagine what she concealed?

His face was moist with perspiration. Following, he could not take his eyes off her. That lady was his wife. He had but to claim her, and all her sham dignity fell to nothing. But he could not command her obedience. He had no more power over her will than any stranger. She might bid him do his worst—

and so vanish with her chosen companion utterly beyond his reach.

Again he thought of the Court-house. For it was too certain that the sight of him would inspire her only with horror. Should he not hold her up to infamy? If *he* did not, another would; Marks was plainly to be trusted; this day was the last of Mrs. Quarrier's grandeur.

And to remember that was to pause. Could he afford to throw away a great opportunity for the sake of malicious satisfaction?

She walked on, and he followed, keeping thirty or forty paces behind her. He saw at length that she was not going into the town. The fine morning had perhaps invited her to a country walk. So much the better; he would wait till they were in a part where observation was less to be feared; then he would speak to her.

Lilian never looked back. It was indeed the bright sunshine that had suggested a walk out to Pear-tree Cottage, where before noon she would probably find Mrs. Wade among her books. She felt light of heart. Within this hour Glazzard would be gone from Polterham. Four days hence, Denzil would be a Member of Parliament. Had she no claim to happiness—she whose girlhood had suffered such monstrous wrong? Another reason there was for the impulse of joy that possessed her—a hope once already disappointed—a voice of nature bidding her regard this marriage as true and eternal, let the world say what it would.

She was within sight of the cottage, when Mrs.

Wade herself appeared, coming towards her. Lilian waved her hand, quickened her step. They met.

"I was going for a walk in the fields," said Mrs. Wade. "Shall we "——

Lilian had turned round, and at this moment her eyes fell upon Northway, who was quite near. A stifled cry escaped her, and she grasped at her friend's arm.

"What is it, dear?"

Mrs. Wade looked at her with alarm, imagining an attack of illness. But the next instant she was aware of the stranger, who stood in obvious embarrassment. She examined him keenly, then again turned her eyes upon Lilian.

"Is this some one you know?" she asked, in a low voice.

Lilian could not reply, and reply was needless. Northway, who had kept postponing the moment of address, now lost himself between conflicting motives. Seeing Lilian's consternation and her friend's surprise, he nervously raised his hat, drew a step or two nearer, tried to smile.

"Mrs. Wade," Lilian uttered, with desperate effort to seem self-possessed, "I wish to speak to this gentleman. Will you—do you mind?"

Her face was bloodless and wrung with anguish. The widow again looked at her, then said:

"I will go in again. If you wish to see me, I shall be there."

And at once she turned away.

Northway came forward, a strange light in his eyes.

" I'm the last person you thought of seeing, no doubt. But we must have a talk. I'm sorry that happened before some one else."

" Come with me out of the road. There's a field-path just here."

They crossed the stile, and walked a short distance in the direction of Bale Water. Then Lilian stopped.

" Who told you where to find me ? "

Already Northway had decided upon his course of action. Whilst he followed Lilian, watching her every movement, the old amorous feeling had gradually taken strong hold upon him. He no longer thought of revenge. His one desire was to claim this beautiful girl as his wife. In doing so, it seemed to him, he took an unassailable position, put himself altogether in the right. Marks's plot did not concern him ; he threw it aside, and followed the guidance of his own discretion.

"I have found you," he said, fingering his throat nervously, " by mere chance. I came here in search of employment—something in a newspaper. And I happened to see you in the streets. I asked who you were. Then, this morning, I watched you and followed you."

" What do you want ? "

" That's a strange question, I think."

" You know there can't be anything between us."

"I don't see that."

He breathed hard ; his eyes never moved from her

face. Lilian, nerved by despair, spoke in almost a
steady voice; but the landscape around her was veiled
in mist; she saw only the visage which her memory had
identified with repugnance and dread.

"If you want my money," she said, "you can have
it—you shall have it at once. I give you it all."

"No, I don't ask for your money," Northway
answered, with resentment. "Here's some one coming;
let us walk out into the field."

Lilian followed the direction of his look, and saw a
man whom she did not recognize. She left the path
and moved whither her companion was leading, over
the stubby grass; it was wet, but for this she had no
thought.

"How long have you been living in this way?" he
asked, turning to her again.

"You have no right to question me."

"What!—no right? Then who *has* a right I should
like to know?"

He did not speak harshly; his look expressed sincere
astonishment.

"I don't acknowledge," said Lilian, with quivering
voice, "that that ceremony made me your wife."

"What do you mean? It was a legal marriage.
Who has said anything against it?"

"You know very well that you did me a great wrong.
The marriage was nothing but a form of words."

"On whose part? Certainly not on mine. I meant
everything I said and promised. It's true I hadn't
been living in the right way; but that was all done

with. If nothing had happened, I should have begun a respectable life. I had made up my mind to do so. I shouldn't have deceived you in anything."

"Whether that's true or not, I don't know. I *was* deceived, and cruelly. You did me an injury you could never have made good."

Northway drew in his cheeks, and stared at her persistently. He had begun to examine the details of her costume—her pretty hat, her gloves, the fur about her neck. In face she was not greatly changed from what he had known, but her voice and accent were new to him—more refined, more mature, and he could not yet overcome the sense of strangeness. He felt as though he were behaving with audacity; it was necessary to remind himself again and again that this was no other than Lilian Allen—nay, Lilian Northway; whose hand he had held, whose lips he had kissed.

A thrill went through him.

"But you are my wife!" he exclaimed, earnestly. "What right have you to call yourself Mrs. Quarrier? Have you pretended to marry that man?"

Lilian's eyes fell; she made no answer.

"You must tell me—or I shall have no choice but to go and ask him. And if you have committed bigamy"——

"There has been no marriage," she hastened to say. "I have done what I thought right."

"Right? I don't know how you can call that right. I suppose you were persuaded into it. Does he know all the truth?"

She was racked with doubt as to what she should disclose. Her thoughts would not be controlled, and whatever words she uttered seemed to come from her lips of their own accord.

" What do you expect of me ? " she cried, in a voice of utmost distress. " I have been living like this for more than two years. Right or wrong, it can't be changed—it can't be undone. You know that. It was natural you should wish to speak to me ; but why do you pretend to think that we can be anything to each other ? You have a right to my money—it shall be yours at once."

He stamped, and his eyes shot anger.

" What do you take me for ? Do you suppose I shall consent to give you up for money ? Tell me what I have asked. Does that man know your history ? "

" Of course he knows it—everything."

" And he thinks I shall never succeed in finding you out ! Well, he is mistaken, you see—things of this kind are always found out, as you and he might have known. You can't do wrong and live all your life as if you were innocent."

The admonition came rather inappropriately from him, but it shook Lilian in spite of her better sense.

" It can't be changed," she exclaimed. " It can't be undone."

" That's all nonsense ! "

" I will die rather than leave him ! "

Hot jealousy began to rage in him. He was not a man of vehement passions, but penal servitude had wrought the natural effect upon his appetites. The egotism of a conceited disposition tended to the same result. He swore within himself a fierce oath that, come what might, this woman should be his. She contrasted him with her wealthy lover, despised him; but right and authority were on his side.

"Leave him you must—and shall: so there's plain speaking! You will never go into that house again."

Lilian turned as if to flee from him. No one was within sight; and how could she have appealed to any one for help? In the distance she saw the roof of Mrs. Wade's cottage; it allayed her despair for the moment. There, at all events, was a friend who would intervene for her, a strong and noble-minded woman, capable of offering the best counsel, of acting with decision. Vain now to think of hiding her secret from that friend— and who could be more safely trusted with it?

But she still had the resource of entreaty.

"You talk of right and wrong—is it right to be merciless? What can I ever be to you? Would you take me away by force, and compel me to live with you? I have told you I would die rather. When you think of everything, have you no pity for me? Whatever you intended, wasn't our marriage a terrible injustice to me? Oughtn't you to give a thought to that?"

"You are living an immoral life," replied Northway, with tremulous emphasis. "I could hold you up to shame. No, I don't ask you to come and live with me at once; I don't expect that. But you must leave that man, and live a respectable life, and—then in time

I shall forgive you, instead of disgracing you in the divorce court. I ask only what is right. You used to be religious "——

"Oh, how can you talk to me like that! If you really think me wicked and disgraced, leave me to my own conscience! Have *you* no sins that ask for forgiveness?"

"It isn't for you to speak of them," he retorted, with imbecile circling. "All I know is that you are my wife by law, and it is my duty to save you from this position. I sha'n't let you go back. If you resist my authority, I shall explain everything to any one who asks, that's all.—Who was that lady you were talking to?"

"She lives in the little house over there. I must go and speak to her."

"Does she know?"

"No."

"What have you to say to her, then?"

They looked into each other's eyes for a moment. Northway was gauging the strength of her character, and he half believed that by an exertion of all his energy he might overcome her, lead her away at once. He remembered that before the close of this day Quarrier's secret would be universally known, and when that had come to pass, he would have no hold upon either the man or the woman. They would simply turn their backs upon him, and go beyond his reach.

He laid his hand upon her, and the touch, the look in his eyes, drove Lilian to the last refuge.

" You must go with me, then, to Mr. Quarrier," she said, firmly. " You have no power to stop me. I shall go home, and you must follow me, if you choose."

"No, you will go with *me!* Do you hear? I command you to come with me!"

It was his best imitation of resistless authority, and he saw, even in speaking, that he had miscalculated. Lilian drew back a step and looked at him with defiance.

" Command me, you cannot. I am as free from your control as any stranger."

" Try, and see. If you attempt to go back into the town, I shall hold you by force, and the consequences will be worse to you than to me. Do as you please."

Again her eyes turned to the distant roof of Peartree Cottage. She, too, had estimated her strength and his. She knew by instinct what his face meant—the swollen, trembling lips, the hot eyes; and understood that he was capable of any baseness. To attempt to reach her home would be an abandonment of all hope, the ruin of Denzil. A means of escape from worst extremity, undiscoverable by her whirling brain, might suggest itself to such a mind as Mrs. Wade's. If only she could communicate with the cottage!

"Then I shall go to my friend here," she said, pointing.

He hesitated.

" Who is she ? "

" A lady who lives quite alone."

" What's the good of your going there ? "

She had recourse to artifice, and acted weakness much better than he had simulated strength.

" I *must* have some one's advice ! I must know how others regard your claim."

He saw no possibility of restraining her, and it might befall that this lady, intentionally or not, would use her influence on his side. Those last words signified a doubt in Lilian's mind. Was it not pretty certain that any respectable woman, on learning how matters stood, must exclaim against that pretended marriage? Northway's experience lay solely among the representatives of English morality, and the frankly vicious; he could hardly imagine a " lady " whose view of the point at issue would admit pleas on Lilian's behalf.

" If you go there," he said, " I must be with you."

Lilian made no answer, but moved away. They passed into the road, turned towards the cottage. On reaching the gate, Lilian saw Mrs. Wade standing just before her.

" I must speak to you ! " she said, holding out her hands impulsively.

Mrs. Wade looked from her to the man in the background, who again had awkwardly raised his hat—a cheap but new cylinder, which, together with his slop-made coat and trousers, classed him among uncertain specimens of humanity.

" Will you let him come in ? " Lilian whispered, a sob at length breaking her voice.

The widow was perfectly self-possessed. Her eyes gleamed very brightly and glanced hither and thither with the keenest scrutiny. She held Lilian's hand, answering in a low voice :

"Trust me, dear! I'm so glad you have come. What is his name?"

"Mr. Northway."

Mrs. Wade addressed him, and invited him to enter; but Northway, having ascertained that there was no escape from the cottage which he could not watch, drew back.

"Thank you," he said; "I had rather wait out here. If that lady wants me, I shall be within reach."

Mrs. Wade nodded, and drew her friend in. Lilian of a sudden lost her physical strength; she had to be supported, almost carried, into the sitting-room. The words of kindness with which Mrs. Wade sought to recover her had a natural enough effect; they invited an hysterical outbreak, and for several minutes the sufferer wailed helplessly. In the meantime she was disembarrassed of her out-door clothing. A stimulant at length so far restored her that she could speak connectedly.

"I don't know what you will think of me.—I am obliged to tell you something I hoped never to speak of. Denzil ought to know first what has happened; but I can't go to him.—I must tell you, and trust your friendship. Perhaps you can help me; you will—I know you will if you can."

"Anything in my power," replied the listener, soothingly. "Whatever you tell me is perfectly safe. I think you know me well enough, Lily."

Then Lilian began, and told her story from first to last.

XXI.

TOLD it rapidly, now and then confusedly, but with
omission of nothing essential. So often she had
reviewed her life, at successive stages of culture and
self-knowledge. Every step had been debated in
heart and conscience. She had so much to say, yet
might not linger in the narration, and feared to seem
eager in the excuse of what she had done. To
speak of these things to one of her own sex was in
itself a great relief, yet from time to time the
recollection that she was betraying Denzil's secret
struck her with cold terror. Was not this necessity
a result of her weakness? A stronger woman would
perhaps have faced the situation in some other
way.

Mrs. Wade listened intently, and the story seemed
to move her in no slight degree. Lilian, anxiously
watching her face, found it difficult to interpret
the look of suppressed excitement. Censure she
could not read there; pain, if ever visible, merely
flitted over brow and lips; at moments she half
believed that her hearer was exulting in this defiance
of accepted morality—what else could be the significance of that flash in the eyes; that quiver of the
nostrils—all but a triumphant smile? They sat close
to each other, Lilian in the low basket-chair, the

widow on a higher seat, and when the story came to an end, their hands met.

"How can I save Denzil?" was Lilian's last word. "Anything—any sacrifice! If this becomes known, his whole life is ruined!"

Mrs. Wade pressed the soft, cold fingers, and kept a thoughtful silence.

"It's a strange coincidence," she said at length, "very strange that this should happen on the eve of the election."

"The secret *must* be kept until"——

Lilian's voice failed. She looked anxiously at her friend, and added:

"What would be the result if it were known afterwards—when Denzil is elected?"

"It's hard to say. But tell me, Lily: is there *no* one who has been admitted to your confidence?"

What purpose would be served by keeping back the name? Lilian's eyes fell as she answered.

"Mr. Glazzard knows."

"Mr. Eustace Glazzard?"

Lilian explained how and when it had become necessary to make him a sharer in the secret.

"Do you believe," Mrs. Wade asked, "that Northway really discovered you by chance?"

"I don't know. He says so. I can only feel absolutely sure that Mr. Glazzard has nothing to do with it."

Mrs. Wade mused doubtfully.

"Absolutely sure?"

"Oh, how is it possible? If you knew him as well as we do!—Impossible!—He came to see us this very morning, on his way to be married, and laughed and talked!"

"You are right, no doubt," returned the other, with quiet reassurance. "If it wasn't chance, some obscure agency has been at work. You must remember, Lily, that only by a miracle could you have lived on in security."

"I have sometimes felt that," whispered the sufferer, her head falling.

"And it almost seems," went on Mrs. Wade, "as if Northway really had no intention of using his power to extort money. To be sure, your own income is not to be despised by a man in his position; but most rascals would have gone to Mr. Quarrier.—He is still in love with you, I suppose."

The last words were murmured in a tone which caused the hearer to look up uneasily. Mrs. Wade at once averted her face, which was curiously hard and expressionless.

"What do you think?" she said a moment after. "Would it be any use if I had a talk with him?"

"Will you?" asked Lilian, eagerly. "You may perhaps influence him. You can speak so well—so persuasively. I don't think he is utterly depraved. As you say, he would have gone first to Denzil. Perhaps he can be moved to have pity on me."

"Perhaps—but I have more faith in an appeal to his interests."

"It would be dreadful if Denzil had to live henceforth at his mercy."

"It would. But it's a matter of—of life and death."

Mrs. Wade's voice sank on those words, shaking just a little. She put her face nearer to Lilian's, but without looking at her.

"Suppose no argument will prevail with him, dear?" she continued in that low, tremulous tone. "Suppose he persists in claiming you?"

The voice had a strange effect upon Lilian's nerves. She shook with agitation, and drew away a little.

"He cannot! He has no power to take me! At the worst, we can only be driven back into solitude."

"True, dear; but it would not be the same kind of solitude as before. Think of the huge scandal, the utter ruin of brilliant prospects."

Lilian lay back and moaned in anguish. Her eyes were closed, and in that moment Mrs. Wade gazed at her for a moment only; then the widow rose from her chair, and spoke in a voice of encouragement.

"I will see him, Lily. You remain here; I'll call him into the dining-room."

She stepped to the window, and saw that Northway was standing only at a little distance. After meditating for a minute or two, she left the room very quietly, crossed the passage, and entered the room opposite, where she generally took her meals. Here again she went to the window, and again had a good view of the man on guard. A smile rose to her face.

Then she went out and signalled to Northway, who approached in an embarrassed way, doing his best to hold his head up and look dignified. Mrs. Wade regarded him with contemptuous amusement, but was careful to show nothing of this; her face and tone as she greeted him expressed more than civility—all but deference.

" Will you do me the kindness to enter for a few minutes, Mr. Northway ? "

He doffed his hat, smiled sourly, and followed her into the little dining-room. But as she was closing the door, he interfered.

" Excuse me—I don't want that lady to go away until I have seen her again."

Mrs. Wade none the less closed the door, holding herself with imperturbable politeness.

" She is resting in the next room. I give you my word, Mr. Northway, that you will find her there when our conversation is over."

He looked about him with sullen uneasiness, but could not resist this lady's manner.

" Pray sit down. Quite a spring day, isn't it ? "

Her tone was melancholy, tempered with the consideration of a hostess. Northway seated himself much as if he were in church. He tried to examine Mrs. Wade's face, but could not meet her look. She, in the meantime, had got the young man's visage by heart, had studied the meaning of every lineament—narrow eyes, sunken cheeks, forehead indicative of conceited intelligence, lips as clearly expressive of another characteristic.

Here, at all events, was a creature she could manage—
an instrument—though to what purpose she was not yet
perfectly clear.

"Mr. Northway, I have been listening to a sad, sad
story."

"Yes, it is sad," he muttered, feeling his inferiority to
this soft-spoken woman, and moving his legs awkwardly.

"I must mention to you that my name is Mrs. Wade.
I have known Lilian since she came to live at Polterham—only since then. That's a very short time ago,
but we have seen a good deal of each other, and have
become intimate friends. I need not tell you that I
never had the faintest suspicion of what I have just
learnt."

This was said certainly not in a voice of indignation
but with a sadness which implied anything but approval.
Northway, after trying to hold his hat in a becoming
way, placed it on the floor, clicking with his tongue the
while and betraying much nervousness.

"You are of course aware," pursued the lady, "that
Mr. Denzil Quarrier is Liberal candidate for this
borough?"

"Yes, I know."

"Until to-day, he had every prospect of being elected.
It is a shocking thing—I hardly know how to express
myself about it."

"If this gets known," said Northway, "I suppose he
has no chance?"

"How would it be possible to vote for a man who has

outraged the law on which all social life is based? He would retire immediately—no doubt."

Regarding this event as certain in any case, the listener merely nodded.

"That, I dare say, doesn't interest you?"

"I take no part in politics."

"And it is quite a matter of indifference to you whether Mr. Quarrier's career is ruined or not?"

"I don't see why I should think much about a man who has injured me as he has."

"No," conceded Mrs. Wade, sadly. "I understand that you have nothing whatever in view but recovering your wife?"

"That's all I want."

"And yet, Mr. Northway, I'm sure you see how very difficult it will be for you to gain this end."

She leaned towards him sympathetically. Northway shuffled, sucked in his cheeks, and spoke in as civil a tone as he could command.

"There are difficulties, I know. I don't ask her to come at once and live with me. I couldn't expect that. But I am determined she sha'n't go back to Mr. Quarrier. I have a right to forbid it."

"Indeed—abstractly speaking—I think you have," murmured Mrs. Wade, with a glance towards the door. "But I grieve to tell you that there seems to me no possibility of preventing her return."

"I shall have to use what means I can. You say Mr. Quarrier wouldn't care to have this made public just now."

He knew (or imagined) that the threat was idle, but it seemed to him that Mrs. Wade, already favourably disposed, might be induced to counsel Lilian for the avoidance of a scandal at this moment.

"Mr. Northway," replied the widow, "I almost think that he would care less for such a disclosure *before* this election than *after* it."

He met her eyes, and tried to understand her. But whatever she meant, it could be of no importance to him. Quarrier was doomed by the Tory agent; on this knowledge he congratulated himself, in spite of the fact that another state of things would have been more to his interest.

" I have really nothing to do with that," he replied. "My wife is living a life of wickedness—and she shall be saved from it at once."

Mrs. Wade had much difficulty in keeping her countenance. She looked down, and drew a deep sigh.

"That is only too true. But I fear—indeed I fear —that you won't succeed in parting them. There is a reason—I cannot mention it."

Northway was puzzled for a moment, then his face darkened; he seemed to understand.

"I do so wish," pursued Mrs. Wade, with a smile of sympathy, "that I could be of some use in this sad affair. My advice—I am afraid you will be very unwilling to listen to it."

She paused, looking at him wistfully.

" What would it be ? " he asked.

" I feel so strongly—just as you do—that it is dreadful to have to countenance such a state of things ; but I am convinced that it would be very, very *unwise* if you went *at once* to extremities, Mr. Northway. I am a woman of the world ; I have seen a good deal of life ; if you allowed yourself to be guided by me, you would not regret it."

" You want to save your friends from the results of their behaviour," he replied, uneasily.

" I assure you, it's not so much that—no, I have *your* interests in view quite as much as theirs. Now, seeing that Lilian cannot possibly take her place as your wife in fact, and that it is practically impossible to part her from Mr. Quarrier, wouldn't it be well to ask yourself what is the most prudent course that circumstances allow ? "

" If it comes to that, I can always get a divorce."

Mrs. Wade reflected, but with no sign of satisfaction.

" Yes, that is open to you. You would then, of course, be enabled to marry again.—May I ask if you are quite at ease with regard to your prospects in life ? "

The tone was so delicately impertinent that Northway missed its significance.

" I haven't quite decided upon anything yet."

" Judging from your conversation, I should say that you will yet find a place among active and successful men. But the beginning is everything. If I could be of any assistance to you—I would put it to you frankly, Mr. Northway : is it worth while sacrificing very solid possibilities to your—your affection for a woman who has deserted you?"

He shuffled on the chair, clicked with his tongue, and looked about him undecidedly.

"I am not to be bribed to act against my conscience," he said at length.

Mrs. Wade heard this with pleasure. The blunt, half-blustering declaration assured her that Northway's " conscience " was on the point of surrender.

"Now, let me tell you what I should like to do," she continued, bending towards him. " Will you allow me to go at once and see Mr. Quarrier?"

"And tell him ? "

" Yes, let him know what has happened. I quite understand," she added, caressingly, " how very painful it would be for you to go directly to him. Will you allow me to be your intermediary ? That you and he must meet is quite certain ; may I smooth away the worst difficulties? I could explain to him your character, your natural delicacy, your conscientiousness. I could make him understand that he has to meet a person quite on his own level—an educated man of honourable feeling. After that, an interview between you would be comparatively easy. I should be really grateful to you if you would allow me to do you this service."

Northway was like clay in her hands. Every word had precisely the effect on which she calculated. His forehead unwrinkled itself, his lips hung loose like the mouth of a dog that is fondled, he tried not to smile

Though he thought himself as far as ever from renouncing Lilian, he began to like the idea of facing Quarrier—of exhibiting his natural delicacy, conscientiousness, and so on. Something was in the background, but of that he took no deliberate account.

A few minutes more, and Mrs. Wade had him entirely at her disposal. It was arranged that, whilst she went into the town to discover Quarrier, Northway should remain on guard, either in or about the cottage. Luncheon would be provided for him. He promised not to molest Lilian, on condition that she made no attempt to escape.

"She will stay where she is," Mrs. Wade assured him. "Your natural delicacy will, I am sure, prevent you from seeking to hold conversation with her. She is very weak, poor thing! I do hope no serious illness will follow on this shock."

Thereupon she returned to the sitting-room, where Lilian stood in an anguish of impatience.

"I think I shall manage it, dear," she whispered, in a tone of affectionate encouragement. "He has consented to see Mr. Quarrier, provided I go first and break the news."

"You, Mrs. Wade? You are going to see Denzil?"

"Dearest girl, leave it all in my hands. You cannot think what difficulties I have overcome. If I am allowed to act freely, I shall save you and him."

She explained the articles of truce, Lilian listening with distressful hope.

"And I don't think he will interfere with you meanwhile. But you can keep the door locked, you know. Annie shall bring you something to eat; I will tell her to give him *his* luncheon first, and then to come very quietly with yours. It is half-past twelve. I can hardly be back in less than an hour and a half. No doubt, Mr. Quarrier will come with me."

"How good you are, dear Mrs. Wade! Oh, if you can save him!"

"Trust me, and try to sit quietly. Now, I will be off at once."

She pressed the hand that was held to her, nodded, and left the room.

XXII.

It was striking one when Mrs. Wade came in sight of the Quarriers' house. At this hour Quarrier was expected at home for luncheon. He arrived whilst the visitor still waited for an answer to her ring at the door.

"But haven't you seen Lily? She told me"——

"Yes, I have seen her. She is at the cottage."

A peculiarity in her tone arrested his attention, and the look of joyous excitement which had been fixed upon his face these last few days changed to anxious inquiry.

"What's the matter?"

"She is quite well—don't imagine accidents. But I must speak to you in private."

The door had opened. Denzil led straightway to the library, where he flung aside hat and overcoat.

"What is it, Mrs. Wade?"

She stood close before him, her eyes on his. The rapid walk had brought colour to her cheek, and perhaps to the same cause was attributable her quickened breathing.

"Lily has been discovered by an enemy of hers and yours. A man named Northway."

"Damnation!"

He felt far too strongly to moderate his utterance

out of regard for the listener. His features were distorted; he stared wrathfully.

"And you have left her with him? Where is she?"

"She is quite safe in my sitting-room—the key turned to protect her. He, too, is in the house, in another room. I have gained time; I "——

He could not listen.

"How did it happen?—You had no right to leave her alone with him!—How has he found her?"

"Please don't eat me up, Mr. Quarrier! I have been doing my very best for you."

And she told him the story of the morning as briefly as possible. Her endeavour to keep a tone of perfect equanimity failed in the course of the narrative; once or twice there was a catching in her breath, and, as if annoyed with herself, she made an impatient gesture.

"And this fellow," cried Quarrier, when she ceased, "imagines that I am at his mercy! Let him do what he likes—let him go into the market-place and shout his news!—We'll go back at once."

"You are prepared, then, to have this known all over Polterham?" Mrs. Wade asked, looking steadily at him.

"I don't care a jot! Let the election go to the devil! Do you think I will submit Lily to a day of such torture? This very evening we go to London. How does she bear it?"

"Very well indeed."

"Like a brave, good girl! Do you think I would weigh the chance of election against her misery?"

"It seems to me," was the cold answer, "that you have done so already."

"Has she complained to you?"

"Oh, no! But I understand now what always puzzled me. I understand her "——

She checked herself, and turned quietly from him. Strategy must always be liable to slips from one cause or another, and Mrs. Wade's prudence had, for the moment, yielded to her impulses.

"You think she has all along been unhappy?"

"No, nothing of the kind. But when we have been speaking of the position of women—that kind of thing—I have noticed something strange—an anxiety. I was only going to say that, after having succeeded thus far, it seems a pity to lose everything when a little prudence "——

She waved her hand.

"Do you believe," Denzil asked, "that his story of finding her by mere chance is true?"

"Lilian tells me that only your most intimate friend shared the secret."

"Glazzard? Of course *he* has nothing to do with it. But some one else may have"——

He walked apart, brooding. Mrs. Wade seated herself, and became thoughtful.

"What sort of a fellow is this?" Quarrier asked, of a sudden.

"It depends who is dealing with him," she answered, meeting his look with eyes full of sympathetic expression. "I read him at once, and managed him. He is too weak for serious villainy. He doesn't seem to have thought of extorting money from you. Lilian was his only object. He would have taken her away by force."

" Come—we mustn't lose time."

" Mr. Quarrier, do be calm, and let us talk before we go. She is quite safe. And as for Northway, I am perfectly sure that you can keep him silent.

" You think it possible ? "

" If you will consent to follow in the path I have prepared. I have taken no small trouble."

She looked up at him and smiled.

" You have behaved like a true friend, Mrs. Wade— it is no more than I should have expected of you. But what have you planned ? Think how this secret has already spread—what hope is there of finally hushing it up? Glazzard and you would never breathe a syllable ; but how, short of manslaughter, could I assure the silence of a blackguard like this Northway ? If I let him blackmail me, I am done for : I should be like the fools in plays and novels, throwing half my possessions away, and all in vain."

" Pray remember," urged the other, " that this Northway is by no means the rascal of melodrama. He has just enough brains to make him conceited, and is at the disposal of any one who plays upon his conceit. With much trouble I induced him to regard you as a source of profit." She broke off and seemed to falter. " I think you won't find fault with me, Mr. Quarrier, for trying to do this ? "

" You did it in the friendliest spirit."

" And not indiscreetly, I hope." She looked at him for a moment, and continued : " He is bribable, but you must go to work carefully. For instance, I think if you offered to give him a good start in a commercial career— by your personal recommendation, I mean—that would have more effect than an offer of money. And then, again, in this way you guard yourself against the perils of which you were speaking. Place him well, so that he considers himself a respectable, responsible man, and for his own sake he won't torment you. Couldn't you send him to some one over in Sweden—some house of business ? "

Denzil pondered, with knitted brows.

" I have no faith in it ! " he exclaimed at length, beginning to walk about. " Come—I want to get to Lilian ; she must be in misery. I will order the carriage ; it will be needed to bring her back."

He rang the bell violently ; a servant appeared, and hurried away to do his bidding.

" Mrs. Wade," he said, as soon as the door had closed, " shouldn't I do better to throw up the game ? I hate these underhand affairs ! I don't think I could go through with the thing—I don't, indeed ! Speak your whole mind. I am not a slave of ambition—at bottom I care precious little for going into Parliament. I enjoyed the excitement of it—I believe I have a knack of making speeches; but what does it all amount to ? Tell me your true thought." He drew near to her. " Shall I throw it up and go abroad with my wife?—my *wife*! that is her true name!"

He looked a fine fellow as he spoke this; better than he had looked on the platform. Mrs. Wade gazed at him fixedly, as if she could not take away her eyes. She trembled, and her forehead was wrung with pain.

"Do this," she replied, eagerly, "if you wish to make Lilian unhappy for the rest of her life."

"What do you mean?"

"It seems I understand her better than you do—perhaps because I am a woman. She dreads nothing so much as the thought that *she* has been the ruin of your prospects. You have taught her to believe that you are made for politics; you can never undo that. The excitement of this election had fixed the belief in her for ever. For *her* sake, you are bound to make every attempt to choke this scandal! Be weak—give in—and (she is weak too) it's all over with her happiness. Her life would be nothing but self-reproach."

"No, no, no! For a short time, perhaps, but security would be the best thing of all for her."

"Try, then—try, and see the result!"

She spoke with suppressed passion, her voice shaking. Denzil turned away, struggled with his thoughts, again faced her. Mrs. Wade read his features as if her life depended on what he would resolve. Seeing him in a misery of indecision, she repeated, at greater length and more earnestly still, her cogent reasonings. Quarrier argued in reply, and they were still thus engaged when it was announced that the carriage waited.

"Let us go!" He threw his overcoat on to his shoulders.

Mrs. Wade caught his hand.

"Are you bent on doing the hopeless thing?"

"Let us talk in the carriage. I can't wait any longer."

But in the carriage both kept silence. Mrs. Wade, exhausted by stress of emotion, by the efforts of her scheming brain, lay back as if she had abandoned the contest; Denzil, his face working ceaselessly, stared through the windows. When they were nearing their destination, the widow leaned towards him.

"I have done my best for you. I have nothing so much at heart as your welfare—and Lilian's."

He pressed her hand, too much disturbed to think of the singular way in which she spoke. Then the vehicle stopped. Denzil assisted his companion to alight, and, whilst she was opening the house-door, bade the coachman go up and down till he was summoned. Then he sprang after Mrs. Wade, learnt from her where Lilian was, and at once tried to enter the sitting-room. The door was locked.

"Lily!" he called, in a low voice. "Open, dear! It is I!"

The key turned rapidly. He rushed in, and clasped Lilian in his arms. She could not utter a word, but clung to him sobbing and wailing.

"Don't!—don't, dear girlie! Try to be quiet—try to command yourself."

"Can you do anything?" she uttered at length. "Is there any hope?"

"What do you wish, Lily, dearest? What shall I do?"

The common sense of manliness urged him to put no such questions, to carry her away without a word, save of tender devotion, to escape with her into quietness, and let all else go as it would. But Mrs. Wade's warning had impressed him deeply. It went with his secret inclination; for, at this stage of the combat, to lose all his aims would be a bitter disappointment. He thought of the lifelong ostracism, and feared it in a vague way.

"Mrs. Wade thinks he can be persuaded to leave us alone," Lilian replied, hurriedly, using simple words which made her seem childlike, though at the same moment she was nerving herself to heroic effort. "See him, and do what you can, Denzil. I did my utmost, dear. Oh, this cruel chance that brought him here!"

She would have given years of her life to say "Sacrifice all, and let us go!" He seemed even to invite her to say it, but she strove with herself. Sacrifice of his career meant sacrifice of the whole man. Not in *her* eyes, oh no !—but she had studied him so well, and knew that he could no longer be content in obscurity. She choked her very soul's desire.

"Shall I try to buy him off, Lily?"

"Do try, darling!"

"But can you face what will come afterwards—the constant risks?"

"Anything rather than you shall be ruined!"

A syllable would have broken down her heroism. It was on his tongue. He had but to say "Ruin!— what do I care for ruin in *that* sense?" and she would have cried with delight. But he kept it back.

"Sit down and wait for me. I will go and see him."

One more embrace, and he left her. Mrs. Wade was talking with Northway in the dining-room, talking hurriedly and earnestly. She heard Quarrier's step and came to the door.

"In here?" Denzil asked.

She nodded and came out. Then the door closed behind him.

Northway stood near the window. He had eaten —luncheon was still on the table—and had been smoking to calm his nerves, but at the sight of Quarrier he became agitated. They inspected each other. Denzil's impulse was to annihilate his contemptible enemy with fierceness of look and word; and in Northway jealousy fought so strongly with prudence that a word of anger would have driven him to revengeful determination. But a few moments of silence averted this danger. Quarrier said to himself that there was no use in half measures. He had promised Lilian to do his best, and his own desire pointed to the same end. Swallowing his gall, he spoke quietly.

"Mr. Northway, we can't talk as if we were

friends; but I must remember that you have never intentionally done me any wrong—that it is *I* who am immediately to blame for this state of things. I hope you will talk it over with me "——

His voice failed, but the first step had been taken. He sat down, motioning the other to a chair.

"I can't allow my wife to live any longer in this way," began the adversary, with blundering attempt at dignified speech.

"My wife" was like a blow to Denzil; he flushed, started, yet controlled himself. What Mrs. Wade had told him of Northway's characteristics came into his mind, and he saw that this address might be mere bluster.

"It's very natural for you to speak in that way; but there is no undoing what has happened. I must say that at once, and as firmly as possible. We may talk of how I can compensate you for—for the injury; but of nothing else."

He ended with much mental objurgation, which swelled his throat.

"You can't compensate a man," returned Northway, "for an injury of this kind."

"Strictly speaking, no. But as it can't be helped— as I wronged you without knowing you—I think I may reasonably offer to do you whatever good turn is in my power. Please to tell me one thing. Have you spoken to any one except Mrs. Wade of what you have discovered?"

"No—to no one."

It might be true or not. Denzil could only hope it was, and proceed on that assumption.

"I am sure I may trust your word," he said, beginning to use diplomacy, with the immediate result that Northway's look encouraged him. "Now, please tell me another thing, as frankly. Can I, as a man of some means and influence, offer you any acceptable service?"

There was silence. Northway could not shape a reply.

"You have been in commerce, I think?" proceeded the other. "Should you care to take a place in some good house of business on the Continent, or elsewhere abroad? I think it's in my power to open a way for you such as you would not easily make by your own exertions."

The listener was suffering. But for one thing, this offer would have tempted him strongly; but that one thing made it idle for him to think of what was proposed. To-day or to-morrow Quarrier would be exposed by his plotting enemies, and thereupon any bargain made with reference to the future must collapse. If he were to profit by Quarrier at all, it must needs be in the shape of a payment which could not be recovered.

"I don't care to go into business again," he said, with a mingling of real annoyance and affected superiority. "I have other views."

"Can I help to advance them?" asked Denzil, sickening under the necessity of speaking fair.

The dialogue lasted for half an hour more. Jealousy notwithstanding, Northway had made up his mind to gain what was to be gained. Lilian was beyond his reach; it would be foolish to go back to his poverty and cloudy, outlook when solid assistance was held out to him. With much posturing and circumlocution, he came at length to the avowal that a sum of ready money would not be refused.

" Are you wise in preferring this to the other kind of help ? " Denzil urged.

" I have my own views."

Quarrier ridiculed himself for what he was doing. How could he pretend to trust such a fellow ? Again, there was only the hope that a bribe might be efficacious.

" I will give you five hundred pounds," he said, " on condition that you leave England at once."

The bid was too low. Northway would be satisfied with twice as much, provided it were paid forthwith. Pondering, Quarrier decided that he was about to commit an absurdity. A thousand pounds—and how much more in future ? He looked Northway in the eyes.

" Here is my last word. I don't greatly care whether this secret comes out or not. If I am to be at your mercy henceforth, I had rather bid you do what you like ; it really doesn't matter much to me. I will give you five hundred pounds at once—a cheque on a Polterham banker ; moreover, if my secret is kept, I will do you the other service I offered. But that's all I have to say. If it doesn't suit you, you must do what you please."

His boldness was successful. Northway could gain nothing by betrayal of the secret—which he believed to be no secret at all. With show of indifference, he accepted what was obtainable.

" Then come and drive with me into the town," said Denzil.

Thereupon he stepped out and entered the sitting-room, where the two women were together. They looked eager inquiry, and he smiled.

" Managed, I think. He goes with me. Lily, I'll be back for you as soon as possible."

A moment, and they watched the carriage roll away.

XXIII.

THIS evening there was a great dinner-party at Colonel Catesby's; a political dinner. Lilian had carefully prepared for the occasion. In Quarrier's opinion, she would far outshine her previous appearances; she was to wear certain jewels which he had purchased on a recent visit to town—at an outlay of which he preferred to say nothing definite. " They are the kind of thing," he remarked, with a significant smile, "that can be passed on to one's children."

But would it be possible for her to keep the engagement ? Through the afternoon she lay in her bedroom with drawn blinds, endeavouring to sleep. Once or twice Denzil entered, very softly, and stood by her for a moment; she looked at him and smiled, but did not speak. At half-past six he brought her tea with his own hand. Declaring herself quite recovered, she rose.

"This is no such important affair that you must go at all costs," he said, regarding her anxiously. " Say you feel unable, and I'll send a message at once."

Already she had assured him that it would disappoint her greatly not to go. Lilian meant, of course, that she could not bear to disappoint *him*, and to make confusion in their hostess's arrangements. There was a weight upon her heart which made it a great effort even to

move, to speak; but she hoped to find strength when
the time came.

"You are quite sure that he has gone, Denzil— gone
for good?"

"I am perfectly sure of it. You needn't have another
moment's fear."

He tried to believe it. By this time, if he had kept
his promise, Northway was in London. But what faith
was to be put in such a man's declarations? It might
be that the secret was already known to other people;
between now and polling-day there might come the
crowning catastrophe. Yet the man's interest seemed
to impose silence upon him, and for Lilian's sake it was
necessary to affect absolute confidence.

They went to the dinner, and the evening passed
without accident. Lilian was universally admired;
pallor heightened her beauty, and the assurance of out-
lived danger which Denzil had succeeded in imparting
gave to her conversation a life and glow that excited
interest in all who spoke with her.

"Mr. Quarrier," said the hostess, playfully, in an
aside, "if you were defeated at Polterham, I don't
think you ought to care much. You have already been
elected by such a charming constituency!"

But there followed a night of sleeplessness. If
exhaustion pressed down her eyelids for a moment,
some image of dread flashed upon her brain and caused
her to start up with a cry. Himself worn out and
suffering a reaction of despondency, Quarrier more than
once repented what he had done. In Lilian's state of

health such a shock as this might have results that would endanger her life. She had not a strong constitution; he recalled the illness of a year ago, and grew so anxious that his fits of slumber gave him no refreshment. In the early dawn, finding that she was awake, he spoke to her of the necessity of avoiding excitement during the next few days.

"I wish you could go away till the affair is over."

"Oh, there is no need of that! I couldn't be away from you."

"Then at all events keep quietly at home. There'll be the deuce of an uproar everywhere to-day."

"We shall lunch at Mary's, you know. I had rather be there than sitting alone."

"Well, Molly will be good company for you, I dare say. But do try not to excite yourself. Don't talk much; we'll tell them you are very tired after last night. As soon as ever the fight is done, we'll be off somewhere or other for a few weeks. Don't get up till midday; anything interesting you shall know at once."

At breakfast Denzil received a note from Mrs. Wade, sent by hand. "Do let me know how Lilian is. The messenger will wait for a reply." He wrote an answer of warm friendliness, signing it, "Ever sincerely yours." Mrs. Wade had impressed him with her devotion; he thought of her with gratitude and limitless confidence.

"If it had been Molly, instead," he said to himself, "I can't be at all sure how she would have behaved. Religion and the proprieties might have been too much for her good nature; yes, they *would* have been. After all, these emancipated women are the most trustworthy, and Mrs. Wade is the best example I have yet known."

When Mrs. Liversedge welcomed her sister-in-law at luncheon, she was stricken with alarm.

"My dear girl, you look like a ghost! This won't do," she added, in a whisper, presently. "You *must* keep quiet!"

But the Liversedges' house was no place for quietness. Two or three vigorous partisans put in an appearance at the meal, and talked with noisy exhilaration. Tobias himself had yielded to the spirit of the hour; he told merry stories of incidents that had come under his notice that morning. One of these concerned a well-known publican, a stalwart figure on the Tory side.

"I am assured that three voters have been drinking steadily for the last week at his expense. He calculates that delirium tremens will have set in, in each case, by the day after to-morrow."

"Who are these men?" asked Lilian, eagerly. "Why can't we save them in time?"

"Oh, the thing is too artfully arranged. They are old topers; no possibility of interfering."

"I can't see "——

"Lilian," interposed Mrs. Liversedge, "what was the material of that wonderful dress Mrs. Kay wore last night?"

"I don't know, Mary; I didn't notice it.—But surely if it is *known* that these men are "——

It was a half-holiday for the Liversedge boys, and they were anticipating the election with all the fervour of British youth. That morning there had been a splendid fight at the Grammar School; they described it with great vigour and amplitude, waxing Homeric in their zeal. Dickinson junior had told Tom Harte that Gladstone was a " blackguard"; whereupon Tom smote him between the eyes, so that the vile calumniator measured his length in congenial mud. The conflict spread. Twenty or thirty boys took coloured rosettes from their pockets (they were just leaving school) and pinned them to their coats, then rushed to combat with party war-cries. Fletcher senior had behaved like a brutal coward (though alas! a Gladstonian—it was sorrowfully admitted), actually throwing a stone at an enemy who was engaged in single fight, with the result that he had cut open the head of one of his own friends— a most serious wound. An under-master (never a favourite, and now loathed by the young Liversedges as a declared Tory) had interposed in the unfairest way— what else could be expected of him? To all this Mrs. Liversedge gave ear not without pride, but as soon as possible she drew Lilian apart into a quiet room, and did her best to soothe the feverishness which was constantly declaring itself.

About three o'clock Mrs. Wade called. She had not expected to find Lilian here. There was a moment's embarrassment on both sides. When they sat down to talk, the widow's eyes flitted now and then over Lilian's face, but she addressed herself almost exclusively to

Mrs. Liversedge, and her visit lasted only a quarter of an hour. On leaving, she went into the town to make some purchases, and near the Liberal committee-rooms it was her fortune to meet with Quarrier.

"I have wanted to see you," he said, regarding her anxiously. "Lily has got over it much better than I expected; but it won't do—she can't go on in this excitement."

"I have just seen her at your sister's. She doesn't look very well."

"Could I venture to ask one more kindness of you, Mrs. Wade? May she come to you, say the day after to-morrow, and stay over night, and over polling-day?"

"I shall be very glad indeed," faltered the widow, with something in her face which did not seem to be reluctance, though it was unlike pleasure.

"Are you quite sure that it isn't asking too much of you? At my sister's she is in a perpetual uproar; it's worse than at home. And I don't know where else to send her—indeed I don't. But I am getting frightened, that's the truth. If she could be with you during the polling-day"——

"How can you hesitate to ask such a simple thing?" broke in Mrs. Wade. "Shall I ask her myself?"

"You are a good friend. Your conversation will have a soothing effect. She likes you so much, and gives such weight to everything you say. Try to set her mind at ease, Mrs. Wade; you can do it if any one can."

"I will write to her, and then call to-morrow."

Again Lilian had a night without thorough rest, and for the greater part of the next day she was obliged to keep her room. There Mrs. Wade visited her, and they talked for a long time; it was decided that Lilian should go to Pear-tree Cottage on the following afternoon, and remain in seclusion until the contest was over.

She came down at five o'clock. Denzil, who had instructed the servants that she was at home to no one, sat with her in the library, holding her hand.

"I am quite well," Lilian declared again and again. "I feel quite easy in mind—indeed I do. As you wish it, I will go to Mrs. Wade's, but "——

"It will be very much better. To tell you the truth, girlie, I shall feel so much freer—knowing you are out of the row, and in such good care."

She looked at him.

"How wretched to be so weak, Denzil! I might have spared you more than half what you have suffered, if I hadn't given way so."

"Nonsense! Most women would have played the coward—and *that* you never could! You have stood it bravely, dear. But it's your health I fear for. Take care of it for my sake."

Most of the evening he was away, and again the whole of next morning. But when the time came for her to leave, they were sitting once more, as they had done so often, hand in hand, their love and trust stronger than ever, too strong to find expression in mere words.

"If I go into Parliament," said Denzil, "it's you I have to thank for it. You have faced and borne everything rather than disappoint my aims."

He raised her fingers to his lips. Then the arrival of the carriage was announced, and when the door had closed again, they held each other for a moment in passionate embrace.

"Good-bye for a night and a day at longest," he whispered by the carriage door. "I shall come before midnight to-morrow."

She tried to say good-bye, but could not utter a sound. The wheels grated, and she was driven rapidly away.

XXIV.

Arthur James Northway reached London in a mood of imperfect satisfaction. On the principle that half a cake was better than nothing, he might congratulate himself that he carried in his pocket-book banknotes to the value of five hundred pounds; but it was a bitter necessity that had forbidden his exacting more. The possession of a sum greater than he had ever yet owned fired his imagination; he began to reflect that, after all, Quarrier's defiance was most likely nothing but a ruse; that by showing himself resolved, he might have secured at least the thousand pounds. Then he cursed the man Marks, whose political schemes would betray the valuable secret, and make it certain that none of that more substantial assistance promised by Quarrier would ever be given. And yet, it was not disagreeable to picture Quarrier's rage when he found that the bribe had been expended to no purpose. If he had felt animosity against the wealthy man before meeting him face to face, he now regarded him with a fiercer malevolence. It was hard to relinquish Lilian, and harder still to have no means of revenging himself upon her and her pretended husband. Humiliated by consciousness of the base part he had played, he wished it in his power to inflict upon them some signal calamity.

On the next day, when he was newly arrayed from head to foot, and jingled loose sovereigns in his pocket, this tumult of feelings possessed him even more strongly. Added to his other provocations was the uncertainty whether Marks had yet taken action. Save by returning to Polterham, he knew not how to learn what was happening there. To-morrow a Polterham newspaper would be published; he must wait for that source of intelligence. Going to a news-agent's, he discovered the name of the journal, and at once posted an order for a copy to be sent to him.

In the meantime, he was disposed to taste some of the advantages of opulence. His passions were awakened; he had to compensate himself for years lost in suffering of body and mind. With exultant swagger he walked about the London streets, often inspecting his appearance in a glass; for awhile he could throw aside all thought of the future, relish his freedom, take his licence in the way that most recommended itself to him.

The hours did not lag, and on the following afternoon he received the newspaper for which he was waiting. He tore it open, and ran his eye over the columns, but they contained no extraordinary matter. Nothing unexpected had befallen; there was an account of the nomination, and plenty of rancour against the Radicals, but assuredly, up to the hour of the *Mercury's* going to press, no public scandal had exploded in Polterham.

What did it mean? Was Marks delaying for some definite reason? Or had he misrepresented his motives?

Was it a private enmity he had planned to gratify—now frustrated by the default of his instrument?

He had given Marks an address in Bristol, that of a shop at which letters were received. Possibly some communication awaited him there. He hastened to Paddington and took the first westward train.

On inquiry next morning, he found he had had his journey for nothing. As he might have anticipated, Marks was too cautious a man to have recourse to writing.

There were still two days before the poll at Polterham. Thither he must return, that was certain; for if the election passed without startling events, he would again be in a position to catch Quarrier by the throat.

To be sure, there was the promise of assistance in a commercial career, but his indulgence of the last day or two had inclined him to prefer sums of ready money. Once elected, Quarrier would not submit to social disgrace for the sake of a thousand pounds—nor for two thousand—possibly not for five. Cupidity had taken hold upon Northway. With a few thousands in his pocket, he might aim at something more to his taste than a life of trading. Five thousand it should be, not a penny less! This time he was not to be fobbed off with bluster and posturing.

He spent the day in Bristol, and at nightfall journeyed towards Polterham.

No; even yet nothing had happened. Conversation at an inn to which he betook himself assured him that things were going their orderly way. Had Marks himself been *bought off?*

The next day—that before the election—he wandered about the town and its vicinity, undetermined how to act, thinking on the whole that he had better do nothing till after the morrow. Twice, morning and afternoon, did he view Mrs. Wade's cottage from a distance. Just after sunset he was once more in that neighbourhood, and this time with a purpose.

At that hour Mrs. Wade and her guest were together in the sitting-room. The lamp had just been lighted, the red blind drawn down. Lilian reclined on a couch; she looked worse in health than when she had taken leave of Denzil; her eyes told of fever, and her limbs were relaxed. Last night she had not enjoyed an hour of sleep; the strange room and the recollection of Northway's visit to this house (Quarrier, in his faith that Mrs. Wade's companionship was best for Lilian, had taken no account of the disagreeable association) kept her nerves in torment, and with the morning she had begun to suffer from a racking headache.

Mrs. Wade was talking, seated by the table, on which her arms rested. She, too, had a look of nervous tension, and her voice was slightly hoarse.

"Ambition," she said, with a slow emphasis, "is the keynote of Mr. Quarrier's character. If you haven't understood that, you don't yet know him—indeed you don't! A noble ambition, mind. He is above all meanness. In wishing to take a foremost part in politics, he cares, at heart, very little for the personal

dignity it will bring him; his desire—I am convinced
—is to advance all causes that appeal to an honest and
feeling man. He has discovered that he can do this in
a way he had never before suspected—by the exercise
of a splendid gift of eloquence. What a deplorable
thing if that possibility had been frustrated!"

Lilian murmured an assent. Silence followed, and
she closed her eyes. In a minute or two Mrs. Wade
turned to look; the expression which grew upon her
face as she watched furtively was one of subtlest malice.
Of scorn, too. Had *she* been in the position of that
feeble creature, how differently would she have encountered its perils!

"Is your head any better?" she asked, just above
her breath.

"It burns!—Feel my hand, how hot it is!"

"You are feverish. We have talked too much, I
fear."

"No; I like to hear you talk. And it passes the
time. Oh, I hope Denzil won't be very late!"

There sounded a knock at the front door, a heavy rap
such as would be given by some rustic hand.

"What can that be?" Lilian exclaimed, raising
herself.

"Nothing, dear—nothing. Some errand boy."

The servant was heard in the passage. She brought
a letter, and said a messenger waited for the reply.
Mrs. Wade looked at the address; the hand was
unknown to her.

"From Denzil?" asked Lilian.

The other made no reply. What she found in the envelope was a note from Northway, saying he was close by and wished to see her. After a moment's hesitation she went to the door, where a boy was standing.

"Will you tell the person who gave you this note that he may come here?"

Then she bade her servant put a light in the dining-room, and returned to Lilian. Her look excited the sufferer's alarm.

"Has anything happened, Mrs. Wade?"

"Hush! Try to command yourself. He is here again; wishes to see me."

"He is here again?"

Lilian rose to her feet, and moaned despairingly.

"You won't let him come into this room? What does he want? He told us he would never come again. Is he seeking more money?"

"He sha'n't come in here. I'll see him as I did before."

As she spoke, a rat-tat sounded from without, and, having advised Lilian to lock the door, Mrs. Wade crossed to the other room. Northway entered, grave and nervous.

"I hope you will excuse my coming again," he began, as the widow regarded him with silent interrogation. "You spoke to me last time in such a very kind and friendly way. Being in a difficulty, I thought I couldn't do better than ask your advice."

"What is the difficulty, Mr. Northway?"

Her suave tone reassured him, and he seated himself. His real purpose in coming was to discover, if possible, whether Quarrier's position was still unassailed. He had a vague sense that this Mrs. Wade, on whatever grounds, was sympathetically disposed to him; by strengthening the acquaintance, he might somehow benefit himself.

" First, I should like to know if all has gone smoothly since I went away ?"

" Smoothly ?—Quite, I think."

" It still seems certain that Mr. Quarrier will be elected to-morrow ? "

" Very likely indeed."

" He looked about him, and smoothed his silk hat— a very different article from that he had formerly worn. Examining him, Mrs. Wade was amused at the endeavour he had made to equip himself like a gentleman.

" What else did you wish to ask me, Mr. Northway ? "

" It's a point of conscience. If you remember, Mrs. Wade, it was you who persuaded me to give up all thought of parting those persons."

" I tried to do so," she answered, with a smile. " I thought it best for your interests as well as for theirs."

" Yes, but I fear that I had no right to do it. My conscience rebukes me."

" Does it, really ?—I can't quite see "——

She herself was so agitated that features and voice would hardly obey her will. She strove to concentrate her attention upon Northway's words, and divine their secret meaning. His talk continued for awhile in the same strain, but confused, uncertain, rambling. Mrs. Wade found it impossible to determine what he aimed at; now and then she suspected that he had been drinking. At length he stood up.

" You still think I am justified in—in making terms with Mr. Quarrier ? "

" What else are you inclined to do ? " the widow asked, anxiously.

" I can't be sure yet what I shall eventually do. Perhaps you would let me see you again, when the election is over ? "

" If you promise me to do nothing—but keep out of sight—in the meanwhile."

" Yes, I'll promise that," he said, with deliberation.

She was loth to dismiss him, yet saw no use in further talk. At the door he shook hands with her, and said that he was going into the town.

Lilian opened the door of the sitting-room.

" He has gone ? "

Her companion nodded.

" Where ?—What will he do ? "

Mrs. Wade answered with a gesture of uncertainty, and sat down by the table, where she propped her forehead upon her hands. Lilian was standing, her countenance that of one distraught. Suddenly the widow looked up and spoke in a voice hoarser than before.

" I see what he means. He enjoys keeping you both at his mercy. It's like an animal that has tasted blood—and if his desire is balked, he'll revenge himself in the other way."

"You think he has gone to Denzil?"

"Very likely. If not to-night, he will to-morrow. Will Mr. Quarrier pay him again, do you think?" She put the question in a tone which to Lilian sounded strange, all but hostile.

"I can't say," was the weary, distracted answer.

"Oh, I am sorry for you, Lilian!" pursued the other, in agitation, though again her voice was curiously harsh. "You will reproach yourself so if his life's purpose is frustrated! But remember, it's not your fault. It was he who took the responsibility from the first. It was he who chose to brave this possible danger. If the worst comes, you must strengthen yourself."

Lilian sank upon a chair, and leaned forward with stupefied gaze at the speaker.

"The danger is," pursued Mrs. Wade, in lower tones, "that he may be unjust—feel unjustly—as men are wont to. You—in spite of himself, he may feel that *you* have been the cause of his failure. You must be prepared for that; I tell it you in all kindness. If he again consents to pay Northway, he will be in constant fear. The sense of servitude will grow intolerable—embarrassing all he tries to do—all his public and private life. In that case, too, he *must* sometimes think of you as in the way of his ambition. A most difficult task is before you—a duty that will tax all your powers. You will be equal to it, I have no doubt.

Just now you see everything darkly and hopelessly, but that's because your health has suffered of late."

" Perhaps this very night," said Lilian, without looking at her companion, " he will tell people."

" He is more likely to succeed in getting money, and then he will keep the threat held over you. He seems to have come at this moment just because he knows that your fear of him will be keenest now. That will always be his aim—to appear with his threats just when a disclosure would be hardest to bear. But I suppose Mr. Quarrier will rather give up everything than submit to this. Oh, the pity! the pity!"

Lilian let her hands fall and sat staring before her.

She felt as though cast out into a terrible solitude. Mrs. Wade's voice came from a distance; and it was not a voice of true sympathy, but of veiled upbraiding. Unspeakably remote was the image of the man she loved, and he moved still away from her. A cloud of pain fell between her and all the kindly world.

In these nights of sleepless misery she had thought of her old home. The relatives from whom she was for ever parted—her sister, her kind old aunt—looked at her with reproachful eyes; and now, in anguish which bordered upon delirium, it was they alone who seemed real to her; all her recent life had become a vague suffering, a confused consciousness of desire and terror. Her childhood returned; she saw her parents and heard them talk. A longing for the peace and love of those dead days rent her heart.

She could neither speak nor move. Torture born in

the brain throbbed through every part of her body. But worse was that ghastly sense of utter loneliness, of being forsaken by human sympathy. The cloud about her thickened; it muffled light and sound, and began to obscure even her memories.

For a long time Mrs. Wade had sat silent. At length she rose, glanced at Lilian, and, without speaking, left the room.

She went upstairs and into her bed-chamber, and here stood for a few minutes in the dark, purposeless. Then she seated herself in a low chair that was by the bed-side. For her, too, the past night had been one of painful watching; her nerves threatened danger if she stayed in the same room with Lilian. Here she could recover something of self-control, and think over the latest aspect of affairs.

Thus had she sat for nearly half an hour, when her reverie was broken by a sound from below. It was the closing of the front door. She sprang up and ran to the window, to see if any one passed out into the road; but no figure became visible. The gate was closed; no one could have gone forth so quickly. A minute or two passed, yet she heard and saw nothing.

Then she quickly descended the stairs. The door of the sitting-room was open; the room was vacant.

"Lilian!" she called aloud, involuntarily.

She sprang to the front door and looked about in the little garden. Some one moving behind caused her to turn round; it was the servant.

"Annie, has Mrs. Quarrier left the house?"

"Yes, m'm, she has. I just had the kitchen door open, and I saw her go out—without anything on her head."

"Where can she be, then? The gate hasn't been opened; I should have heard it."

One other way there was out of the garden. By passing along a side of the cottage, one came into the back-yard, and thence, by a gate, into one of the fields which spread towards Bale Water. Mrs. Wade remembered that Lilian had discovered this exit one day not long ago.

"I don't understand it," she continued, hurriedly. "You run and put your hat on, and then look up and down the road. I'll go to the back."

Regardless of the cold night air, she hastened in the direction that Lilian must necessarily have taken. Reaching the field, she could at first distinguish no object in the dark space before her. But the sky was clear and starry, and in a few moments, running on the while, she caught sight of a figure not very far in advance. That undoubtedly was Lilian, escaping, speeding over the meadows—whither?

The ground rose gradually, and at a distance of less than a quarter of a mile cut clearly across the sky. Still advancing, though with less speed, she saw Lilian's form gain the top of the rise, and there stand, a black, motionless projection from the ground. If now she called in a loud voice, the fugitive must certainly hear her; but she kept silence. By running quickly over the grass she might overtake her friend, who still lingered ; but, as if her limbs had failed, she crouched down, and so remained until the dark figure all at once disappeared.

Immediately she started to her feet again, and pressed forward. A few minutes, and she was at the top of the field, where Lilian had paused ; panting, her heart throbbing, a cold sweat on her forehand. From this point she looked over a grassy slope, towards the trees which shadowed Bale Water. But her eye could discern nothing save outlines against the starry heaven. All the ground before her lay in a wide-spreading hollow, and darkness cloaked it.

Again she crouched down, pressing her hand against her heart, listening. It was a very still night, and few sounds disturbed its peacefulness. Somewhere, far off, a cart rumbled along; presently one of the Polterham clocks began to strike, faintly but clearly. That caused her to look in the direction of the town ; she saw the radiance of lights, and thought of what was going on over there—the shouting, rushing, fighting.

A night-insect buzzed against her, and, almost in the same moment, there came from down in the hollow, from beyond the trees, a sound which chilled her blood, stopped the wild beating of her heart. It seemed to echo with dreadful clearness from end to end of the heavens. A dull splash of water, that was all ; in reality, scarcely to be heard at this distance save by an ear straining in dreadful expectation.

She made one effort to rise, but could not. Another,

and she was fleeing back to the cottage as if chased for her life.

The back-door was locked; she had to go round into the garden, and there the servant was waiting.

"Have you found her, m'm?"

"No—I can't think—go in, Annie."

The girl was frightened; yet more so when, by the light from the sitting-room, she saw her mistress's face.

"Do you think she's gone home, m'm?"

"Yes, no doubt. Go into the kitchen. I'll call you again."

Mrs. Wade entered the parlour, and closed the door. Her dress was in disorder; her hair had in part fallen loose; on her hands were traces of mud. She did not sit down, and remained just within the door; her look and attitude were those of a terrified listener.

Presently she moved towards the fire, and knelt before it—though she had no need of warmth. Starts and shudders indicated her mental anguish. Yet no sound escape her, until, in a sudden convulsion of her frame, she gave a cry of terror, and threw herself at full length upon the ground. There she lay, struggling with hysterical passion, half choked by sobs, now and then uttering a hoarse wail, at length weeping with the self-abandonment of a child.

It lasted for ten minutes or more, and then followed a long silence. Her body still quivered; she lay with her face half hidden against the hearth-rug, lips parted, but teeth set, breathing heavily.

The clock upon her mantelpiece sounded the third quarter—a quarter to nine. It drew her attention, and at length she half raised herself. Still she had the look of one who listens. She stood up, mechanically smoothed her hair, and twice walked the length of the room. Nearing the door yet again, she opened it, and went upstairs.

Five minutes, and she had made herself ready to go out. At the foot of the stairs she called to her servant.

"I must go into Polterham, Annie. If Mr. Quarrier should come whilst I'm away, say that Mrs. Quarrier and I have gone out, but shall be back very soon. You understand that?"

Then she set forth, and hurried along the dark road.

XXV.

ONLY one vehicle passed her before she came within sight of the streets; it was a carriage and pair, and she recognized the coachman of a family who lived towards Rickstead. Quarrier was doubtless still in the town, but to find him might be difficult. Perhaps she had better go to his house and despatch a servant in search of him. But that was away on the other side of Polterham, and in the meantime he might be starting for Pear-tree Cottage. The polling was long since over; would he linger with his friends at the committee-room?

Yet she must go to the house first of all; there was a reason for it which only now occurred to her.

The main thoroughfares, usually silent and forsaken at this hour, were alive with streams of pedestrians, with groups of argumentative electors, with noisy troops of lads and girls who occasionally amused themselves with throwing mud at some unpopular person, or even breaking a window and rushing off with yells into the darkness of byways. Public-houses were doing a brisk trade, not without pugilism for the entertainment of such as lounged about the doors. For these sights and sounds Mrs. Wade had no attention, but frequently her ear was smitten with the name " Quarrier," spoken or roared by partisan or adversary. Her way led her through the open place where stood the Town Hall ; here had gathered some hundreds of people, waiting for the result of the poll. As she hurried along the ragged edge of the crowd, a voice from somewhere close at hand checked her.

" If you imagine that Quarrier will do more for the people than any other politician, you will find your-selves mistaken. Party politics are no good—no good at all. You working men ought to have the sense to form a party of your own."

It was Northway, addressing a cluster of mill-hands, and evidently posing as one of a superior class who deigned to give them disinterested advice. She listened for a minute longer, but heard nothing that could excite her alarm.

When she reached the house it was a quarter to ten. This part of the town lay in obscurity and quietness; not a shout sounded in her hearing.

Mr. Quarrier had not been at home since early in the afternoon.

"He must be found at once," said Mrs. Wade, adding quickly, "I suppose Mrs. Quarrier hasn't come ? "

The servant gave a surprised negative.

"You must please send some one to find Mr. Quarrier, without a moment's delay. I will come in and wait."

The coachman happened to be in the kitchen. Mrs. Wade had him summoned, and despatched him for his master. Though her limbs shook with fatigue, she could not remain seated for more than a few minutes at a time; she kept the drawing-room door open, and kept going out to listen. Her suspense lasted for more than half an hour; then at length she heard a cab rattle up the drive, and in another moment Quarrier stood before her. This was the second time within a few days that her face had been of ill omen to him; he frowned an anxious inquiry.

"You haven't seen Lilian?" she began.

"Seen her?"

"She has gone—left the cottage—I can't find her."

"Gone? When did she go?"

"I have bad news for you. Northway has come back; he called at the cottage about seven o'clock. I didn't let him know Lilian was there, and soon got rid of him; he said he would have to see you again. Lilian was dreadfully agitated, and when I happened to leave the room, she went out—disappeared—I thought she must have come home"——

"What do the servants say?"

"They haven't seen her."

"But she may have gone to Mary's?"

Arrested in the full flow of his jubilant spirits by this extraordinary announcement, Denzil could not admit grave alarm. If Lilian had fled from the proximity of her pursuer, she must of course have taken refuge with some friend.

"Let us go to the Liversedges'," he exclaimed. "I have a cab"——

"Stop, Mr. Quarrier.—I haven't told you the worst. She ran from the house just as she was, without her hat"——

" What do you mean ?   Why should she——? "

" She was in a dreadful state.   I had done my best to soothe her.   I was just going to send for you.   My servant saw her run out from the sitting-room into the garden, and the gate wasn't opened—she must have gone the back way—into the fields."

" Into the fields——? "

He stared at her with a look of gathering horror, and his tongue failed him.

" I followed that way.   I searched everywhere.   I went a long way over towards "——

She broke off, quivering from head to foot.

" But she *must* have gone somewhere for refuge—to some one's house."

" I hope so !   Oh, I hope so ! "

Her voice choked ; tears started from her eyes.

" What do you fear ?   Tell me at once, plainly ! "

She caught his hand, and replied with sobs of anguish.

" Why should she have gone into the fields ?—without anything on her head—into the fields that lead over to "——

" To—you don't mean to—the water ? "

Still clinging to his hand, she sobbed, tried to utter words of denial, then again of fear.   For the instant Denzil was paralyzed, but rapidly he released himself, and in a voice of command bade her follow.   They entered the cab and were driven towards the Town Hall.

" Did you go to the water," he asked, " and look about there ? "

" Yes," she answered, "I did.—I could see nothing."

As they drew near, a roar of triumphant voices became audible; presently they were in the midst of the clamour, and with difficulty their vehicle made its way through a shouting multitude. It stopped at length by the public building, and Quarrier alighted. At once he was recognized. There rose yells of " Quarrier for ever ! " Men pressed upon him, wanted to shake hands with him, bellowed congratulations in his ear. Heedless, he rushed on, and was fortunate enough to find very quickly the man he sought, his brother-in-law.

" Toby ! " he whispered, drawing him aside, " we have lost Lilian ! She may be at your house; come with us ! "

Voiceless with astonishment, Mr. Liversedge followed, seated himself in the cab. Five minutes brought them to his house.

" Go in and ask," said Quarrier.

Toby returned in a moment, followed by his wife.

" She hasn't been here. What the deuce does it all mean ? I can't understand you. Why, where should she have gone ? "

Again Denzil drew him aside.

" Get a boatman, with lights and drags, and row round as fast as possible to Bale Water ! "

" Good heavens ! What are you talking about ? "

" Do as I tell you, without a minute's delay ! Take this cab. I shall be there long before you."

Mrs. Liversedge was talking with Mrs. Wade, who would say nothing but that Lilian had disappeared.

At Denzil's bidding the cab was transferred to Toby, who, after whispering with his wife, was driven quickly away. Quarrier refused to enter the house.

"We shall find another cab near the Town Hall," he said to Mrs. Wade. "Good-night, Molly! I can't talk to you now."

The two hastened off. When they were among the people again, Mrs. Wade caught sentences that told her the issue of the day. "Majority of over six hundred!— Well done, Quarrier!—Quarrier for ever!" Without exchanging a word, they gained the spot where one or two cabs still waited, and were soon speeding along the Rickstead Road.

"She may be at the cottage," was all Denzil said on the way.

But no; Lilian was not at the cottage. Quarrier stood in the porch, looking about him as if he imagined that the lost one might be hiding somewhere near.

"I shall go—over there," he said. "It will take a long time."

"What?"——

"Liversedge is rowing round, with drags.—Go in and wait.—You may be wrong."

"I didn't say I *thought* it! It was only a fear—a dreadful possibility."

Again she burst into tears.

"Go in and rest, Mrs. Wade," he said, more gently. "You shall know—if anything "——

And, with a look of unutterable misery, he turned away.

Lilian might have taken refuge somewhere in the fields. It seemed a wild unlikelihood, but he durst not give up hope. Though his desire was to reach the waterside as quickly as possible, he searched on either hand as he went by the path, and once or twice he called in a loud voice "Lilian!" The night was darker now than when Mrs. Wade had passed through the neighbouring field; clouds had begun to spread, and only northwards was there a space of starry brilliance.

He came in sight of the trees along the bank, and proceeded at a quicker step, again calling Lilian's name more loudly. Only the soughing wind replied to him.

The nearest part of the water was that where it was deepest, where the high bank had a railing; the spot where Mrs. Wade and Lilian had stood together on their first friendly walk. Denzil went near, leaned across the rail, and looked down into featureless gloom. Not a sound beneath.

He walked hither and thither, often calling and standing still to listen. The whole sky was now obscured, and the wind grew keener. Afraid of losing himself, he returned to the high bank and there waited, his eyes fixed in the direction whence the boat must come. The row along the river Bale from Polterham would take more than an hour.

As he stood sunk in desperate thoughts, a hand touched him. He turned round, exclaiming "Lilian!"

"It is I," answered Mrs. Wade's voice.

"Why have you come? What good can you do here?"

"Don't be angry with me!" she implored. "I couldn't stay at home—I couldn't!"

"I don't mean to speak angrily.—Think," he added, in low shaken voice, "if that poor girl is lying "——

A sob broke off his sentence; he pointed down into the black water. Mrs. Wade uttered no reply, but he heard the sound of her weeping.

They stood thus for a long time, then Denzil raised his hand.

"Look! They are coming!"

There was a spot of light far off, moving slowly.

"I can hear the oars," he added presently.

It was in a lull of the soughing wind. A minute after there came a shout from far across the black surface. Denzil replied to it, and so at length the boat drew near.

Mr. Liversedge stood up, and Quarrier talked with him in brief, grave sentences. Then a second lantern was lighted by the boatman, and presently the dragging began.

Wrapped in a long cloak, Mrs. Wade stood at a distance, out of sight of the water, but able to watch Denzil. When cold and weariness all but overcame her, she first leaned against the trunk of a tree, then crouched there on the ground. For how long, she had no idea. A little rain fell, and afterwards the sky showed signs of clearing; stars were again visible here and there.　She had sunk into a half-unconscious state, when Quarrier's voice spoke to her.

"You must go home," he said, hoarsely.　"It's over."

She started up.

"Have they found"——

"Yes.—Go home at once."

He turned away, and she hurried from the spot with bowed head.

XXVI.

"Oh, depend upon it," said Mrs. Tenterden, in her heavy, consequential way, "there's more behind than *we* shall ever know! 'Unsound mind,' indeed! She was no more of unsound mind than *I* am!'"

It was after church, and Mrs. Mumbray, alone this morning, had offered the heavy lady a place in her brougham. The whole congregation had but one topic as they streamed into the unconsecrated daylight. Never was such eagerness for the strains of the voluntary which allowed them to start up from attitudes of profound meditation, and look round for their acquaintances. Yesterday's paper—the *Polterham Examiner* unfortunately—reported the inquest, and people had to make the most of those meagre paragraphs—until the *Mercury* came out, when fuller and less considerate details might be hoped for. The whispering, the nodding, the screwing up of lips, the portentous frowning and the shaking of heads—no such excitement was on record!

"To me," remarked Mrs. Mumbray, with an air of great responsibility, "the mystery is too plain. I don't hint at *the worst*—it would be uncharitable—but the poor creature had undoubtedly made some discovery in that woman's house which drove her to despair."

Mrs. Tenterden gave a start.

" You really think so ? That has occurred to me.
Mrs. Wade's fainting when she gave her evidence—oh
dear, oh dear ! I'm afraid there *can* be only one
explanation."

" That is our *honourable* member, my dear ! " threw
out Mrs. Mumbray. " These are Radical principles—
in man and woman. Why, I am told that scarcely a
day passed without Mrs. Wade calling at the house."

" And they tell me that *he* was frequently at
hers ! "

" That poor young wife ! Oh, it is shameful ! The
matter oughtn't to end here. Something ought to be
done. If that man is allowed to keep his seat "——

Many were the conjectures put forward and discussed
throughout the day, but this of Mrs. Mumbray's—
started of course in several quarters—found readiest
acceptance in Conservative circles. Mrs. Wade was
obviously the cause of what had happened—no wonder
she fainted at the inquest ; no wonder she hid herself in
her cottage ! When she ventured to come out, virtuous
Polterham would let her know its mind. Quarrier
shared in the condemnation, but not even political
animosity dealt so severely with him as social opinion did
with Mrs. Wade.

Mr. Chown—who would on no account have been
seen in a place of worship—went about all day among
his congenial gossips, and scornfully contested the
rumour that Quarrier's relations with Mrs. Wade would
not bear looking into. At the house of Mr. Murgatroyd,
the Radical dentist, he found two or three friends who

were very anxious not to think evil of their victorious leader, but felt wholly at a loss for satisfactory explanations. Mr. Vawdrey, the coal-merchant, talked with gruff discontent.

"I don't believe there's been anything wrong; I couldn't think it—neither of him nor her. But I do say it's a lesson to you men who go in for Female Suffrage. Now, this is just the kind of thing that 'ud always be happening. If there isn't wrong-doing, there'll be wrong-speaking. Women have no business in politics, that's the plain moral of it. Let them keep at home and do their duty."

"Humbug!" cried Mr. Chown, who cared little for the graces of dialogue. "A political principle is not to be at the mercy of party scandal. I, for my part, have never maintained that women were ripe for public duties; but Radicalism involves the certainty that they some day will be. The fact of the matter is that Mrs. Quarrier was a woman of unusually feeble physique. We all know—those of us, at all events, who keep up with the science of the day—that the mind is entirely dependent upon the body—entirely!" He looked round, daring his friends to contradict this. "Mrs. Quarrier had overtaxed her strength, and it's just possible—I say it's just possible—that her husband was not very prudent in sending her for necessary repose to the house of a woman so active-minded and so excitable as Mrs. Wade. We must remember the peculiar state of her health. As far as *I* am concerned, Dr. Jenkins's evidence is final, and entirely satisfactory. As for the dirty calumnies of dirty-minded reactionists, *I* am not the man to give ear to them! "

One man there was who might have been expected to credit such charges, yet surprised his acquaintances by what seemed an unwonted exercise of charity. Mr. Scatchard Vialls, hitherto active in defamation of Quarrier, with amiable inconsistency refused to believe him guilty of conduct which had driven his wife to suicide. It was some days before the rumour reached his ears. Since the passage of arms with Serena, he had held aloof from Mrs. Mumbray's drawing-room, and his personality did not invite the confidence of ordinary scandal-mongers. When at length his curate hinted to him what was being said, he had so clearly formulated his own theory of Mrs. Quarrier's death that only the strongest evidence would have led him to reconsider it. Obstinacy and intellectual conceit forbade him to indulge his disposition to paint an enemy's character in the darkest colours.

" No, Mr. Blenkinsop," he replied to the submissive curate, standing on his hearth-rug at full height and regarding the cornice as his habit was when he began to monologize—"no, I find it impossible to entertain such an accusation. I have little reason to think well of Mr. Quarrier; he is intemperate, in many senses of the word, and intemperance, it is true, connects closely with the most odious crimes. But in this case censure has been too quick to interpret suspicious circumstances— suspicious, I admit. Far be it from me to speak in defence of such a person as Mrs. Wade; I think she is a source of incalculable harm to all who are on friendly terms with her—especially young and impressionable women; but you must trust my judgment in this instance : I am convinced she is not guilty. Her agitation in the coroner's court has no special significance. No; the solution of the mystery is not so simple; it involves wider issues—calls for a more profound interpretation of character and motives. Mrs. Quarrier—pray attend to this, Mr. Blenkinsop—represents a type of woman becoming, I have reason to think, only too common in our time, women who cultivate the intellect at the expense of the moral nature, who abandon religion and think they have found a substitute for it in the so-called humanitarianism of the day. Strong-minded women, you will hear them called; in truth, they are the weakest of their sex. Let their energies be submitted to any unusual strain, let their nerves (they are always morbid) be overwrought, and they snap ! " He illustrated the catastrophe with his hands. " Unaided by religion, the female nature is irresponsible, unaccountable." Mr. Vialls had been severe of late in his judgment of women. "Mrs. Quarrier, poor creature, was the victim of immoderate zeal for worldly ends. She was abetted by her husband and by Mrs. Wade ; they excited her to the point of frenzy, and in the last moment she—snapped! Mrs. Wade's hysterical display is but another illustration of the same thing. These women have no support outside themselves— they have deliberately cast away everything of the kind."

"Let me exhibit my meaning from another point of view. Consider, Mr. Blenkinsop "——

Quarrier, in the meantime, was very far from suspecting the accusation which hostile ingenuity had brought against him. Decency would in any case have necessitated his withdrawal for the present from public affairs, and, in truth, he was stricken down by his calamity. The Liversedges had brought him to their house; he transacted no business, and saw no one beyond the family circle. At the funeral people had thought him strangely unmoved; pride forbade him to make an exhibition of grief, but in secret he suffered as only a strong man can. His love for Lilian was the deepest his life would know. Till now, he had not understood how unspeakably precious she was to him; for the most part he had treated her with playful good-humour, seldom, if ever, striking the note of passion in his speech. With this defect he reproached himself. Lilian had not learnt to trust him sufficiently; she feared the result upon him of such a blow as Northway had it in his power to inflict. It was thus he interpreted her suicide, for Mrs. Wade had told him that Lilian believed disaster to be imminent. Surely he was to blame for it that, at such a pass, she had fled *away* from him instead of hastening to his side. How perfectly had their characters harmonized! He could recall no moment of mutual dissatisfaction, and that in spite of conditions which, with most women, would have made life very difficult. He revered her purity; her intellect he esteemed far subtler and nobler than his own. With such a woman for companion, he might have done great things; robbed for ever of her beloved presence, he felt lame, purposeless, indifferent to all but the irrecoverable past.

In a day or two he was to leave Polterham. Whether Northway would be satisfied with the result of his machinations remained to be seen; as yet nothing more had been heard of him. The fellow was perhaps capable of demanding more hush-money, of threatening the memory of the woman he had killed. Quarrier hoped more earnestly than ever that the secret would not be betrayed; he scorned vulgar opinion, so far as it affected himself, but could not bear the thought of Lilian's grave being defiled by curiosity and reprobation. The public proceedings had brought to light nothing whatever that seemed in conflict with medical evidence and the finding of the coroner's jury. One dangerous witness had necessarily come forward—Mrs. Wade's servant; but the girl made no kind of allusion to Northway's visit—didn't, in her own mind, connect it with Mrs. Quarrier's behaviour. She was merely asked to describe in what way the unfortunate lady had left the house. In Glazzard and Mrs. Wade, Denzil of course reposed perfect confidence. Northway, if need were, could and should be bought off.

Toby Liversedge got wind of the scandal in circulation, and his rage knew no bounds. Lest his wife should somehow make the discovery, he felt obliged to speak to her—representing the change in its mildest form.

"There's a vile story going about that Lilian was jealous of Mrs. Wade's influence with Denzil; that the two quarrelled that day at the cottage, and the poor girl drowned herself in despair."

Mary looked shocked, but was silent.

"I suppose," added her husband, "we must be prepared for all sorts of rumours. The thing is unintelligible to people in general. Any one who knew her, and saw her those last days, can understand it only too well."

"Yes," murmured Mrs. Liversedge, with sad thoughtfulness.

She would not speak further on the subject, and Toby concluded that the mere suggestion gave her offence.

On the day after Denzil departed, leaving by a night train for London.

He was in town for a week, then took a voyage to Madeira, where he remained until there was only time enough to get back for the opening of Parliament. The natural plea of shaken health excused him to his constituents, many of whom favoured him with their unsolicited correspondence. (He had three or four long letters from Mr. Chown, who thought it necessary to keep the borough member posted in the course of English politics.) From Glazzard he heard twice, with cheerful news. "How it happened," he had written to his newly-married friend, in telling of Lilian's death, "I will explain some day; I cannot speak of it yet." Glazzard's response was full of manly sympathy. "I don't pretend," wrote the connoisseur, "that I am ideally mated, but my wife is a good girl, and I understand enough of happiness in marriage to appreciate to the full how terrible is your loss. Let confidences be for the future; if they do not come naturally, be assured I shall never pain you by a question."

Denzil's book had now been for several weeks before the public; it would evidently excite little attention. "A capital present for a schoolboy," was one of the best things the critics had yet found to say of it. He suffered disappointment, but did not seriously resent the world's indifference. Honestly speaking, was the book worth much? The writing had at first amused him; in the end it had grown a task. Literature was not his field.

Back, then, to politics! There he knew his force. He was looking to the first taste of Parliament with decided eagerness.

In Madeira he chanced to make acquaintance with an oldish man who had been in Parliament for a good many years; a Radical, an idealist, sore beset with physical ailments. This gentleman found pleasure in Denzil's society, talked politics to him with contagious fervour, and greatly aided the natural process whereby Quarrier was recovering his interest in the career before him.

"My misfortune is," Denzil one day confided to this friend, "that I detest the town and the people that have elected me."

"Indeed?" returned the other, with a laugh. "Then lay yourself out to become my successor at ——

when a general election comes round again. I hope to live out this Parliament, but sha'n't try for another."

About the same time he had a letter from Mrs. Wade, now in London, wherein, oddly enough, was a passage running thus:

"You say that the thought of representing Polterham spoils your pleasure in looking forward to a political life. Statesmen (and you will become one) have to be trained to bear many disagreeable things. But you are not bound to Polterham for ever—the gods forbid! Serve them in this Parliament, and in the meantime try to find another borough."

It was his second letter from Mrs. Wade; the first had been a mere note, asking if he could bear to hear from her, and if he would let her know of his health. He replied rather formally, considering the terms on which they stood; and, indeed, it not gratify him much to be assured of the widow's constant friendship.

XXVII.

SOMETHING less than a year after his marriage, Glazzard was summoned back to England by news of his brother's death. On the point of quitting Highmead, with Ivy, for a sojourn abroad, William Glazzard had an apoplectic seizure and died within the hour. His affairs were in disorder; he left no will; for some time it would remain uncertain whether the relatives inherited anything but debt.

Eustace and his wife took a house in the north of London, a modest temporary abode. There, at the close of March, Serena gave birth to a child.

During the past year Glazzard had returned to his old amusement of modelling in clay. He drew and painted, played and composed, at intervals; but plastic art seemed to have the strongest hold upon him. Through April he was busy with a head for which he had made many studies —a head of Judas; in Italy he had tried to paint the same subject, but ineffectually. The face in its latest development seemed to afford him some satisfaction.

One morning, early in May, Serena was sitting with him in the room he used as a studio. Experience of life, and a certain measure of happiness, had made the raw girl a very pleasing and energetic woman; her face was comely, her manner refined, she spoke softly and thoughtfully, but with spirit.

"It is wonderful," she said, after gazing long, with knitted brows, at the Judas, "but horrible. I wish it hadn't taken hold of you so."

"Taken hold of me? I care very little about it."

"Oh, nonsense! That's your worst fault, Eustace. You seem ashamed of being in earnest. I wish you had found a pleasanter subject, but I am delighted to see you *do* something. Is it quite finished?"

A servant appeared at the door.

"Mr. Quarrier wishes to see you, sir."

Denzil entered, and had a friendly greeting. The Glazzards did not see much of him, for he was over head and ears in politics, social questions, philanthropic undertakings—these last in memory of Lilian, whose spirit had wrought strongly in him since her death. He looked a much riper and graver man than a year ago. His language was moderate; he bore himself reservedly, at moments with diffidence. But there was the old frank cordiality undiminished. To Serena he spoke with the gentle courtesy which marks a man's behaviour to women when love and grief dwell together in his heart.

"Our friend Judas?" he said, stepping up to the model. "Finished at last?"

"Something like it." Glazzard replied, tapping the back of his hand with a tool.

"Discontented, as usual! I know nothing about this kind of thing, but I should say it was very good. Makes one uncomfortable—doesn't it, Mrs. Glazzard? Do something pleasanter next time."

"Precisely what I was saying," fell from Serena.

They talked awhile, and Mrs. Glazzard left the room.

"I want to know your mind on a certain point," said Denzil. "Mrs. Wade has been asking me to bring her together with your wife and you. Now, what is your feeling?"

The other stood in hesitation, but his features expressed no pleasure.

"What is *your* feeling?" he asked, in return.

"Why, to tell you the truth, I can't advise you to make a friend of her. I'm sorry to say she has got into a very morbid state of mind. I see more of her than I care to. She has taken up with a lot of people I don't like—rampant women—extremists of many kinds. There's only one thing: it's perhaps my duty to try and get her into a more sober way of life, and if all steady-going people reject her —— Still, I don't think either you or your wife would like to have her constantly coming here."

"I think not," said Glazzard, with averted face.

"Well, I shall tell her that she would find you very unsympathetic. I'm sorry for her; I wish she could recover a healthy mind."

He brooded for a moment, and the lines that came into his face gave it an expression of unrest and melancholy out of keeping with its natural tone.

In a few minutes he was gone, and presently Serena returned to the studio. She found her husband in a dark reverie, a mood to which he often yielded, which she always did her best to banish.

"Do you think, Eustace," she asked, "that Mr. Quarrier will marry again?"

"Oh, some day, of course."

"I shall be sorry. There's something I have often meant to tell you about his wife; I will now."

He looked up attentively. Serena had never been admitted to his confidence regarding Lilian's story; to her, the suicide was merely a woful result of disordered health.

"But for her," she continued, smiling archly, "I should perhaps not have married you. I was destracted with doubts about myself and about you. Then I went to Mrs. Quarrier, and—what a thing to do!—asked her what she thought of you! She told me, and I came away without a doubt left.—That's why I cried so much when we heard of her death. I should have told you then if you hadn't got vexed with me—I'm sure I don't know why."

Glazzard laughed, and dismissed the subject carelessly.

Not long after, he was alone. After much pacing about the room, he came to a stand before his clay masterpiece, and stared at it as though the dull eyes fascinated him. Of a sudden he raised his fist and with one blow beat the head into a shapeless mass.

Then he went out, locking the door behind him.

On leaving the Glazzards, Quarrier pursued the important business that had brought him into this part of London. He drove to a hospital, newly opened, with which he was connected in the capacity of treasurer. Talk with the secretary occupied him for half an hour; about to set forth again, he encountered on the staircase two ladies, the one a hospital nurse, the other Mrs. Wade.

"Could you grant me five minutes?" asked the widow, earnestly. "I didn't hope to see you here, and must have called upon you—but you are so busy."

There was a humility in her suppressed voice which, had the speaker been another person, would have prepared Denzil for some mendicant petition of the politer kind. She spoke hurriedly, as if fearing a rebuff.

"Let us step this way," he said, opening a door which led into an unoccupied room.

Mrs. Wade was dressed rather more simply than had been her wont when she lived at Polterham. One conjectured that her circumstances were not improved. She looked tired, harassed; her eyes wanted something of their former brightness, and she had the appearance of a much older woman.

There were no seats in the room. Quarrier did not refer to the fact, but stood in an attitude of friendly attention.

"I saw Northway yesterday," Mrs. Wade began.

The listener's face expressed annoyance.

"Need we speak of him?" he said, briefly.

"I am obliged to. He told me something which I had long suspected — something you certainly must learn."

"Is it a fresh attack on my pocket?" asked Denzil, with resignation.

"No, but something that will grieve you far more. I have been trying for a long time to get it out of him, and now that I have succeeded I almost wish the thought had never occurred to me."

"Pray, pray don't keep me in suspense, Mrs. Wade."

"Northway did *not* make his discovery by chance. You were betrayed to him—by a seeming friend."

Denzil looked steadily at her.

"A friend?—He has deceived you. Only one acquaintance of mine knew."

"Mr. Glazzard. It was he who laid a plot for your downfall."

Quarrier moved impatiently.

"Mrs. Wade, you are being played upon by this scoundrel. There is no end to his contrivances."

"No, he has told me the truth," she pursued, with agitated voice. "Listen to the story, first of all."

She related to him, in accurate detail, all that had passed between Northway and Mr. Marks.

"And Mr. Marks was Mr. Glazzard, undoubtedly. His description tallies exactly."

Denzil broke out indignantly.

"The whole thing is a fabrication! I not only *won't* believe it, but simply *can't*. You say that you have suspected this?"

"I have—from the moment when Lilian told me that Mr. Glazzard knew."

"That's astounding!—Then why should you have desired to be on friendly terms with the Glazzards?"

Mrs. Wade sank her eyes.

"I hoped," she made answer, "to find out something. I had only in view to serve you."

"You have deluded yourself, and been deluded, in the strangest way. Now, I will give you one reason (a very odd, but a very satisfactory one) why it is impossible to believe Glazzard guilty of such baseness—setting aside the obvious fact that he had no motive. He goes in for modelling in clay, and for some time he has been busy on a very fine head. What head do you think? —That of Judas Iscariot."

He laughed.

"Now, a man guilty of abominable treachery would not choose for an artistic subject the image of an archtraitor."

Mrs. Wade smiled strangely as she listened to his scornful demonstration.

"You have given me," she said, "a most important piece of evidence in support of Northway's story."

Denzil was ill at ease. He could not dismiss this lady with contempt. Impossible that he should not have learnt by this time the meaning of her perpetual assiduity on his behalf; the old friendliness (never very warm) had changed to a compassion which troubled him. Her image revived such painful memories that he would have welcomed any event which put her finally at a distance from him The Polterham scandal, though not yet dead, had never come to his ears; had he known it, he could scarcely have felt more constrained in her society.

" Will you oblige me," he said, with kindness, " by never speaking of this again ? "

" If you will first grant me one test of my opinion. Will you meet Northway in some public place where Mr. Glazzard can be easily seen, and ask the man to point out his informant—Mr. Marks ? "

After much debate, and with great reluctance, he consented. From his conversation of an hour ago he knew that Glazzard would be at the Academy on the morrow. He had expressed a hope for a meeting there. At the Academy, accordingly, the test should be applied. It was all a fabrication; Northway, laying some new plot, might already know Glazzard by sight. But the latter should be put on his guard, and Mrs. Wade should then be taught that henceforth she was forbidden to concern herself with his—Quarrier's— affairs.

He went home and passed a cheerless time until the next morning. Suspicion, in spite of himself, crept into his thoughts. He was sick at heart under the necessity, perhaps life-long, of protecting Lilian's name against a danger which in itself was a sort of pollution. His sanguine energy enabled him to lose the thought, at ordinary times, of the risks to which he himself was exposed; but occasionally he reflected that public life might even yet be made impossible for him, and then he cursed the moral stupidity of people in general.

At eleven o'clock next morning he entered Burlington House. In the vestibule at the head of the stairs stood

Mrs. Wade, and Northway, indistinguishable from ordinary frequenters of the exhibition, was not far off. This gentleman had a reason for what he was doing; he wished to discover who Mr. Marks really was, and what (since the political plea could no longer be credited) had been his interest in Lilian.

" He is here already," said Mrs. Wade, as she joined Denzil. " Among the sculpture—the inner room."

" Then I shall follow you at a distance. Challenge that fellow to go up to Glazzard and address him as Mr. Marks."

The widow led in the direction she had indicated, through the central hall, then to the right, Northway following close. Denzil had, of course, to take it for granted that Mrs. Wade was acting honourably; he did not doubt her good faith. If it came to a mere conflict of assertions between his friend and Northway, he knew which of them to believe. But he was much perturbed, and moved forward with a choking in his throat.

Arrived at the threshold of the Lecture Room, he saw that only some dozen people were standing about. No sooner had he surveyed them than he became aware that Northway was sauntering directly towards the place where Glazzard stood; Mrs. Wade remained in the doorway. Unperceived, the informer came close behind his confederate and spoke quietly.

Glazzard turned as if some one had struck him.

It was forcible evidence, confirmed moreover by the faces of the two men as they exchanged a few words.

Seeing Northway retire, Quarrier said to Mrs. Wade :

" Please to go away. You have done your part."

With a look of humble entreaty, she obeyed him. Denzil, already observed by Glazzard, stepped forward.

" Do you know that man ? " he asked, pointing to Northway, who affected a study of some neighbouring work of art.

" I have met him," was the subdued answer.

It was necessary to speak so that attention should not be drawn hither. Though profoundly agitated, Quarrier controlled himself sufficiently to use a very low tone.

" He has told an incredible story, Glazzard. I sha'n't believe it unless it is confirmed by your own lips."

" I have no doubt he has told the truth."

Denzil drew back.

" But do you know *what* he has said ? "

" I guess from the way he addressed me—as Mr. Marks."

Glazzard was deadly pale, but he smiled persistently, and with an expression of relief.

" You—*you*—betrayed us to him ? "

" I did."

Each could hear the other's breathing.

" Why did you do that ? " asked Denzil, the excess of his astonishment declaring itself in a tone which would have suited some every-day inquiry. He could not speak otherwise.

" I can't tell you why I did it. I'm not sure that I quite understand now. I did it, and there's no more to be said."

Denzil turned away, and stood with his eyes fixed on the ground. A minute passed, and Glazzard's voice again sounded close to him.

" Quarrier, you can't forgive me, and I don't wish you to. But may I hope that you won't let my wife know of it?"

" You are safe from me," answered Denzil, barely glancing at him, and at once walked away.

He returned to the vestibule, descended the stairs, went out into the court. There, aside from vehicles and people, he let his thoughts have their way. Presently they summed themselves in a sentence which involuntarily he spoke aloud :

" Now I understand the necessity for social law!"

THE END.

PRINTED BY HENDERSON & SPALDING, LIMITED, MARYLEBONE LANE, W.

Notes to the Text

The holograph manuscript of *Denzil Quarrier,* which is in the Huntington Library, San Marino, California, consists of 133 leaves, many of which actually are two and occasionally three pieces of paper pasted together to uniform size. A number of the pieces are wholly uncorrected, which suggests that Gissing may have done some of his rough work elsewhere and then transferred finished passages to the main manuscript. Throughout there are remarkably few corrections, no cancelled passages of substantive length, and very few insertions: the overall impression is that Gissing wrote *Denzil Quarrier* quickly and easily and revised it hardly at all. (External evidence suggests that it was written in less than two months of concentrated work in October and November of 1891.) Most of the MS. is written in plain black ink; the few corrections and insertions are made in ink a slightly darker black. The first English edition reproduced here follows the MS. faithfully, except in several minor instances, which are indicated in notes.

Title page:
The novel's original title, *The Radical Candidate,* is cancelled on the title page of the holograph MS., and the final title, *Denzil Quarrier,* is written, in a hand probably not Gissing's, below and to the right of the original title, which is in Gissing's hand. The decision to change the title was made by Lawrence & Bullen, with Gissing's concurrence (see the Bibliographical Note to this edition).

Page 10, line 4:
Eutropius, a Latin historian of the late fourth century AD, was the author of a popular – because abbreviated – history of Rome.

Page 10, lines 21–22:
Beaconsfield (Disraeli) was Prime Minister in 1879 – in which year the novel opens – and, after the Congress of Berlin in 1878, at the height of his influence and reputation. He was born in 1804 and died in 1881.

Page 11, line 3:

Originally this paragraph contained more exposition, but Gissing cancelled six holograph lines between the penultimate and final sentences of the paragraph.

Page 14, line 30, and page 15, line 1:

Between the last paragraph on p. 14 and the first paragraph on p. 15 two holograph lines extending the argument are cancelled.

Page 16, lines 25–8:

These lines were inserted by Gissing into the MS. during revision.

Page 18, line 8:

In keeping with his other revisions of this scene, Gissing here cancelled three more holograph lines in the interest of foreshortening.

Page 20, line 8:

This is a misprint. The MS. reads, 'but do you know whose it is?'; the first edition omits 'you'.

Page 22, line 10:

Brummagem, i.e., Birmingham.

Page 23, line 22:

H.M.S. *Britannia,* anchored in the River Dart, was part of the Royal Naval College, Dartmouth, 1863–1905.

Page 24, line 27:

The *Heimskringla*, a history of Norse kings from mythical times to 1177, takes its title ('the round world') from the first words in the manuscript.

Page 25, line 25:

Clement's Inn was an Inn of Chancery, founded before the reign of Edward IV. It is now part of the Inner Temple.

Page 26, line 6:

Christiania, i.e., Oslo.

Page 28, line 10:

There was bad blood between England and Russia throughout much of the nineteenth century, especially after the Crimean War in the 1850s and again when they found themselves at odds in the 1870s over what became known as the Eastern Question – that is, the question of what to do with the crumbling Ottoman Empire. Disraeli supported the Turks and made a number of inflammatory speeches against Russia in the late 1870s; Gladstone and the Liberals supported Russia against Turkey. The possibility of war with Russia is mentioned again later in the novel; see below, p. 183.

Page 30, lines 3–4
Jens Peter Jacobsen (1847–85), Danish writer, published *Marie Grubbe,* a novel, in 1876.

Page 36, line 16:
William Laud (1573–1645), Charles I's Archbishop of Canterbury, was famous for the zeal with which he enforced uniformity in the Church of England before his impeachment for treason by the Long Parliament.

Page 36, line 26:
Workman is John Workman, a puritan preacher of Gloucester, who in 1633 was suspended, excommunicated, and imprisoned by Laud's (see above) High Commission. The persecution of Workman was later one of the articles in Laud's own impeachment. In his *Commonplace Book* Gissing quotes a passage on Workman from Guizot's *English Revolution,* which he was reading in the Autumn of 1891.

Page 39, lines 9-10:
David Hume (1711-76) was considered by many nineteenth-century conservatives a godless radical largely because of his insistence on secular and natural explanations for apparently miraculous phenomena. Henry Thomas Buckle (1821–62), in his *History of Civilisation in England* (2 vols, 1857–61), emphasized scientific methods of obtaining information and insight into historical questions.

Page 40, lines 25-8:
The election of 1868 was a great victory for the Liberals; in 1874 the Conservatives gained an even bigger majority.

Page 41, line 9:
Good Words, founded in 1868, was an illustrated, monthly, family magazine specializing in secular literature. Its largely scientific content sometimes made it offensive to fundamentalists. One of Gissing's stories was turned down by the editor of *Good Words;* it could not have been one of his favourite publications.

Page 41, line 21:
Gissing cancelled three holograph lines between the two sentences here; the excised passage is an extension of the account of Polterham journalism.

Page 47, line 18:
For discussion of the female-suffrage movement and Gissing's complicated feelings about women's rights, see the Introduction.

Page 47, line 28:
Disestablishment was one of the great political controversies of the latter half of the nineteenth century. W.E. Gladstone (1809 – 98) felt 'called' to disestablish the protestant episcopal Church of Ireland; Disraeli and the Tories resisted. The Irish Church was not disestablished.

Page 54, line 4:
Revivalism was an outgrowth of evangelicalism and essentially low-Church in flavour. George Eliot's *Adam Bede* (1859) opens with a Wesleyan prayer meeting presided over by a woman (Dinah Morris).

Page 54, lines 14-19:
The last two sentences of this paragraph were a late insert (alluded to in the Introduction).

Page 67, line 30:
The election of 1880 ended in a great Liberal victory. See below, p. 193 and accompanying notes.

Page 73, Chapter VII:
This chapter, a substantial part of which is Quarrier's long lecture on women, has remarkably few corrections in the MS. Either Gissing worked on it separately and then transferred it to the main MS. or he knew pretty much what he wanted to say and simply wrote it out without much tinkering.

Page 86, lines 10–14:
This is the central theme of *The Odd Women,* published by Gissing the following year (1893).

Page 96, line 3:
Gissing, a classical scholar and sometime tutor, could of course 'read the originals' himself.

Page 105, line 6:
The Jotuns were giants of Scandinavian mythology who lived in Jötunheim.

Page 107, line 29:
The Christian Socialists were left-wing high-church Anglicans who advocated strenuous programmes of self-improvement. Charles Kingsley and F.D. Maurice were among their number.

Page 108, lines 20-1:
A misprint; should read 'About so long ago, I suppose?', as in MS.

Page 111, lines 5-13:
This entire paragraph was a late insertion into the holograph MS.

Page 111, lines 15-19:
These four sentences also were a late insert. Gissing's theme here is discussed in the Introduction.

Page 145, line 7:
Between the first and second sentences of this paragraph three holograph lines of dialogue were cancelled in the MS. Gissing was apparently wary here of letting Lilian talk too much.

Page 149, lines 5–6:
Blue was (and is) the colour of the Conservatives, yellow of the Liberals. Cf. below, p. 293.

Page 165, lines 8–11:
Sir Stafford Northcote (1818–87; later first Earl of Iddesleigh) in 1880 introduced a measure designed to prevent Parnell and his followers from obstructing the business of the House of Commons, a tactic the Irish members and their allies had taken to as a means of forcing Parliament's hand on the Irish Home Rule question. The Radicals at this time were allied with Parnell's faction against the Government. Northcote's measure was passed but rescinded later in calmer weather.

Page 168, line 3:
'hommasse,' i.e., masculine.

Page 172, line 2:
The Irish Question was that of Home Rule; see above, p. 165 and accompanying note.

Page 172, line 19:
Disraeli dissolved on 24 March 1880; the election ended in a resounding triumph for the Liberals.

Page 174, lines 15–24:
Disraeli, who on several occasions misread the mood of the country on Irish matters, openly opposed Home Rule at a time when Gladstone and the Liberals were flirting with Parnell's faction and the Radicals in the Commons for political support. Disraeli campaigned in 1880 largely on the issue of imperialism and the expansion of British influence abroad – a policy he wished to continue – and he and his party were soundly defeated. The letter to the seventh Duke of Marlborough, who at the time was Viceroy of Ireland, issued on 9 March, was in effect the opening salvo of the Prime Minister's own election campaign. It warned of the dangers of Irish separatism.

Page 175, lines 1–2:
See above, p. 174 and accompanying note. The mood of the electorate in 1880 was decidedly anti-jingoist (that is, against further imperialist adventures abroad). Gladstone's bungling pacifist policy was soon to drive public opinion back into a jingoist mood, however.

Page 179, lines 1–3:
The famous phrase was purloined from Burke's *Reflections on the Revolution in France.*

Page 179, line 21:
Disraeli's ancestors were mostly Portuguese and Italian Jews. He himself was baptised into Christianity at the age of nine as a result of a bitter dispute between his father (who cared nothing about religion) and the leaders of a local synagogue. This accident enabled Disraeli to pursue a political career.

Page 182, line 20:
This is a reference to Tennyson's dialect poem, 'Northern Farmer, Old Style'.

Page 183, line 23:
Lilian refers to Disraeli's continuing cultivation of British Russophobia. See above, p. 28 and accompanying note.

Page 193, lines 14–15:
Gladstone's Midlothian campaign, as it came to be called, was probably the most galvanizing event of the 1880 election. The Grand Old Man's astonishing and virtually uninterrupted eloquence on behalf of Liberal principles during a period of two weeks in the final days of 1879 made it possible for him to take away and occupy himself the seat of the Tory Lord Dalkeith. The Midlothian campaign gave Gladstone's comeback a splendid start and signalled the beginning of the end of the Tory dominance of the late 1870s. By the time of the actual balloting (March 1880) Conservative policies had taken a considerable public drubbing, and the Liberals won a large majority.

Page 198, line 9:
Between the end of this line and the beginning of the next one Gissing cancelled two more holograph lines; the effect is to foreshorten and tighten up his description here of Glazzard's feelings.

Page 203, line 12:
The quotation is from *Paradise Lost,* I, 157 (Satan addressing Beelzebub).

Page 205, lines 24–30:
Thomas Chatterton (1752-70), the Bristol poet who poisoned himself at the age of 17, was baptized and buried in the cathedral of St Mary Redcliffe. His poetic inspiration was derived in part from documents discovered in this church.

Page 206, lines 14–20:
Gissing uses here some authentic geography and topography of the Bristol region and its environs. He went house-hunting in this area on 17 and 18 August 1891.

Page 208, line 11:
Cf. above, p. 206, and accompanying note.

Page 209, line 11:
See above, p. 107, and note.

Page 223, line 15:
After the word 'but' there are three cancelled holograph lines of further exposition in the MS.

Page 224, line 11:
See above, p. 193, and note.

Page 227, lines 7-9:
The Marquis of Hartington (1833–1908), immortalized in Lytton Strachey's *Eminent Victorians,* had been for a time Liberal leader of the House of Commons in the 1870s and led the Whig section of the Liberal party in the 1880s. Hartington and his faction deserted Gladstone over Home Rule, which Hartington opposed – though his 'answer' to Cross, a Tory, would have been given before he broke with Gladstone. R.A. Cross (1823–1914) was a Lancashire banker and a Tory MP who vigorously opposed Gladstone on Home Rule. John Bright (1811–89), the rich and eloquent manufacturer who led the Radical forces in the Commons for many years and served in several Liberal Cabinets, was well-known also as a teetotaler, and made a number of speeches throughout his career in support of the temperance movement.

Page 227, line 19:
Sir Wilfred Lawson (1829-1906), Liberal MP (for Carlisle) and temperance advocate, was known for the humour and genial sarcasm with which he seasoned his speeches. In the 1860s and 1870s Lawson favoured, and frequently reintroduced, his 'local veto' bill, which mandated local control over Sunday opening and closing of public houses.

Page 238, lines 7-9:
These lines, up to 'are you disposed to serve me?', are a late insert into the MS.

Page 293, 10:
The 'coloured rosettes' – cf. above, p. 149, and note.

Page 294, lines 25–9:
The last three sentences of this paragraph are a late insertion.

Page 315, lines 29–30, and p. 316, line 1:
These lines are late insertions into the MS.

Page 318, lines 3–6:
These lines are heavily corrected in the MS., suggesting that Gissing had trouble getting this scene down the way he wanted it. The original version has Quarrier calling loudly across the water.

Page 327, lines 8–15:
These lines are also heavily corrected in the MS. The description of Quarrier's state of mind at this point obviously gave Gissing trouble.

Page 330, line 17:
This is a misprint. The MS. reads, 'it did not gratify him much', etc.

Page 334, line 11:
The mis-spelling is Gissing's.

Page 338, lines 29–30:
The MS. says Somerset House; the correction was probably made in proof. Somerset House for many years housed the Royal Academy of Arts. From 1869 Burlington House was, and has remained, the address of the Royal Academy (in which, presumably, the exhibition referred to takes place). The Royal Society, the Royal Geographical Society, and several other institutions are also housed there.

Bibliography

Note: *Denzil Quarrier* was reviewed widely and for the most part favourably when it appeared in February 1892. As letters to his friend Bertz and his sister Ellen make clear, Gissing was pleased with the critical reception accorded the novel – never one of his own favourites – and by its quick publication in America. Among reviews of the first English edition (all published in 1892) listed below, the most important are probably those which appeared in the *Daily Chronicle*, the *Saturday Review*, *The Times*, and the *Guardian* (London). All four of these are reprinted in the *Critical Heritage* volume on Gissing, also listed below.

I — Articles and reviews dealing with the first English edition

Globe, 10 February, p.3.
Publishers' Circular, 13 February, p. 183.
Daily Chronicle, 20 February, p.3.
Glasgow Herald, 20 February, p. 9.
World, 24 February, p. 24.
Manchester Guardian, 1 March, p. 10.
Bookseller, 4 March, p. 210b.
Saturday Review, 5 March, p. 276.
The Times, 12 March, p. 5.
Whitehall Review, 19 March, pp. 18-19.
Guardian (London), 23 March, p. 439.
St James's Gazette, 25 March, p. 6.
National Review, March, pp. 131-2.
Bookman (London), March, p. 215.
Review of Reviews (London), March, p. 308.
New Review, March, p. 378 (by H.D. Traill).
Athenaeum, 9 April, p. 466.
Academy, 9 April, p. 347 (by George Cotterell).
Graphic, 23 April, p. 528.
Illustrated London News, 28 May, p. 659.

II – Reviews of the first American edition (all published in 1892)

Chicago Tribune, 13 February, p. 13 (reprinted in the *Literary News,*
     March 1892, p. 74, and in the *Critical Heritage* volume).
Literary World (Boston), 12 March, p. 88.
New York Times, 13 March, p. 19.
New York Daily Tribune, 27 March, p. 18.
Nation, 28 April, p. 327 (by Annie R.M. Logan)

III–The following items contain material helpful to the reader of
Denzil Quarrier:

Michael Collie, *George Gissing: A Biography* (London, 1977).

Pierre Coustillas (ed.), *Collected Articles on George Gissing* (London and
     New York, 1968).

Pierre Coustillas (ed.), *George Gissing: Essays and Fiction* (Baltimore,
     1970).

Pierre Coustillas (ed.), *London and the Life of Literature in Late Victorian
England: The Diary of George Gissing, Novelist* (Hassocks, Sussex, 1978).

Pierre Coustillas and Colin Partridge (eds), *Gissing: The Critical Heritage*
     (London and Boston, 1972).

Oswald H. Davis, *George Gissing: A Study in Literary Leanings* (London,
     1966).

Mabel Collins Donnelly, *George Gissing: Grave Comedian* (Cambridge,
     Mass., 1954).

Samuel Vogt Gapp, *George Gissing: Classicist* (Philadelphia, 1936).

Royal A. Gettmann (ed.), *George Gissing and H.G. Wells: Their Friendship
     and Correspondence* (Urbana, Ill., and London, 1961).

Algernon and Ellen Gissing (eds), *Letters of George Gissing to Members of
     His Family* (London, 1927).

John D. Gordan, *George Gissing 1857-1903: An Exhibition from the Berg
     Collection* (New York, 1954).

John Halperin, 'The Gissing Revival, 1961 – 1974', *Studies in the Novel,*
     Vol. 8, No. 1 (Spring 1976).

John Halperin, 'How to Read Gissing,' *English Literature in Transition,*
     Vol. 20, No. 4 (Fall 1977).

James Haydock, '*Denzil Quarrier* and the Woman Question,' *Gissing
     Newsletter,* Vol. 3, No. 2 (June 1967).

Granville Hicks, *Figures of Transition* (New York, 1939).

Norman Kelvin, *A Troubled Eden: Nature and Society in the Works of George
     Meredith* (Stanford, Ca., 1961).

Jacob Korg, *George Gissing: A Critical Biography* (Seattle, 1963).

Jacob Korg (ed.), *George Gissing's Commonplace Book* (New York, 1962).

Jacob and Cynthia Korg (eds.), *George Gissing on Fiction* (London, 1978).

P.F. Kropholler, 'Notes on *Denzil Quarrier*', *Gissing Newsletter,* Vol. 9, No.
     1 (January 1973).

Stanley P. Kurman, 'The Hero as Politcian', *Gissing Newsletter,* Vol. 9, No. 2 (April 1973).

Q.D. Leavis, 'Gissing and the English Novel', *Scrutiny* (June 1938).

Jack Lindsay, *George Meredith: His Life and Work* (London, 1956).

Ruth Capers McKay, *George Gissing and His Critic Frank Swinnerton* (Philadelphia, 1933).

Adrian Poole, *Gissing in Context* (London and Totowa, N.J., 1975).

Morley Roberts, *The Private Life of Henry Maitland* (London, 1912).

John Spiers and Pierre Coustillas, *The Rediscovery of George Gissing* (London, 1971).

Frank Swinnerton, *George Gissing: A Critical Study* (London, 1912).

Gillian Tindall, *The Born Exile: George Gissing* (London and New York, 1974).

Arthur C. Young (ed.), *The Letters of George Gissing to Eduard Bertz, 1887-1903* (New Brunswick, N.J., 1961).